COLLECTED WORKS OF
MAXIM GORKY

CONTENTS

TWENTY-SIX AND ONE AND OTHER STORIES

THE MAN WHO WAS AFRAID

TWENTY-SIX AND ONE AND OTHER STORIES

From the Vagabond Series
Translated from the Russian
Preface by Ivan Strannik

PREFACE

MAXIME GORKY

Russian literature, which for half a century has abounded in happy surprises, has again made manifest its wonderful power of innovation. A tramp, Maxime Gorky, lacking in all systematic training, has suddenly forced his way into its sacred domain, and brought thither the fresh spontaneity of his thoughts and character. Nothing as individual or as new has been produced since the first novels of Tolstoy. His work owes nothing to its predecessors; it stands apart and alone. It, therefore, obtains more than an artistic success, it causes a real revolution.

Gorky was born of humble people, at Nizhni-Novgorod, in 1868 or 1869,—he does not know which—and was early left an orphan. He was apprenticed to a shoemaker, but ran away, a sedentary life not being to his taste. He left an engraver's in the same manner, and then went to work with a painter of *ikoni*, or holy pictures. He is next found to be a cook's boy, then an assistant to a gardener. He tried life in these diverse ways, and not one of them pleased him. Until his fifteenth year, he had only had the time to learn to read a little; his grandfather taught him to read a prayer-book in the old Slav dialect. He retained from his first studies only a distaste for anything printed until the time when, cook's boy on board a steam-boat, he was initiated by the chief cook into more attractive reading matter. Gogol, Glebe Ouspenski, Dumas *pere* were revelations to him. His imagination took fire; he was seized with a "fierce desire" for instruction. He set out for Kazan, "as though a poor child could receive instruction gratuitously," but he soon perceived that "it was contrary to custom." Discouraged, he became a baker's boy with the wages of three rubles (about $1.50) a month. In the midst of worse fatigue and ruder privations, he always recalls the bakery of Kazan with peculiar bitterness; later, in his story, "Twenty-Six and One," he utilized this painful remembrance: "There were twenty-six of us—twenty-six living machines, locked up in a damp cellar, where we patted dough from morning till night, making biscuits and cakes. The windows of our cellar looked out into a ditch, which was covered with bricks grown green from dampness, the window frames were obstructed from the outside by a dense iron netting, and the light of the sun could not peep in through the panes, which were covered with flour dust . . ."

Gorky dreamed of the free air. He abandoned the bakery. Always reading, studying feverishly, drinking with vagrants, expending his strength in every possible manner, he is one day at work in a saw-mill, another, 'longshoreman on the quays . . . In 1888, seized with despair, he attempted to kill himself. "I was," said he, "as ill as I could be, and I continued to live to sell apples . . ." He afterward became a gate-keeper and later retailed *kvass* in the streets. A happy chance brought him to the notice of a lawyer, who interested himself in him, directed his reading and organized his instruction. But his restless disposition drew him back to his wandering life; he traveled over Russia in every direction and tried his hand at every trade, including, henceforth, that of man of letters.

He began by writing a short story, "Makar Tchoudra," which was published by a provincial newspaper. It is a rather interesting work, but its interest lies more, frankly speaking, in what it promises than in what it actually gives. The subject is rather too suggestive of certain pieces of fiction dear to the romantic school.

Gorky's appearance in the world of literature dates from 1893. He had at this time, the acquaintance of the writer Korolenko, and, thanks to him, soon published "Tchelkache," which met with a resounding success. Gorky henceforth rejects all traditional methods, and free and untrammeled devotes himself to frankly and directly interpreting life as he sees it. As he has, so far, lived only in the society of tramps, himself a tramp, and one of the most refractory, it has been reserved for him to write the poem of vagrancy.

His preference is for the short story. In seven years, he has written thirty, contained in three volumes, which in their expressive brevity sometimes recall Maupassant.

The plot is of the simplest. Sometimes, there are only two personages: an old beggar and his grandson, two workmen, a tramp and a Jew, a baker's boy and his assistant, two companions in misery.

The interest of these stories does not lie in the unraveling of an intricate plot. They are rather fragments of life, bits of biography covering some particular period, without reaching the limits of a real drama. And these are no more artificially combined than are the events of real life.

Everything that he relates, Gorky has seen. Every landscape that he describes has been seen by him in the course of his adventurous existence. Each detail of this scenery is fraught for him with some remembrance of distress or suffering. This vagrant life has been his own. These tramps have been his companions, he has loved or hated them. Therefore his work is alive with what he has almost unconsciously put in of himself. At the same time, he knows how to separate himself from his work; the characters introduced live their own lives, independent of his, having their own characters and their own individual way of reacting against the common misery. No writer has to a greater degree the gift of objectivity, while at the same time freely introducing himself into his work.

Therefore, his tramps are strikingly truthful. He does not idealise them; the sympathy that their strength, courage, and independence inspire in him does not blind him. He conceals neither their faults, vices, drunkenness nor boastfulness. He is without indulgence for them, and judges them discriminatingly. He paints reality, but without, for all that, exaggerating ugliness. He does not avoid painful or coarse scenes; but in the most cynical passages he does not revolt because it is felt that he only desires to be truthful, and not to excite the emotions by cheap means.

He simply points out that things are as they are, that there is nothing to be done about it, that they depend upon immutable laws. Accordingly all those sad, even horrible spectacles are accepted as life itself. To Gorky, the spectacle presented by these characters is only natural: he has seen them shaken by passion as the waves by the wind, and a smile pass over their souls like the sun piercing the clouds. He is, in the true acceptation of the term, a realist.

The introduction of tramps in literature is the great innovation of Gorky. The Russian writers first interested themselves in the cultivated classes of society; then they went as far as the moujik. The "literature of the moujik," assumed a social importance. It had a political influence and was not foreign to the abolition of serfdom.

In the story "Malva," Gorky offers us two characteristic types of peasants who become tramps by insensible degrees; almost without suspecting it, through the force of circumstances. One of them is Vassili. When he left the village, he fully intended to return. He went away to earn a little money for his wife and children. He found employment in a fishery. Life was easy and joyous. For a while he sent small sums of money home, but gradually the village and the old life faded away and became less and less real. He ceased to think of them. His son Iakov came to seek him and to procure work for himself for a season. He had the true soul of a peasant.

Later he falls, like the others, under the spell of this easy, free life, and one feels that Iakov will never more return to the village.

In Gorky's eyes, his work is tainted by a capital vice. It is unsuited to producing the joy that quickens. Humanity has forgotten joy; what has he done beyond pitying or rallying suffering? . . . These reflections haunt him, and this doubt of his beneficent efficacy imparts extreme sadness to his genius.

IVAN STRANNIK.

14

TWENTY-SIX AND ONE

BY MAXIME GORKY

There were twenty-six of us—twenty-six living machines, locked up in a damp cellar, where we patted dough from morning till night, making biscuits and cakes. The windows of our cellar looked out into a ditch, which was covered with bricks grown green from dampness, the window frames were obstructed from the outside by a dense iron netting, and the light of the sun could not peep in through the panes, which were covered with flour-dust. Our proprietor stopped up our windows with iron that we might not give his bread to the poor or to those of our companions who, being out of work, were starving; our proprietor called us cheats and gave us for our dinner tainted garbage instead of meat.

It was stifling and narrow in our box of stone under the low, heavy ceiling, covered with smoke-black and spider-webs. It was close and disgusting within the thick walls, which were spattered with stains of mud and mustiness . . . We rose at five o'clock in the morning, without having had enough sleep, and, dull and indifferent, we seated ourselves by the table at six to make biscuits out of the dough, which had been prepared for us by our companions while we were asleep. And all day long, from morning till ten o'clock at night, some of us sat by the table rolling out the elastic dough with our hands, and shaking ourselves that we might not grow stiff, while the others kneaded the dough with water. And the boiling water in the kettle, where the cracknels were being boiled, was purring sadly and thoughtfully all day long; the baker's shovel was scraping quickly and angrily against the oven, throwing off on the hot bricks the slippery pieces of dough. On one side of the oven, wood was burning from morning till night, and the red reflection of the flame was trembling on the wall of the workshop as though it were silently mocking us. The huge oven looked like the deformed head of a fairy-tale monster. It looked as though it thrust itself out from underneath the floor, opened its wide mouth full of fire, and breathed on us with heat and stared at our endless work through the two black air-holes above the forehead. These two cavities were like eyes—pitiless and impassible eyes of a monster: they stared at us with the same dark gaze, as though they had grown tired of looking at slaves, and expecting nothing human from them, despised them with the cold contempt of wisdom. Day in and day out, amid flour-dust and mud and thick, bad-odored suffocating heat, we rolled out the dough and made biscuits, wetting them with our sweat, and we hated our work with keen hatred; we never ate the biscuit that came out of our hands, preferring black bread to the cracknels. Sitting by a long table, one opposite the other—nine opposite nine—we mechanically moved our hands, and fingers during the long hours, and became so accustomed to our work that we no longer ever followed the motions of our hands. And we had grown so tired of looking at one another that each of us knew all the wrinkles on the faces of the others. We had nothing to talk about, we were used to this and were silent all the time, unless abusing one another—for there is always something for which to abuse a man, especially a companion. But we even abused one another very seldom. Of what can a man be guilty when he is half dead, when he is like a statue, when all his feelings are crushed under the weight of toil? But silence is terrible and painful only to those who have said all and have nothing more to speak of; but to those who never had anything to say—to them silence is simple and easy . . . Sometimes we sang, and our song began thus: During work some one would suddenly heave a sigh, like that of a tired horse, and would softly start one of those drawling songs, whose touchingly caressing tune always gives ease to the troubled soul of the singer. One of us sang, and at first we listened in silence to his lonely song, which was drowned and deafened underneath the heavy ceiling of the cellar, like the small fire of a wood-pile in the steppe on a damp autumn night, when the gray sky is hanging over the earth like a leaden roof. Then another joined the singer, and now, two voices soar softly and mournfully over the suffocating heat of our narrow ditch. And suddenly a few more voices take up the song—and the song bubbles up like a wave, growing stronger, louder, as though moving asunder the damp, heavy walls of our stony prison.

All the twenty-six sing; loud voices, singing in unison, fill the workshop; the song has no room there; it strikes against the stones of the walls, it moans and weeps and reanimates the heart by a soft tickling pain, irritating old wounds and rousing sorrow.

The singers breathe deeply and heavily; some one unexpectedly leaves off his song and listens for a long time to the singing of his companions, and again his voice joins the general wave. Another mournfully exclaims, Eh! sings, his eyes closed, and it may be that the wide, heavy wave of sound appears to him like a road leading somewhere far away, like a wide road, lighted by the brilliant sun, and he sees himself walking there . . .

The flame is constantly trembling in the oven, the baker's shovel is scraping against the brick, the water in the kettle is purring, and the reflection of the fire is trembling on the wall, laughing in silence . . . And we sing away, with some one else's words, our dull sorrow, the heavy grief of living men, robbed of sunshine, the grief of slaves. Thus we lived, twenty-six of us, in the cellar of a big stony house, and it was hard for us to live as though all the three stories of the house had been built upon our shoulders.

But besides the songs, we had one other good thing, something we all loved and which, perhaps, came to us instead of the sun. The second story of our house was occupied by an embroidery shop, and there, among many girl workers, lived the sixteen year old chamber-maid, Tanya. Every morning her little, pink face, with blue, cheerful eyes, leaned against the pane of the little window in our hallway door, and her ringing, kind voice cried to us: "Little prisoners! Give me biscuits!"

We all turned around at this familiar, clear sound and joyously, kind-heartedly looked at the pure maiden face as it smiled to us delightfully. We were accustomed and pleased to see her nose flattened against the window-pane, and the small, white teeth that flashed from under her pink lips, which were open with a smile. We rush to open the door for her, pushing one another; she enters, cheerful and amiable, and holding out her apron. She stands before us, leaning her head somewhat on one side and smiles all the time. A thick, long braid of chestnut hair, falling across her shoulder, lies on her breast. We, dirty, dark, deformed men, look up at her from below—the threshold was four steps higher than the floor—we look at her, lifting our heads upwards, we wish her a good morning. We say to her some particular words, words we use for her alone. Speaking to her our voices are somehow softer, and our jokes lighter. Everything is different for her. The baker takes out a shovelful of the brownest and reddest biscuits and throws them cleverly into Tanya's apron.

"Look out that the boss doesn't see you!" we always warn her. She laughs roguishly and cries to us cheerfully:

"Good-by, little prisoners!" and she disappears quickly, like a little mouse. That's all. But long after her departure we speak pleasantly of her to one another. We say the very same thing we said yesterday and before, because she, as well as we and everything around us, is also the same as yesterday and before. It is very hard and painful for one to live, when nothing changes around him, and if it does not kill his soul for good, the immobility of the surroundings becomes all the more painful the longer he lives. We always spoke of women in such a manner that at times we were disgusted at our own rude and shameless words, and this is quite clear, for the women we had known, perhaps, never deserved any better words. But of Tanya we never spoke ill. Not only did none of us ever dare to touch her with his hand, she never even heard a free jest from us. It may be that this was because she never stayed long with us; she flashed

18

before our eyes like a star coming from the sky and then disappeared, or, perhaps, because she was small and very beautiful, and all that is beautiful commands the respect even of rude people. And then, though our hard labor had turned us into dull oxen, we nevertheless remained human beings, and like all human beings, we could not live without worshipping something. We had nobody better than she, and none, except her, paid any attention to us, the dwellers of the cellar; no one, though tens of people lived in the house. And finally—this is probably the main reason—we all considered her as something of our own, as something that existed only because of our biscuits. We considered it our duty to give her hot biscuits and this became our daily offering to the idol, it became almost a sacred custom which bound us to her the more every day. Aside from the biscuits, we gave Tanya many advices—to dress more warmly, not to run fast on the staircase, nor to carry heavy loads of wood. She listened to our advice with a smile, replied to us with laughter and never obeyed us, but we did not feel offended at this. All we needed was to show that we cared for her. She often turned to us with various requests. She asked us, for instance, to open the heavy cellar door, to chop some wood. We did whatever she wanted us to do with joy, and even with some kind of pride.

But when one of us asked her to mend his only shirt, she declined, with a contemptuous sneer.

We laughed heartily at the queer fellow, and never again asked her for anything. We loved her; all is said in this. A human being always wants to bestow his love upon some one, although he may sometime choke or slander him; he may poison the life of his neighbor with his love, because, loving, he does not respect the beloved. We had to love Tanya, for there was no one else we could love.

At times some one of us would suddenly begin to reason thus:

"And why do we make so much of the girl? What's in her? Eh? We have too much to do with her." We quickly and rudely checked the man who dared to say such words. We had to love something. We found it out

19

and loved it, and the something which the twenty-six of us loved had to be inaccessible to each of us as our sanctity, and any one coming out against us in this matter was our enemy. We loved, perhaps, not what was really good, but then we were twenty-six, and therefore we always wanted the thing dear to us to be sacred in the eyes of others. Our love is not less painful than hatred. And perhaps this is why some haughty people claim that our hatred is more flattering than our love. But why, then, don't they run from us, if that is true?

Aside from the biscuit department our proprietor had also a shop for white bread; it was in the same house, separated from our ditch by a wall; the *bulochniks* (white-bread bakers), there were four of them, kept aloof, considering their work cleaner than ours, and therefore considering themselves better than we were; they never came to our shop, laughed at us whenever they met us in the yard; nor did we go to them. The proprietor had forbidden this for fear lest we might steal loaves of white bread. We did not like the *bulochniks*, because we envied them. Their work was easier than ours, they were better paid, they were given better meals, theirs was a spacious, light workshop, and they were all so clean and healthy—repulsive to us; while we were all yellow, and gray, and sickly. During holidays and whenever they were free from work they put on nice coats and creaking boots; two of them had harmonicas, and they all went to the city park; while we had on dirty rags and burst shoes, and the city police did not admit us into the park—could we love the *bulochniks*?

One day we learned that one of their bakers had taken to drink, that the proprietor had discharged him and hired another one in his place, and that the other one was a soldier, wearing a satin vest and a gold chain to his watch. We were curious to see such a dandy, and in the hope of seeing him we, now and again, one by one, began to run out into the yard.

But he came himself to our workshop. Kicking the door open with his foot, and leaving it open, he stood on the threshold, and smiling, said to us:

20

"God help you! Hello, fellows!" The cold air, forcing itself in at the door in a thick, smoky cloud, was whirling around his feet; he stood on the threshold, looking down on us from above, and from under his fair, curled moustache, big, yellow teeth were flashing. His waistcoat was blue, embroidered with flowers; it was beaming, and the buttons were of some red stones. And there was a chain too. He was handsome, this soldier, tall, strong, with red cheeks, and his big, light eyes looked good—kind and clear. On his head was a white, stiffly-starched cap, and from under his clean apron peeped out sharp toes of stylish, brightly shining boots.

Our baker respectfully requested him to close the door; he did it without haste, and began to question us about the proprietor. Vieing with one another, we told him that our "boss" was a rogue, a rascal, a villain, a tyrant, everything that could and ought to be said of our proprietor, but which cannot be repeated here. The soldier listened, stirred his moustache and examined us with a soft, light look.

"And are there many girls here?" he asked, suddenly.

Some of us began to laugh respectfully, others made soft grimaces; some one explained to the soldier that there were nine girls.

"Do you take advantage?" . . . asked the soldier, winking his eye.

Again we burst out laughing, not very loud, and with a confused laughter. Many of us wished to appear before the soldier just as clever as he was, but not one was able to do it. Some one confessed, saying in a low voice:

"It is not for us." . . .

"Yes, it is hard for you!" said the soldier with confidence, examining us fixedly. "You haven't the bearing for it . . . the figure—you haven't the appearance, I mean! And a woman likes a good appearance in a man. To her it must be perfect, everything perfect! And then she respects strength . . . A hand should be like this!" The soldier pulled his right hand out of his pocket. The shirt sleeve was rolled up to his elbow. He showed his hand to us . . . It was white, strong, covered with glossy, golden hair.

"A leg, a chest, in everything there must be firmness. And then, again, the man must be dressed according to style . . . As the beauty of things requires it. I, for instance, I am loved by women. I don't call them, I don't lure them, they come to me of themselves." He seated himself on a bag of flour and told us how the women loved him and how he handled them boldly. Then he went away, and when the door closed behind him with a creak, we were silent for a long time, thinking of him and of his stories. And then suddenly we all began to speak, and it became clear at once that he pleased every one of us. Such a kind and plain fellow. He came, sat awhile and talked. Nobody came to us before, nobody ever spoke to us like this; so friendly . . . And we all spoke of him and of his future successes with the embroidery girls, who either passed us by, closing their lips insultingly, when they met us in the yard, or went straight on as if we had not been in their way at all. And we always admired them, meeting them in the yard, or when they went past our windows—in winter dressed in some particular hats and in fur coats, in summer in hats with flowers, with colored parasols in their hands. But thereafter among ourselves, we spoke of these girls so that had they heard it, they would have gone mad for shame and insult.

"However, see that he doesn't spoil Tanushka, too!" said the baker, suddenly, with anxiety.

We all became silent, dumb-founded by these words. We had somehow forgotten Tanya; it looked as though the soldier's massive, handsome figure prevented us from seeing her. Then began a noisy dispute. Some said that Tanya would not submit herself to this, others argued that she would not hold out against the soldier; still others said that they would break the soldier's bones in case he should annoy Tanya, and finally all decided to look after the soldier and Tanya, and to warn the girl to be on guard against him . . . This put an end to the dispute.

About a month went by. The soldier baked white bread, walked around with the embroidery girls, came quite often to our workshop, but never told us of his success with the girls; he only twisted his moustache and licked his lips with relish.

Tanya came every morning for the biscuits and, as always, was cheerful, amiable, kind to us. We attempted to start a conversation with her about the soldier, but she called him a "goggle-eyed calf," and other funny names, and this calmed us. We were proud of our little girl, seeing that the embroidery girls were making love to the soldier. Tanya's relation toward him somehow uplifted all of us, and we, as if guided by her relation, began to regard the soldier with contempt. And we began to love Tanya still more, and, meet her in the morning more cheerfully and kind-heartedly.

But one day the soldier came to us a little intoxicated, seated himself and began to laugh, and when we asked him what he was laughing at he explained: "Two had a fight on account of me . . . Lidka and Grushka . . . How they disfigured each other! Ha, ha! One grabbed the other by the hair, and knocked her to the ground in the hallway, and sat on her . . . Ha, ha, ha! They scratched each other's faces . . . It is laughable! And why cannot women fight honestly? Why do they scratch? Eh?"

He sat on the bench, strong and clean and jovial; talking and laughing all the time. We were silent. Somehow or other he seemed repulsive to us this time.

"How lucky I am with women, Eh? It is very funny! Just a wink and I have them!"

His white hands, covered with glossy hair, were lifted and thrown back to his knees with a loud noise. And he stared at us with such a pleasantly surprised look, as though he really could not understand why he was so lucky in his affairs with women. His stout, red face was radiant with happiness and self-satisfaction, and he kept on licking his lips with relish.

Our baker scraped the shovel firmly and angrily against the hearth of the oven and suddenly said, sarcastically:

"You need no great strength to fell little fir-trees, but try to throw down a pine." . . .

"That is, do you refer to me?" asked the soldier.

"To you . . ."

"What is it?"

"Nothing . . . Too late!"

"No, wait! What's the matter? Which pine?"

Our baker did not reply, quickly working with his shovel at the oven. He would throw into the oven the biscuits from the boiling kettle, would take out the ready ones and throw them noisily to the floor, to the boys who put them on bast strings. It looked as though he had forgotten all about the soldier and his conversation with him. But suddenly the soldier became very restless. He rose to his feet and walking up to the oven, risked striking his chest against the handle of the shovel, which was convulsively trembling in the air.

"No, you tell me—who is she? You have insulted me . . . I? . . . Not a single one can wrench herself from me, never! And you say to me such offensive words." . . . And, indeed, he looked really offended. Evidently there was nothing for which he might respect himself, except for his ability to lead women astray; it may be that aside from this ability there was no life in him, and only this ability permitted him to feel himself a living man.

There are people to whom the best and dearest thing in life is some kind of a disease of either the body or the soul. They make much of it during all their lives and live by it only; suffering from it, they are nourished by it, they always complain of it to others and thus attract the attention of their neighbors. By this they gain people's compassion for themselves, and aside from this they have nothing. Take away this disease from them, cure them, and they are rendered most unfortunate, because they thus lose their sole means of living, they then become empty. Sometimes a man's life is so poor that he is involuntarily compelled to prize his defect and live by it. It may frankly be said that people are often depraved out

24

of mere weariness. The soldier felt insulted, and besetting our baker, roared:

"Tell me—who is it?"

"Shall I tell you?" the baker suddenly turned to him.

"Well?"

"Do you know Tanya?"

"Well?"

"Well, try." . . .

"I?"

"You!"

"Her? That's easy enough!"

"We'll see!"

"You'll see! Ha, ha!"

"She'll . . ."

"A month's time!"

"What a boaster you are, soldier!"

"Two weeks! I'll show you! Who is it? Tanya! Tfoo!" . . .

"Get away, I say."

"Get away, . . . you're bragging!"

"Two weeks, that's all!"

Suddenly our baker became enraged, and he raised the shovel against the soldier. The soldier stepped back, surprised, kept silent for awhile, and, saying ominously, in a low voice: "Very well, then!" he left us.

During the dispute we were all silent, interested in the result. But when the soldier went out, a loud, animated talk and noise was started among us.

Some one cried to the baker:

"You contrived a bad thing, Pavel!"

"Work!" replied the baker, enraged.

We felt that the soldier was touched to the quick and that a danger was threatening Tanya. We felt this, and at the same time we were seized with a burning, pleasant curiosity—what will happen? Will she resist the soldier? And almost all of us cried out with confidence:

"Tanya? She will resist! You cannot take her with bare hands!"

We were very desirous of testing the strength of our godling; we persistently proved to one another that our godling was a strong godling, and that Tanya would come out the victor in this combat. Then, finally, it appeared to us that we did not provoke the soldier enough, that he might forget about the dispute, and that we ought to irritate his self-love the more. Since that day we began to live a particular, intensely nervous life—a life we had never lived before. We argued with one another all day long, as if we had grown wiser. We spoke more and better. It seemed to us that we were playing a game with the devil, with Tanya as the stake on our side. And when we had learned from the *bulochniks* that the soldier began to court "our Tanya," we felt so dreadfully good and were so absorbed in our curiosity that we did not even notice that the proprietor, availing himself of our excitement, added to our work fourteen *poods* (a *pood* is a weight of forty Russian pounds) of dough a day. We did not even get tired of working. Tanya's name did not leave our lips all day long. And each morning we expected her with especial impatience. Sometimes we imagined that she might come to us—and that she would be no longer the same Tanya, but another one.

However, we told her nothing about the dispute. We asked her no questions and treated her as kindly as before. But something new and foreign to our former feelings for Tanya crept in stealthily into our relation toward her, and this new *something* was keen curiosity, sharp and cold like a steel knife.

"Fellows! Time is up to-day!" said the baker one morning, commencing to work.

We knew this well without his calling our attention to it, but we gave a start, nevertheless.

"Watch her! . . . She'll come soon!" suggested the baker. Some one exclaimed regretfully: "What can we see?"

And again a lively, noisy dispute ensued. To-day we were to learn at last how far pure and inaccessible to filth was the urn wherein we had placed all that was best in us. This morning we felt for the first time that we were really playing a big game, that this test of our godling's purity might destroy our idol. We had been told all these days that the soldier was following Tanya obstinately, but for some reason or other none of us asked how she treated him. And she kept on coming to us regularly every morning for biscuits and was the same as before. This day, too, we soon heard her voice:

"Little prisoners! I've come . . ."

We hastened to let her in, and when she entered we met her, against our habit, in silence. Staring at her fixedly, we did not know what to say to her, what to ask her; and as we stood before her we formed a dark, silent crowd. She was evidently surprised at our unusual reception, and suddenly we noticed that she turned pale, became restless, began to bustle about and asked in a choking voice:

"Why are you . . . such?

"And you?" asked the baker sternly, without taking his eyes off the girl.

"What's the matter with me?"

"Nothing . . ."

"Well, quicker, give me biscuits . . ."

She had never before hurried us on . . .

"There's plenty of time!" said the baker, his eyes fixed, on her face.

Then she suddenly turned around and disappeared behind the door.

The baker took up his shovel and said calmly, turning towards the oven:

"It is done, it seems! . . . The soldier! . . . Rascal! . . . Scoundrel!" . . .

Like a herd of sheep, pushing one another, we walked back to the table, seated ourselves in silence and began to work slowly. Soon some one said:

"And perhaps not yet." . . .

"Go on! Talk about it!" cried the baker.

We all knew that he was a clever man, cleverer than any of us, and we understood by his words that he was firmly convinced of the soldier's victory . . . We were sad and uneasy. At twelve o'clock, during the dinner hour, the soldier came. He was, as usual, clean and smart, and, as usual, looked straight into our eyes. We felt awkward to look at him.

"Well, honorable gentlemen, if you wish, I can show you a soldier's boldness," . . . said he, smiling proudly. "You go out into the hallway and look through the clefts. . . . Understand?"

We went out and, falling on one another, we stuck to the cleft, in the wooden walls of the hallway, leading to the yard. We did not have to wait long . . . . Soon Tanya passed with a quick pace, skipping over the plashes of melted snow and mud. Her face looked troubled. She disappeared behind the cellar door. Then the soldier went there slowly and whistling. His hands were thrust into his pockets, and his moustache was stirring.

A rain was falling, and we saw the drops fall into plashes, and the plashes were wrinkling under their blows. It was a damp, gray day—a very dreary day. The snow still lay on the roofs, while on the ground, here and there, were dark spots of mud. And the snow on the roofs, too, was covered with a brownish, muddy coating. The rain trickled slowly, producing a mournful sound. We felt cold and disagreeable.

The soldier came first out of the cellar; he crossed the yard slowly, Stirring his moustache, his hands in his pockets—the same as always.

Then Tanya came out. Her eyes . . . her eyes were radiant with joy and happiness, and her lips were smiling. And she walked as though in sleep, staggering, with uncertain steps. We could not stand this calmly. We all rushed toward the door, jumped out into the yard, and began to hiss and bawl at her angrily and wildly. On noticing us she trembled and stopped short as if petrified in the mud under her feet. We surrounded her and malignantly abused her in the most obscene language. We told her shameless things.

We did this not loud but slowly, seeing that she could not get away, that she was surrounded by us and we could mock her as much as we pleased. I don't know why, but we did not beat her. She stood among us, turning her head one way and another, listening to our abuses. And we kept on throwing at her more of the mire and poison of our words.

The color left her face. Her blue eyes, so happy a moment ago, opened wide, her breast breathed heavily and her lips were trembling.

And we, surrounding her, avenged ourselves upon her, for she had robbed us. She had belonged to us, we had spent on her all that was best in us, though that best was the crusts of beggars, but we were twenty-six, while she was one, and therefore there was no suffering painful enough to punish her for her crime! How we abused her! She was silent, looked at us wild-eyed, and trembling in every limb. We were laughing, roaring, growling. Some more people ran up to us. Some one of us pulled Tanya by the sleeve of her waist . . .

Suddenly her eyes began to flash; slowly she lifted her hands to her head, and, adjusting her hair, said loudly, but calmly, looking straight into our eyes:

"Miserable prisoners!"

And she came directly toward us, she walked, too, as though we were not in front of her, as though we were not in her way. Therefore none of us were in her way, and coming out of our circle, without turning to us, she said aloud, and with indescribable contempt:

"Rascals! . . . Rabble!" . . .

Then she went away.

We remained standing in the centre of the yard, in the mud, under the rain and the gray, sunless sky . . .

Then we all went back silently to our damp, stony ditch. As before, the sun never peeped in through our windows, and Tanya never came there again! . . .

TCHELKACHE

The sky is clouded by the dark smoke rising from the harbor. The ardent sun gazes at the green sea through a thin veil. It is unable to see its reflection in the water so agitated is the latter by the oars, the steamer screws and the sharp keels of the Turkish feluccas, or sail boats, that plough the narrow harbor in every direction. The waves imprisoned by stone walls, crushed under the enormous weights that they carry, beat against the sides of the vessels and the quays; beat and murmur, foaming and muddy.

The noise of chains, the rolling of wagons laden with merchandise, the metallic groan of iron falling on the pavements, the creaking of windlasses, the whistling of steamboats, now in piercing shrieks, now in muffled roars, the cries of haulers, sailors and custom-house officers— all these diverse sounds blend in a single tone, that of work, and vibrate and linger in the air as though they feared to rise and disappear. And still the earth continues to give forth new sounds; heavy, rumbling, they set in motion everything about them, or, piercing, rend the hot and smoky air.

Stone, iron, wood, vessels and men, all, breathe forth a furious and passionate hymn to the god of Traffic. But the voices of the men, scarcely distinguishable, appear feeble and ridiculous, as do also the men, in the midst of all this tumult. Covered with grimy rags, bent under their burdens, they move through clouds of dust in the hot and noisy atmosphere, dwarfed to insignificance beside the colossal iron structures, mountains of merchandise, noisy wagons and all the other things that they have themselves created. Their own handiwork has reduced them to subjection and robbed them of their personality.

The giant vessels, at anchor, shriek, or sigh deeply, and in each sound there is, as it were, an ironical contempt for the men who crawl over their decks and fill their sides with the products of a slaved toil. The long files of 'longshoremen are painfully absurd; they carry huge loads of corn on their shoulders and deposit them in the iron holds of the vessels so that they may earn a few pounds of bread to put in their famished stomachs. The men, in rags, covered with perspiration, are stupefied by fatigue, noise and heat; the machines, shining, strong and impassive, made by the hands of these men, are not, however, moved by steam, but by the muscles and blood of their creators—cold and cruel irony!

The noise weighs down, the dust irritates nostrils and eyes; the heat burns the body, the fatigue, everything seems strained to its utmost tension, and ready to break forth in a resounding explosion that will clear the air and bring peace and quiet to the earth again—when the town, sea and sky will be calm and beneficent. But it is only an illusion, preserved by the untiring hope of man and his imperishable and illogical desire for liberty.

Twelve strokes of a bell, sonorous and measured, rang out. When the last one had died away upon the air, the rude tones of labor were already half softened. At the end of a minute, they were transformed into a dull murmur. Then, the voices of men and sea were more distinct. The dinner hour had come.

* * * * *

When the longshoremen, leaving their work, were dispersed in noisy groups over the wharf, buying food from the open-air merchants, and settling themselves on the pavement, in shady corners, to eat, Grichka Tchelkache, an old jail-bird, appeared among them. He was game often hunted by the police, and the entire quay knew him for a hard drinker and a clever, daring thief. He was bare-headed and bare-footed, and wore a worn pair of velvet trousers and a percale blouse torn at the neck, showing his sharp and angular bones covered with brown skin. His touseled black hair, streaked with gray, and his sharp visage, resembling a bird of prey's, all rumpled, indicated that he had just awakened. From his moustache hung a straw, another clung to his unshaved cheek, while behind his ear was a fresh linden leaf. Tall, bony, a little bent, he walked slowly over the stones, and, turning his hooked nose from side to side, cast piercing glances about him, appearing to be seeking someone among the 'longshoremen. His long, thick, brown moustache trembled like a cat's, and his hands, behind his back, rubbed each other, pressing closely together their twisted and knotty fingers. Even here, among hundreds of his own kind, he attracted attention by his resemblance to a sparrow-hawk of the steppes, by his rapacious leanness, his easy stride, outwardly calm but alert and watchful as the flight of the bird that he recalled.

When he reached a group of tatterdemalions, seated in the shade of some baskets of charcoal, a broad-shouldered and stupid looking boy rose to meet him. His face was streaked with red and his neck was scratched; he bore the traces of a recent fight. He walked along beside Tchelkache, and said under his breath:

"The custom-house officers can't find two boxes of goods. They are looking for them. You understand, Grichka?"

"What of it?" asked Tchelkache, measuring him calmly with his eyes.

"What of it? They are looking, that's all."

"Have they inquired for me to help them in their search?"

Tchelkache gazed at the warehouses with a meaning smile.

"Go to the devil!"

The other turned on his heel.

"Hey! Wait!—Who has fixed you up in that fashion? Your face is all bruised—Have you seen Michka around here?"

"I haven't seen him for a long time!" cried the other, rejoining the 'longshoremen.

Tchelkache continued on his way, greeted in a friendly manner by all. But he, usually so ready with merry word or biting jest, was evidently out of sorts to-day, and answered all questions briefly.

Behind a bale of merchandise appeared a custom-house officer, standing in his dark-green, dusty uniform with military erectness. He barred Tchelkache's way, placing himself before him in an offensive attitude, his left hand on his sword, and reached out his right hand to take Tchelkache by the collar.

"Stop, where are you going?"

Tchelkache fell back a step, looked at the officer and smiled drily.

The red, cunning and good-natured face of the custom-house officer was making an effort to appear terrible; with the result that swollen and purple, with wrinkling eyebrows and bulging eyes, it only succeeded in being funny.

"You've been warned before: don't you dare to come upon the wharf, or I'll break every rib in your body!" fiercely exclaimed the officer.

"How do you do, Semenitch! I haven't seen you for a long time," quietly replied Tchelkache, extending his hand.

"I could get along without ever seeing you! Go about your business!"

However, Semenitch shook the hand that was extended to him.

"You're just the one I want to see," pursued Tchelkache, without loosening the hold of his hooked fingers on Semenitch's hand, and shaking it familiarly. "Have you seen Michka?"

"What Michka? I don't know any Michka! Get along with you, friend, or the inspector'll see you; he—"

"The red-haired fellow who used to work with me on board the 'Kostroma,'" continued Tchelkache, unmoved.

"Who stole with you would be nearer the truth! Your Michka has been sent to the hospital: his leg was crushed under a bar of iron. Go on, friend, take my advice or else I shall have to beat you."

"Ah!—And you were saying: I don't know Michka! You see that you do know him. What's put you out, Semenitch?"

"Enough, Grichka, say no more and off with you—"

The officer was getting angry and, darting apprehensive glances on either side, tried to free his hand from the firm grasp of Tchelkache. The last named looked at him calmly from under his heavy eyebrows, while a slight smile curved his lips, and without releasing his hold of the officer's hand, continued talking.

"Don't hurry me. When I'm through talking to you I'll go. Tell me how you're getting on. Are your wife and children well?"

Accompanying his words with a terrible glance, and showing his teeth in a mocking grin, he added:

"I'm always intending to make you a visit, but I never have the time: I'm always drunk—"

"That'll do, that'll do, drop that—Stop joking, bony devil! If you don't, comrade, I—Or do you really intend to rob houses and streets?"

"Why? There's enough here for both of us. My God, yes!—Semenitch! You've stolen two boxes of goods again?—Look out, Semenitch, be careful! Or you'll be caught one of these days!"

Semenitch trembled with anger at the impudence of Tchelkache; he spat upon the ground in a vain effort to speak. Tchelkache let go his hand and turned back quietly and deliberately at the entrance to the wharf. The officer, swearing like a trooper, followed him.

Tchelkache had recovered his spirits; he whistled softly between his teeth, and, thrusting his hands in his trousers' pockets, walked slowly, like a man who has nothing to do, throwing to the right and left scathing remarks and jests. He received replies in kind.

"Happy Grichka, what good care the authorities take of him!" cried someone in a group of 'longshoremen who had eaten their dinner and were lying, stretched out on the ground.

"I have no shoes; Semenitch is afraid that I may hurt my feet," replied Tchelkache.

34

They reached the gate. Two soldiers searched Tchelkache and pushed him gently aside.

"Don't let him come back again!" cried Semenitch, who had remained inside.

Tchelkache crossed the road and seated himself on a stepping-block in front of the inn door. From the wharf emerged an interminable stream of loaded wagons. From the opposite direction arrived empty wagons at full speed, the drivers jolting up and down on the seats. The quay emitted a rumbling as of thunder; accompanied by an acrid dust. The ground seemed to shake.

Accustomed to this mad turmoil, stimulated by his scene with Semenitch, Tchelkache felt at peace with all the world. The future promised him substantial gain without great outlay of energy or skill on his part. He was sure that neither the one nor the other would fail him; screwing up his eyes, he thought of the next day's merry-making when, his work accomplished, he should have a roll of bills in his pocket. Then his thoughts reverted to his friend Michka, who would have been of so much use to him that night, if he had not broken his leg. Tchelkache swore inwardly at the thought that for want of Michka he might perhaps fail in his enterprise. What was the night going to be?—He questioned the sky and inspected the street.

Six steps away, was a boy squatting in the road near the sidewalk, his back against a post; he was dressed in blue blouse and trousers, tan shoes, and a russet cap. Near him lay a little bag and a scythe, without a handle, wrapped in hay carefully bound with string. The boy was broad shouldered and fairhaired with a sun-burned and tanned face; his eyes were large and blue and gazed at Tchelkache confidingly and pleasantly.

Tchelkache showed his teeth, stuck out his tongue, and, making a horrible grimace, stared at him persistently.

The boy, surprised, winked, then suddenly burst out laughing and cried:

"O! how funny he is!"

Almost without rising from the ground, he rolled heavily along toward Tchelkache, dragging his bag in the dust and striking the stones with his scythe.

"Eh! say, friend, you've been on a good spree!" said he to Tchelkache, pulling his trousers.

"Just so, little one, just so!" frankly replied Tchelkache. This robust and artless lad pleased him from the first.

"Have you come from the hay-harvest?"

"Yes. I've mowed a verst and earned a kopek! Business is bad! There are so many hands! The starving folks have come—have spoiled the prices. They used to give sixty kopeks at Koubagne. As much as that! And formerly, they say, three, four, even five rubles."

"Formerly!—Formerly, they gave three rubles just for the sight of a real Russian. Ten years ago, I made a business of that. I would go to a village, and I would say: 'I am a Russian!' At the words, everyone came flocking to look at me, feel of me, marvel at me—and I had three rubles in my pocket! In addition, they gave me food and drink and invited me to stay as long as I liked."

The boy's mouth had gradually opened wider and wider, as he listened to Tchelkache, and his round face expressed surprised admiration; then, comprehending that he was being ridiculed by this ragged man, be brought his jaws together suddenly and burst, out laughing. Tchelkache kept a serious face, concealing a smile under his moustache.

"What a funny fellow! . . . You said that as though it was true, and I believed you. But, truly, formerly, yonder . . ."

"And what did I say? I said that formerly, yonder . . ."

"Get along with you!" said the boy, accompanying his words with a gesture. "Are you a shoemaker? or a tailor? Say?"

"I?" asked Tchelkache; then after a moment's reflection, he added: "I'm a fisherman."

"A fisherman? Really! What do you catch, fish?"

"Why should I catch fish? Around here the fishermen catch other things besides that. Very often drowned men, old anchors, sunken boats—everything, in fact! There are lines for that . . ."

"Invent, keep on inventing! Perhaps you're one of those fishermen who sing about themselves:

"We are those who throw our nets
Upon dry banks,
Upon barns and stables!"

"Have you ever seen any of that kind?" asked Tchelkache, looking ironically at him, and thinking that this honest boy must be very stupid.

"No, I've never seen any; but I've heard them spoken of."

"Do you like them?"

"Why not? They are fearless and free."

"Do you feel the need of freedom? Do you like freedom?"

"How could I help liking it? One is his own master, goes where he likes, and does what he pleases. If he succeeds in supporting himself and has no weight dragging at his neck, what more can he ask? He can have as good a time as he likes provided he doesn't forget God."

Tchelkache spat contemptuously and interrupted the boy's questions by turning his back to him.

"Look at me, for instance," said the other, with sudden animation. "When my father died, he left little. My mother was old, the land worn out, what could I do? One must live. But how? I don't know. A well-to-do family would take me in as a son-in-law, to be sure! If the daughter only received her share! But no! The devil of a father-in-law never wants to divide the property. So then, I must toil for him . . . a long time . . . years. Do you see how it stands? While if I could put by a hundred and fifty rubles, I should feel independent and be able to talk to the old man. 'Will you give Marfa her share?' No! 'All right! She's not the only girl in the village, thank God.' And so I'd be perfectly free, my own master. Yes!"

The lad sighed. "As it is, there's nothing for it but to go into a family. I've thought that if I were to go to Koubagne, I'd easily make two hundred rubles. Then I should have a chance for myself. But no, nothing has come my way, I've failed in everything! So now it's necessary to enter a family, be a slave, because I can't get along with what I have—impossible! Ehe! . . ."

The lad detested the idea of becoming the husband of some rich girl who would remain at home. His face grew dull and sad. He moved restlessly about on the ground; this roused Tchelkache from the reflections in which his speech had plunged him.

Tchelkache felt that he had no more desire to talk, but he nevertheless asked:

"Where are you going, now?"

"Where am I going? Home, of course!"

"Why of course? . . . Perhaps you'd like to go to Turkey."

"To Turkey?" drawled the boy. "Do Christians go there? What do you mean by that?"

"What an imbecile you are!" sighed Tchelkache, and he again turned his back on his interlocutor, thinking this time that he would not vouchsafe him another word. This robust peasant awakened something obscure within him.

A confused feeling was gradually growing up, a kind of vexation was stirring the depths of his being and preventing him from concentrating his thoughts upon what he had to do that night.

The lad whom he had just insulted muttered something under his breath and looked askance at him. His cheeks were comically puffed out, his lips pursed up, and he half closed his eyes in a laughable manner. Evidently he had not expected that his conversation with this moustached person would end so quickly and in a manner so humiliating for him.

Tchelkache paid no more attention to him. Sitting on the block, he whistled absent-mindedly and beat time with his bare and dirty heel.

The boy longed to be revenged.

"Hey! Fisherman! Are you often drunk?" he began; but at the same instant the fisherman turned quickly around and asked:

"Listen, youngster! Do you want to work with me to-night? Eh? Answer quick."

"Work at what?" questioned the boy, distrustfully.

"At what I shall tell you . . . We'll go fishing. You shall row . . ."

"If that's it . . . why not? All right! I know how to work . . . Only suppose anything happens to me with you; you're not reassuring, with your mysterious airs . . ."

Tchelkache felt a burning sensation in his breast and said with concentrated rage:

"Don't talk about what you can't understand, or else, I'll hit you on the head so hard that your ideas will soon clear up."

He jumped up, pulling his moustache with his left hand and doubling his right fist all furrowed with knotted veins and hard as iron; his eyes flashed.

The lad was afraid. He glanced quickly around him and, blinking timidly, also jumped up on his feet. They measured each other with their eyes in silence.

"Well?" sternly demanded Tchelkache.

He was boiling over with rage at being insulted by this young boy, whom he had despised even when talking with him, and whom he now began to hate on account of his pure blue eyes, his healthy and sun-burned face and his short, strong arms; because he had, somewhere yonder, a village and a home in that village; because it had been proposed to him to enter as son-in-law in a well-to-do family, and, above all, because this being, who was only a child in comparison with himself, should presume to like liberty, of which he did not know the worth and which was useless to him. It is always disagreeable to see a person whom we consider our inferior like, or dislike, the same things that we do and to be compelled to admit that in that respect they are our equals.

The lad gazed at Tchelkache and felt that he had found his master.

39

"Why . . ." said he; "I consent. I'm willing. It's work that I'm looking for. It's all the same to me whether I work with you or someone else. I only said that because you don't seem like a man that works . . . you are far too ragged. However, I know very well that that may happen to anyone. Have I never seen a drunkard? Eh! How many I've seen, and much worse than you!"

"Good! Then you consent?" asked Tchelkache, somewhat mollified.

"I, why yes, with pleasure. Name your price."

"My price depends upon the work. It's according to what we do and take. You may perhaps receive five rubles. Do you understand?"

But now that it was a question of money, the peasant wanted a clear understanding and exacted perfect frankness on the part of his master. He again became distrustful and suspicious.

"That's scarcely to my mind, friend. I must have those five rubles in my hand how."

Tchelkache humored him.

"Enough said, wait a little. Let us go to the tavern."

They walked side by side along the street; Tchelkache twisting his moustache with the important air of an employer, the lad submissively, but at the same time filled with distrust and fear.

"What's your name?" asked Tchelkache.

"Gavrilo," replied the lad.

When they had entered the dirty and smoky ale-house Tchelkache went up to the bar and ordered, in the familiar tone of a regular customer, a bottle of brandy, cabbage soup, roast beef and tea, and, after enumerating the order, said briefly: "to be charged!" To which the boy responded by a silent nod. At this, Gavrilo was filled with great respect for his master, who, despite his knavish exterior, was so well known and treated with so much confidence.

"There, let us eat a bite, and talk afterward. Wait for me an instant, I will be back directly."

He went out. Gavrilo looked around him. The ale-house was in a basement; it was damp and dark and reeking with tobacco smoke, tar and a musty odor. In front of Gavrilo, at another table, was a drunken sailor, with a red beard, all covered with charcoal and tar. He was humming, interrupted by frequent hiccoughs, a fragment of a song very much out of tune. He was evidently not a Russian.

Behind him were two ragged women from Moldavia, black-haired and sun-burned; they were also grinding out a song.

Further on, other faces started out from the darkness, all dishevelled, half drunk, writhing, restless . . .

Gavrilo was afraid to remain alone. He longed for his master's return. The divers noises of the ale-house blended in one single note: it seemed like the roaring of some enormous animal with a hundred voices, struggling blindly and furiously in this stone box and finding no issue. Gavrilo felt himself growing heavy and dull as though his body had absorbed intoxication; his head swam and he could not see, in spite of his desire to satisfy his curiosity.

Tchelkache returned; he ate and drank while he talked. At the third glass Gavrilo was drunk. He grew lively; he wanted to say something nice to his host, who, worthy man that he was, was treating him so well, before he had availed himself of his services. But the words, which vaguely mounted to his throat, refused to leave his suddenly thick tongue.

Tchelkache looked at him. He said, smiling sarcastically.

"So you're done for, already! . . . it isn't possible! Just for five small glasses! How will you manage to work?"

"Friend," stammered Gavrilo, "don't be afraid! I will serve you. Ah, how I'll serve you! Let me embrace you, come?"

"That's right, that's right! . . . One more glass?"

Gavrilo drank. Everything swam before his eyes in unequal waves. That was unpleasant and gave him nausea. His face had a stupid expression. In his efforts to speak, he protruded his lips comically and roared. Tchelkache looked at him fixedly as though he was recalling something, then without turning aside his gaze twisted his moustache and smiled, but this time, moodily and viciously.

The ale-house was filled with a drunken uproar. The red-haired sailor was asleep with his elbows on the table.

"Let us get out of here!" said Tchelkache rising.

Gavrilo tried to rise, but not succeeding, uttered a formidable oath and burst out into an idiotic, drunken laugh.

"See how fresh you are!" said Tchelkache, sitting down again. Gavrilo continued to laugh, stupidly contemplating his master. The other looked at him lucidly and penetratingly. He saw before him a man whose life he held in his hands. He knew that he had it in his power to do what he would with him. He could bend him like a piece of cardboard, or help him to develop amid his staid, village environments. Feeling himself the master and lord of another being, he enjoyed this thought and said to himself that this lad should never drink of the cup that destiny had made him, Tchelkache, empty. He at once envied and pitied this young existence, derided it and was moved to compassion at the thought that it might again fall into hands like his own. All these feelings were finally mingled in one—paternal and authoritative. He took Gavrilo by the arm, led and gently pushed him from the public house and deposited him in the shade of a pile of cut wood; he sat down beside him and lighted his pipe. Gavrilo stirred a little, muttered something and went to sleep.

* * * * *

"Well, is it ready?" asked Tchelkache in a low voice to Gavrilo who was looking after the oars.

"In a moment! one of the thole-pins is loose; may I pound it down with an oar?"

"No, no! No noise! Push it down with your hands, it will be firm."

They noiselessly cut loose the boat fastened to the bow of a sailing vessel. There was here a whole fleet of sailing vessels, loaded with oak bark, and Turkish feluccas still half full of palma, sandal-wood and great cypress logs.

The night was dark; the sky was overspread with shreds of heavy clouds, and the sea was calm, black and thick as oil. It exhaled a humid and salt aroma, and softly murmured as it beat against the sides of the vessels and the shore and gently rocked Tchelkache's boat. Far out at sea rose the black forms of ships; their sharp masts, surmounted with colored lanterns, were outlined against the sky. The sea reflected the lights and appeared to be sown with yellow spots, which trembled upon its soft velvety black bosom, rising and falling regularly. The sea was sleeping the healthy sound sleep of the laborer after his day's work.

"We're off!" said Gavrilo, dipping his oars.

"Let us pull!"

Tchelkache, with a strong stroke of the oar, drove the boat into an open space between two fishing-boats; he pulled rapidly over the shining water, which glowed, at the contact of the oars, with a blue phosphorescent fire. A long trail of softly scintillating light followed the boat windingly.

"Well! does your head ache very much?" asked Tchelkache, kindly.

"Horribly! It rings like a clock . . . I'm going to wet it with a little water."

"What good will that do? Wet it rather inside; you'll come to quicker."

Tchelkache handed the bottle to Gavrilo.

"Do you think so? With the blessing of God! . . ." A soft gurgle was heard.

"Eh! you're not sorry to have the chance? Enough!" cried Tchelkache, stopping him.

The boat shot on again, noiselessly; it moved easily between the ships . . . All at once it cleared itself from the other craft, and the immense shining sea lay before them. It disappeared in the blue distance, where from its waters rose lilac-gray clouds to the sky; these were edged with down, now yellow, again green as the sea, or again slate-colored, casting those gloomy shadows that oppress soul and mind. The clouds slowly crept over one another, sometimes melting in one, sometimes dispersing each other; they mingled their forms and colors, dissolving or reappearing with new contours, majestic and mournful. This slow moving of inanimate masses had something fatal about it. It seemed as though yonder at the confines of the sea, there was an innumerable quantity of them always crawling indifferently over the sky, with the wicked and stupid intention of never allowing it to illumine the sleeping sea with the million golden eyes of its many-colored stars, which awaken the noble desires of beings in adoration before their holy and pure light.

"Isn't the sea beautiful?" asked Tchelkache.

"Not bad! Only one is afraid on it," replied Gavrilo, rowing evenly and strongly. The sea could scarcely be heard; it dripped from the long oars and still shone with its warm, blue phosphorescent lights.

"Afraid? Simpleton!" growled Tchelkache.

He, the cynical robber, loved the sea. His ardent temperament, greedy for impressions, never tired of contemplating its infinite, free and powerful immensity. It offended him to receive such a reply to his question concerning the beauty of the sea that he loved. Seated at the tiller, he cleaved the water with his oar and gazed tranquilly before him, filled with the desire to thus continue rowing forever over this velvet plain.

On the sea, warm and generous impulses rose within him, filled his soul and in a measure purified it of the defilements of life. He enjoyed this effect and liked to feel himself better, out here, amid the waves and air where the thoughts and occupations of life lose their interest and life itself sinks into insignificance. In the night, the sound of its soft breathing is wafted over the slumbering sea, and this infinite murmur fills the soul with peace, checks all unworthy impulses and brings forth mighty dreams.

"The nets, where are they, eh?" suddenly asked Gavrilo, inspecting the boat.

44

Tchelkache shuddered.

"There's the net, at the rudder."

"What kind of a net's that?" asked Gavrilo, suspiciously.

"A sweep-net . . ."

But Tchelkache was ashamed to lie to this child to conceal his real purpose; he also regretted the thoughts and feelings that the lad had put to flight by his question. He became angry. He felt the sharp burning sensation that he knew so well, in his breast; his throat contracted. He said harshly to Gavrilo:

"You're there; well, remain there! Don't meddle with what doesn't concern you. You've been brought to row, now row. And if you let your tongue wag, no good will come of it. Do you understand?"

For one minute, the boat wavered and stopped. The oars stood still in the foaming water around them, and Gavrilo moved uneasily on his seat.

"Row!"

A fierce oath broke the stillness. Gavrilo bent to the oars. The boat, as though frightened, leaped ahead rapidly and nervously, noisily cutting the water.

"Better than that!"

Tchelkache had risen from the helm and, without letting go his oar, he fixed his cold eyes upon the pale face and trembling lips of Gavrilo. Sinuous and bending forward, he resembled a cat ready to jump. A furious grinding of teeth and rattling of bones could be heard.

"Who goes there?"

This imperious demand resounded over the sea.

"The devil! Row, row! No noise! I'll kill you, dog. Row, can't you! One, two! Dare to cry out! I'll tear you from limb to limb! . . ." hissed Tchelkache.

"Oh, Holy Virgin," murmured Gavrilo, trembling and exhausted.

The boat turned, obedient to his touch; he pulled toward the harbor where the many-colored lanterns were grouped together and the tall masts were outlined against the sky.

"Hey! Who calls?" was again asked. This time the voice was further away; Tchelkache felt relieved.

"It's you, yourself, friend, who calls!" said he, in the direction of the voice. Then, he turned to Gavrilo, who continued to murmur a prayer. "Yes, brother, you're in luck. If those devils had pursued us, it would have been the end of you. Do you hear? I'd have soon sent you to the fishes."

Now that Tchelkache again spoke quietly and even good-naturedly, Gavrilo, still trembling with fear, begged him:

"Listen, let me go! In the name of Christ, let me go. Set me down somewhere. Oh dear! oh, dear! I'm lost! For God's sake, let me go. What do you want of me? I can't do this, I've never done anything like it. It's the first time, Lord! I'm lost! How did you manage, comrade, to get around me like this? Say? It's a sin, you make me lose my soul! . . . Ah! what a piece of business!"

"What business?" sternly questioned Tchelkache. "Speak, what business do you mean?"

The lad's terror amused him; he also enjoyed the sensation of being able to provoke such fear.

"Dark transactions, brother . . . Let me go, for the love of Heaven. What am I to you? Friend . . ."

"Be quiet! If I hadn't needed you, I shouldn't have brought you! Do you understand? Eh! Well, be quiet!"

"Oh, Lord!" sobbed Gavrilo.

"Enough!"

Gavrilo could no longer control himself and his breath came in broken and painful gasps; he wept and moved restlessly about on his seat, but rowed hard, in despair. The boat sped ahead like an arrow. Again the black hulls of the ships arose before them, and the boat, turning like a top in the narrow channels that separated them, was soon lost among them.

"Hey! You, listen: If anyone speaks to us, keep still, if you value your skin. Do you understand?"

"Alas!" hopelessly sighed Gavrilo, in response to this stern command, and he added: "It was my lot to be lost!"

"Stop howling!" whispered Tchelkache.

These words completely robbed Gavrilo of all understanding and he remained crushed under the chill presentiment of some misfortune. He mechanically dipped his oars and sending them back and forth through the water in an even and steady stroke did not lift his eyes again.

The slumbering murmur of the waves was gloomy and fearsome. Here is the harbor . . . From behind its stone wall, comes the sound of human voices, the plashing of water, singing and shrill whistling."

"Stop!" whispered Tchelkache.

"Drop the oars! Lean your hands against the wall! Softly, devil!"

Gavrilo caught hold of the slippery stone and guided the boat along the wall. He advanced noiselessly, just grazing the slimy moss of the stone.

"Stop, give me the oars! Give them here! And your passport, where have you put it? In your bag! Give me the bag! Quicker! . . . That, my friend, is so that you'll not run away . . . Now I hold you. Without oars you could have made off just the same, but, without a passport you'll not dare. Wait! And remember that if you so much as breathe a word I'll catch you, even though at the bottom of the sea."

Suddenly, catching hold of something, Tchelkache rose in the air; he disappeared over the wall.

Gavrilo shuddered . . . It had been so quickly done! He felt that the cursed weight and fear that he experienced in the presence of this moustached and lean bandit had, as it were, slipped off and rolled away from him. Could he escape, now? Breathing freely, he looked around him. On the left rose a black hull without masts, like an immense empty, deserted coffin. The waves beating against its sides awakened heavy echoes therein, resembling long-drawn sighs. On the right, stretched the damp wall of the quay, like a cold heavy serpent. Behind were visible black skeletons, and in front, in the space between the wall and the coffin, was the sea, silent and deserted, with black clouds hanging over it. These clouds were slowly advancing, their enormous, heavy masses, terrifying in the darkness, ready to crush man with their weight. All was cold, black and of evil omen. Gavrilo was afraid. This fear was greater than that imposed on him by Tchelkache; it clasped Gavrilo's breast in a tight embrace, squeezed him to a helpless mass and riveted him to the boat's bench.

Perfect silence reigned. Not a sound, save the sighs of the seas; it seemed as though this silence was about to be suddenly broken by some frightful, furious explosion of sound that would shake the sea to its depths, tear apart the dark masses of clouds floating over the sky and bury under the waves all those black craft. The clouds crawled over the sky as slowly and as wearily as before, but the sea gradually emerged from under them, and one might fancy, looking at the sky, that it was also a sea, but an angry sea overhanging a peaceful, sleeping one. The clouds resembled waves whose gray crests touched the earth; they resembled abysses hollowed by the wind between the waves and nascent billows not yet covered with the green foam of fury.

Gavrilo was oppressed by this dark calm and beauty; he realized that he desired his master's return. But he did not come! The time passed slowly, more slowly than crawled the clouds up in the sky . . . And the length of time augmented the agony of the silence. But just now behind the wall, the plashing of water was heard, then a rustling, and something like a whisper. Gavrilo was half dead from fright.

"Hey, there! Are you asleep? Take this! Softly!" said Tchelkache's hoarse voice.

From the wall descended a solid, square, heavy object. Gavrilo put it in the boat, then another one like it. Across the wall stretched Tchelkache's long figure. The oars reappeared mysteriously, then Gavrilo's bag fell at his feet and Tchelkache out of breath seated himself at the tiller.

Gavrilo looked at him with a timid and glad smile.

"Are you tired?" said he.

"A little, naturally, simpleton! Row firm, with all your might. You have a pretty profit, brother! The affair is half done, now there only remains to pass unseen under the eyes of those devils, and then you'll receive your money and fly to your Machka . . . You have a Machka, say, little one?"

"N-no!"

Gavrilo did not spare himself; his breast worked like a bellows and his arms like steel springs. The water foamed under the boat and the blue trail that followed in the wake of the stern had become wider. Gavrilo was bathed in perspiration, but he continued to row with all his strength. After twice experiencing the fright that he had on this night, he dreaded a repetition of it and had only one desire: to finish this accursed task as soon as possible, regain the land, and flee from this man before he should be killed by him or imprisoned on account of his misdeeds. He resolved not to speak to him, not to contradict him in anything, to execute all his commands and if he succeeded in freeing himself from him unmolested, to sing a Te Deum to Saint Nicholas. An earnest prayer was on his lips. But he controlled himself, puffed like a steamboat, and in silence cast furtive glances at Tchelkache.

The other, bending his long, lean body forward, like a bird poising for flight, gazed ahead into the darkness with his hawk's eyes. Turning his fierce, aquiline nose from side to side, he held the tiller with one hand and with the other tugged at his moustache which by a constant trembling betrayed the quiet smile on the thin lips. Tchelkache was pleased with his success, with himself and with this lad, whom he had terrified into becoming his slave. He enjoyed in advance to-morrow's feast and now he rejoiced in his strength and the subjection of this young, untried boy. He saw him toil; he took pity on him and tried to encourage him.

"Hey! Say there!" he asked softly. "Were you very much afraid?"

"It doesn't matter!" sighed Gavrilo, coughing.

"You needn't keep on rowing so hard. It's ended, now. There's only one more bad place to pass . . . Rest yourself."

Gavrilo stopped docilely, wiped the perspiration from his face with the sleeve of his blouse and again dipped the oars in the water.

"That's right, row more gently. So that the water tells no tales. There's a channel to cross. Softly, softly. Here, brother, are serious people. They are quite capable of amusing themselves with a gun, They could raise a fine lump on your forehead before you'd have time to cry out."

The boat glided over the water almost without sound. Blue drops fell from the oars and when they touched the sea there flamed up for an instant a little blue spot. The night was growing darker and more silent. The sky no longer resembled a rough sea; the clouds extended over its surface, forming a thick, even curtain, hanging motionless above the ocean. The sea was calmer and blacker, its warm and salty odor was stronger and it did not appear as vast as before.

"Oh! if it would only rain!" murmured Tchelkache; "we would be hidden by a curtain."

On the right and left of the boat, the motionless, melancholy, black hulls of ships emerged from the equally black water. A light moved to and fro on one; someone was walking with a lantern. The sea, caressing their sides, seemed to dully implore them while they responded by a cold, rumbling echo, as though they were disputing and refusing to yield.

"The custom-house," whispered Tchelkache.

From the moment that he had ordered Gavrilo to row slowly, the lad had again experienced a feeling of feverish expectation. He leaned forward, toward the darkness and it seemed to him that he was growing larger; his bones and veins stretched painfully; his head, filled with one thought, ached; the skin on his back shivered and in his legs were pricking sensations as though small sharp, cold needles were being thrust into them. His eyes smarted from having gazed too long into the darkness out of which he expected to see someone rise up and cry out: "Stop thieves!"

When Tchelkache murmured: "the custom-house!" Gavrilo started: he was consumed by a sharp, burning thought; his nerves were wrought up to the highest pitch; he wanted to cry out, to call for help, he had already opened his mouth and straightened himself up on the seat. He thrust forward his chest, drew a long breath, and again opened his mouth; but suddenly, overcome by sharp fear, he closed his eyes and fell from his seat.

Ahead of the boat, far off on the horizon, an immense, flaming blue sword sprang up from the black water. It rose, cleaved the darkness; its blade flashed across the clouds and illumined the surface of the sea with a broad blue hand. In this luminous ray stood out the black, silent ships, hitherto invisible. It seemed as though they had been waiting at the bottom of the sea, whither they had been dragged by an irresistible tempest, and that now they arose in obedience to the sword of fire to which the sea had given birth. They had ascended to contemplate the sky and all that was above the water. The rigging clinging to the mast seemed like seaweed that had left the water with these black giants, covering them with their meshes. Then the wonderful blue sword again arose in the air, cleaved the night and descended in a different place. Again, on the spot where it rested, appeared the skeletons of ships until then invisible.

Tchelkache's boat stopped and rocked on the water as though hesitating. Gavrilo lay flat on the bottom of the boat, covering his face with his hands, and Tchelkache prodded him with his oar, hissing furiously, but quite low.

"Idiot, that's the custom-house cruiser. The electric lantern! Get up, row with all your might! They'll throw the light upon us! You'll ruin us, devil, both of us!"

When the sharp edge of the oar had been brought down once more, harder this time, on Gavrilo's back, he arose and, not daring to open his eyes, resumed his seat and feeling for the oars, sent the boat ahead.

"Softly, or I'll kill you! Softly! Imbecile, may the devil take you! What are you afraid of? Say? A lantern and a mirror. That's all! Softly with those oars, miserable wretch! They incline the mirror at will and light the sea to find out if any folks like us are roving over it. They're on the watch for smugglers. We're out of reach; they're too far away, now. Don't be afraid, boy, we're safe! Now, we . . ."

Tchelkache looked around him triumphantly.

"Yes, we're safe. Out! You were in luck, you worthless stick!"

Gavrilo rowed in silence; breathing heavily, he cast sidelong glances at the spot where still rose and fell the sword of fire. He could not believe that it was only, as Tchelkache said, a lantern with a reflector. The cold, blue light, cutting the darkness, awoke silver reflections upon the sea; there seemed something mysterious about it, and Gavrilo again felt his faculties benumbed with fear. The presentiment of some misfortune oppressed him a second time. He rowed like a machine, bent his shoulders as though expecting a blow to descend and felt himself void of every desire, and without soul. The emotions of that night had consumed all that was human in him.

Tchelkache was more triumphant than ever: his success was complete! His nerves, accustomed to shocks, were already calmed. His lips trembled and his eyes shone with an eager light. He felt strong and well, whistled softly, inhaled long breaths of the salt sea air, glanced about from right to left and smiled good-naturedly when his eyes fell upon Gavrilo.

A light breeze set a thousand little waves to dancing. The clouds became thinner and more transparent although still covering the sky. The wind swept lightly and freely over the entire surface of the sea, but the clouds remained motionless, and seemed to be plunged in a dull, gray reverie.

"Come, brother, wake up, it's time! Your soul seems to have been shaken out of your skin; there's nothing left but a bag of bones. My dear fellow! We have hold of the good end, eh?"

Gavrilo was glad to hear a human voice, even though it was that of Tchelkache.

"I know it," said he, very low.

"That's right, little man! Take the tiller, I'll row; You're tired, aren't you?"

Gavrilo mechanically changed places, and when Tchelkache saw that he staggered, he pitied him more still and patted him on the shoulder,

"Don't be afraid! You've made a good thing out of it. I'll pay you well. Would you like to have twenty-five rubles, eh?"

"I—I don't need anything. All I ask is to reach land!"

Tchelkache removed his hand, spat and began to row; his long arms sent the oars far back of him.

The sea had awakened. It sported with its tiny waves, brought them forth, adorned them with a fringe of foam, tumbled them over each other and broke them into spray. The foam as it melted sighed and the air was filled with harmonious sounds and the plashing of water. The darkness seemed to be alive.

"Well! tell me . . ." began Tchelkache. "You'll return to the village, you'll marry, you'll set to work to plough and sow, your wife'll present you with many children, you'll not have enough bread and you'll just manage to keep soul and body together all your life! So . . . is it such a pleasant prospect?"

"What pleasure can there be in that?" timidly and shudderingly replied Gavrilo. "What can one do?"

Here and there, the clouds were rent by the wind and, through the spaces, the cold sky studded with a few stars looked down. Reflected by the joyous sea, these stars leaped upon the waves, now disappearing, now shining brightly.

"More to the left!" said Tchelkache. "We shall soon be there, Yes! . . . it is ended. We've done a good stroke of work. In a single night, you understand—five hundred rubles gained! Isn't that doing well, say?"

"Five hundred rubles!" repeated Gavrilo, distrustfully, but he was immediately seized with fright and quickly asked, kicking the bales at the bottom of the boat: "What are those things?"

"That's silk. A very dear thing. If it were to be sold for its real value, it would bring a thousand rubles. But I don't raise the price . . . clever that, eh?"

"Is it possible?" asked Gavrilo. "If I only had as much!"

He sighed at the thought of the country, of his miserable life, his toil, his mother and all those far-distant and dear things for which he had gone away to work, and for which he had suffered so much that night. A wave of memory swept over him: he saw his village on a hill-side with the river at the bottom, hidden by birches, willows, mountain-ash and wild cherry trees. The picture breathed some life in him and gave him a little strength.

"Oh, Lord, how much good it would do!" he sighed, sadly.

"Yes! I imagine that you'd very quickly board the train and—good-evening! Oh, how the girls would love you, yonder, in the village! You could have your pick. You could have a new house built. But for a new house, there might not be enough . . ."

"That's true. A house, no; wood is very dear with us."

"Never mind, you could have the one that you have repaired. Do you own a horse?"

"A horse? Yes, there's one, but he's very old!"

"Then a horse, a good horse! A cow . . . sheep . . . poultry . . . eh?"

"Why do you say that? If only! . . . Ah! Lord, how I might enjoy life."

"Yes, brother, life under those circumstances would not be bad . . . I, too, I know a little about such things. I also have a nest belonging to me. My father was one of the richest peasants of his village."

Tchelkache rowed slowly. The boat danced upon the waves which beat against its sides; it scarcely advanced over the somber sea, now disporting itself harder than ever. The two men dreamed, rocked upon the water and gazing vaguely around them. Tchelkache had spoken to Gavrilo of his village with the purpose of quieting him and helping him to recover from his emotion. He at first spoke with a sceptical smile hidden under his moustache, but as he talked and recalled the joys of country life, in regard to which he himself had long since been disabused, and that he had forgotten until this moment, he became carried away, and instead of talking to the lad, he began unconsciously to harangue:

"The essential part of the life of a peasant, brother, is liberty. You must be your own master. You own your house: it is not worth much, but it belongs to you. You possess a piece of ground, a little corner, perhaps, but it is yours. Your chickens, eggs, apples are yours. You are a king upon the earth. Then you must be methodical . . . As soon as you are up in the morning, you must go to work. In the spring it is one thing, in the summer another, in the autumn and winter still another. From wherever you may be you always return to your home. There is warmth, rest! . . . You are a king, are you not?"

Tchelkache had waxed enthusiastic over this long enumeration of the privileges and rights of the peasant, forgetting only to speak of his duties.

Gavrilo looked at him with curiosity, and was also aroused to enthusiasm. He had already had time in the course of this conversation to forget with whom he was dealing; he saw before him only a peasant like himself, attached to the earth by labor, by several generations of laborers, by memories of childhood, but who had voluntarily withdrawn from it and its cares and who was now suffering the punishment of his ill-advised act.

"Yes, comrade, that's true! Oh! how true that is! See now, take your case, for instance: what are you now, without land? Ah! friend, the earth is like a mother: one doesn't forget it long."

Tchelkache came to himself. He felt within him that burning sensation that always seized upon him when his self-love as a dashing devil-may-care fellow was wounded, especially when the offender was of no account in his eyes.

"There he goes again!" he exclaimed fiercely. "You imagine, I suppose that I'm speaking seriously. I'm worth more than that, let me tell you!"

"Why, you funny fellow!" replied Gavrilo, again intimidated, "am I speaking of you? There are a great many like you! My God, how many unfortunate persons, vagabonds there are on the earth!"

"Take the oars again, dolt!" commanded Tchelkache shortly, restraining himself from pouring forth a string of fierce oaths that rose in his throat.

They again changed places. Tchelkache, while clambering over the bales to return to the helm, experienced a sharp desire to give Gavrilo a good blow that would send him overboard, and, at the same time, he could not muster strength to look him in the face.

The short conversation was ended; but now Gavrilo's silence even savored to Tchelkache of the village. He was lost in thoughts of the past and forgot to steer his boat; the waves had turned it and it was now going out to sea. They seemed to understand that this boat had no aim, and they played with it and lightly tossed it, while their blue fires flamed up under the oars. Before Tchelkache's inward vision, was rapidly unfolded a series of pictures of the past—that far distant past separated from the present by a wall of eleven years of vagrancy. He saw himself again a child, in the village, he saw his mother, red-cheeked, fat, with kind gray eyes,— his father, a giant with a tawny beard and stern countenance,—himself betrothed to Amphissa, black-eyed with a long braid down her back, plump, easy-going, gay . . . And then, himself, a handsome soldier of the guard; later, his father, gray and bent by work, and his mother, wrinkled and bowed. What a merry-making there was at the village when he had returned after the expiration of his service! How proud the father was of his Gregori, the moustached, broad-shouldered soldier, the cock of the village! Memory, that scourge of the unfortunate, brings to life even the stones of the past, and, even to the poison, drunk in former days, adds drops of honey; and all this only to kill man by the consciousness of his faults, and to destroy in his soul all faith in the future by causing him to love the past too well.

Tchelkache was enveloped in a peaceful whiff of natal air that was wafting toward him the sweet words of his mother, the sage counsel of his father, the stern peasant, and many forgotten sounds and savory odors of the earth, frozen as in the springtime, or freshly ploughed, or lastly, covered with young wheat, silky, and green as an emerald . . . Then he felt himself a pitiable, solitary being, gone astray, without attachments and an outcast from the life where the blood in his veins had been formed.

"Hey! Where are we going?" suddenly asked Gavrilo.

Tchelkache started and turned around with the uneasy glance of a wild beast.

"Oh! the devil! Never mind . . . Row more cautiously . . . We're almost there."

"Were you dreaming?" asked Gavrilo, smiling.

Tchelkache looked searchingly at him. The lad was entirely himself again; calm, gay, he even seemed complacent. He was very young, all his life was before him. That was bad! But perhaps the soil would retain him. At this thought, Tchelkache grew sad again, and growled out in reply:

"I'm tired! . . . and the boat rocks!"

"Of course it rocks! So, now, there's no danger of being caught with this?"

Gavrilo kicked the bales.

"No, be quiet. I'm going to deliver them at once and receive the money. Yes!"

"Five hundred?"

"Not less, probably . . ."

"It's a lot! If I had it, poor beggar that I am, I'd soon let it be known."

"At the village? . . ."

"Sure! without delay . . ."

Gavrilo let himself be carried away by his imagination. Tchelkache appeared crushed. His moustache hung down straight; his right side was all wet from the waves, his eyes were sunken in his head and without life. He was a pitiful and dull object. His likeness to a bird of prey had disappeared; self-abasement appeared in the very folds of his dirty blouse.

"I'm tired, worn out!"

"We are landing . . . Here we are."

Tchelkache abruptly turned the boat and guided it toward something black that arose from the water.

The sky was covered with clouds, and a fine, drizzling rain began to fall, pattering joyously on the crests of the waves.

"Stop! . . . Softly!" ordered Tchelkache.

The bow of the boat hit the hull of a vessel.

"Are the devils sleeping?" growled Tchelkache, catching the ropes hanging over the side with his boat-hook. "The ladder isn't lowered. In this rain, besides . . . It couldn't have rained before! Eh! You vermin, there! Eh!"

"Is that you Selkache?" came softly from above.

"Lower the ladder, will you!"

"Good-day, Selkache."

"Lower the ladder, smoky devil!" roared Tchelkache.

"Oh! Isn't he ill-natured to-day . . . Eh! Oh!"

"Go up, Gavrilo!" commanded Tchelkache to his companion.

In a moment they were on the deck, where three dark and bearded individuals were looking over the side at Tchelkache's boat and talking animatedly in a strange and harsh language. A fourth, clad in a long gown, advanced toward Tchelkache, shook his hand in silence and cast a suspicious glance at Gavrilo.

"Get the money ready for to-morrow morning," briefly said Tchelkache. "I'm going to sleep, now. Come Gavrilo. Are you hungry?"

"I'm sleepy," replied Gavrilo,

In five minutes, he was snoring on the dirty deck; Tchelkache sitting beside him, was trying on an old boot that he found lying there. He softly whistled, animated both by sorrow and anger. Then he lay down beside Gavrilo, without removing the boot from his foot, and putting his hands under the back of his neck he carefully examined the deck, working his lips the while.

The boat rocked joyously on the water; the sound of wood creaking dismally was heard, the rain fell softly on the deck, the waves beat against the sides. Everything resounded sadly like the lullaby of a mother who has lost all hope for the happiness of her son.

Tchelkache, with parted lips, raised his head and gazed around him . . . and murmuring a few words, lay down again.

* * * * *

He was the first to awaken, starting up uneasily; then suddenly quieting down he looked at Gavrilo, who was still sleeping. The lad was smiling in his sleep, his round, sun-burned face irradiated with joy.

Tchelkache sighed and climbed up a narrow rope ladder. The opening of the trap-door framed a piece of leaden sky. It was daylight, but the autumn weather was gray and gloomy.

It was two hours before Tchelkache reappeared. His face was red, his moustache curled fiercely upward; his eyes beamed with gaiety and good-nature. He wore high, thick boots, a coat and leather trowsers; he looked like a hunter. His costume, which, although a little worn, was still in good condition and fitted him well, made him appear broader, concealed his too angular lines and gave him a martial air.

"Hey! Youngster, get up!" said he touching Gavrilo with his foot.

The last named started up, and not recognizing him just at first, gazed at him vacantly. Tchelkache burst out laughing.

"How you're gotten up! . . ." finally exclaimed Gavrilo, smiling broadly. "You are a gentleman!"

"We do that quickly here! What a coward you are! Dear, dear! How many times did you make up your mind to die last night, eh? Say . . ."

"But you see, it's the first time I've ever done anything like this! One might lose his soul for the rest of his days!"

"Would you be willing to go again?"

"Again? I must know first what there would be in it for me."

"Two hundred."

"Two hundred, you say? Yes I'd go."

"Stop! . . . And your soul?"

"Perhaps I shouldn't lose it!" said Gavrilo, smiling. "And then one would be a man for the rest of his days!"

Tchelkache burst out laughing. "That's right, but we've joked long enough! Let us row to the shore. Get ready."

"I? Why I'm ready . . ."

They again took their places in the boat. Tchelkache at the helm, Gavrilo rowing.

The gray sky was covered with clouds; the troubled, green sea, played with their craft, tossing it on its still tiny waves that broke over it in a shower of clear, salt drops. Far off, before the prow of the boat, appeared the yellow line of the sandy beach; back of the stern was the free and joyous sea, all furrowed by the troops of waves that ran up and down, already decked in their superb fringe of foam. In the far distance, ships were rocking on the bosom of the sea and, on the left, was a whole forest of masts mingled with the white masses of the houses of the town. Prom there, a dull murmur is borne out to sea and blending with the sound of the waves swelled into rapturous music. Over all stretched a thin veil of mist, widening the distance between the different objects.

"Eh! It'll be rough to-night!" said Tchelkache, nodding his head in the direction of the sea.

"A storm?" asked Gavrilo. He was rowing hard. He was drenched from head to foot by the drops blown by the wind.

"Ehe!" affirmed Tchelkache.

Gavrilo looked at him curiously.

"How much did they give you?" he asked at last, seeing that Tchelkache was not disposed to talk.

"See!" said Tchelkache. He held out toward Gavrilo something that he drew from his pocket.

Gavrilo saw the variegated banknotes, and they assumed in his eyes all the colors of the rainbow.

"Oh! And I thought you were boasting! How much?"

"Five hundred and forty! Isn't that a good haul?"

"Certain!" murmured Gavrilo, following with greedy eyes the five hundred and forty roubles as they again disappeared in the pocket. "Ah! If it was only mine!" He sighed dejectedly.

"We'll have a lark, little one!" enthusiastically exclaimed Tchelkache! "Have no fear: I'll pay you, brother. I'll give you forty rubles! Eh? Are you pleased? Do you want your money now?"

"If you don't mind. Yes, I'll accept it!"

Gavrilo trembled with anticipation; a sharp, burning pain oppressed his breast.

"Ha! ha! ha! Little devil! You'll accept it? Take it, brother, I beg of you! I implore you, take it! I don't know where to put all this money; relieve me, here!"

Tchelkache handed Gavrilo several ten ruble notes. The other took them with a shaking hand, dropped the oars and proceeded to conceal his booty in his blouse, screwing up his eyes greedily, and breathing noisily as though he were drinking something hot. Tchelkache regarded him ironically. Gavrilo seized the oars; he rowed in nervous haste, his eyes lowered, as though he were afraid. His shoulders shook.

"My God, how greedy you are! That's bad. Besides, for a peasant . . ."

"Just think of what one can do with money!" exclaimed Gavrilo, passionately. He began to talk brokenly and rapidly, as though pursuing an idea, and seizing the words on the wing, of life in the country with and without money. "Respect, ease, liberty, gaiety . . ."

Tchelkache listened attentively with a serious countenance and inscrutable eyes. Occasionally, he smiled in a pleased manner.

"Here we are!" he said at last.

A wave seized hold of the boat and landed it high on the sand.

"Ended, ended, quite ended! We must draw the boat up farther, so that it will be out of reach of the tide. They will come after it. And, now, good-bye. The town is eight versts from here. You'll return to town, eh?"

Tchelkache's face still beamed with a slily good-natured smile; he seemed to be planning something pleasant for himself and a surprise for Gavrilo. He put his hand in his pocket and rustled the bank-notes.

"No, I'm not going . . . I . . ."

Gavrilo stifled and choked. He was shaken by a storm of conflicting desires, words and feelings. He burned as though on fire.

Tchelkache gazed at him with astonishment.

"What's the matter with you?" he asked.

"Nothing."

But Gavrilo's face grew red and then ashy pale. The lad moved his feet restlessly as though he would have thrown himself upon Tchelkache, or as though he were torn by Borne secret desire difficult to realize.

His suppressed excitement moved Tchelkache to some apprehension. He wondered what form it would take in breaking out.

Gavrilo gave a laugh, a strange laugh, like a sob. His head was bent, so that Tchelkache could not see the expression of his face; he could only perceive Gavrilo's ears, by turns red and white.

"Go to the devil!" exclaimed Tchelkache, motioning with his hand. "Are you in love with me? Say? Look at you mincing like a young girl. Are you distressed at leaving me? Eh! youngster, speak, or else I'm going!"

"You're going?" cried Gavrilo, in a sonorous voice. The deserted and sandy beach trembled at this cry, and the waves of sand brought by the waves of the sea seemed to shudder. Tchelkache also shuddered. Suddenly Gavrilo darted from his place, and throwing himself at Tchelkache's feet, entwined his legs with his arms and drew him toward him. Tchelkache tottered, sat down heavily on the sand, and gritting his teeth, brandished his long arm and closed fist in the air. But before he had time to strike, he was stopped by the troubled and suppliant look of Gavrilo.

"Friend! Give me . . . that money! Give it to me, in the name of Heaven. What need have you of it? It is the earnings of one night . . . a single night . . . And it would take me years to get as much as that . . . Give it to me . . . I'll pray for you . . . all my life . . . in three churches . . . for the safety of your soul. You'll throw it to the winds, and I'll give it to the earth. Oh! give me that money. What will you do with it, say? Do you care about it as much as that? One night . . . and you are rich! Do a good deed! You are lost, you! . . . You'll never come back again to the way, while I! . . . Ah! give it to me!"

Tchelkache frightened, astonished and furious threw himself backward, still seated on the sand, and leaning on his two hands silently gazed at him, his eyes starting from their orbits; the lad leaned his head on his knees and gasped forth his supplications. Tchelkache finally pushed him away, jumped to his feet, and thrusting his hand into his pocket threw the multi-colored bills at Gavrilo.

"There, dog, swallow them!" he cried trembling with mingled feelings of anger, pity and hate for this greedy slave. Now that he had thrown him the money, he felt himself a hero. His eyes, his whole person, beamed with conscious pride.

"I meant to have given you more. I pitied you yesterday. I thought of the village. I said to myself: 'I'll help this boy.' I was waiting to see what you'd do, whether you'd ask me or not. And now, see! tatterdemalion, beggar, that you are! . . . Is it right to work oneself up to such a state for money . . . to suffer like that? Imbeciles, greedy devils who forget . . . who would sell themselves for five kopeks, eh?"

63

"Friend . . . Christ's blessing on you! What is this? What? Thousands? . . . I'm a rich man, now!" screamed Gavrilo, in a frenzy of delight, hiding the money in his blouse. "Ah! dear man! I shall, never forget this! never! And I'll beg my wife and children to pray for you."

Tchelkache listened to these cries of joy, gazed at this face, irradiated and disfigured by the passion of covetousness; he felt that he himself, the thief and vagabond, freed from all restraining influence, would never become so rapacious, so vile, so lost to all decency. Never would he sink so low as that! Lost in these reflections, which brought to him the consciousness of his liberty and his audacity, he remained beside Gavrilo on the lonely shore.

"You have made me happy!" cried Gavrilo, seizing Tchelkache's hand and laying it against his cheek.

Tchelkache was silent and showed his teeth like a wolf. Gavrilo continued to pour out his heart.

"What an idea that was of mine! We were rowing here . . . I saw the money . . . I said to myself:

"Suppose I were to give him . . . give you . . . a blow with the oar . . . just one! The money would be mine; as for him, I'd throw him in the sea . . . you, you understand? Who would ever notice his disappearance? And if you were found, no inquest would be made: who, how, why had you been killed? You're not the kind of man for whom any stir would be made! You're of no use on the earth! Who would take your part? That's the way it would be! Eh?"

"Give back that money!" roared Tchelkache, seizing Gavrilo by the throat.

Gavrilo struggled, once, twice . . . but Tchelkache's other arm entwined itself like a serpent around him . . . a noise of tearing linen,—and Gavrilo slipped to the ground with bulging eyes, catching at the air with his hands and waving his legs. Tchelkache, erect, spare, like a wild beast, showed his teeth wickedly and laughed harshly, while his moustache worked nervously on his sharp, angular face. Never, in his whole life, had he been so deeply wounded, and never had his anger been so great.

"Well! Are you happy, now?" asked he, still laughing, of Gavrilo, and turning his back to him, he walked away in the direction of the town.

But he had hardly taken two steps when Gavrilo, crouching like a cat, threw a large, round stone at him, crying furiously:

"O—one!"

Tchelkache groaned, raised his hands to the back of his neck and stumbled forward, then turned toward Gavrilo and fell face downward on the sand. He moved a leg, tried to raise his head and stiffened, vibrating like a stretched cord. At this, Gavrilo began to run, to run far away, yonder, to where the shadow of that ragged cloud overhung the misty steppe. The murmuring waves, coursing over the sands, joined him and ran on and on, never stopping. The foam hissed, the spray flew through the air.

The rain fell. Slight at first, it soon came down thickly, heavily and came from the sky in slender streams. They crossed, forming a net that soon shut off the distance on land and water. For a long time there was nothing to be seen but the rain and this long body lying on the sand beside the sea . . . But suddenly, behold Gavrilo coming from out the rain, running; he flew like a bird. He went up to Tchelkache, fell upon his knees before him, and tried to turn him over. His hand sank into a sticky liquid, warm and red. He trembled and drew back, pale and distracted.

"Get up, brother!" he whispered amid the noise of the falling rain into the ear of Tchelkache.

Tchelkache came to himself and, repulsing Gavrilo, said in a hoarse voice:

"Go away!"

"Forgive me, brother: I was tempted by the devil . . ." continued Gavrilo, trembling and kissing Tchelkache's hand.

"Go, go away!" growled the other.

"Absolve my sin! Friend . . . forgive me!"

"Go, go to the devil!" suddenly cried out Tchelkache, sitting up on the sand. His face was pale, threatening; his clouded eyes closed as though he were very sleepy . . . "What do you want, now? You've finished your business . . . go! Off with you!"

He tried to kick Gavrilo, prostrated by grief, but failed, and would have fallen if Gavrilo hadn't supported him with his shoulders. Tchelkache's face was now on a level with Gavrilo's. Both were pale, wretched and terrifying.

"Fie!"

Tchelkache spat in the wide opened eyes of his employe.

The other humbly wiped them with his sleeve, and murmured:

"Do what you will . . . I'll not say one word. Pardon me, in the name of Heaven!"

"Fool, you don't even know how to steal!" cried Tchelkache, contemptuously. He tore his shirt under his waistcoat and, gritting his teeth in silence, began to bandage his head.

"Have you taken the money?" he asked, at last.

"I haven't taken it, brother; I don't want it! It brings bad luck!"

Tchelkache thrust his hand into his waistcoat pocket, withdrew the package of bills, put one of them in his pocket and threw all the rest at Gavrilo.

"Take that and be off!"

"I cannot take it . . . I cannot! Forgive me!"

"Take it, I tell you!" roared Tchelkache, rolling his eyes frightfully.

"Pardon me! When you have forgiven me I'll take it," timidly said Gavrilo, falling on the wet sand at Tchelkache's feet.

"You lie, fool, you'll take it at once!" said Tchelkache, confidently, and raising his head, by a painful effort, he thrust the money before his face. "Take it, take it! You haven't worked for nothing! Don't be ashamed of having failed to assassinate a man! No one will claim anyone like me. You'll be thanked, on the contrary, when it's learned what you've done.

There, take it! No one'll know what you've done and yet it deserves some reward! Here it is!"

Gavrilo saw that Tchelkache was laughing, and he felt relieved. He held the money tightly in his hand.

"Brother! Will you forgive me? Won't you do it? Say?" he supplicated tearfully.

"Little brother!" mimicked Tchelkache, rising on his tottering limbs. "Why should I pardon you? There's no occasion for it. To-day it's you, to-morrow it'll be me . . ."

"Ah! brother, brother!" sighed Gavrilo, sorrowfully, shaking his head.

Tchelkache was standing before him, smiling strangely; the cloth wrapped around his head, gradually reddening, resembled a Turkish head-dress.

The rain fell in torrents. The sea complained dully and the waves beat angrily against the beach.

The two men were silent.

"Good-bye!" said Tchelkache, with cold irony.

He staggered, his legs trembled, and he carried his head oddly, as though he was afraid of losing it.

"Pardon me, brother!" again repeated Gavrilo.

"It's nothing!" drily replied Tchelkache, as he supported his head with his left hand and gently pulled his moustache with his right.

Gavrilo stood gazing after him until he had disappeared in the rain that still fell in fine, close drops, enveloping the steppe in a mist as impenetrable and gray as steel.

Then Gavrilo took off his wet cap, made the sign of the cross, looked at the money pressed tightly in his hand and drew a long, deep sigh; he concealed his booty in his blouse and began to walk, taking long strides, in the opposite direction to that in which Tchelkache had gone.

The sea thundered, threw great heavy waves upon the sand and broke them into foam and spray. The rain lashed the sea and land pitilessly;

the wind roared. All the air around was filled with plaints, cries and dull sounds. The rain masked sea and sky . . .

The rain and the breaking waves soon washed away the red spot where Tchelkache had been struck to the ground; they soon effaced his footprints and those of the lad on the sand, and the lonely beach was left without the slightest trace of the little drama that had been played between these two men.

MALVA

BY MAXIME GORKY

The sea laughed.

It trembled at the warm and light breath of the wind and became covered with tiny wrinkles that reflected the sun in blinding fashion and laughed at the sky with its thousands of silvery lips. In the deep space between sea and sky buzzed the deafening and joyous sound of the waves chasing each other on the flat beach of the sandy promontory. This noise and brilliancy of sunlight, reverberated a thousand times by the sea, mingled harmoniously in ceaseless and joyous agitation. The sky was glad to shine; the sea was happy to reflect the glorious light.

The wind caressed the powerful and satin-like breast of the sea, the sun heated it with its rays and it sighed as if fatigued by these ardent caresses; it filled the burning air with the salty aroma of its emanations. The green waves, coursing up the yellow sand, threw on the beach the white foam of their luxurious crests which melted with a gentle murmur, and wet it.

At intervals along the beach, scattered with shells and sea weed, were stakes of wood driven into the sand and on which hung fishing nets, drying and casting shadows as fine as cobwebs. A few large boats and a small one were drawn up beyond high-water mark, and the waves as they ran up towards them seemed as if they were calling to them. Gaffs, oars, coiled ropes, baskets and barrels lay about in disorder and amidst it all was a cabin built of yellow branches, bark and matting. Above the general chaos floated a red rag at the extremity of a tall mast.

Under the shade of a boat lay Vassili Legostev, the watchman at this outpost of the Grebentchikov fishing grounds. Lying on his stomach, his head resting on his hands, he was gazing fixedly out to sea, where away in the distance danced a black spot. Vassili saw with satisfaction that it grew larger and was drawing nearer.

Screwing up his eyes on account of the glare caused by the reflection on the water, he grunted with pleasure and content. Malva was coming. A few minutes more and she would be there, laughing so heartily as to strain every stitch of her well-filled bodice. She would throw her robust and gentle arms around him and kiss him, and in that rich sonorous voice that startles the sea gulls would give him the news of what was going on yonder. They would make a good fish soup together, and drink brandy as they chatted and caressed each other. That is how they spent every Sunday and holiday. And at daylight he would row her back over the sea in the sharp morning air. Malva, still nodding with sleep, would hold the tiller and he would watch her as he pulled. She was amusing at those times, funny and charming both, like a cat which had eaten well. Sometimes she would slip from her seat and roll herself up at the bottom of the boat like a ball.

As Vassili watched the little black spot grow larger it seemed to him that Malva was not alone in the boat. Could Serejka have come along with her? Vassili moved heavily on the sand, sat up, shaded his eyes with his hands, and with a show of ill humor began to strain his eyes to see who was coming. No, the man rowing was not Serejka. He rows strong but clumsily. If Serejka were rowing Malva would not take the trouble to hold the rudder.

"Hey there!" cried Vassili impatiently.

The sea gulls halted in their flight and listened.

"Hallo! Hallo!" came back from the boat. It was Malva's sonorous voice.

"Who's with you?"

A laugh replied to him.

"Jade!" swore Vassili under his breath.

He spat on the ground with vexation.

He was puzzled. While he rolled a cigarette he examined the neck and back of the rower who was rapidly drawing nearer. The sound of the water when the oars struck it resounded in the still air, and the sand crunched under the watchman's bare feet as he stamped about in his impatience.

"Who's with you?" he cried, when he could discern the familiar smile on Malva's pretty plump face.

"Wait. You'll know him all right," she replied laughing.

The rower turned on his seat and, also laughing, looked at Vassili.

The watchman frowned. It seemed to him that he knew the fellow.

"Pull harder!" commanded Malva.

The stroke was so vigorous that the boat was carried up the beach on a wave, fell over on one side and then righted itself while the wave rolled back laughing into the sea. The rower jumped out on the beach, and going up to Vassili said:

"How are you, father?"

"Iakov!" cried Vassili, more surprised than pleased.

They embraced three times. Afterwards Vassili's stupor became mingled with both joy and uneasiness. The watchman stroked his blond beard with one hand and with the other gesticulated:

"I knew something was up; my heart told me so. So it was you! I kept asking myself if it was Serejka. But I saw it was not Serejka. How did you come here?"

Vassili would have liked to look at Malva, but his son's rollicking eyes were upon him and he did not dare. The pride he felt at having a son so strong and handsome struggled in him with the embarrassment caused by the presence of Malva. He shuffled about and kept asking Iakov one question after another, often without waiting for a reply. His head felt awhirl, and he felt particularly uneasy when he heard Malva say in a mocking tone.

"Don't skip about—for joy. Take him to the cabin and give him something to eat."

The father examined his son from head to foot. On the latter's lips hovered that cunning smile Vassili knew so well. Malva turned her green eyes from the father to the son and munched melon seeds between her small white teeth. Iakov smiled and for a few seconds, which were painful to Vassili, all three were silent.

"I'll come back in a moment," said Vassili suddenly going towards the cabin. "Don't stay there in the sun, I'm going to fetch some water. We'll make some soup. I'll give you some fish soup, Iakov."

He seized a saucepan that was lying on the ground and disappeared behind the fishing nets.

Malva and the peasant followed him.

"Well, my fine young fellow, I brought you to your father, didn't I?" said Malva, brushing up against Iakov's robust figure.

He turned towards her his face framed in its curled blond beard, and with a brilliant gleam in his eyes said:

"Yes, here we are—It's fine here, isn't it? What a stretch of sea!"

"The sea is great. Has the old man changed much?"

"No, not much. I expected to find him more grey. He's still pretty solid."

"How long is it since you saw him?"

"About five years. I was nearly seventeen when he left the village."

They entered the cabin, the air of which was suffocating from the heat and the odor of cooking fish. They sat down. Between them there was a roughly-hewn oak table. They looked at each other for a long time without speaking.

"So you want to work here?" said Malva at last.

"I don't know. If I find something, I'll work."

"You'll find work," replied Malva with assurance, examining him critically with her green eyes.

He paid no attention to her, and with his sleeve wiped away the perspiration that covered his face.

She suddenly began to laugh.

"Your mother probably sent messages for your father by you?"

Iakov gave a shrug of ill humor and replied:

"Of course. What if she did?"

"Oh, nothing."

And she laughed the louder.

Her laugh displeased Iakov. He paid no attention to her and thought of his mother's instructions. When she accompanied him to the end of the village she had said quickly, blinking her eyes:

"In Christ's name, Iakov say to him: 'Father, mother is alone yonder. Five years have gone by and she is always alone. She is getting old.' Tell him that, Iakov, my little Iakov, for the love of God. Mother will soon be an old woman. She's always alone, always at work. In Christ's name, tell him that."

And she had wept silently, hiding her face in her apron.

Iakov had not pitied her then, but he did now. And his face took on a hard expression before Malva, as if he were about to abuse her.

"Here I am!" cried Vassili, bursting in on them with a wriggling fish in one hand and a knife in the other.

He had not got over his uneasiness, but had succeeded in dissimulating it deep within him. Now he looked at his guests with serenity and good nature; only his manner was more agitated than usual.

"I'll make a bit of a fire in a minute, and we'll talk. Why, Iakov, what a fine fellow you've grown!"

Again he disappeared.

Malva went on munching her melon seeds. She stared familiarly at Iakov. He tried not to meet her eyes, although he would have liked to, and he thought to himself:

"Life must come easy here. People seem to eat as much as they want to. How strong she is and father, too!"

Then intimidated by the silence, he said aloud:

"I forgot my bag in the boat. I'll go and get it."

Iakov rose leisurely and went out. Vassili appeared a moment later. He bent down towards Malva and said rapidly with anger:

"What did you want to bring him for? What shall I tell him about you?"

"What's that to me? Am I afraid of him? Or of you?" she asked, closing her green eyes with disdain. Then she laughed: "How you went on when you saw him. It was so funny!"

"Funny, eh?"

The sand crunched under Iakov's steps and they had to suspend their conversation. Iakov had brought a bag which he threw into a corner. He cast a hostile look at the young woman.

She went on munching her seeds. Vassili, seating himself on the woodbin, said with a forced smile:

"What made you think of coming?"

"Why, I just came. We wrote you."

"When? I haven't received any letter."

"Really? We wrote often."

"The letter must have got lost," said Vassili regretfully. "It always does when it's important."

"So you don't know how things are at home?" asked Iakov, suspiciously.

"How should I know? I received no letter."

Then Iakov told him that the horse was dead, that all the corn had been eaten before the beginning of February, and that he himself had been unable to find any work. Hay was also short, and the cow had almost perished from hunger. They had managed as best they could until April and then they decided that Iakov should join the father far away

74

and work three months with him. That is what they had written. Then they sold three sheep, bought flour and hay and Iakov had started.

"How is that possible?" cried Vassali. "I sent you some money."

"Your money didn't go far. We repaired the cottage, we had to marry sister off and I bought a plough. You know five years is a long time."

"Hum," said Vassili, "wasn't it enough? What a tale of woe! Ah, there's my soup boiling over!"

He rose and stooping before the fire on which was the saucepan, Vassili meditated while throwing the scum into the flame. Nothing in his son's recital had touched him particularly, and he felt irritated against his wife and Iakov. He had sent them a great deal of money during the last five years, and yet they had not been able to manage. If Malva had not been present he would have told his son what he thought about it. Iakov was smart enough to leave the village on his own responsibility and without the father's permission, but he had not been able to get a living out of the soil. Vassili sighed as he stirred the soup, and as he watched the blue flames he thought of his son and Malva. Henceforward, he thought, his life would be less agreeable, less free. Iakov had surely guessed what Malva was.

Meanwhile Malva, in the cabin, was trying to arouse the rustic with her bold eyes.

"Perhaps you left a girl in the village?" she asked suddenly.

"Perhaps," he responded surlily.

Inwardly he was abusing Malva.

"Is she pretty?" she asked with indifference.

Iakov made no reply.

"Why don't you answer? Is she better looking than I, or no?"

He looked at her in spite of himself. Her cheeks were sunburnt and plump, her lips red and tempting and now, parted in a malicious smile, showing the white even teeth, they seemed to tremble. Her bust was full and firm under a pink cotton waist that set off to advantage her trim waist and well-rounded arms. But he did not like her green and cynical eyes.

"Why do you talk like that?" he asked.

He sighed without reason and spoke in a beseeching tone, yet he wanted to speak brutally to her.

"How shall I talk?" she asked laughing.

"There you are, laughing—at what?"

"At you—."

"What have I done to you?" he said with irritation. And once more he lowered his eyes under her gaze.

She made no reply.

Iakov understood her relations towards his father perfectly well and that prevented him from expressing himself freely. He was not surprised. It would have been difficult for a man like his father to have been long without a companion.

"The soup is ready," announced Vassili, at the threshold of the cabin. "Get the spoons, Malva."

When she found the spoons she said she must go down to the sea to wash them.

The father and son watched her as she ran down the sands and both were silent.

"Where did you meet her?" asked Vassili, finally.

"I went to get news of you at the office. She was there. She said to me: 'Why go on foot along the sand? Come in the boat. I'm going there.' And so we started."

"And—what do you think of her?"

"Not bad," said Iakov, vaguely, blinking his eyes.

"What could I do?" asked Vassili. "I tried at first. But it was impossible. She mends my clothes and so on. Besides it's as easy to escape from death as from a woman when once she's after you."

"What's it to me?" said Iakov. "It's your affair. I'm not your judge."

Malva now returned with the spoons, and they sat down to dinner. They ate without talking, sucking the bones noisily and spitting them out on the sand, near the door. Iakov literally devoured his food, which seemed to please Malva vastly; she watched with tender interest his sunburnt cheeks extend and his thick humid lips moving quickly. Vassili was not hungry. He tried, however, to appear absorbed in the meal so as to be able to watch Malva and Iakov at his ease.

After awhile, when Iakov had eaten his fill he said he was sleepy.

"Lie down here," said Vassili. "We'll wake you up."

"I'm willing," said Iakov, sinking down on a coil of rope. "And what will you do?"

Embarrassed by his son's smile, Vassili left the cabin hastily, Malva frowned and replied to Iakov:

"What's that to you? Learn to mind your own business, my lad."

Then she went out.

Iakov turned over and went to sleep.

Vassili had fixed three stakes in the sand, and with a piece of matting had rigged up a shelter from the sun. Then he lay down flat on his back and contemplated the sky. When Malva came up and dropped on the sand by his side he turned towards her with vexation plainly written on his face.

"Well, old man," she said laughing, "you don't seem pleased to see your son."

"He mocks me. And why? Because of you," replied Vassili testily.

"Oh, I am sorry. What can we do? I mustn't come here again, eh? All right. I'll not come again."

"Siren that you are! Ah, you women! He mocks me and you too—and yet you are what I have dearest to me."

He moved away from her and was silent. Squatting on the sand, with her legs drawn up to her chin, Malva balanced herself gently to and fro, idly gazing with her green eyes over the dazzling joyous sea, and she smiled with triumph as all women do when they understand the power of their beauty.

"Why don't you speak?" asked Vassili.

"I'm thinking," said Malva. Then after a pause she added:

"Your son's a fine fellow."

"What's that to you?" cried Vassili, jealously.

"Who knows?"

He glanced at her suspiciously. "Take care," he said, menacingly. "Don't play the imbecile. I'm a patient man, but I mustn't be crossed."

He ground his teeth and clenched his fists.

"Don't frighten me, Vassili," she said indifferently, without looking up at him.

"Well, stop your joking."

"Don't try to frighten me."

"I'll soon make you dance if you begin any foolishness."

"Would you beat me?"

She went up to him and gazed with curiosity at his frowning face.

"One would think you were a countess. Yes, I would beat you."

"Yet I'm not your wife," said Malva, calmly. "You have been accustomed to beat your wife for nothing, and you imagine that you can do the same with me. No, I am free. I belong only to myself, and I am afraid of no one. But you are afraid of your son, and now you dare threaten me."

She shook her head with disdain. Her careless manner cooled Vassili's anger. He had never seen her look so beautiful.

"I have something else to tell you," she went on. "You boasted to Serejka that I could no more get along without you than without bread, and that I cannot live without you. You are mistaken. Perhaps it is not you that I love and not for you that I come. Perhaps I love the peace of this deserted beach. (Here she made a wide gesture with her arms.) Perhaps I love these lonely sands, with their vast stretch of sea and sky, and to be away from vile beings. Because you are here is nothing to me. If this were Serejka's place I should come here. If your son lived here, I should come too. It would be better still if no one were here, for I am disgusted with you all. But if I take it into my head one day—beautiful as I am—I can always choose a man, and one who'll please me better than you."

"So, so!" hissed Vassili, furiously, and he seized her by the throat. "So that's your game, is it?"

He shook her, and she did not strive to get away from his grasp, although her face was congested and her eyes bloodshot. She merely placed her two hands on the rough hands that were around her throat.

"Ah, now I know you!" Vassili was hoarse with rage. "And yet you said you loved me, and you kissed me and caressed me? Ah, I'll show you!"

Holding her down to the ground, he struck her repeatedly with his clenched fist. Finally, fatigued with the exertion, he pushed her away from him crying:

"There, serpent. Now you've got what you deserved."

Without a complaint, silent and calm, Malva fell back on her back, all crumpled, red and still beautiful. Her green eyes watched him furtively under the lashes, and burned with a cold flame full of hatred, but he, gasping with excitement and satisfied with the punishment he had inflicted, did not notice the look, and when he stooped down towards her to see if she was crying, she smiled up at him gently.

He looked at her, not understanding and not knowing what to do next. Should he beat her again? But his fury was appeased, and he had no desire to recommence.

"How you love me!" she whispered.

Vassili felt hot all over.

"All right! all right! the devil take you," he said gloomily. "Are you satisfied now?"

"Was I not foolish, Vassili? I thought you no longer loved me! I said to myself, 'now his son is here he will neglect me for him.'"

And she burst out laughing, a strange forced laugh.

"Foolish girl!" said Vassili, smiling in spite of himself.

He felt himself at fault, and was sorry for her, but remembering what she had said, he went on crossly:

"My son has nothing to do with it. If I beat you it was your own fault. Why did you cross me?"

"I did it on purpose to try you."

And purring like a cat she rubbed herself against his shoulder.

He glanced furtively towards the cabin and bending down embraced the young woman.

"To try me?" he repeated. "As if you wanted to do that? You see the result?"

"Oh, that's nothing!" said Malva, half closing her eyes. "I'm not angry. You beat me only because you loved me. You'll make it up to me."

She gave him a long look, trembled and lowering her voice repeated:

"Oh, yes, you'll make it up to me."

Vassili interpreted her words in a sense agreeable to him.

"How?" he asked.

"You'll see," replied Malva calmly, very calmly, but her lips trembled.

"Ah, my darling!" cried Vassili, clasping her close in his arms. "Do you know that since I have beaten you I love you better." Her head fell back on his shoulders and he placed his lips on her trembling mouth.

The sea gulls whirled about over their heads uttering hoarse cries. From the distance came the regular and gentle splash of the tiny waves breaking on the sand.

When, at last, they broke from their long embrace, Malva sat up on Vassili's knee. The peasant's face, tanned by wind and sun, was bent close to hers and his great blond beard tickled her neck. The young woman was motionless; only the gradual and regular rise and fall of her bosom showed her to be alive. Vassili's eyes wandered in turn from the sea to this woman by his side. He told Malva how tired he was of living alone and how painful were his sleepless nights filled with gloomy thoughts. Then he kissed her again on the mouth with the same sound that he might have made in chewing a hot piece of meat.

They stayed there three hours in this way, and finally, when he saw the sun setting, Vassili said with a bored look:

"I must go and make some tea. Our guest will soon he awake."

Malva rose with the indolent gesture of a languorous cat, and with a gesture of regret he started towards the cabin. Through her half-open lids the young woman watched him as he moved away, and sighed as people sigh when they have borne too heavy a burden.

* * * * *

Fifteen days later it was again Sunday and again Vassili Legostev, stretched out on the sand near his hut, was gazing out to sea, waiting for Malva. And the deserted sea laughed, playing with the reflections of the sun, and legions of waves were born to run on the sand, deposit the foam of their crests and return to the sea, where they melted.

All was as before. Only Vassili, who the last time awaited her coming with peaceful security, was now filled with impatience. Last Sunday she had not come; to-day she would surely come. He did not doubt it for a moment, but he wanted to see her as soon as possible. Iakov, at least, would not be there to embarrass them. The day before yesterday, as he passed with the other fishermen, he said he would go to town on Sunday to buy a blouse. He had found work at fifteen roubles a month.

Except for the gulls, the sea was still deserted. The familiar little black spot did not appear,

"Ah, you're not coming!" said Vassili, with ill humor. "All right, don't. I don't want you."

And he spat with disdain in the direction of the water.

The sea laughed.

"If, at least, Serejka would come," he thought. And he tried to think only of Serejka. "What a good-for-nothing the fellow is! Robust, able to read, seen the world—but what a drunkard! Yet good company. One can't feel dull in his company. The women are mad for him; all run after him. Malva's the only one that keeps aloof. No, no sign of her! What a cursed woman! Perhaps she's angry because I beat her."

Thus, thinking of his son, of Serejka, but more often of Malva, Vassili paced up and down the sandy beach, turning every now and then to look anxiously out to sea. But Malva did not come.

This is what had happened.

Iakov rose early, and on going down to the beach as usual to wash himself, he saw Malva. She was seated on the bow of a large fishing boat anchored in the surf and letting her bare feet hang, sat combing her damp hair.

Iakov stopped to watch her.

"Have you had a bath?" he cried.

She turned to look at him, and glanced down at her feet: then, continuing to comb herself, she replied:

"Yes, I took a bath. Why are you up so early?"

"Aren't you up early?"

"I am not an example for you. If you did all I do, you'd be in all kinds of trouble."

"Why do you always wish to frighten me?" he asked.

"And you, why do you make eyes at me?"

Iakov had no recollection of having looked at her more than at the other women on the fishing grounds, but now he said to her suddenly:

"Because you are so—appetizing."

"If your father heard you, he'd give you an appetite! No, my lad, don't run after me, because I don't want to be between you and Vassili. You understand?"

"What have I done?" asked Iakov. "I haven't touched you."

"You daren't touch me," retorted Malva.

There was such a contemptuous tone in her voice that he resented this.

"So I dare not?" he replied, climbing up on the boat and seating himself at her side.

"No, you dare not."

"And if I touch you?"

"Try!"

"What would you do?"

"I'd give you such a box on the ear that you would fall into the water."

"Let's see you do it"

"Touch me if you dare!"

Throwing his arm around her waist, he pressed her to his breast.

"Here I am. Now box my ears."

"Let me be, Iakov," she said, quickly, trying to disengage herself from his arms which trembled.

"Where is the punishment you promised me?"

"Let go or take care!"

"Oh, stop your threats—luscious strawberry that you are!"

He drew her to him and pressed his thick lips into her sunburnt cheek.

She gave a wild laugh of defiance, seized Iakov's arms and suddenly, with a quick movement of her whole body threw herself forward. They fell into the water enlaced, forming a single heavy mass, and disappeared under the splashing foam. Then from beneath the agitated water Iakov appeared, looking half drowned. Malva, at his side swimming like a fish, eluded his grasp, and tried to prevent him regaining the boat. Iakov struggled desperately, striking the water and roaring like a walrus, while Malva, screaming with laughter, swam round and round him, throwing the salt water in his face, and then diving to avoid his vigorous blows.

At last he caught her and pulled her under the water, and the waves passed over both their heads. Then they came to the surface again both panting with the exertion. Thus they played like two big fish until, finally, tired out and full of salt water, they climbed up the beach and sat down in the sun to dry.

Malva laughed and twisted her hair to get the water out.

The day was growing. The fishermen, after their night of heavy slumber, were emerging from their huts, one by one. From the distance all looked alike. One began to strike blows on an empty barrel at regular intervals. Two women were heard quarrelling. Dogs barked.

"They are getting up," said Iakov. "And I wanted to start to town early. I've lost time with you."

"One does nothing good in my company," she said, half in jest, half seriously.

"What a habit you have of scaring people," replied Iakov.

"You'll see when your father—."

This allusion to his father angered him.

"What about my father? I'm not a boy. And I'm not blind, either. He's not a saint, either; he deprives himself of nothing. If you don't mind I'll steal you from my father."

"You?"

"Do you think I wouldn't dare?"

"Really?"

"Now, look you," he began furiously, "don't defy me. I—."

"What now?" she asked with indifference.

"Nothing."

He turned away with a determined look on his face.

"How brave you are," she said, tauntingly. "You remind me of the inspector's little dog. At a distance he barks and threatens to bite, but when you get near him he puts his tail between his legs and runs away."

"All right," cried Iakov, angrily. "Wait! you'll see what I am."

Advancing towards them came a sunburnt, tattered and muscular-looking individual. He wore a ragged red shirt, his trousers were full of holes, and his feet were bare. His face was covered with freckles and he had big saucy blue eyes and an impertinent turned-up nose. When he came up he stopped and made a grimace.

"Serejka drank yesterday, and today Serejka's pocket is empty. Lend me twenty kopeks. I'll not return them."

Iakov burst out laughing; Malva smiled.

"Give me the money," went on the tramp. "I'll marry you for twenty kopeks if you like."

"You're an odd fellow," said Iakov, "are you a priest?"

"Imbecile question," replied Serejka. "Wasn't I servant to a priest at Ouglitch?"

"I don't want to get married," said Iakov.

"Give the money all the same, and I won't tell your father you're paying court to his queen," replied Serejka, passing his tongue over his dry and cracked lips.

Iakov did not want to give twenty kopeks, but they had warned him to be on his guard when dealing with Serejka, and to put up with his whims. The tramp never demanded much, but if he was refused he spread evil tales about you or else he would beat you. So Iakov, sighing, put his hand in his pocket.

"That's right," said Serejka, with a tone of encouragement, and he sat down beside them on the sand. "Always do what I tell you and you'll be happy. And you," he went on, turning to Malva—"when are you going to marry me? Better be quick. I don't like to wait long."

"You are too ragged. Begin by sewing up your holes and then we'll see," replied Malva.

Serejka regarded his rents with a reproachful air and shook his head.

"Give me one of your skirts, that'll be better."

"Yes, I can," said Malva, laughing.

"I'm serious. You must have an old one you don't want."

"You'd do better to buy yourself a pair of trousers."

"I prefer to drink the money."

Serejka rose and, jingling his twenty kopeks, shuffled off, followed by a strange smile from Malva.

When he was some distance away, Iakov said:

"In our village such a braggart would goon have been put in his place. Here, every one seems afraid of him."

Malva looked at Iakov and replied, disdainfully:

"You don't know his worth."

"There's nothing to know. He's worth five kopeks a hundred."

She did not reply, but watched the play of the waves as they chased one after the other, swaying the fishing boat. The mast inclined now to right, now to left, and the bow rose and then fell suddenly, striking the water with a loud splash.

"Why don't you go?" asked Malva.

"Where?" he asked.

"You wanted to go to town."

"I shan't go now."

"Well, go to your father's."

"And you?"

"What?"

"Shall you go, too?"

"No."

"Then I shan't either."

"Are you going to stay round me all day?"

"I don't want your company so much as that," replied Iakov, offended.

He rose and moved away. But he was mistaken in saying that he did not need her, for when away from her he felt lonely. A strange feeling had come to him after their conversation, a secret desire to protest against the father. Only yesterday this feeling had not existed, nor even to-day, before he saw Malva. Now it seemed to him that his father embarrassed him and stood in his way, although he was far away over the sea yonder, on a narrow tongue of sand almost invisible to the eye. Then it seemed to him, too, that Malva was afraid of the father; if she were not afraid she would talk differently. Now she was missing in his life while only that morning he had not thought of her.

And so he wandered for several hours along the beach, stopping here and there to chat with fishermen he knew. At noon he took a siesta under the shade of an upturned boat. When he awoke he took another stroll and came across Malva far from the fishing ground, reading a tattered book under the shade of the willows.

She looked up at Iakov and smiled.

"Ah, there you are," he said, sitting down beside her.

"Have you been looking for me long?" she asked, demurely.

"Looking for you? What an idea?" replied Iakov, who was only just beginning to realize that it was the truth.

"Do you know how to read?" she asked.

"Yes—I used to, but I've forgotten everything."

"So have I."

"Why didn't you go to the headland to-day?" asked Iakov, suddenly.

"What's that to you?"

Iakov plucked a leaf and chewed it.

"Listen," he said in a low tone and drawing near her. "Listen to what I'm going to say. I'm young and I love you."

"You're a silly lad, very silly," said Malva, shaking her head.

"I may be a fool," cried Iakov, passionately. "But I love you, I love you."

"Be silent! Go away!"

"Why?"

"Because."

"Don't be obstinate." He took her gently by the shoulders. "Can't you understand?"

"Go away, Iakov," she cried, severely. "Go away!"

"Oh, if that's the tone you take I don't care a rap. You're not the only woman here. You imagine that you are better than the others."

She made no reply, rose and brushed the dust off her skirt.

"Come," she said.

And they went back to the fishing grounds side by side.

They walked slowly on account of the soft sand. Suddenly, as they were nearing the boats, Iakov stopped short and seized Malva by the arms.

"Are you driving me desperate on purpose? Why do you play with me like this?" he demanded.

"Leave me alone, I tell you," she said, calmly disengaging herself from his grasp.

Serejka appeared from behind a boat. He shook his fist at the couple, and said, threateningly:

"So, that's how you go off together. Vassili shall know of this."

"Go to the devil, all of you!" cried Malva. And she left them, disappearing among the boats.

Iakov stood facing Serejka, and looked him square in the face. Serejka boldly returned the stare and so they remained for a minute or two, like two rams ready to charge on each other. Then without a word each turned away and went off in a different direction.

The sea was calm and crimson with the rays of the setting sun. A confused sound hovered over the fishing ground. The voice of a drunken woman sang hysterically words devoid of sense.

* * * * *

In the dawn's pure light the sea still slumbered, reflecting the pearl-like clouds. On the headland a party of fishermen still only half awake moved slowly about, getting ready the rigging of their boat.

Serejka, bareheaded and tattered as usual, stood in the bow hurrying the men on with a hoarse voice, the result of his drunken orgy of the previous night.

"Where are the oars, Vassili?"

Vassili, moody as a dark autumn day, was arranging the net at the bottom of the boat. Serejka watched him and, when he looked his way, smacked his lips, signifying that he wanted to drink.

"Have you any brandy," he asked.

"Yes," growled Vassili.

"Good. I'll take a nip when they've gone."

"Is all ready?" cried the fishermen.

"Let go!" commanded Serejka, jumping to the ground. "Be careful. Go far out so as not to entangle the net."

The big boat slid down the greased planks to the water, and the fishermen, jumping in as it went, seized the oars, ready to strike the water directly she was afloat. Then with a big splash the graceful bark forged ahead through the great plain of luminous water.

"Why didn't you come Sunday?" said Vassili, as the two men went back to the cabin.

"I couldn't."

"You were drunk?"

"No, I was watching your son and his step-mother," said Serejka, phlegmatically.

"A new worry on your shoulders," said Vassili, sarcastically and with a forced smile. "They are only children." He was tempted to learn where and how Serejka had seen Malva and Iakov the day before, but he was ashamed.

"Why don't you ask news of Malva?" asked Serejka, as he gulped down a glass of brandy.

"What do I care what she does?" replied Vassili, with indifference, although he trembled with a secret presentiment.

"As she didn't come Sunday, you should ask what she was doing. I know you are jealous, you old dog!"

"Oh, there are many like her," said Vassili, carelessly.

"Are there?" said Serejka, imitating him. "Ah, you peasants, you're all alike. As long as you gather your honey, it's all one to you."

"What's she to you?" broke in Vassili with irritation. "Have you come to ask her hand in marriage?"

"I know she's yours," said Serejka. "Have I ever bothered you? But now Iakov, your son, is all the time dancing around her, it's different. Beat him, do you hear? If not, I will. You've got a strong fist if you are a fool."

Vassili did not reply, but watched the boat as it turned about and made toward the beach again.

"You are right," he said finally. "Iakov will hear from me."

"I don't like him. He smells too much of the village," said Serejka.

In the distance, on the sea, was opening out the pink fan formed by the rays of the rising sun. The glowing orb was already emerging from the water. Amid the noise of the waves was heard from the boat the distant cry:

"Draw in!"

"Come, boys!" cried Serejka, to the other fishermen on the beach. "Let's pull together."

"When you see Iakov tell him to come here to-morrow," said Vassili.

The boat grounded on the beach and the fishermen, jumping out, pulled their end of the net so that the two groups gradually met, the cork floats bobbing up and down on the water forming a perfect semi-circle.

* * * * *

Very late on the evening of the same day, when the fishermen had finished their dinner, Malva, tired and thoughtful, had seated herself on an old boat turned upside down and was watching the sea, already screened in twilight. In the distance a fire was burning, and Malva knew that Vassili had lighted it. Solitary and as if lost in the darkening shadows, the flame leaped high at times and then fell back as if broken. And Malva felt a certain sadness as she watched that red dot abandoned in the desert of ocean, and palpitating feebly among the indefatigable and incomprehensible murmur of the waves.

"What are you doing there?" asked Serejka's voice behind her.

90

"What's that to you?" she replied dryly, without stirring.

He lighted a cigarette, was silent a moment and then said in a friendly tone:

"What a funny woman you are! First you run away from everybody, and then you throw yourself round everyone's neck."

"Not round yours," said Malva, carelessly.

"Not mine, perhaps, but round Iakov's."

"It makes you envious."

"Hum! do you want me to speak frankly?"

"Speak."

"Have yon broken off with Vassili?"

"I don't know," she replied, after a silence. "I am vexed with him."

"Why?"

"He beat me."

"Really? And you let him?"

Serejka could not understand it. He tried to catch a glimpse of Malva's face, and made an ironical grimace.

"I need not have let him beat me," she said. "I did not want to defend myself."

"So you love the old grey cat as much as that?" grinned Serejka, puffing out a cloud of smoke. "I thought better of you than that."

"I love none of you," she said, again indifferent and wafting the smoke away with her hand.

"But if you don't love him, why did you let him beat you?"

"Do you suppose I know? Leave me alone."

"It's funny," said Serejka, shaking his head.

Both remained silent.

Night was falling. The shadows came down from the slow-moving clouds to the seas beneath. The waves murmured.

Vassili's fire had gone out on the distant headland, but Malva continued to gaze in that direction.

* * * * *

The father and son were seated in the cabin facing each other, and drinking brandy which the youth had brought with him to conciliate the old man and so as not to be weary in his company.

Serejka had told Iakov that his father was angry with him on account of Malva, and that he had threatened to beat Malva until she was half dead. He also said that was the reason she resisted Iakov's advances.

This story had excited Iakov's resentment against his father. He now looked upon him as an obstacle in his road that he could neither remove nor get around.

But feeling himself of equal strength as his adversary, Iakov regarded his father boldly, with a look that meant: "Touch me if you dare!"

They had both drunk two glasses without exchanging a word, except a few commonplace remarks about the fisheries. Alone amidst the deserted waters each nursed his hatred, and both knew that this hate would soon burst forth into flame.

"How's Serejka?" at last Vassili blurted out.

"Drunk as usual," replied Iakov, pouring our some more brandy for his father.

"He'll end badly—and if you don't take care you'll do the same."

"I shall never become like him," replied Iakov, surlily.

"No?" said Vassili, frowning. "I know what I'm talking about. How long are you here already? Two months. You must soon think of going back. How much money have you saved?"

"In so little time I've not been able to save any," replied Iakov.

"Then you don't want to stay here any longer, my lad, go back to the village."

Iakov smiled.

"Why these grimaces?" cried Vassili threateningly, and impatient at his son's coolness. "Your father's advising you and you mock him. You're in too much of a hurry to play the independent. You want to be put in the traces again."

Iakov poured out some more brandy and drank it. These coarse reproaches offended him, but he mastered himself, not wanting to arouse his father's anger.

Seeing that his son had drunk again, alone, without filling his glass, made Vassili more angry than ever.

"Your father says to you, 'Go home,' and you laugh at him. Very well, I'll speak differently. You'll get your pay Saturday and trot—home to the village—do you understand?"

"I won't go," said Iakov, firmly.

"What!" cried Vassili, and leaning his two hands on the edge of the table he rose to his feet. "Have I spoken, yes or no? You dog, barking at your father! Do you forget that I can do what I please with you?"

His mouth trembled with passion, his face was convulsed, and two swollen veins stood out on his temples.

"I forget nothing," said Iakov, in a low tone and not looking at his father. "And you—have you forgotten nothing?"

"It's not your place to preach to me. I'll break every bone in your body."

Iakov avoided the hand that his father raised over his head and a feeling of savage hatred arose in him. He said, between his clenched teeth:

"Don't touch me. We're not in the village now."

"Be silent. I'm your father everywhere."

They stood facing each other, Vassili, his eyes bloodshot, his neck outstretched, his fists clenched, panted his brandy-smelling breath in his son's face. Iakov stepped back. He was watching his father's movements, ready to ward off blows, peaceful outwardly, but steaming with perspiration. Between them was the table.

"Perhaps I won't give you a good beating?" cried Vassili hoarsely, and bending his back like a cat about to make a spring.

"Here we are equal," said Iakov, watching him warily. "You are a fisherman, I too. Why do you attack me like this? Do you think I do not understand? You began."

Vassili howled with passion, and raised his arm to strike so rapidly that Iakov had no time to avoid it. The blow fell on his head. He staggered and ground his teeth in his father's face.

"Wait!" cried the latter, clenching his fists and again threatening him.

They were now at close quarters, and their feet were entangled in the empty sacks and cordage on the floor. Iakov, protecting himself as best he could against his father's blows, pale and bathed in perspiration, his teeth clenched, his eyes brilliant as a wolf's, slowly retreated, and as his father charged upon him, gesticulating with ferocity and blind with rage, like a wild boar, he turned and ran out of the cabin, down towards the sea.

Vassili started in pursuit, his head bent, his arms extended, but his foot caught in some rope, and he fell all his length on the sand. He tried to rise, but the fall had taken all the fight out of him and he sank back on the beach, shaking his fist at Iakov, who remained grinning at a safe distance. He shouted:

"Be cursed! I curse you forever!"

Bitterness came into Vassili's soul as he realized his own position. He sighed heavily. His head bent low as if an immense weight had crushed him. For an abandoned woman he had deserted his wife, with whom he had lived faithfully for fifteen years, and the Lord had punished him by this rebellion of his son. His son had mocked him and trampled on his heart. Yes, he was punished for the past. He made the sign of the cross and remained seated, blinking his eyes to free them from the tears that were blinding them.

And the sun went down into the sea, and the crimson twilight faded away in the sky. A warm wind caressed the face of the weeping peasant. Deep in his resolutions of repentance he stayed there until he fell asleep shortly before dawn.

94

* * * * *

The day following the quarrel, Iakov went off with a party to fish thirty miles out at sea. He returned alone five days later for provisions. It was midday when he arrived, and everyone was resting after dinner. It was unbearably hot. The sand burned his feet and the shells and fish bones pricked them. As Iakov carefully picked his way along the beach he regretted he had no boots on. He did not want to return to the bark as he was in a hurry to eat and to see Malva. Many a time had he thought of her during the long lonely hours on the sea. He wondered if she and his father had seen each other again and what they had said. Perhaps the old man had beaten her.

The deserted fisheries were slumbering, as if overcome by the heat. In the inspector's office a child was crying. From behind a heap of barrels came the sound of voices.

Iakov turned his steps in that direction. He thought he recognised Malva's voice, but when he arrived at the barrels he recoiled a step and stopped.

In the shade, lying on his back, with his arms under his head, was Serejka. Near him were, on one side, Vassili and, on the other, Malva.

Iakov thought to himself: "Why is father here. Has he left his post so as to be nearer Malva and to watch her? Should he go up to them or not."

"So, you've decided!" said Serejka to Vassili. "It's goodbye to us all? Well, go your way and scratch the soil."

A thrill went through Iakov and he made a joyous grimace.

"Yes, I'm going;" said Vassili.

Then Iakov advanced boldly.

"Good-day, all!"

The father gave him a rapid glance and then turned away his eyes. Malva did not stir. Serejka moved his leg and raising his voice said:

"Here's our dearly beloved son, Iakov, back from a distant shore."

95

Then he added in his ordinary voice:

"You should flay him alive and make drums with his skin."

Malva laughed.

"It's hot," said Iakov, sitting beside them.

"I've been waiting for you since this morning, Iakov. The inspector told me you were coming."

The young man thought his voice seemed weaker than usual and his face seemed changed. He asked Serejka for a cigarette.

"I have no tobacco for an imbecile like you," replied the latter, without stirring.

"I'm going back home, Iakov," said Vassili, gravely digging into the sand with his fingers.

"Why," asked the son, innocently.

"Never mind why, shall you stay?"

"Yes. I'll remain. What should we both do at home?"

"Very well. I have nothing to say. Do as you please. You are no longer a child. Only remember that I shall not get about long. I shall live, perhaps, but I do not know how long I shall work. I have lost the habit of the soil. Remember, too, that your mother is there."

Evidently it was difficult for him to talk. The words stuck between his teeth. He stroked his beard and his hand trembled.

Malva eyed him. Serejka had half closed one eye and with the other watched Iakov. Iakov was jubilant, but afraid of betraying himself; he was silent and lowered his head.

"Don't forget your mother, Iakov. Remember, you are all she has."

"I know," said Iakov, shrugging his shoulders.

"It is well if you know," said the father, with a look of distrust. "I only warn you not to forget it."

Vassili sighed deeply. For a few minutes all were silent.

Then Malva said:

"The work bell will soon ring."

"I'm going," said Vassili, rising.

And all rose.

"Goodbye, Serejka. If you happen to be on the Volga, maybe you'll drop in to see me."

"I'll not fail," said Serejka.

"Goodbye."

"Goodbye, dear friend."

"Goodbye, Malva," said Vassili, not raising his eyes.

She slowly wiped her lips with her sleeve, threw her two white arms round his neck and kissed him three times on the lips and cheeks.

He was overcome with emotion and uttered some indistinct words. Iakov lowered his head, dissimulating a smile. Serejka was impassible, and he even yawned a little, at the same time gazing at the sky.

"You'll find it hot walking," he said.

"No matter. Goodbye, you too, Iakov."

"Goodbye!"

They stood facing each other, not knowing what to do. The sad word "goodbye" aroused in Iakov a feeling of tenderness for his father, but he did not know how to express it. Should he embrace his father as Malva had done or shake his hand like Serejka? And Vassili felt hurt at this hesitation, which was visible in his son's attitude.

"Remember your mother," said Vassili, finally.

"Yes, yes," replied Iakov, cordially. "Don't worry. I know."

"That's all. Be happy. God protect you. Don't think badly of me. The kettle, Serejka, is buried in the sand near the bow of the green boat."

"What does he want with the kettle?" asked Iakov.

"He has taken my place yonder on the headland," explained Vassili.

Iakov looked enviously at Serejka, then at Malva.

"Farewell, all! I'm going."

Vassili waved his hand to them and moved away. Malva followed him.

"I'll accompany you a bit of the road."

Serejka sat down on the ground and seized the leg of Iakov, who was preparing to accompany Malva.

"Stop! where are you going?"

"Let me alone," said Iakov, making a forward movement. But Serejka had seized his other leg.

"Sit down by my side."

"Why? What new folly is this?"

"It is not folly. Sit down."

Iakov obeyed, grinding his teeth.

"What do you want?"

"Wait. Be silent, and I'll think, and then I'll talk."

He began staring at Iakov, who gave way.

Malva and Vassili walked for a few minutes in silence. Malva's eyes shone strangely. Vassili was gloomy and preoccupied. Their feet sank in the sand and they advanced slowly.

"Vassili!"

"What?"

He turned and looked at her.

"I made you quarrel with Iakov on purpose. You might both have lived here without quarrelling," she said in a calm tone.

There was not a shade of repentance in her words.

"Why did you do that?" asked Vassili, after a silence.

"I do not know—for nothing."

She shrugged her shoulders and smiled.

"What you have done was noble!" he said, with irritation.

She was silent.

"You will ruin my boy, ruin him entirely. You do not fear God, you have no shame! What are you going to do?"

"What should I do?" she said.

There was a ring of anguish, or vexation, in her voice.

"What you ought to do!" cried Vassili, seized suddenly with a fierce rage.

He felt a passionate desire to strike her, to knock her down and bury her in the sand, to kick her in the face, in the breast. He clenched his fists and looked back.

Yonder, near the barrels, he saw Iakov and Serejka. Their faces were turned in his direction.

"Get away with you! I could crush you!"

He stopped and hissed insults in her face. His eyes were bloodshot, his beard trembled and his hands seemed to advance involuntarily towards Malva's hair, which emerged from beneath her shawl.

She fixed her green eyes on him.

"You deserve killing," he said. "Wait, some one will break your head yet."

She smiled, still silent. Then she sighed deeply and said:

"That's enough! now farewell!"

And suddenly turning on her heels she left him and came back.

Vassili shouted after her and shook his fists. Malva, as she walked, took pains to place each foot in the deep impressions of Vassili's feet, and when she succeeded she carefully effaced the traces. Thus she continued on until she came to the barrels where Serejka greeted her with this question:

"Well, have you seen the last of him?"

She gave an affirmative sign, and sat down beside him. Iakov looked at her and smiled, gently moving his lips as if he were saying things that he alone heard.

"When will you go to the headland?" she asked Serejka, indicating the sea with a movement of her head.

"This evening."

"I will go with you."

"Bravo, that suits me."

"And I, too—I'll go," cried Iakov.

"Who invited you?" asked Serejka, screwing up his eyes.

The sound of a cracked bell called the men to work.

"She will invite me," said Iakov.

He looked defiantly at Malva.

"I? what need have I of you?" she replied, surprised.

"Let us he frank, Iakov," said Serejka. "If you annoy her, I'll beat you to a jelly. And if you as much as touch her with a finger, I'll kill you like a fly. I am a simple man."

His face, all his person, his knotty and muscular arms proved eloquently that killing a man would be a very simple thing for him.

Iakov recoiled a step and said, in a choking voice:

"Wait! That is for Malva to—"

"Keep quiet, that's all. You are not the dog that will eat the lamb. If you get the bones you may be thankful."

Iakov looked at Malva. Her green eyes laughed in a humiliating way at him and she fondled Serejka so that Iakov felt himself grow hot and cold.

Then they went away side by side and both burst out laughing. Iakov dug his foot deep in the sand and remained glued to the spot, his body stretched forward, his face red, his heart beating wildly.

In the distance, on the dead waves of sand, was a small dark human figure moving slowly away; on his right beamed the sun and the powerful sea, and on the left, to the horizon, there was sand, nothing but sand, uniform, deserted,—gloomy. Iakov watched the receding figure of the lonely man and blinked his eyes, filled with tears—tears of humiliation and painful uncertainty.

On the fishing grounds everyone was busy at work. Iakov heard Malva's sonorous voice ask, angrily:

"Who has taken my knife?"

The waves murmured, the sun shone and the sea laughed.

THE MAN WHO WAS AFRAID

Foma Gordyeff

Translated by Herman Bernstein

INTRODUCTORY NOTE.

OUT of the darkest depths of life, where vice and crime and misery abound, comes the Byron of the twentieth century, the poet of the vagabond and the proletariat, Maxim Gorky. Not like the beggar, humbly imploring for a crust in the name of the Lord, nor like the jeweller displaying his precious stones to dazzle and tempt the eye, he comes to the world,—nay, in accents of Tyrtaeus this commoner of Nizhni Novgorod spurs on his troops of freedom-loving heroes to conquer, as it were, the placid, self-satisfied literatures of to-day, and bring new life to pale, bloodless frames.

Like Byron's impassioned utterances, "borne on the tones of a wild and quite artless melody," is Gorky's mad, unbridled, powerful voice, as he sings of the "madness of the brave," of the barefooted dreamers, who are proud of their idleness, who possess nothing and fear nothing, who are gay in their misery, though miserable in their joy.

Gorky's voice is not the calm, cultivated, well-balanced voice of Chekhov, the Russian De Maupassant, nor even the apostolic, well-meaning, but comparatively faint voice of Tolstoy, the preacher: it is the roaring of a lion, the crash of thunder. In its elementary power is the heart. rending cry of a sincere but suffering soul that saw the brutality of life in all its horrors, and now flings its experiences into the face of the world with unequalled sympathy and the courage of a giant.

For Gorky, above all, has courage; he dares to say that he finds the vagabond, the outcast of society, more sublime and significant than society itself.

His Bosyak, the symbolic incarnation of the Over-man, is as naive and as bold as a child—or as a genius. In the vehement passions of the magnanimous, compassionate hero in tatters, in the aristocracy of his soul, and in his constant thirst for Freedom, Gorky sees the rebellious and irreconcilable spirit of man, of future man,—in these he sees something beautiful, something powerful, something monumental, and is carried away by their strange psychology. For the barefooted dreamer's life is Gorky's life, his ideals are Gorky's ideals, his pleasures and pains, Gorky's pleasures and pains.

And Gorky, though broken in health now, buffeted by the storms of fate, bruised and wounded in the battle-field of life, still like Byron and like Lermontov,

> "—seeks the storm
> As though the storm contained repose."

And in a leonine voice he cries defiantly:

> "Let the storm rage with greater force and fury!"

HERMAN BERNSTEIN.
September 20, 1901.

FOMA GORDYEEF

Dedicated to

ANTON P. CHEKHOV

By

Maxim Gorky

CHAPTER I

ABOUT sixty years ago, when fortunes of millions had been made on the Volga with fairy-tale rapidity, Ignat Gordyeeff, a young fellow, was working as water-pumper on one of the barges of the wealthy merchant Zayev.

Built like a giant, handsome and not at all stupid, he was one of those people whom luck always follows everywhere—not because they are gifted and industrious, but rather because, having an enormous stock of energy at their command, they cannot stop to think over the choice of means when on their way toward their aims, and, excepting their own will, they know no law. Sometimes they speak of their conscience with fear, sometimes they really torture themselves struggling with it, but conscience is an unconquerable power to the faint-hearted only; the strong master it quickly and make it a slave to their desires, for they unconsciously feel that, given room and freedom, conscience would fracture life. They sacrifice days to it; and if it should happen that conscience conquered their souls, they are never wrecked, even in defeat—they are just as healthy and strong under its sway as when they lived without conscience.

At the age of forty Ignat Gordyeeff was himself the owner of three steamers and ten barges. On the Volga he was respected as a rich and clever man, but was nicknamed "Frantic," because his life did not flow along a straight channel, like that of other people of his kind, but now and again, boiling up turbulently, ran out of its rut, away from gain— the prime aim of his existence. It looked as though there were three Gordyeeffs in him, or as though there were three souls in Ignat's body. One of them, the mightiest, was only greedy, and when Ignat lived according to its commands, he was merely a man seized with untamable passion for work. This passion burned in him by day and by night, he was completely absorbed by it, and, grabbing everywhere hundreds and thousands of roubles, it seemed as if he could never have enough of the jingle and sound of money. He worked about up and down the Volga, building and fastening nets in which he caught gold: he bought up grain in the villages, floated it to Rybinsk on his barges; he plundered, cheated, sometimes not noticing it, sometimes noticing, and, triumphant, be openly laughed at by his victims; and in the senselessness of his thirst for money, he rose to the heights of poetry. But, giving up so much strength to this hunt after the rouble, he was not greedy in the narrow sense, and sometimes he even betrayed an inconceivable but sincere indifference to his property. Once, when the ice was drifting down the Volga, he stood on the shore, and, seeing that the ice was breaking his new barge, having crushed it against the bluff shore, he ejaculated:

"That's it. Again. Crush it! Now, once more! Try!"

"Well, Ignat," asked his friend Mayakin, coming up to him, "the ice is crushing about ten thousand out of your purse, eh?"

"That's nothing! I'll make another hundred. But look how the Volga is working! Eh? Fine? She can split the whole world, like curd, with a knife. Look, look! There you have my 'Boyarinya!' She floated but once. Well, we'll have mass said for the dead."

The barge was crushed into splinters. Ignat and the godfather, sitting in the tavern on the shore, drank vodka and looked out of the window, watching the fragments of the "Boyarinya" drifting down the river together with the ice.

"Are you sorry for the vessel, Ignat?" asked Mayakin.

"Why should I be sorry for it? The Volga gave it to me, and the Volga has taken it back. It did not tear off my hand."

"Nevertheless."

"What—nevertheless? It is good at least that I saw how it was all done. It's a lesson for the future. But when my 'Volgar' was burned—I was really sorry—I didn't see it. How beautiful it must have looked when such a woodpile was blazing on the water in the dark night! Eh? It was an enormous steamer."

"Weren't you sorry for that either?"

"For the steamer? It is true, I did feel sorry for the steamer. But then it is mere foolishness to feel sorry! What's the use? I might have cried; tears cannot extinguish fire. Let the steamers burn. And even though everything be burned down, I'd spit upon it! If the soul is but burning to work, everything will be erected anew. Isn't it so?"

"Yes," said Mayakin, smiling. "These are strong words you say. And whoever speaks that way, even though he loses all, will nevertheless be rich."

Regarding losses of thousands of roubles so philosophically, Ignat knew the value of every kopeika; he gave to the poor very seldom, and only to those that were altogether unable to work. When a more or less healthy man asked him for alms, Ignat would say, sternly:

"Get away! You can work yet. Go to my dvornik and help him to remove the dung. I'll pay you for it."

Whenever he had been carried away by his work he regarded people morosely and piteously, nor did he give himself rest while hunting for roubles. And suddenly—it usually happened in spring, when everything on earth became so bewitchingly beautiful and something reproachfully wild was breathed down into the soul from the clear sky—Ignat Gordyeeff would feel that he was not the master of his business, but its low slave. He would lose himself in thought and, inquisitively looking about himself from under his thick, knitted eyebrows, walk about for days, angry and morose, as though silently asking something, which he feared to ask aloud. They awakened his other soul, the turbulent and lustful soul of a hungry beast. Insolent and cynical, he drank, led a depraved life, and made drunkards of other people. He went into ecstasy, and something like a volcano of filth boiled within him. It looked as though he was madly tearing the chains which he himself had forged and carried, and was not strong enough to tear them. Excited and very dirty, his face swollen from drunkenness and sleeplessness, his eyes wandering madly, and roaring in a hoarse voice, he tramped about the town from one tavern to another, threw away money without counting it, cried and danced to the sad tunes of the folk songs, or fought, but found no rest anywhere—in anything.

It happened one day that a degraded priest, a short, stout little bald-headed man in a torn cassock, chanced on Ignat, and stuck to him, just as a piece of mud will stick to a shoe. An impersonal, deformed and nasty creature, he played the part of a buffoon: they smeared his bald head with mustard, made him go upon all-fours, drink mixtures of different brandies and dance comical dances; he did all this in silence, an idiotic smile on his wrinkled face, and having done what he was told to do, he invariably said, outstretching his hand with his palm upward:

"Give me a rouble."

They laughed at him and sometimes gave him twenty kopeiks, sometimes gave him nothing, but it sometimes happened that they threw him a ten-rouble bill and even more.

"You abominable fellow," cried Ignat to him one day. "Say, who are you?"

The priest was frightened by the call, and bowing low to Ignat, was silent.

"Who? Speak!" roared Ignat.

"I am a man—to be abused," answered the priest, and the company burst out laughing at his words.

"Are you a rascal?" asked Ignat, sternly.

"A rascal? Because of need and the weakness of my soul?"

"Come here!" Ignat called him. "Come and sit down by my side."

Trembling with fear, the priest walked up to the intoxicated merchant with timid steps and remained standing opposite him.

"Sit down beside me!" said Ignat, taking the frightened priest by the hand and seating him next to himself. "You are a very near man to me. I am also a rascal! You, because of need; I, because of wantonness. I am a rascal because of grief! Understand?"

"I understand," said the priest, softly. All the company were giggling.

"Do you know now what I am?"

"I do."

"Well, say, 'You are a rascal, Ignat!'"

The priest could not do it. He looked with terror at the huge figure of Ignat and shook his head negatively. The company's laughter was now like the rattling of thunder. Ignat could not make the priest abuse him. Then he asked him:

"Shall I give you money?"

"Yes," quickly answered the priest.

"And what do you need it for?"

He did not care to answer. Then Ignat seized him by the collar, and shook out of his dirty lips the following speech, which he spoke almost in a whisper, trembling with fear:

"I have a daughter sixteen years old in the seminary. I save for her, because when she comes out there won't be anything with which to cover her nakedness."

"Ah," said Ignat, and let go the priest's collar. Then he sat for a long time gloomy and lost in thought, and now and again stared at the priest. Suddenly his eyes began to laugh, and he said:

"Aren't you a liar, drunkard?"

The priest silently made the sign of the cross and lowered his head on his breast.

"It is the truth!" said one of the company, confirming the priest's words.

"True? Very well!" shouted Ignat, and, striking the table with his fist, he addressed himself to the priest:

"Eh, you! Sell me your daughter! How much will you take?"

The priest shook his head and shrank back.

"One thousand!"

111

The company giggled, seeing that the priest was shrinking as though cold water was being poured on him.

"Two!" roared Ignat, with flashing eyes.

"What's the matter with you? How is it?" muttered the priest, stretching out both hands to Ignat.

"Three!"

"Ignat Matveyich!" cried the priest, in a thin, ringing voice. "For God's sake! For Christ's sake! Enough! I'll sell her! For her own sake I'll sell her!"

In his sickly, sharp voice was heard a threat to someone, and his eyes, unnoticed by anybody before, flashed like coals. But the intoxicated crowd only laughed at him foolishly.

"Silence!" cried Ignat, sternly, straightening himself to his full length and flashing his eyes.

"Don't you understand, devils, what's going on here? It's enough to make one cry, while you giggle."

He walked up to the priest, went down on his knees before him, and said to him firmly:

"Father now you see what a rascal I am. Well, spit into my face!"

Something ugly and ridiculous took place. The priest too, knelt before Ignat, and like a huge turtle, crept around near his feet, kissed his knees and muttered something, sobbing. Ignat bent over him, lifted him from the floor and cried to him, commanding and begging:

"Spit! Spit right into my shameless eyes!"

The company, stupefied for a moment by Ignat's stern voice, laughed again so that the panes rattled in the tavern windows.

"I'll give you a hundred roubles. Spit!"

And the priest crept over the floor and sobbed for fear, or for happiness, to hear that this man was begging him to do something degrading to himself.

Finally Ignat arose from the floor, kicked the priest, and, flinging at him a package of money, said morosely, with a smile:

"Rabble! Can a man repent before such people? Some are afraid to hear of repentance, others laugh at a sinner. I was about to unburden myself completely; the heart trembled. Let me, I thought. No, I didn't think at all. Just so! Get out of here! And see that you never show yourself to me again. Do you hear?"

"Oh, a queer fellow!" said the crowd, somewhat moved.

Legends were composed about his drinking bouts in town; everybody censured him strictly, but no one ever declined his invitation to those drinking bouts. Thus he lived for weeks.

And unexpectedly he used to come home, not yet altogether freed from the odour of the kabaks, but already crestfallen and quiet. With humbly downcast eyes, in which shame was burning now, he silently listened to his wife's reproaches, and, humble and meek as a lamb, went away to his room and locked himself in. For many hours in succession he knelt before the cross, lowering his head on his breast; his hands hung helplessly, his back was bent, and he was silent, as though he dared not pray. His wife used to come up to the door on tiptoe and listen. Deep sighs were heard from behind the door—like the breathing of a tired and sickly horse.

"God! You see," whispered Ignat in a muffled voice, firmly pressing the palms of his hands to his broad breast.

During the days of repentance he drank nothing but water and ate only rye bread.

In the morning his wife placed at the door of his room a big bottle of water, about a pound and a half of bread, and salt. He opened the door, took in these victuals and locked himself in again. During this time he was not disturbed in any way; everybody tried to avoid him. A few days later he again appeared on the exchange, jested, laughed, made contracts to furnish corn as sharp-sighted as a bird of prey, a rare expert at anything concerning his affairs.

But in all the moods of Ignat's life there was one passionate desire that never left him—the desire to have a son; and the older he grew the greater was this desire. Very often such conversation as this took place between him and his wife. In the morning, at her tea, or at noon during dinner hour he gloomily glared at his wife, a stout, well-fed woman, with a red face and sleepy eyes, and asked her:

"Well, don't you feel anything?"

She knew what he meant, but she invariably replied:

"How can I help feeling? Your fists are like dumb-bells."

"You know what I'm talking about, you fool."

"Can one become pregnant from such blows?"

"It's not on account of the blows that you don't bear any children; it's because you eat too much. You fill your stomach with all sorts of food—and there's no room for the child to engender."

"As if I didn't bear you any children?"

"Those were girls," said Ignat, reproachfully. "I want a son! Do you understand? A son, an heir! To whom shall I give my capital after my death? Who shall pray for my sins? Shall I give it to a cloister? I have given them enough! Or shall I leave it to you? What a fine pilgrim you are! Even in church you think only of fish pies. If I die, you'll marry again, and my money will be turned over to some fool. Do you think this is what I am working for?"

And he was seized with sardonic anguish, for he felt that his life was aimless if he should have no son to follow him.

During the nine years of their married life his wife had borne him four daughters, all of whom had passed away. While Ignat had awaited their birth tremblingly, he mourned their death but little—at any rate they were unnecessary to him. He began to beat his wife during the second year of their married life; at first he did it while being intoxicated and without animosity, but just according to the proverb: "Love your wife like your soul and shake her like a pear-tree;" but after each confinement, deceived in his expectation, his hatred for his wife grew stronger, and he began to beat her with pleasure, in revenge for not bearing him a son.

114

Once while on business in the province of Samarsk, he received a telegram from relatives at home, informing him of his wife's death. He made the sign of the cross, thought awhile and wrote to his friend Mayakin:

"Bury her in my absence; look after my property."

Then he went to the church to serve the mass for the dead, and, having prayed for the repose of the late Aquilina's soul, he began to think that it was necessary for him to marry as soon as possible.

He was then forty-three years old, tall, broad-shouldered, with a heavy bass voice, like an arch-deacon; his large eyes looked bold and wise from under his dark eyebrows; in his sunburnt face, overgrown with a thick, black beard, and in all his mighty figure there was much truly Russian, crude and healthy beauty; in his easy motions as well as in his slow, proud walk, a consciousness of power was evident—a firm confidence in himself. He was liked by women and did not avoid them.

Ere six months had passed after the death of his wife, he courted the daughter of an Ural Cossack. The father of the bride, notwithstanding that Ignat was known even in Ural as a "pranky" man, gave him his daughter in marriage, and toward autumn Ignat Gordyeeff came home with a young Cossack-wife. Her name was Natalya. Tall, well-built, with large blue eyes and with a long chestnut braid, she was a worthy match for the handsome Ignat. He was happy and proud of his wife and loved her with the passionate love of a healthy man, but he soon began to contemplate her thoughtfully, with a vigilant eye.

Seldom did a smile cross the oval, demure face of his wife—she was always thinking of something foreign to life, and in her calm blue eyes something dark and misanthropic was flashing at times. Whenever she was free from household duties she seated herself in the most spacious room by the window, and sat there silently for two or three hours. Her face was turned toward the street, but the look of her eyes was so indifferent to everything that lived and moved there beyond the window, and at the same time it was so fixedly deep, as though she were looking into her very soul. And her walk, too, was queer. Natalya moved about the spacious room slowly and carefully, as if something invisible restrained the freedom of her movements. Their house was filled with heavy and coarsely boastful luxury; everything there was resplendent, screaming of the proprietor's wealth, but the Cossack-wife walked past the costly furniture and the silverware in a shy and somewhat frightened manner, as though fearing lest they might seize and choke her. Evidently, the noisy life of the big commercial town did not interest this silent woman, and whenever she went out driving with her husband, her eyes were fixed on the back of the driver. When her husband took her visiting she went and behaved there just as queerly as at home; when guests came to her house, she zealously served them refreshments, taking no interest whatever in what was said, and showing preference toward none. Only Mayakin, a witty, droll man, at times called forth on her face a smile, as vague as a shadow. He used to say of her:

"It's a tree—not a woman! But life is like an inextinguishable wood-pile, and every one of us blazes up sometimes. She, too, will take fire; wait, give her time. Then we shall see how she will bloom."

"Eh!" Ignat used to say to her jestingly. "What are you thinking about? Are you homesick? Brighten up a bit!"

She would remain silent, calmly looking at him.

"You go entirely too often to the church. You should wait. You have plenty of time to pray for your sins. Commit the sins first. You know, if you don't sin you don't repent; if you don't repent, you don't work out your salvation. You better sin while you are young. Shall we go out for a drive?"

"I don't feel like going out."

He used to sit down beside her and embrace her. She was cold, returning his caresses but sparingly. Looking straight into her eyes, he used to say:

"Natalya! Tell me—why are you so sad? Do you feel lonesome here with me?"

"No," she replied shortly.

"What then is it? Are you longing for your people?"

No, it's nothing."

"What are you thinking about?"

"I am not thinking."

"What then?"

"Oh, nothing!"

Once he managed to get from her a more complete answer:

"There is something confused in my heart. And also in my eyes. And it always seems to me that all this is not real."

She waved her hand around her, pointing at the walls, the furniture and everything. Ignat did not reflect on her words, and, laughing, said to her:

"That's to no purpose! Everything here is genuine. All these are costly, solid things. If you don't want these, I'll burn them, I'll sell them, I'll give them away—and I'll get new ones! Do you want me to?"

"What for?" said she calmly.

He wondered, at last, how one so young and healthy could live as though she were sleeping all the time, caring for nothing, going nowhere, except to the church, and shunning everybody. And he used to console her:

"Just wait. You'll bear a son, and then an altogether different life will commence. You are so sad because you have so little anxiety, and he will give you trouble. You'll bear me a son, will you not?

"If it pleases God," she answered, lowering her head.

Then her mood began to irritate him.

"Well, why do you wear such a long face? You walk as though on glass. You look as if you had ruined somebody's soul! Eh! You are such a succulent woman, and yet you have no taste for anything. Fool!"

Coming home intoxicated one day, he began to ply her with caresses, while she turned away from him. Then he grew angry, and exclaimed:

"Natalya! Don't play the fool, look out!"

She turned her face to him and asked calmly:

"What then?"

Ignat became enraged at these words and at her fearless look.

"What?" he roared, coming up close to her.

"Do you wish to kill me?" asked she, not moving from her place, nor winking an eye.

Ignat was accustomed to seeing people tremble before his wrath, and it was strange and offensive to him to see her calm.

"There," he cried, lifting his hand to strike her. Slowly, but in time, she eluded the blow; then she seized his hand, pushed it away from her, and said in the same tone:

"Don't you dare to touch me. I will not allow you to come near me!"

Her eyes became smaller and their sharp, metallic glitter sobered Ignat. He understood by her face that she, too, was a strong beast, and if she chose to she wouldn't admit him to her, even though she were to lose her life.

"Oh," he growled, and went away.

But having retreated once, he would not do it again: he could not bear that a woman, and his wife at that, should not bow before him—this would have degraded him. He then began to realise that henceforth his wife would never yield to him in any matter, and that an obstinate strife for predominance must start between them.

"Very well! We'll see who will conquer," he thought the next day, watching his wife with stern curiosity; and in his soul a strong desire was already raging to start the strife, that he might enjoy his victory the sooner.

But about four days later, Natalya Fominichna announced to her husband that she was pregnant.

Ignat trembled for joy, embraced her firmly, and said in a dull voice:

"You're a fine fellow, Natalya! Natasha, if it should be a son! If you bear me a son I'll enrich you! I tell you plainly, I'll be your slave! By God! I'll lie down at your feet, and you may trample upon me, if you like!"

"This is not within our power; it's the will of the Lord," said she in a low voice.

"Yes, the Lord's!" exclaimed Ignat with bitterness and drooped his head sadly.

From that moment he began to look after his wife as though she were a little child.

"Why do you sit near the window? Look out. You'll catch cold in your side; you may take sick," he used to say to her, both sternly and mildly. "Why do you skip on the staircase? You may hurt yourself. And you had better eat more, eat for two, that he may have enough."

And the pregnancy made Natalya more morose and silent, as though she were looking still deeper into herself, absorbed in the throbbing of new life within her. But the smile on her lips became clearer, and in her eyes flashed at times something new, weak and timid, like the first ray of the dawn.

When, at last, the time of confinement came, it was early on an autumn morning. At the first cry of pain she uttered, Ignat turned pale and started to say something, but only waved his hand and left the bedroom, where his wife was shrinking convulsively, and went down to the little room which had served his late mother as a chapel. He ordered vodka, seated himself by the table and began to drink sternly, listening to the alarm in the house and to the moans of his wife that came from above. In the corner of the room, the images of the ikons, indifferent and dark, stood out confusedly, dimly illumined by the glimmering light of the image lamp. There was a stamping and scraping of feet over his head, something heavy was moved from one side of the floor to the other, there was a clattering of dishes, people were bustling hurriedly, up and down the staircase. Everything was being done in haste, yet time was creeping slowly. Ignat could hear a muffled voice from above

"As it seems, she cannot be delivered that way. We had better send to the church to open the gates of the Lord."

Vassushka, one of the hangers-on in his house, entered the room next to Ignat's and began to pray in a loud whisper:

"God, our Lord, descend from the skies in Thy benevolence, born of the Holy Virgin. Thou dost divine the helplessness of human creatures. Forgive Thy servant."

And suddenly drowning all other sounds, a superhuman, soul-rending cry rang out, and a continuous moan floated softly over the room and died out in the corners, which were filled now with the twilight. Ignat cast stern glances at the ikons, heaved a deep sigh and thought:

"Is it possible that it's again a daughter?"

At times he arose, stupidly stood in the middle of the room, and crossed himself in silence, bowing before the ikons; then he went back to the table, drank the vodka, which had not made him dizzy during these hours, dozed off, and thus passed the whole night and following morning until noon.

And then, at last, the midwife came down hastily, crying to him in a thin, joyous voice.

"I congratulate you with a son, Ignat Matveyich!"

"You lie!" said he in a dull voice. "What's the matter with you, batushka!" Heaving a sigh with all the strength of his massive chest, Ignat went down on his knees, and clasping his hands firmly to his breast, muttered in a trembling voice:

"Thank God! Evidently Thou didst not want that my stem should be checked! My sins before Thee shall not remain without repentance. I thank Thee, Oh Lord. Oh!" and, rising to his feet, he immediately began to command noisily:

"Eh! Let someone go to St. Nicholas for a priest. Tell him that Ignat Matveyich asked him to come! Let him come to make a prayer for the woman."

The chambermaid appeared and said to him with alarm:

"Ignat Matveyich, Natalya Fominichna is calling you. She is feeling bad."

"Why bad? It'll pass!" he roared, his eyes flashing cheerfully. "Tell her I'll be there immediately! Tell her she's a fine fellow! I'll just get a present for her and I'll come! Hold on! Prepare something to eat for the priest. Send somebody after Mayakin!"

His enormous figure looked as though it had grown bigger, and intoxicated with joy, he stupidly tossed about the room; he was smiling, rubbing his hands and casting fervent glances at the images; he crossed himself swinging his hand wide. At last he went up to his wife.

His eyes first of all caught a glimpse of the little red body, which the midwife was bathing in a tub. Noticing him, Ignat stood up on tiptoes, and, folding his hands behind his back, walked up to him, stepping carefully and comically putting forth his lips. The little one was whimpering and sprawling in the water, naked, impotent and pitiful.

"Look out there! Handle him more carefully! He hasn't got any bones yet," said Ignat to the midwife, softly.

She began to laugh, opening her toothless mouth, and cleverly throwing the child over from one hand to the other.

"You better go to your wife."

He obediently moved toward the bed and asked on his way:

"Well, how is it, Natalya?"

Then, on reaching her, he drew back the bed curtain, which had thrown a shadow over the bed.

"I'll not survive this," said she in a low, hoarse voice.

Ignat was silent, fixedly staring at his wife's face, sunk in the white pillow, over which her dark locks were spread out like dead snakes. Yellow, lifeless, with black circles around her large, wide-open eyes—her face was strange to him. And the glance of those terrible eyes, motionlessly fixed somewhere in the distance through the wall—that, too, was unfamiliar to Ignat. His heart, compressed by a painful foreboding, slackened its joyous throbbing.

"That's nothing. That's nothing. It's always like this," said he softly, bending over his wife to give her a kiss. But she moaned right into his face:

"I'll not survive this."

Her lips were gray and cold, and when he touched them with his own he understood that death was already within her.

"Oh, Lord!" he uttered, in an alarmed whisper, feeling that fright was choking his throat and suppressing his breath.

"Natasha? What will become of him? He must be nursed! What is the matter with you?"

He almost began to cry at his wife. The midwife was bustling about him; shaking the crying child in the air. She spoke to him reassuringly, but he heard nothing—he could not turn his eyes away from the frightful face of his wife. Her lips were moving, and he heard words spoken in a low voice, but could not understand them. Sitting on the edge of the bed, he spoke in a dull and timid voice: "Just think of it! He cannot do without you; he's an infant! Gather strength! Drive this thought away from you! Drive it away."

He talked, yet he understood he was speaking useless words. Tears welled up within him, and in his breast there came a feeling heavy as stone and cold as ice.

"Forgive me. Goodbye! Take care. Look out. Don't drink," whispered Natalya, soundlessly.

The priest came, and, covering her face with something, and sighing, began to read gentle, beseeching words:

"0h God, Almighty Lord, who cureth every disease, cure also Thy servant Natalya, who has just given birth to a child; and restore her from the bed on which she now lies, for in the words of David, 'We indulge in lawlessness and are wicked in Thine eyes.'"

The old man's voice was interrupted now and then, his thin face was stern and from his clothes came the odour of rock-rose.

"Guard the infant born of her, guard him from all possible temptation, from all possible cruelty, from all possible storms, from evil spirits, night and day."

Ignat listened to the prayer, and wept silently. His big, hot tears fell on the bare hand of his wife. But the hand, evidently, did not feel that the tears were dropping upon it: it remained motionless, and the skin did not tremble from the fall of the tears. After the prayer Natalya became unconscious and a day later she died, without saying another word—she died just as quietly as she had lived. Having arranged a pompous funeral, Ignat christened his son, named him Foma, and unwillingly gave his boy into the family of the godfather, his old friend Mayakin, whose wife, too, had given birth to a child not long before. The death of his wife had sown many gray hairs in Ignat's dark beard, but in the stern glitter of his eyes appeared a new expression, gentle, clear and mild.

CHAPTER II

MAYAKIN lived in an enormous two-story house near a big palisade, where sturdy, old spreading linden trees were growing magnificently. The rank branches covered the windows with a dense, dark embroidery, and the sun in broken rays peeped into the small rooms, which were closely crowded with miscellaneous furniture and big trunks, wherefore a stern and melancholy semi-darkness always reigned there supreme. The family was devout—the odour of wax, of rock-rose and of image-lamp oil filled the house, and penitent sighs and prayers soared about in the air. Religious ceremonials were performed infallibly, with pleasure, absorbing all the free power of the souls of the dwellers of the house. Feminine figures almost noiselessly moved about the rooms in the half-dark, stifling, heavy atmosphere. They were dressed in black, wore soft slippers on their feet, and always had a penitent look on their faces.

The family of Yakov Tarazovich Mayakin consisted of himself, his wife, a daughter and five kinswomen, the youngest of whom was thirty-four years old. These were alike devout and impersonal, and subordinate to Antonina Ivanovna, the mistress of the house. She was a tall, thin woman, with a dark face and with stern gray eyes, which had an imperious and intelligent expression. Mayakin also had a son Taras, but his name was never mentioned in the house; acquaintances knew that since the nineteen-year-old Taras had gone to study in Moscow—he married there three years later, against his father's will—Yakov disowned him. Taras disappeared without leaving any trace. It was rumoured that he had been sent to Siberia for something.

Yakov Mayakin was very queerly built. Short, thin, lively, with a little red beard, sly greenish eyes, he looked as though he said to each and every one:

"Never mind, sir, don't be uneasy. Even though I know you for what you are, if you don't annoy me I will not give you away."

His beard resembled an egg in shape and was monstrously big. His high forehead, covered with wrinkles, joined his bald crown, and it seemed as though he really had two faces—one an open, penetrating and intellectual face, with a long gristle nose, and above this face another one, eyeless and mouthless, covered with wrinkles, behind which Mayakin seemed to hide his eyes and his lips until a certain time; and when that time had arrived, he would look at the world with different eyes and smile a different smile.

He was the owner of a rope-yard and kept a store in town near the harbour. In this store, filled up to the ceiling with rope, twine, hemp and tow, he had a small room with a creaking glass door. In this room stood a big, old, dilapidated table, and near it a deep armchair, covered with oilcloth, in which Mayakin sat all day long, sipping tea and always reading the same "Moskovskiya Vedomosty," to which he subscribed, year in and year out, all his life. Among merchants he enjoyed the respect and reputation of a "brainy" man, and he was very fond of boasting of the antiquity of his race, saying in a hoarse voice:

"We, the Mayakins, were merchants during the reign of 'Mother' Catherine, consequently I am a pure-blooded man."

In this family Ignat Gordyeeff's son lived for six years. By the time he was seven years old Foma was a big-headed, broad-shouldered boy, seemingly older that his years, both in his size and in the serious look of his dark, almond-shaped eyes. Quiet, silent and persistent in his childish desires, he spent all his days over his playthings, with Mayakin's daughter, Luba, quietly looked after by one of the kinswomen, a stout, pock-marked old maid, who was, for some reason or other, nicknamed "Buzya." She was a dull, somewhat timid creature; and even to the children she spoke in a low voice, in words of monosyllables. Having devoted her time to learning prayers, she had no stories to tell Foma.

Foma was on friendly terms with the little girl, but when she angered or teased him he turned pale, his nostrils became distended, his eyes stared comically and he beat her audaciously. She cried, ran to her mother and complained to her, but Antonina loved Foma and she paid but little attention to her daughter's complaints, which strengthened the friendship between the children still more. Foma's day was long and uniform. Getting out of bed and washing himself, he used to place himself before the image, and under the whispering of the pock-marked Buzya he recited long prayers. Then they drank tea and ate many biscuits, cakes and pies. After tea—during the summer—the children went to the big palisade, which ran down to a ravine, whose bottom always looked dark and damp, filling them with terror. The children were not allowed to go even to the edge of the ravine, and this inspired in them a fear of it. In winter, from tea time to dinner, they played in the house when it was very cold outside, or went out in the yard to slide down the big ice hill.

They had dinner at noon, "in Russian style," as Mayakin said. At first a big bowl of fat, sour cabbage soup was served with rye biscuits in, but without meat, then the same soup was eaten with meat cut into small pieces; then they ate roast meat—pork, goose, veal or rennet, with gruel—then again a bowl of soup with vermicelli, and all this was usually followed by dessert. They drank kvass made of red bilberries, juniper-berries, or of bread—Antonina Ivanovna always carried a stock of different kinds of kvass. They ate in silence, only now and then uttering a sigh of fatigue; the children each ate out of a separate bowl, the adults eating out of one bowl. Stupefied by such a dinner, they went to sleep; and for two or three hours Mayakin's house was filled with snoring and with drowsy sighs.

Awaking from sleep, they drank tea and talked about local news, the choristers, the deacons, weddings, or the dishonourable conduct of this or that merchant. After tea Mayakin used to say to his wife:

"Well, mother, hand me the Bible."

126

Yakov Tarasovich used to read the Book of Job more often than anything else. Putting his heavy, silver-framed spectacles on his big, ravenous nose, he looked around at his listeners to see whether all were in their places.

They were all seated where he was accustomed to see them and on their faces was a familiar, dull and timid expression of piety.

"There was a man in the land of Uz," began Mayakin, in a hoarse voice, and Foma, sitting beside Luba on the lounge in the corner of the room, knew beforehand that soon his godfather would become silent and pat his bald head with his hand. He sat and, listening, pictured to himself this man from the land of Uz. The man was tall and bare, his eyes were enormously large, like those of the image of the Saviour, and his voice was like a big brass trumpet on which the soldiers played in the camps. The man was constantly growing bigger and bigger; and, reaching the sky, he thrust his dark hands into the clouds, and, tearing them asunder, cried out in a terrible voice:

"Why is light given to a man whose way is hid, and whom God hath hedged in?"

Dread fell on Foma, and he trembled, slumber fled from his eyes, he heard the voice of his godfather, who said, with a light smile, now and then pinching his beard:

"See how audacious he was!"

The boy knew that his godfather spoke of the man from the land of Uz, and the godfather's smile soothed the child. So the man would not break the sky; he would not rend it asunder with his terrible arms. And then Foma sees the man again—he sits on the ground, "his flesh is clothed with worms and clods of dust, his skin is broken." But now he is small and wretched, he is like a beggar at the church porch.

Here he says:

"What is man, that he should be clean? And he which is born of woman, that he should be righteous?" [These words attributed by Mayakin to Job are from Eliphaz the Temanite's reply—Translator's Note.]

127

"He says this to God," explained Mayakin, inspired. "How, says he, can I be righteous, since I am made of flesh? That's a question asked of God. How is that?"

And the reader, triumphantly and interrogatively looks around at his listeners.

"He merited it, the righteous man," they replied with a sigh.

Yakov Mayakin eyes them with a smile, and says:

"Fools! You better put the children to sleep."

Ignat visited the Mayakins every day, brought playthings for his son, caught him up into his arms and hugged him, but sometimes dissatisfied he said to him with ill-concealed uneasiness:

"Why are you such a bugbear? Oh! Why do you laugh so little?"

And he would complain to the lad's godfather:

"I am afraid that he may turn out to be like his mother. His eyes are cheerless."

"You disturb yourself rather too soon," Mayakin smilingly replied.

He, too, loved his godson, and when Ignat announced to him one day that he would take Foma to his own house, Mayakin was very much grieved.

"Leave him here," he begged. "See, the child is used to us; there! he's crying."

"He'll cease crying. I did not beget him for you. The air of the place is disagreeable. It is as tedious here as in an old believer's hermitage. This is harmful to the child. And without him I am lonesome. I come home—it is empty. I can see nothing there. It would not do for me to remove to your house for his sake. I am not for him, he is for me. So. And now that my sister has come to my house there will be somebody to look after him."

And the boy was brought to his father's house.

There he was met by a comical old woman, with a long, hook-like nose and with a mouth devoid of teeth. Tall, stooping, dressed in gray, with gray hair, covered by a black silk cap, she did not please the boy at

128

first; she even frightened him. But when he noticed on the wrinkled face her black eyes, which beamed so tenderly on him, he at once pressed his head close to her knees in confidence.

"My sickly little orphan!" she said in a velvet-like voice that trembled from the fulness of sound, and quietly patted his face with her hand, "stay close to me, my dear child!"

There was something particularly sweet and soft in her caresses, something altogether new to Foma, and he stared into the old woman's eyes with curiosity and expectation on his face. This old woman led him into a new world, hitherto unknown to him. The very first day, having put him to bed, she seated herself by his side, and, bending over the child, asked him:

"Shall I tell you a story, Fomushka?"

And after that Foma always fell asleep amid the velvet-like sounds of the old woman's voice, which painted before him a magic life. Giants defeating monsters, wise princesses, fools who turned out to be wise—troops of new and wonderful people were passing before the boy's bewitched imagination, and his soul was nourished by the wholesome beauty of the national creative power. Inexhaustible were the treasures of the memory and the fantasy of this old woman, who oftentimes, in slumber, appeared to the boy—now like the witch of the fairy-tales—only a kind and amiable old witch—now like the beautiful, all-wise Vasilisa. His eyes wide open, holding his breath, the boy looked into the darkness that filled his chamber and watched it as it slowly trembled in the light of the little lamp that was burning before the image. And Foma filled this darkness with wonderful pictures of fairy-tale life. Silent, yet living shadows, were creeping over the walls and across the floor; it was both pleasant and terrible to him to watch their life; to deal out unto them forms and colours, and, having endowed them with life, instantly to destroy them all with a single twinkle of the eyelashes. Something new appeared in his dark eyes, something more childish and naive, less grave; the loneliness and the darkness, awaking in him a painful feeling of expectation, stirred his curiosity, compelled him to go out to the dark corner and see what was hidden there beyond the thick veils of darkness. He went and found nothing, but he lost no hope of finding it out.

He feared his father and respected him. Ignat's enormous size, his harsh, trumpet-like voice, his bearded face, his gray-haired head, his powerful, long arms and his flashing eyes—all these gave to Ignat the resemblance of the fairy-tale robbers.

Foma shuddered whenever he heard his voice or his heavy, firm steps; but when the father, smiling kind-heartedly, and talking playfully in a loud voice, took him upon his knees or threw him high up in the air with his big hands the boy's fear vanished.

Once, when the boy was about eight years old, he asked his father, who had returned from a long journey:

"Papa, where were you?"

"On the Volga."

"Were you robbing there?" asked Foma, softly.

"Wha-at?" Ignat drawled out, and his eyebrows contracted.

"Aren't you a robber, papa? I know it," said Foma, winking his eyes slyly, satisfied that he had already read the secret of his father's life.

"I am a merchant!" said Ignat, sternly, but after a moment's thought he smiled kind-heartedly and added: "And you are a little fool! I deal in corn, I run a line of steamers. Have you seen the 'Yermak'? Well, that is my steamer. And yours, too."

"It is a very big one," said Foma with a sigh.

"Well, I'll buy you a small one while you are small yourself. Shall I?"

"Very well," Foma assented, but after a thoughtful silence he again drawled out regretfully: "But I thought you were a robber or a giant."

"I tell you I am a merchant!" repeated Ignat, insinuatingly, and there was something discontented and almost timorous in his glance at the disenchanted face of his son.

"Like Grandpa Fedor, the Kalatch baker?" asked Foma, having thought awhile.

"Well, yes, like him. Only I am richer than he. I have more money than Fedor."

"Have you much money?"

Well, some people have still more."

"How many barrels do you have?"

"Of what?"

"Of money, I mean."

"Fool! Is money counted by the barrel?"

"How else?" exclaimed Foma, enthusiastically, and, turning his face toward his father, began to tell him quickly: "Maksimka, the robber, came once to a certain town and filled up twelve barrels with money belonging to some rich man there. And he took different silverware and robbed a church. And cut up a man with his sword and threw him down the steeple because he tried to sound an alarm."

"Did your aunt tell you that?" asked Ignat admiring his son's enthusiasm.

"Yes! Why?"

"Nothing!" said Ignat, laughing. "So you thought your father was a robber."

"And perhaps you were a robber long ago?"

Foma again returned to his theme, and it was evident on his face that he would be very glad to hear an affirmative answer.

"I was never a robber. Let that end it."

"Never?"

"I tell you I was not! What a queer little boy you are! Is it good to be a robber? They are all sinners, the robbers. They don't believe in God—they rob churches. They are all cursed in the churches. Yes. Look here, my son, you'll have to start to study soon. It is time; you'll soon be nine years old. Start with the help of God. You'll study during the winter and in spring I'll take you along with me on the Volga."

"Will I go to school?" asked Foma, timidly.

"First you'll study at home with auntie." Soon after the boy would sit down near the table in the morning and, fingering the Slavonic alphabet, repeat after his aunt:

"Az, Buky, Vedy."

When they reached "bra, vra, gra, dra" for a long time the boy could not read these syllables without laughter. Foma succeeded easily in gaining knowledge, almost without any effort, and soon he was reading the first psalm of the first section of the psalter: "Blessed is the man that walketh not in the counsel of the ungodly."

"That's it, my darling! So, Fomushka, that's right!" chimed in his aunt with emotion, enraptured by his progress.

"You're a fine fellow, Foma!" Ignat would approvingly say when informed of his son's progress. "We'll go to Astrakhan for fish in the spring, and toward autumn I'll send you to school!"

The boy's life rolled onward, like a ball downhill. Being his teacher, his aunt was his playmate as well. Luba Mayakin used to come, and when with them, the old woman readily became one of them.

They played at "hide and seek and "blind man's buff;" the children were pleased and amused at seeing Anfisa, her eyes covered with a handkerchief, her arms outstretched, walking about the room carefully, and yet striking against chairs and tables, or looking for them in each and every commodious corner, saying:

"Eh, little rascals. Eh, rogues. Where have they hidden themselves? Eh?"

And the sun shone cheerfully and playfully upon the old worn-out body, which yet retained a youthful soul, and upon the old life, that was adorning, according to its strength and abilities, the life-path of two children.

Ignat used to go to the Exchange early in the morning and sometimes stayed away until evening; in the evening he used to go to the town council or visiting or elsewhere. Sometimes he returned home intoxicated. At first Foma, on such occasions, ran from him and hid himself, then he became accustomed to it, and learned that his father was better when drunk than sober: he was kinder and plainer and was somewhat comical. If it happened at night, the boy was usually awakened by his trumpet-like voice:

"Anfisa! Dear sister! Let me in to my son; let me in to my successor!"

And auntie answered him in a crying and reproachful voice:

"Go on. You better go to sleep, you cursed devil! Drunk again, eh? You are gray already?"

"Anfisa! May I see my son, with one eye?" Foma knew that Anfisa would not let him in, and he again fell asleep in spite of the noise of their voices. But when Ignat came home intoxicated during the day he immediately seized his son with his enormous paws and carried him about the rooms, asking him with an intoxicated, happy laughter:

"Fomka! What do you wish? Speak! Presents? Playthings? Ask! Because you must know there's nothing in this world that I wouldn't buy for you. I have a million! Ha, ha, ha! And I'll have still more! Understand? All's yours! Ha, ha!"

And suddenly his enthusiasm was extinguished like a candle put out by a violent puff of the wind. His flushed face began to shake, his eyes, burning red, filled with tears, and his lips expanded into a sad and frightened smile.

"Anfisa, in case he should die, what am I to do then?"

And immediately after these words he was seized with fury.

"I'd burn everything!" he roared, staring wildly into some dark corner of the room. "I'd destroy everything! I'd blow it up with dynamite!"

"Enough, you ugly brute! Do you wish to frighten the child? Or do you want him to take sick?" interposed Anfisa, and that was sufficient for Ignat to rush off hastily, muttering:

"Well, well, well! I am going, I am going, but don't cry! Don't make any noise. Don't frighten him."

And when Foma was somewhat sick, his father, casting everything aside, did not leave the house for a moment, but bothered his sister and his son with stupid questions and advice; gloomy, sighing, and with fear in his eyes, he walked about the house quite out of sorts.

"Why do you vex the Lord?" said Anfisa. "Beware, your grumblings will reach Him, and He will punish you for your complaints against His graces."

"Eh, sister!" sighed Ignat. "And if it should happen? My entire life is crumbling away! Wherefore have I lived? No one knows."

Similar scenes and the striking transitions of his father from one mood to another frightened the child at first, but he soon became accustomed to all this, and when he noticed through the window that his father, on coming home, was hardly able to get out of the sledge, Foma said indifferently:

"Auntie, papa came home drunk again."

* * * * *

Spring came, and, fulfilling his promise, Ignat took his son along on one of his steamers, and here a new life, abounding in impressions, was opened before Foma's eyes.

The beautiful and mighty "Yermak," Gordyeeff's steam tow-boat, was rapidly floating down the current, and on each side the shores of the powerful and beautiful Volga were slowly moving past him—the left side, all bathed in sunshine, stretching itself to the very end of the sky like a pompous carpet of verdure; the right shore, its high banks overgrown with woods, swung skyward, sinking in stern repose.

The broad-bosomed river stretched itself majestically between the shores; noiselessly, solemnly and slowly flowed its waters, conscious of their invincible power; the mountainous shore is reflected in the water in a black shadow, while on the left side it is adorned with gold and with verdant velvet by a border of sand and the wide meadows. Here and there villages appear on mountain and on meadow, the sun shines bright on the window-panes of the huts and on the yellow roofs of straw, the church crosses sparkle amid the verdure of the trees, gray wind-mill wings revolve lazily in the air, smoke from the factory chimney rises skyward in thick, black curling clouds. Crowds of children in blue, red or white shirts, standing on the banks, shouted loudly at the sight of the steamer, which had disturbed the quiet of the river, and from under the steamer's wheels the cheerful waves are rushing toward the feet of the children and splash against the bank. Now a crowd of children, seated in a boat, rowed toward the middle of the river to rock there on the waves as in a cradle. Trees stood out above the water; sometimes many of them are drowned in the overflow of the banks, and these stand in the water like islands. From the shore a melancholy song is heard:

"Oh, o-o-o, once more!"

The steamer passes many rafts, splashing them with waves. The beams are in continual motion under the blows of the waves; the men on the rafts in blue shirts, staggering, look at the steamer and laugh and shout something. The big, beautiful vessel goes sidewise on the river; the yellow scantlings with which it is loaded sparkle like gold and are dimly reflected in the muddy, vernal water. A passenger steamer comes from the opposite side and whistles—the resounding echo of the whistle loses itself in the woods, in the gorges of the mountainous bank, and dies away there. In the middle of the river the waves stirred up by the two vessels strike against one another and splash against the steamers' sides, and the vessels are rocked upon the water. On the slope of the mountainous bank are verdant carpets of winter corn, brown strips of fallow ground and black strips of ground tilled for spring corn. Birds, like little dots, soar over them, and are clearly seen in the blue canopy of the sky; nearby a flock is grazing; in the distance they look like children's toys; the small figure of the shepherd stands leaning on a staff, and looks at the river.

The glare of the water—freedom and liberty are everywhere, the meadows are cheerfully verdant and the blue sky is tenderly clear; a restrained power is felt in the quiet motion of the water; above it the generous May sun is shining, the air is filled with the exquisite odour of fir trees and of fresh foliage. And the banks keep on meeting them, caressing the eyes and the soul with their beauty, as new pictures constantly unfold themselves.

Everything surrounding them bears the stamp of some kind of tardiness: all—nature as well as men—live there clumsily, lazily; but in that laziness there is an odd gracefulness, and it seems as though beyond the laziness a colossal power were concealed; an invincible power, but as yet deprived of consciousness, as yet without any definite desires and aims. And the absence of consciousness in this half-slumbering life throws shades of sadness over all the beautiful slope. Submissive patience, silent hope for something new and more inspiriting are heard even in the cry of the cuckoo, wafted to the river by the wind from the shore. The melancholy songs sound as though imploring someone for help. And at times there is in them a ring of despair. The river answers the songs with sighs. And the tree-tops shake, lost in meditation. Silence.

Foma spent all day long on the captain's bridge beside his father. Without uttering a word, he stared wide-eyed at the endless panorama of the banks, and it seemed to him he was moving along a broad silver path in those wonderful kingdoms inhabited by the sorcerers and giants of his familiar fairy-tales. At times he would load his father with questions about everything that passed before them. Ignat answered him willingly and concisely, but the boy was not pleased with his answers; they contained nothing interesting and intelligible to him, and he did not hear what he longed to hear. Once he told his father with a sigh:

"Auntie Anfisa knows better than you."

"What does she know?" asked Ignat, smiling.

"Everything," replied the boy, convincedly.

No wonderful kingdom appeared before him. But often cities appeared on the banks of the river, just such cities as the one where Foma lived. Some of them were larger, some smaller, but the people, and the houses, and the churches—all were the same as in his own city. Foma examined them in company with his father, but was still unsatisfied and returned to the steamer gloomy and fatigued.

"Tomorrow we shall be in Astrakhan," said Ignat one day.

"And is it just the same as the other cities?"

"Of course. How else should it be?"

"And what is beyond Astrakhan?"

"The sea. The Caspian Sea it is called."

"And what is there?"

"Fishes, queer fellow! What else can there be in the water?"

"There's the city Kitezh standing in the water."

"That's a different thing! That's Kitezh. Only righteous people live there."

"And are there no righteous cities on the sea?"

No," said Ignat, and, after a moment's silence, added: "The sea water is bitter and nobody can drink it."

"And is there more land beyond the sea?"

"Certainly, the sea must have an end. It is like a cup."

"And are there cities there too?"

"Again cities. Of course! Only that land is not ours, it belongs to Persia. Did you see the Persians selling pistachio-nuts and apricots in the market?"

"Yes, I saw them," replied Foma, and became pensive.

One day he asked his father:

"Is there much more land left?"

"The earth is very big, my dear! If you should go on foot, you couldn't go around it even in ten years."

Ignat talked for a long time with his son about the size of the earth, and said at length:

"And yet no one knows for certain how big it really is, nor where it ends."

"And is everything alike on earth?"

"What do you mean?"

"The cities and all?"

"Well, of course, the cities are like cities. There are houses, streets—and everything that is necessary."

After many similar conversations the boy no longer stared so often into the distance with the interrogative look of his black eyes.

The crew of the steamer loved him, and he, too, loved those fine, sun-burnt and weather-beaten fellows, who laughingly played with him. They made fishing tackles for him, and little boats out of bark, played with him and rowed him about the anchoring place, when Ignat went to town on business. The boy often heard the men talking about his father, but he paid no attention to what they said, and never told his father what he heard about him. But one day, in Astrakhan, while the steamer was taking in a cargo of fuel, Foma heard the voice of Petrovich, the machinist:

"He ordered such a lot of wood to be taken in. What an absurd man! First he loads the steamer up to the very deck, and then he roars. 'You break the machinery too often,' he says. 'You pour oil,' he says, 'at random.'"

The voice of the gray and stern pilot replied:

"It's all his exorbitant greediness. Fuel is cheaper here, so he is taking all he can. He is greedy, the devil!"

"Oh, how greedy!"

This word, repeated many times in succession, fixed itself in Foma's memory, and in the evening, at supper, he suddenly asked his father:

"Papa!"

"What?"

"Are you greedy?"

In reply to his father's questions Foma told him of the conversation between the pilot and the machinist. Ignat's face became gloomy, and his eyes began to flash angrily.

"That's how it is," ejaculated Ignat, shaking his head. "Well, you—don't you listen to them. They are not your equals; don't have so much

138

to do with them. You are their master, they are your servants, understand that. If we choose to, we can put every one of them ashore. They are cheap and they can be found everywhere like dogs. Understand? They may say many bad things about me. But they say them, because I am their master. The whole thing arises because I am fortunate and rich, and the rich are always envied. A happy man is everybody's enemy."

About two days later there was a new pilot and another machinist on the steamer.

"And where is Yakov?" asked the boy.

"I discharged him. I ordered him away."

"For that?" queried Foma.

"Yes, for that very thing."

"And Petrovich, too?"

"Yes, I sent him the same way."

Foma was pleased with the fact that his father was able to change the men so quickly. He smiled to his father, and, coming out on the deck, walked up to a sailor, who sat on the floor, untwisting a piece of rope and making a swab.

"We have a new pilot here," announced Foma.

"I know. Good health to you, Foma Ignatich! How did you sleep?"

"And a new machinist, too."

"And a new machinist. Are you sorry for Petrovich?"

"Really? And he was so good to you."

"Well, why did he abuse my father?"

"Oh? Did he abuse him?"

"Of course he did. I heard it myself."

"Mm—and your father heard it, too?"

"No, I told him."

"You—so"—drawled the sailor and became silent, taking up his work again.

"And papa says to me: 'You,' he says, 'you are master here—you can drive them all away if you wish.'"

"So," said the sailor, gloomily looking at the boy, who was so enthusiastically boasting to him of his supreme power. From that day on Foma noticed that the crew did not regard him as before. Some became more obliging and kind, others did not care to speak to him, and when they did speak to him, it was done angrily, and not at all entertainingly, as before. Foma liked to watch while the deck was being washed: their trousers rolled up to their knees, or sometimes taken off altogether, the sailors, with swabs and brushes in their hands, cleverly ran about the deck, emptying pails of water on it, besprinkling one another, laughing, shouting, falling. Streams of water ran in every direction, and the lively noise of the men intermingled with the gray splash of the water. Before, the boy never bothered the sailors in this playful and light work; nay, he took an active part, besprinkling them with water and laughingly running away, when they threatened to pour water over him. But after Yakov and Petrovich had been discharged, he felt that he was in everybody's way, that no one cared to play with him and that no one regarded him kindly. Surprised and melancholy, he left the deck, walked up to the wheel, sat down there, and, offended, he thoughtfully began to stare at the distant green bank and the dented strip of woods upon it. And below, on the deck, the water was splashing playfully, and the sailors were gaily laughing. He yearned to go down to them, but something held him back.

"Keep away from them as much as possible," he recalled his father's words; "you are their master." Then he felt like shouting at the sailors—something harsh and authoritative, so his father would scold them. He thought a long time what to say, but could not think of anything. Another two, three days passed, and it became perfectly clear to him that the crew no longer liked him. He began to feel lonesome on the steamer, and amid the parti-coloured mist of new impressions, still more often there came up before Foma the image of his kind and gentle Aunt Anfisa, with her stories, and smiles, and soft, ringing laughter, which filled the boy's soul with a joyous warmth. He still lived in the world of fairy-tales, but the invisible and pitiless hand of reality was already at work tearing the beautiful, fine web of the wonderful, through which the boy had looked at everything about him. The incident with the machinist and the pilot directed his attention to his surroundings; Foma's eyes became more sharp-sighted. A conscious searchfulness appeared in them and in his questions to his father rang a yearning to understand which threads and springs were managing the deeds of men.

One day a scene took place before him: the sailors were carrying wood, and one of them, the young, curly-haired and gay Yefim, passing the deck of the ship with hand-barrows, said loudly and angrily:

"No, he has no conscience whatever! There was no agreement that I should carry wood. A sailor—well, one's business is clear—but to carry wood into the bargain—thank you! That means for me to take off the skin I have not sold. He is without conscience! He thinks it is clever to sap the life out of us."

The boy heard this grumbling and knew that it was concerning his father. He also noticed that although Yefim was grumbling, he carried more wood on his stretcher than the others, and walked faster than the others. None of the sailors replied to Yefim's grumbling, and even the one who worked with him was silent, only now and then protesting against the earnestness with which Yefim piled up the wood on the stretchers.

"Enough!" he would say, morosely, "you are not loading a horse, are you?"

"And you had better keep quiet. You were put to the cart—cart it and don't kick—and should your blood be sucked—keep quiet again. What can you say?"

Suddenly Ignat appeared, walked up to the sailor and, stopping in front of him, asked sternly:

"What were you talking about?"

"I am talking—I know," replied Yefim, hesitating. "There was no agreement—that I must say nothing."

"And who is going to suck blood?" asked Ignat, stroking his beard.

The sailor understood that he had been caught unawares, and seeing no way out of it, he let the log of wood fall from his hands, rubbed his palms against his pants, and, facing Ignat squarely, said rather boldly:

"And am I not right? Don't you suck it?"

"I?"

"You."

Foma saw that his father swung his hand. A loud blow resounded, and the sailor fell heavily on the wood. He arose immediately and worked on in silence. Blood was trickling from his bruised face on to the white bark of the birch wood; he wiped the blood off his face with the sleeve of his shirt, looked at his sleeve and, heaving a sigh, maintained silence, and when he went past Foma with the hand-harrows, two big, turbid tears were trembling on his face, near the bridge of his nose, and Foma noticed them.

At dinner Foma was pensive and now and then glanced at his father with fear in his eyes.

"Why do you frown?" asked his father, gently.

"Frown?"

"Are you ill, perhaps? Be careful. If there is anything, tell me."

"You are strong," said Foma of a sudden musingly.

"I? That's right. God has favoured me with strength."

"How hard you struck him!" exclaimed the boy in a low voice, lowering his head.

Ignat was about to put a piece of bread with caviar into his mouth, but his hand stopped, held back by his son's exclamation; he looked interrogatively at Foma's drooping head and asked:

"You mean Yefim, don't you?"

"Yes, he was bleeding. And how he walked afterward, how he cried," said the boy in a low voice.

"Mm," roared Ignat, chewing a bite. "Well, are you sorry for him?"

"It's a pity!" said Foma, with tears in his voice.

"Yes. So that's the kind of a fellow you are," said Ignat.

Then, after a moment's silence, he filled a wineglass with vodka, emptied it, and said sternly, in a slightly reprimanding tone:

"There is no reason why you should pity him. He brawled at random, and therefore got what he deserved. I know him: he is a good fellow, industrious, strong and not a bit foolish. But to argue is not his business; I may argue, because I am the master. It isn't simple to be master. A punch wouldn't kill him, but will make him wiser. That's the way. Eh, Foma! You are an infant, and you do not understand these things. I must teach you how to live. It may be that my days on earth are numbered."

Ignat was silent for awhile, drank some more vodka and went on instinctively:

"It is necessary to have pity on men. You are right in doing so. But you must pity them sensibly. First look at a man, find out what good there is in him, and what use may be made of him! And if you find him to be strong and capable—pity and assist him. And if he is weak and not inclined to work—spit upon him, pass him by. Just keep this in mind—the man who complains against everything, who sighs and moans all the time—that man is worth nothing; he merits no compassion and you will do him no good whatever, even if you help him. Pity for such people makes them more morose, spoils them the more. In your godfather's house you saw various kinds of people—unfortunate travellers and hangers-on, and all sorts of rabble. Forget them. They are not men, they are just shells, and are good for nothing. They are like bugs, fleas and other unclean things. Nor do they live for God's sake—they have no God. They call His name in vain, in order to move fools to pity, and, thus pitied, to fill their bellies with something. They live but for their bellies, and aside from eating, drinking, sleeping and moaning they can do nothing. And all they accomplish is the soul's decay. They are in your way and you trip over them. A good man among them—like fresh apples among bad ones—may soon be spoilt, and no one will profit by it. You are young, that's the trouble. You cannot comprehend my words. Help him who is firm in misery. He may not ask you for assistance, but think of it yourself, and assist him without his request. And if he should happen to be proud and thus feel offended at your aid, do not allow him to see that you are lending him a helping hand. That's the way it should be done, according to common sense! Here, for example, two boards, let us say, fall into the mud—one of them is a rotten one, the other, a good sound board. What should you do? What good is there in the rotten board? You had better drop it, let it stay in the mud and step on it so as not to soil your feet. As to the sound board, lift it up and place it in the sun; if it can be of no use to you, someone else may avail himself of it. That's the way it is, my son! Listen to me and remember. There is no reason why Yefim should be pitied. He is a capable fellow, he knows his value. You cannot knock his soul out with a box on the ear. I'll just watch him for about a week, and then I'll put him at the helm. And there, I am quite sure, he'll be a good pilot. And if he should be promoted to captain, he wouldn't lose courage—he would make a clever captain! That's the way people grow. I have gone through this school myself, dear. I, too, received more than one box on the ear when I was of his age. Life, my son, is not a dear mother to all of us. It is our exacting mistress."

Ignat talked with his son about two hours, telling him of his own youth, of his toils, of men; their terrible power, and of their weakness; of how they live, and sometimes pretend to be unfortunate in order to live on other people's money; and then he told him of himself, and of how he rose from a plain working man to be proprietor of a large concern. The boy listened to his words, looked at him and felt as though his father were coming nearer and nearer to him. And though his father's story did not contain the material of which Aunt Anfisa's fairy-tales were brimful, there was something new in it, something clearer and more comprehensible than in her fairy-tales, and something just as interesting. Something powerful and warm began to throb within his little heart, and he was drawn toward his father. Ignat, evidently, surmised his son's feelings by his eyes: he rose abruptly from his seat, seized him in his arms and pressed him firmly to his breast. And Foma embraced his neck, and, pressing his cheek to that of his father, was silent and breathed rapidly.

"My son," whispered Ignat in a dull voice, "My darling! My joy! Learn while I am alive. Alas! it is hard to live."

The child's heart trembled at this whisper; he set his teeth together, and hot tears gushed from his eyes.

Until this day Ignat had never kindled any particular feeling in his son: the boy was used to him; he was tired of looking at his enormous figure, and feared him slightly, but was at the same time aware that his father would do anything for him that he wanted. Sometimes Ignat would stay away from home a day, two, a week, or possibly the entire summer. And yet Foma did not even notice his absence, so absorbed was he by his love for Aunt Anfisa. When Ignat returned the boy was glad, but he could hardly tell whether it was his father's arrival that gladdened him or the playthings he brought with him. But now, at the sight of Ignat, the boy ran to meet him, grasped him by the hand, laughed, stared into his eyes and felt weary if he did not see him for two or three hours: His father became interesting to him, and, rousing his curiosity, he fairly developed love and respect for himself. Every time that they were together Foma begged his father:

"Papa, tell me about yourself."

* * * * *

The steamer was now going up the Volga. One suffocating night in July, when the sky was overcast with thick black clouds, and everything on the Volga was somewhat ominously calm, they reached Kazan and anchored near Uslon at the end of an enormous fleet of vessels. The clinking of the anchor chains and the shouting of the crew awakened Foma; he looked out of the window and saw, far in the distance, small lights glimmering fantastically: the water about the boat black and thick, like oil—and nothing else could be seen. The boy's heart trembled painfully and he began to listen attentively. A scarcely audible, melancholy song reached his ears—mournful and monotonous as a chant on the caravan the watchmen called to one another; the steamer hissed angrily getting up steam. And the black water of the river splashed sadly and quietly against the sides of the vessels. Staring fixedly into the darkness, until his eyes hurt, the boy discerned black piles and small lights dimly burning high above them. He knew that those were barges, but this knowledge did not calm him and his heart throbbed unevenly, and, in his imagination, terrifying dark images arose.

"O-o-o," a drawling cry came from the distance and ended like a wail.

Someone crossed the deck and went up to the side of the steamer.

"O-o-o," was heard again, but nearer this time.

"Yefim!" some one called in a low voice on the deck. "Yefimka!"

"Well?"

"Devil! Get up! Take the boat-hook."

"O-o-o," someone moaned near by, and Foma, shuddering, stepped back from the window.

The queer sound came nearer and nearer and grew in strength, sobbed and died out in the darkness. While on the deck they whispered with alarm:

"Yefimka! Get up! A guest is floating!"

"Where?" came a hasty question, then bare feet began to patter about the deck, a bustle was heard, and two boat-hooks slipped down past the boy's face and almost noiselessly plunged into the water.

"A gue-e-est!" Some began to sob near by, and a quiet, but very queer splash resounded.

The boy trembled with fright at this mournful cry, but he could not tear his hands from the window nor his eyes from the water.

"Light the lantern. You can't see anything."

"Directly."

146

And then a spot of dim light fell over the water. Foma saw that the water was rocking calmly, that a ripple was passing over it, as though the water were afflicted, and trembled for pain.

"Look! Look!" they whispered on the deck with fright.

At the same time a big, terrible human face, with white teeth set together, appeared on the spot of light. It floated and rocked in the water, its teeth seemed to stare at Foma as though saying, with a smile:

"Eh, boy, boy, it is cold. Goodbye!"

The boat-hooks shook, were lifted in the air, were lowered again into the water and carefully began to push something there.

"Shove him! Shove! Look out, he may be thrown under the wheel."

"Shove him yourself then."

The boat-hooks glided over the side of the steamer, and, scratching against it, produced a noise like the grinding of teeth. Foma could not close his eyes for watching them. The noise of feet stamping on the deck, over his head, was gradually moving toward the stern. And then again that moaning cry for the dead was heard:

"A gue-e-est!"

"Papa!" cried Foma in a ringing voice. "Papa!" His father jumped to his feet and rushed toward him.

"What is that? What are they doing there?" cried Foma.

Wildly roaring, Ignat jumped out of the cabin with huge bounds. He soon returned, sooner than Foma, staggering and looking around him, had time to reach his father's bed.

"They frightened you? It's nothing!" said Ignat, taking him up in his arms. "Lie down with me."

"What is it?" asked Foma, quietly.

"It was nothing, my son. Only a drowned man. A man was drowned and he is floating. That's nothing! Don't be afraid, he has already floated clear of us."

"Why did they push him?" interrogated the boy, firmly pressing close to his father, and shutting his eyes for fright.

"It was necessary to do so. The water might have thrown him under the wheel. Under ours, for instance. Tomorrow the police would notice it, there would be trouble, inquests, and we would be held here for examination. That's why we shoved him along. What difference does it make to him? He is dead; it doesn't pain him; it doesn't offend him. And the living would be troubled on his account. Sleep, my son.

"So he will float on that way?"

"He will float. They'll take him out somewhere and bury him."

"And will a fish devour him?"

"Fish do not eat human bodies. Crabs eat them. They like them."

Foma's fright was melting, from the heat of his father's body, but before his eyes the terrible sneering face was still rocking in the black water.

"And who is he?"

"God knows! Say to God about him: 'Oh Lord, rest his soul!'"

"Lord, rest his soul!" repeated Foma, in a whisper.

"That's right. Sleep now, don't fear. He is far away now! Floating on. See here, be careful as you go up to the side of the ship. You may fall overboard. God forbid! And—"

"Did he fall overboard?"

"Of course. Perhaps he was drunk, and that's his end! And maybe he threw himself into the water. There are people who do that. They go and throw themselves into the water and are drowned. Life, my dear, is so arranged that death is sometimes a holiday for one, sometimes it is a blessing for all."

"Papa."

"Sleep, sleep, dear."

CHAPTER III

DURING the very first day of his school life, stupefied by the lively and hearty noise of provoking mischiefs and of wild, childish games, Foma picked out two boys from the crowd who at once seemed more interesting to him than the others. One had a seat in front of him. Foma, looking askance, saw a broad back; a full neck, covered with freckles; big ears; and the back of the head closely cropped, covered with light-red hair which stood out like bristles.

When the teacher, a bald-headed man, whose lower lip hung down, called out: "Smolin, African!" the red-headed boy arose slowly, walked up to the teacher, calmly stared into his face, and, having listened to the problem, carefully began to make big round figures on the blackboard with chalk.

"Good enough!" said the teacher. "Yozhov, Nicolai. Proceed!"

One of Foma's neighbours, a fidgety little boy with black little mouse-eyes, jumped up from his seat and passed through the aisle, striking against everything and turning his head on all sides. At the blackboard he seized the chalk, and, standing up on the toes of his boots, noisily began to mark the board with the chalk, creaking and filling with chalk dust, dashing off small, illegible marks.

"Not so loud!" said the teacher, wrinkling his yellow face and contracting his fatigued eyes. Yozhov spoke quickly and in a ringing voice:

"Now we know that the first peddler made 17k. profit."

"Enough! Gordyeeff! Tell me what must we do in order to find out how much the second peddler gained?"

Watching the conduct of the boys, so unlike each other, Foma was thus taken unawares by the question and he kept quiet.

"Don't you know? How? Explain it to him, Smolin."

Having carefully wiped his fingers, which had been soiled with chalk, Smolin put the rag away, and, without looking at Foma, finished the problem and again began to wipe his hands, while Yozhov, smiling and skipping along as he walked, returned to his seat.

"Eh, you!" he whispered, seating himself beside Foma, incidentally striking his side with his fist. "Why don't you know it? What was the profit altogether? Thirty kopecks. And there were two peddlers. One of them got 17. Well, how much did the other one get?"

"I know," replied Foma, in a whisper, feeling confused and examining the face of Smolin, who was sedately returning to his seat. He didn't like that round, freckled face, with the blue eyes, which were loaded with fat. And Yozhov pinched his leg and asked:

"Whose son are you? The Frantic's?"

"Yes."

"So. Do you wish me to prompt you always?"

"Yes."

"And what will you give me for it?"

Foma thought awhile and asked:

"And do you know it all yourself?"

"I? I am the best pupil. You'll see for yourself."

"Hey, there! Yozhov, you are talking again?" cried the teacher, faintly.

Yozhov jumped to his feet and said boldly:

"It's not I, Ivan Andreyich—it's Gordyeeff."

"Both of them were whispering," announced Smolin, serenely.

Wrinkling his face mournfully and moving his big lip comically, the teacher reprimanded them all, but his words did not prevent Yozhov from whispering immediately:

"Very well, Smolin! I'll remember you for telling."

"Well, why do you blame it all on the new boy?" asked Smolin, in a low voice, without even turning his head to them.

"All right, all right," hissed Yozhov.

Foma was silent, looking askance at his brisk neighbour, who at once pleased him and roused in him a desire to get as far as possible away from him. During recess he learned from Yozhov that Smolin, too, was rich, being the son of a tan-yard proprietor, and that Yozhov himself was the son of a guard at the Court of Exchequer, and very poor. The last was clearly evident by the adroit boy's costume, made of gray fustian and adorned with patches on the knees and elbows; by his pale, hungry-looking face; and, by his small, angular and bony figure. This boy spoke in a metallic alto, elucidating his words with grimaces and gesticulations, and he often used words whose meaning was known but to himself.

"We'll be friends," he announced to Foma.

"Why did you complain to the teacher about me?" Gordyeeff reminded Yozhov, looking at him suspiciously.

"There! What's the difference to you? You are a new scholar and rich. The teacher is not exacting with the rich. And I am a poor hanger-on; he doesn't like me, because I am impudent and because I never bring him any presents. If I had been a bad pupil he would have expelled me long ago. You know I'll go to the Gymnasium from here. I'll pass the second class and then I'll leave. Already a student is preparing me for the second class. There I'll study so that they can't hold me back! How many horses do you have?"

"Three. What do you need to study so much for?" asked Foma.

"Because I am poor. The poor must study hard so that they may become rich. They become doctors, functionaries, officers. I shall be a 'tinkler.' A sword at my side, spur on my boots. Cling, cling! And what are you going to be?"

"I don't know," said Foma, pensively, examining his companion.

"You need not be anything. And are you fond of pigeons?"

"Yes."

"What a good-for-nothing you are! Oh! Eh!" Yozhov imitated Foma's slow way of speaking. "How many pigeons do you have?"

"I have none."

"Eh, you! Rich, and yet you have no pigeons. Even I have three. If my father had been rich I would have had a hundred pigeons and chased them all day long. Smolin has pigeons, too, fine ones! Fourteen. He made me a present of one. Only, he is greedy. All the rich are greedy. And you, are you greedy, too?"

"I don't know," said Foma, irresolutely.

"Come up to Smolin's and the three of us together will chase the pigeons."

"Very well. If they let me."

"Why, does not your father like you?"

"He does like me."

"Well, then, he'll let you go. Only don't tell him that I am coming. Perhaps he would not let you go with me. Tell him you want to go to Smolin's. Smolin!"

A plump boy came up to them, and Yozhov accosted him, shaking his head reproachfully:

"Eh, you red-headed slanderer! It isn't worth while to be friends with you, blockhead!"

"Why do you abuse me?" asked Smolin, calmly, examining Foma fixedly.

"I am not abusing you; I am telling the truth," Yozhov explained, straightening himself with animation. "Listen! Although you are a kissel, but—let it go! We'll come up to see you on Sunday after mass."

"Come," Smolin nodded his head.

"We'll come up. They'll ring the bell soon. I must run to sell the siskin," declared Yozhov, pulling out of his pocket a paper package, wherein some live thing was struggling. And he disappeared from the school-yard as mercury from the palm of a hand.

"What a queer fellow he is!" said Foma, dumfounded by Yozhov's adroitness and looking at Smolin interrogatively.

"He is always like this. He's very clever," the red-headed boy explained.

"And cheerful, too," added Foma.

"Cheerful, too," Smolin assented. Then they became silent, looking at each other.

"Will you come up with him to my house?" asked the red-headed boy.

"Yes."

"Come up. It's nice there."

Foma said nothing to this. Then Smolin asked him:

"Have you many friends?"

"I have none."

"Neither did I have any friends before I went to school. Only cousins. Now you'll have two friends at once."

"Yes," said Foma.

"Are you glad?"

"I'm glad."

"When you have lots of friends, it is lively. And it is easier to study, too—they prompt you."

"And are you a good pupil?"

"Of course! I do everything well," said Smolin, calmly.

The bell began to bang as though it had been frightened and was hastily running somewhere.

Sitting in school, Foma began to feel somewhat freer, and compared his friends with the rest of the boys. He soon learned that they both were the very best boys in school and that they were the first to attract everybody's attention, even as the two figures 5 and 7, which had not yet been wiped off the blackboard. And Foma felt very much pleased that his friends were better than any of the other boys.

They all went home from school together, but Yozhov soon turned into some narrow side street, while Smolin walked with Foma up to his very house, and, departing, said:

"You see, we both go home the same way, too."

At home Foma was met with pomp: his father made him a present of a heavy silver spoon, with an ingenious monogram on it, and his aunt gave him a scarf knitted by herself. They were awaiting him for dinner, having prepared his favourite dishes for him, and as soon as he took off his coat, seated him at the table and began to ply him with questions.

"Well, how was it? How did you like the school?" asked Ignat, looking lovingly at his son's rosy, animated face.

"Pretty good. It's nice!" replied Foma.

"My darling!" sighed his aunt, with feeling, "look out, hold your own with your friends. As soon as they offend you tell your teachers about it."

"Go on. What else will you tell him?" Ignat smiled. "Never do that! Try to get square with every offender yourself, punish him with your own hand, not with somebody else's. Are there any good fellows there?"

"There are two," Foma smiled, recalling Yozhov. "One of them is so bold—terrible!"

"Whose is he?"

"A guard's son."

"Mm! Bold did you say?"

"Dreadfully bold!"

"Well, let him be! And the other?"

"The other one is red-headed. Smolin."

"Ah! Evidently Mitry Ivanovitch's son. Stick to him, he's good company. Mitry is a clever peasant. If the son takes after his father it is all right. But that other one—you know, Foma, you had better invite them to our house on Sunday. I'll buy some presents and you can treat them. We'll see what sort of boys they are."

"Smolin asked me to come to him this Sunday," said Foma, looking up at his father questioningly.

"So. Well, you may go! That's all right, go. Observe what kind of people there are in the world. You cannot pass your life alone, without friendship. Your godfather and I, for instance, have been friends for more than twenty years, and I have profited a great deal by his common sense. So you, too, try to be friendly with those that are better and wiser than you. Rub against a good man, like a copper coin against silver, and you may then pass for a silver coin yourself."

And, bursting into laughter at his comparison, Ignat added seriously:

"I was only jesting. Try to be, not artificial, but genuine. And have some common sense, no matter how little, but your own. Have you many lessons to do?"

"Many!" sighed the boy, and to his sigh, like an echo, his aunt answered with a heavy sigh.

"Well, study. Don't be worse than others at school. Although, I'll tell you, even if there were twenty-five classes in your school, they could never teach you there anything save reading, writing and arithmetic. You may also learn some naughty things, but God protect you! I shall give you a terrible spanking if you do. If you smoke tobacco I'll cut your lips off."

"Remember God, Fomushka," said the aunt. "See that you don't forget our Lord."

"That's true! Honour God and your father. But I wish to tell you that school books are but a trivial matter. You need these as a carpenter needs an adze and a pointer. They are tools, but the tools cannot teach you how to make use of them. Understand? Let us see: Suppose an adze were handed to a carpenter for him to square a beam with it. It's not enough to have hands and an adze; it is also necessary for him to know how to strike the wood so as not to hit his foot instead. To you the knowledge of reading and writing is given, and you must regulate your life with it. Thus it follows that books alone are but a trifle in this matter; it is necessary to be able to take advantage of them. And it is this ability that is more cunning than any books, and yet nothing about it is written in the books. This, Foma, you must learn from Life itself. A book is a dead thing, you may take it as you please, you may tear it, break it—it will not cry out. While should you but make a single wrong step in life, or wrongly occupy a place in it, Life will start to bawl at you in a thousand voices; it will deal you a blow, felling you to the ground."

Foma, his elbows leaning on the table, attentively listened to his father, and under the sound of his powerful voice he pictured to himself now the carpenter squaring a beam, now himself, his hands outstretched, carefully and stealthily approaching some colossal and living thing, and desiring to grasp that terrible something.

"A man must preserve himself for his work and must be thoroughly acquainted with the road to it. A man, dear, is like the pilot on a ship. In youth, as at high tide, go straight! A way is open to you everywhere. But you must know when it is time to steer. The waters recede—here you see a sandbank, there, a rock; it is necessary to know all this and to slip off in time, in order to reach the harbour safe and sound."

"I will reach it!" said the boy, looking at his father proudly and with confidence.

"Eh? You speak courageously!" Ignat burst into laughter. And the aunt also began to laugh kindly.

Since his trip with his father on the Volga, Foma became more lively and talkative at home, with his father, with his aunt and with Mayakin. But on the street, in a new place, or in the presence of strangers, he was always gloomy, always looking about him with suspicion, as though he felt something hostile to him everywhere, something hidden from him spying on him.

At nights he sometimes awoke of a sudden and listened for a long time to the silence about him, fixedly staring into the dark with wide-open eyes. And then his father's stories were transformed before him into images and pictures. Without being aware of it, he mixed up those stories with his aunt's fairy-tales, thus creating for himself a chaos of adventures wherein the bright colours of fantasy were whimsically intertwined with the stern shades of reality. This resulted in something colossal, incomprehensible; the boy closed his eyes and drove it all away from him and tried to check the play of his imagination, which frightened him. In vain he attempted to fall asleep, and the chamber became more and more crowded with dark images. Then he quietly roused his aunt.

"Auntie! Auntie!"

"What? Christ be with you."

"I'll come to you," whispered Foma.

"Why? Sleep, darling, sleep."

"I am afraid," confessed the boy.

"You better say to yourself, 'And the Lord will rise again,' then you won't be afraid."

Foma lies with his eyes open and says the prayer. The silence of the night pictures itself before him in the form of an endless expanse of perfectly calm, dark water, which has overflowed everything and congealed; there is not a ripple on it, not a shadow of a motion, and neither is there anything within it, although it is bottomlessly deep. It is very terrible for one to look down from the dark at this dead water. But now the sound of the night watchman's mallet is heard, and the boy sees that the surface of the water is beginning to tremble, and, covering the surface with ripples, light little balls are dancing upon it. The sound of the bell on the steeple, with one mighty swing, brings all the water in agitation and it is slightly trembling from that sound; a big spot of light is also trembling, spreading light upon the water, radiating from its centre into the dark distance, there growing paler and dying out. Again there is weary and deathlike repose in this dark desert.

"Auntie," whispers Foma, beseechingly.

"Dearest?"

"I am coming to you."

"Come, then, come, my darling."

Going over into auntie's bed, he presses close to her, begging:

"Tell me something."

"At night?" protests auntie, sleepily.

"Please."

He does not have to ask her long. Yawning, her eyes closed, the old woman begins slowly in a voice grown heavy with sleep:

"Well, my dear sir, in a certain kingdom, in a certain empire, there lived a man and his wife, and they were very poor. They were so unfortunate that they had nothing to eat. They would go around begging, somebody would give them a crust of stale bread and that would keep them for awhile. And it came to pass that the wife begot a child—a child was born—it was necessary to christen it, but, being poor, they could not entertain the godparents and the guests, so nobody came to christen the child. They tried this and they tried that—yet nobody came. And they began to pray to the Lord, 'Oh Lord! Oh Lord!'"

Foma knew this awful story about God's godchild. He had heard it more than once and was already picturing to himself this godchild riding on a white horse to his godfather and godmother; he was riding in the darkness, over the desert, and he saw there all the unbearable miseries to which sinners are condemned. And he heard their faint moans and requests:

"Oh! Man! Ask the Lord yet how long are we to suffer here!"

Then it appeared to Foma that it was he who was riding at night on the white horse, and that the moans and the implorings were addressed to him. His heart contracts with some incomprehensible desire; sorrow compressed his breast and tears gathered in his eyes, which he had firmly closed and now feared to open.

He is tossing about in his bed restlessly,

"Sleep, my child. Christ be with you!" says the old woman, interrupting her tale of men suffering for their sins.

But in the morning after such a night Foma rose sound and cheerful, washed himself hastily, drank his tea in haste and ran off to school, provided with sweet cakes, which were awaited by the always hungry little Yozhov, who greedily subsisted on his rich friend's generosity.

"Got anything to eat?" he accosted Foma, turning up his sharp-pointed nose. "Let me have it, for I left the house without eating anything. I slept too long, devil take it! I studied up to two o'clock last night. Have you solved your problems?"

"No, I haven't."

"Eh, you lazy bones! Well, I'll dash them off for you directly!"

Driving his small, thin teeth into the cakes, he purred something like a kitten, stamped his left foot, beating time, and at the same time solved the problem, rattling off short phrases to Foma:

"See? Eight bucketfuls leaked out in one hour. And how many hours did it leak—six? Eh, what good things they eat in your house! Consequently, we must multiply six by eight. Do you like cake with green onions? Oh, how I like it! So that in six hours forty-eight bucketfuls leaked out of the first gauge-cock. And altogether the tub contained ninety. Do you understand the rest?"

Foma liked Yozhov better than Smolin, but he was more friendly with Smolin. He wondered at the ability and the sprightliness of the little fellow. He saw that Yozhov was more clever and better than himself; he envied him, and felt offended on that account, and at the same time he pitied him with the condescending compassion of a satisfied man for a hungry one. Perhaps it was this very compassion that prevented him from preferring this bright boy to the boring red-headed Smolin. Yozhov, fond of having a laugh at the expense of his well-fed friends, told them quite often: "Eh, you are little trunks full of cakes!"

Foma was angry with him for his sneers, and one day, touched to the quick, said wickedly and with contempt:

"And you are a beggar—a pauper!"

Yozhov's yellow face became overcast, and he replied slowly:

"Very well, so be it! I shall never prompt you again—and you'll be like a log of wood!"

And they did not speak to each other for about three days, very much to the regret of the teacher, who during these days had to give the lowest markings to the son of the esteemed Ignat Matveyich.

Yozhov knew everything: he related at school how the procurator's chambermaid gave birth to a child, and that for this the procurator's wife poured hot coffee over her husband; he could tell where and when it was best to catch perch; he knew how to make traps and cages for birds; he could give a detailed account of how the soldier had hanged himself in the garret of the armoury, and knew from which of the pupils' parents the teacher had received a present that day and precisely what sort of a present it was.

The sphere of Smolin's knowledge and interests was confined to the merchant's mode of life, and, above all, the red-headed boy was fond of judging whether this man was richer than that, valuing and pricing their houses, their vessels and their horses. All this he knew to perfection, and spoke of it with enthusiasm.

Like Foma, he regarded Yozhov with the same condescending pity, but more as a friend and equal. Whenever Gordyeeff quarrelled with Yozhov, Smolin hastened to reconcile them, and he said to Foma one day, on their way home:

"Why do you always quarrel with Yozhov?"

"Well, why is he so self-conceited?" said Foma, angrily.

"He is proud because you never know your lessons, and he always helps you out. He is clever. And because he is poor—is he to blame for that? He can learn anything he wants to, and he will be rich, too."

"He is like a mosquito," said Foma, disdainfully; "he will buzz and buzz, and then of a sudden will bite."

But there was something in the life of these boys that united them all; there were hours when the consciousness of difference in their natures and positions was entirely lost. On Sundays they all gathered at Smolin's, and, getting up on the roof of the wing, where they had an enormous pigeon-house, they let the pigeons loose.

160

The beautiful, well-fed birds, ruffling their snow-white wings, darted out of the pigeon-house one by one, and, seating themselves in a row on the ridge of the roof, and, illumined by the sun, cooing, flaunted before the boys.

"Scare them!" implored Yozhov, trembling for impatience.

Smolin swung a pole with a bast-wisp fastened to its end, and whistled.

The frightened pigeons rushed into the air, filling it with the hurried flapping of their wings. And now, outlining big circles, they easily soar upwards, into the blue depths of the sky; they float higher and higher, their silver and snow-white feathers flashing. Some of them are striving to reach the dome of the skies with the light soaring of the falcon, their wings outstretched wide and almost motionless; others play, turn over in the air, now dropping downward in a snowy lump, now darting up like an arrow. Now the entire flock seems as though hanging motionless in the desert of the sky, and, growing smaller and smaller, seems to sink in it. With heads thrown back, the boys admire the birds in silence, without taking their eyes from them—their tired eyes, so radiant with calm joy, not altogether free from envying these winged creatures, which so freely took flight from earth up into the pure and calm atmosphere full of the glitter of the sun. The small group of scarcely visible dots, now mere specks in the azure of the sky, leads on the imagination of the children, and Yozhov expresses their common feeling when, in a low voice, he says thoughtfully:

"That's the way we ought to fly, friends."

While Foma, knowing that human souls, soaring heavenward, oftentimes assume the form of pigeons, felt in his breast the rising of a burning, powerful desire.

Unified by their joy, attentively and mutely awaiting the return of their birds from the depths of the sky, the boys, pressing close to one another, drifted far away from the breath of life, even as their pigeons were far from earth; at this moment they are merely children, knowing neither envy nor anger; free from everything, they are near to one another, they are mute, judging their feelings by the light in their eyes—and they feel as happy as the birds in the sky.

But now the pigeons come down on the roof again, and, tired out by their flight, are easily driven into the pigeon-house.

"Friends, let's go for apples?" suggests Yozhov, the instigator of all games and adventures.

His call drives out of the children's souls the peacefulness brought into them by the pigeons, and then, like plunderers, carefully listening for each and every sound, they steal quietly across the back yards toward the neighbouring garden. The fear of being caught is balanced by the hope of stealing with impunity. But stealing is work and dangerous work at that, and everything that is earned by your own labour is so sweet! And the more effort required to gain it, the sweeter it is. Carefully the boys climb over the fence of the garden, and, bending down, crawl toward the apple trees and, full of fright, look around vigilantly. Their hearts tremble and their throbbing slackens at the faintest rustle. They are alike afraid of being caught, and, if noticed, of being recognised, but in case they should only see them and yell at them, they would be satisfied. They would separate, each going in a different direction, and then, meeting again, their eyes aglow with joy and boldness, would laughingly tell one another how they felt when they heard some one giving chase to them, and what happened to them when they ran so quickly through the garden, as though the ground were burning under their feet.

Such invasions were more to Foma's liking than all other adventures and games, and his behaviour during these invasions was marked with a boldness that at once astounded and angered his companions. He was intentionally careless in other people's gardens: he spoke loud, noisily broke the branches of apple trees, and, tearing off a worm-eaten apple, threw it in the direction of the proprietor's house. The danger of being caught in the act did not frighten him; it rather encouraged him—his eyes would turn darker, his teeth would clench, and his face would assume an expression of anger and pride.

Smolin, distorting his big mouth contemptibly, would say to him:

"You are making entirely too much fuss about yourself."

"I am not a coward anyway!" replied Foma.

"I know that you are not a coward, but why do you boast of it? One may do a thing as well without boasting."

Yozhov blamed him from a different point of view:

"If you thrust yourself into their hands willingly you can go to the devil! I am not your friend. They'll catch you and bring you to your father—he wouldn't do anything to you, while I would get such a spanking that all my bones would be skinned."

"Coward!" Foma persisted, stubbornly.

And it came to pass one day that Foma was caught by the second captain, Chumakov, a thin little old man. Noiselessly approaching the boy, who was hiding away in his bosom the stolen apples, the old man seized him by the shoulders and cried in a threatening voice:

"Now I have you, little rogue! Aha!"

Foma was then about fifteen years old, and he cleverly slipped out of the old man's hands. Yet he did not run from him, but, knitting his brow and clenching his fist, he said threateningly:

"You dare to touch me!"

"I wouldn't touch you. I'll just turn you over to the police! Whose son are you?"

Foma did not expect this, and all his boldness and spitefulness suddenly left him.

The trip to the police station seemed to him something which his father would never forgive him. He shuddered and said confusedly:

"Gordyeeff."

"Ignat Gordyeeff's?"

"Yes."

Now the second captain was taken aback. He straightened himself, expanded his chest and for some reason or other cleared his throat impressively. Then his shoulders sank and he said to the boy in a fatherly tone:

"It's a shame! The son of such a well-known and respected man! It is unbecoming your position. You may go. But should this happen again! Hm! I should be compelled to notify your father, to whom, by the way, I have the honour of presenting my respects."

Foma watched the play of the old man's physiognomy and understood that he was afraid of his father. Like a young wolf, he looked askance at Chumakov; while the old man, with comical seriousness, twisted his gray moustache, hesitating before the boy, who did not go away, notwithstanding the given permission.

"You may go," repeated the old man, pointing at the road leading to his house.

"And how about the police?" asked Foma, sternly, and was immediately frightened at the possible answer.

"I was but jesting," smiled the old man. "I just wanted to frighten you."

"You are afraid of my father yourself," said Foma, and, turning his back to the old man, walked off into the depth of the garden.

"I am afraid? Ah! Very well!" exclaimed Chumakov after him, and Foma knew by the sound of his voice that he had offended the old man. He felt sad and ashamed; he passed the afternoon in walking, and, coming home, he was met by his father's stern question:

"Foma! Did you go to Chumakov's garden?"

"Yes, I did," said the boy, calmly, looking into his father's eyes.

Evidently Ignat did not expect such an answer and he was silent for awhile, stroking his beard.

"Fool! Why did you do it? Have you not enough of your own apples?"

Foma cast down his eyes and was silent, standing before his father.

"See, you are shamed! Yozhishka must have incited you to this! I'll give it to him when he comes, or I'll make an end of your friendship altogether."

"I did it myself," said Foma, firmly.

"From bad to worse!" exclaimed Ignat. "But why did you do it?"

"Because."

"Because!" mocked the father. "Well, if you did it you ought to be able to explain to yourself and to others the reason for so doing. Come here!"

Foma walked up to his father, who was sitting on a chair, and placed himself between his knees. Ignat put his hand on the boy's shoulders, and, smiling, looked into his eyes.

"Are you ashamed?"

"I am ashamed," sighed Foma.

"There you have it, fool! You have disgraced me and yourself."

Pressing his son's head to his breast, he stroked his hair and asked again:

"Why should you do such a thing—stealing other people's apples?"

"I—I don't know," said Foma, confusedly. "Perhaps because it is so lonesome. I play and play the same thing day after day. I am growing tired of it! While this is dangerous."

"Exciting?" asked the father, smiling.

"Yes."

"Mm, perhaps it is so. But, nevertheless, Foma, look out—drop this, or I shall deal with you severely."

"I'll never climb anywhere again," said the boy with confidence.

"And that you take all the blame on yourself—that is good. What will become of you in the future, only God knows, but meanwhile—it is pretty good. It is not a trifle if a man is willing to pay for his deeds with his own skin. Someone else in your place would have blamed his friends, while you say: 'I did it myself.' That's the proper way, Foma. You commit the sin, but you also account for it. Didn't Chumakov strike you?" asked Ignat, pausing as he spoke.

"I would have struck him back," declared Foma, calmly.

"Mm," roared his father, significantly.

"I told him that he was afraid of you. That is why he complained. Otherwise he was not going to say anything to you about it."

"Is that so?"

"'By God! Present my respects to your father,' he said."

"Did he?"

"Yes."

"Ah! the dog! See what kind of people there are; he is robbed and yet he makes a bow and presents his respects! Ha, ha! It is true it might have been worth no more than a kopeck, but a kopeck is to him what a rouble is to me. And it isn't the kopeck, but since it is mine, no one dares touch it unless I throw it away myself. Eh! The devil take them! Well, tell me—where have you been, what have you seen?"

The boy sat down beside his father and told him in detail all the impressions of that day. Ignat listened, fixedly watching the animated face of his son, and the eyebrows of the big man contracted pensively.

"You are still but floating on the surface, dear. You are still but a child. Eh! Eh!"

"We scared an owl in the ravine," related the boy. "That was fun! It began to fly about and struck against a tree—bang! It even began to squeak so pitifully. And we scared it again; again it rose and flew about here and there, and again it struck against something, so that its feathers were coming out. It flew about in the ravine and at last hid itself somewhere with difficulty. We did not try to look for it, we felt sorry it was all bruised. Papa, is an owl entirely blind in daytime?"

"Blind!" said Ignat; "some men will toss about in life even as this owl in daytime. Ever searching for his place, he strives and strives—only feathers fly from him, but all to no purpose. He is bruised, sickened, stripped of everything, and then with all his might he thrusts himself anywhere, just to find repose from his restlessness. Woe to such people. Woe to them, dear!"

"How painful is it to them?" said Foma in a low voice.

"Just as painful as to that owl."

"And why is it so?"

"Why? It is hard to tell. Someone suffers because he is darkened by his pride—he desires much, but has but little strength. Another because of his foolishness. But then there are a thousand and one other reasons, which you cannot understand."

"Come in and have some tea," Anfisa called to them. She had been standing in the doorway for quite a long while, and, folding her hands, lovingly admired the enormous figure of her brother, who bent over Foma with such friendliness, and the pensive pose of the boy, who clung to his father's shoulder.

Thus day by day Foma's life developed slowly—a quiet, peaceful life, not at all brimful of emotions. Powerful impressions, rousing the boy's soul for an hour or for a day, sometimes stood out strikingly against the general background of this monotonous life, but these were soon obliterated. The boy's soul was as yet but a calm lake—a lake hidden from the stormy winds of life, and all that touched the surface of the lake either sank to the bottom, stirring the placid water for a moment, or gliding over the smooth surface, swam apart in big circles and disappeared.

Having stayed at the district school for five years, Foma passed four classes tolerably well and came out a brave, dark-haired fellow, with a swarthy face, heavy eyebrows and dark down on the upper lip. His big dark eyes had a naive and pensive look, and his lips were like a child's, half-open; but when meeting with opposition to his desires or when irritated by something else, the pupils of his eyes would grow wide, his lips press tight, and his whole face assume a stubborn and resolute expression. His godfather, smiling sceptically, would often say to him:

"To women, Foma, you'll be sweeter than honey, but as yet not much common sense can be seen in you."

Ignat would heave a sigh at these words.

"You had better start out your son as soon as possible."

"There's time yet, wait."

"Why wait? He'll go about the Volga for two or three years and then we'll have him married. There's my Lubov."

Lubov Mayakina was now studying in the fifth class of some boarding school. Foma often met her on the street at which meeting she always bowed condescendingly, her fair head in a fashionable cap. Foma liked her, but her rosy cheeks, her cheerful brown eyes and crimson lips could not smooth the impression of offence given to him by her condescending bows. She was acquainted with some Gymnasium students, and although Yozhov, his old friend, was among them, Foma felt no inclination to be with them, and their company embarrassed him. It seemed to him that they were all boasting of their learning before him and that they were mocking his ignorance. Gathered together in Lubov's house they would read some books, and whenever he found them reading or loudly arguing, they became silent at his sight. All this removed them further from him. One day when he was at Mayakin's, Luba called him to go for a walk in the garden, and there, walking by his side, asked him with a grimace on her face:

"Why are you so unsociable? You never talk about anything."

"What shall I talk about, since I know nothing!" said Foma, plainly.

"Study—read books."

"I don't feel like doing it."

"You see, the Gymnasium students know everything, and know how to talk about everything. Take Yozhov, for instance."

"I know Yozhov—a chatterbox."

"You simply envy him. He is very clever—yes. He will soon graduate from the Gymnasium—and then he'll go to Moscow to study in the University."

"Well, what of it?" said Foma, indifferently.

"And you'll remain just an ignorant man."

168

"Well, be it so."

"That will be nice!" exclaimed Luba, ironically.

"I shall hold my ground without science," said Foma, sarcastically. "And I'll have a laugh at all the learned people. Let the hungry study. I don't need it."

"Pshaw, how stupid you are, bad, disgusting!" said the girl with contempt and went away, leaving him alone in the garden. Offended and gloomy, he looked after her, moved his eyebrows and lowering his head, slowly walked off into the depth of the garden.

He already began to recognise the beauty of solitude and the sweet poison of contemplation. Oftentimes, during summer evenings, when everything was coloured by the fiery tints of sunset, kindling the imagination, an uneasy longing for something incomprehensible penetrated his breast. Sitting somewhere in a dark corner of the garden or lying in bed, he conjured up before him the images of the fairy-tale princesses—they appeared with the face of Luba and of other young ladies of his acquaintance, noiselessly floating before him in the twilight and staring into his eyes with enigmatic looks. At times these visions awakened in him a mighty energy, as though intoxicating him—he would rise and, straightening his shoulders, inhale the perfumed air with a full chest; but sometimes these same visions brought to him a feeling of sadness—he felt like crying, but ashamed of shedding tears, he restrained himself and never wept in silence. Or suddenly his heart began to tremble with the desire to express his gratitude to God, to bow before Him; the words of the prayer flashed through his memory, and beholding the sky, he whispered them for a long time, one by one, and his heart grew lighter, breathing into prayer the excess of his power.

The father patiently and carefully introduced him into commercial circles, took him on the Exchange, told him about his contracts and enterprises, about his co-associates, described to him how they had made their way, what fortunes they now possessed, what natures were theirs. Foma soon mastered it, regarding everything seriously and thoughtfully.

"Our bud is blooming into a blood-red cup-rose!" Mayakin smiled, winking to Ignat.

And yet, even when Foma was nineteen years old, there was something childish in him, something naive which distinguished him from the boys of his age. They were laughing at him, considering him stupid; he kept away from them, offended by their relations toward him. As for his father and Mayakin, who were watching him vigilantly, this uncertainty of Foma's character inspired them with serious apprehensions.

"I cannot understand him!" Ignat would say with contrite heart. "He does not lead a dissipated life, he does not seem to run after the women, treats me and you with respect, listens to everything—he is more like a pretty girl than a fellow! And yet he does not seem to be stupid!"

"No, there's nothing particularly stupid about him," said Mayakin.

"It looks as though he were waiting for something—as though some kind of shroud were covering his eyes. His late mother groped on earth in the same way.

"Just look, there's Afrikanka Smolin, but two years older than my boy—what a man he has become! That is, it is difficult to tell whether he is his father's head or his father his. He wants to go to some factory to study. He swears:

"'Eh,' says he, 'papa, you have not taught me enough.' Yes. While mine does not express himself at all. Oh Lord!"

"Look here," Mayakin advised him, "you had better push him head foremost into some active business! I assure you! Gold is tested in fire. We'll see what his inclinations are when at liberty. Send him out on the Kama—alone."

"To give him a trial?"

"Well, he'll do some mischief—you'll lose something—but then we'll know what stuff he is made of."

"Indeed—I'll send him off," Ignat decided.

And thus in the spring, Ignat sent his son off on the Kama with two barges laden with corn. The barges were led by Gordyeeff's steamer

"Philezhny," under the command of Foma's old acquaintance, the former sailor Yefim—now, Yefim Ilyich, a squarely built man of about thirty with lynx-like eyes—a sober-minded, steady and very strict captain.

They sailed fast and cheerfully, because all were contented. At first Foma was proud of the responsible commission with which he had been charged. Yefim was pleased with the presence of the young master, who did not rebuke or abuse him for each and every oversight; and the happy frame of mind of the two most important persons on the steamer reflected in straight rays on the entire crew. Having left the place where they had taken in their cargo of corn in April, the steamer reached the place of its destination in the beginning of May, and the barges were anchored near the shore with the steamer at their side. Foma's duty was to deliver the corn as soon as possible, and receiving the payments, start off for Perm, where a cargo of iron was awaiting him, which Ignat had undertaken to deliver at the market.

The barges stood opposite a large village, near a pine forest, about two versts distant from the shore. On the very next day after their arrival, a big and noisy crowd of women and peasants, on foot and on horses, came up to the shore early in the morning. Shouting and singing, they scattered on the decks and in an instant work started expeditiously. Having descended into the holds, the women were filling the sacks with rye, the peasants, throwing the sacks upon their shoulders, ran over the gangplanks to the shore, and from the shore, carts, heavily laden with the long-expected corn, went off slowly to the village. The women sang songs; the peasants jested and gaily abused one another; the sailors representing the guardians of peace, scolded the working people now and then; the gangplanks, bending under the feet of the carriers, splashed against the water heavily; while on the shore the horses neighed, and the carts and the sand under the wheels were creaking.

The sun had just risen, the air was fresh and invigorating and densely filled with the odour of pines; the calm water of the river, reflecting the clear sky, was gently murmuring, breaking against the sides of the vessels and the chains of the anchors. The loud and cheerful noise of toil, the youthful beauty of nature, gaily illumined by the sunbeams—all was full of a kind-hearted, somewhat crude, sound power, which pleasantly stirred Foma's soul, awakening in him new and perplexed sensations and desires. He was sitting by the table under the awning of the steamer and drinking tea, together with Yefim and the receiver of the corn, a provincial clerk— a redheaded, short-sighted gentleman in glasses. Nervously shrugging his shoulders the receiver was telling in a hoarse voice how the peasants were starving, but Foma paid little attention to his words, looking now at the work below, now at the other side of the river—a tall, yellow, sandy steep shore, whose edges were covered with pine trees. It was unpeopled and quiet.

"I'll have to go over there," thought Foma. And as though from a distance the receiver's tiresome, unpleasant, harsh voice fell on his ears:

"You wouldn't believe it—at last it became horrible! Such an incident took place! A peasant came up to a certain intelligent man in Osa and brought along with him a girl about sixteen years old.

"'What do you wish?'

"'Here,' he says, 'I've brought my daughter to your Honour.'

"'What for?'

"'Perhaps,' he says, 'you'll take her—you are a bachelor.'

"'That is, how? What do you mean?'

"'I took her around town,' he says. 'I wanted to hire her out as a servant— but nobody would have her—take her at least as your mistress!'

"Do you understand? He offered his own daughter—just think of it! A daughter—as a mistress! The devil knows what that is! Eh? The man, of course, became indignant and began abusing the peasant. But the peasant spoke to him reasonably:

"'Your Honour! Of what use is she to me at this time? Utterly useless. I have,' says he, 'three boys—they will be working men; it is necessary to keep them up. Give me,' says he, 'ten roubles for the girl, and that will improve my lot and that of my boys.'

172

"How is that? Eh? It is simply terrible, I tell you."

"No good!" sighed Yefim. "As they say—hunger will break through stone walls. The stomach, you see, has its own laws."

This story called forth in Foma a great incomprehensible interest in the fate of the girl, and the youth hastened to enquire of the receiver:

"Well, did the man buy her?"

"Of course not!" exclaimed the receiver, reproachfully.

"Well, and what became of her?"

"Some good people took pity on her—and provided for her."

"A-h!" drawled Foma, and suddenly he said firmly and angrily: "I would have given that peasant such a thrashing! I would have broken his head!" And he showed the receiver his big tightly-clenched fist.

"Eh! What for?" cried the receiver in a sickly, loud voice, tearing his spectacles from his eyes. "You do not understand the motive."

"I do understand it!" said Foma, with an obstinate shake of his head.

"But what could he do? It came to his mind."

"How can one allow himself to sell a human being?"

"Ah! It is brutal, I agree with you."

"And a girl at that! I would have given him the ten roubles!"

The receiver waved his hand hopelessly and became silent. His gesture confused Foma. He arose from his seat, walked off to the railing and looked down at the deck of the barge, which was covered with an industriously working crowd of people. The noise intoxicated him, and the uneasy something, which was rambling in his soul, was now defined into a powerful desire to work, to have the strength of a giant, to possess enormous shoulders and put on them at one time a hundred bags of rye, that every one looking at him might be astonished.

"Come now, hurry up there!" he shouted down in a ringing voice. A few heads were raised to him, some faces appeared before him, and one of them—the face of a dark-eyed woman—smiled at him a gentle and enticing smile. Something flared up in his breast at this smile and began to spread over his veins in a hot wave. He drew back from the railing and walked up to the table again, feeling that his cheeks were burning.

"Listen!" said the receiver, addressing him, "wire to your father asking him to allow some grain for waste! Just see how much is lost here. And here every pound is precious! You should have understood this! What a fine father you have," he concluded with a biting grimace.

"How much shall I allow?" asked Foma, boldly and disdainfully. "Do you want a hundred puds? [A pud is a weight of 40 Russian pounds.] Two hundred?"

"I—I thank you!" exclaimed the receiver, overjoyed and confused, "if you have the right to do it."

"I am the master!" said Foma, firmly. "And you must not speak that way about my father—nor make such faces."

"Pardon me! I—I do not doubt that you have full power. I thank you heartily. And your father, too—in behalf of all these men—in behalf of the people!"

Yefim looked cautiously at the young master, spreading out and smacking his lips, while the master with an air of pride on his face listened to the quick-witted speech of the receiver, who was pressing his hand firmly.

"Two hundred puds! That is Russian-like, young man! I shall directly notify the peasants of your gift. You'll see how grateful they will be—how glad." And he shouted down:

"Eh, boys! The master is giving away two hundred puds."

"Three hundred!" interposed Foma.

"Three hundred puds. Oh! Thank you! Three hundred puds of grain, boys!"

But their response was weak. The peasants lifted up their heads and mutely lowered them again, resuming their work. A few voices said irresolutely and as though unwillingly:

"Thanks. May God give you. We thank you very humbly."

And some cried out gaily and disdainfully:

174

"What's the use of that? If they had given each of us a glass of vodka instead—that would be a just favour. For the grain is not for us—but for the country Council."

"Eh! They do not understand!" exclaimed the receiver, confused. "I'll go down and explain it to them."

And he disappeared. But the peasants' regard for his gift did not interest Foma. He saw that the black eyes of the rosy-cheeked woman were looking at him so strangely and pleasingly. They seemed to thank him and caressingly beckoned him, and besides those eyes he saw nothing. The woman was dressed like the city women. She wore shoes, a calico waist, and over her black hair she had a peculiar kerchief. Tall and supple, seated on a pile of wood, she repaired sacks, quickly moving her hands, which were bare up to the elbows, and she smiled at Foma all the time.

"Foma Ignatyich!" he heard Yefim's reproachful voice, "you've showed off too much. Well, if it were only about fifty puds! But why so much? Look out that we don't get a good scolding for this."

"Leave me alone!" said Foma, shortly.

"What is it to me? I'll keep quiet. But as you are so young, and as I was told to keep an eye on you, I may get a rap on the snout for being heedless."

"I'll tell my father all about it. Keep quiet!" said Foma.

"As for me—let it be so—so that you are master here."

"Very well."

"I have said this, Foma Ignatyich, for your own sake—because you are so young and simple-minded."

"Leave me alone, Yefim!"

Yefim heaved a sigh and became silent, while Foma stared at the woman and thought:

"I wish they would bring such a woman for sale to me."

His heart beat rapidly. Though as yet physically pure, he already knew from conversations the mysteries of intimate relations between men and women. He knew by rude and shameful names, and these names kindled in

175

him an unpleasant, burning curiosity and shame; his imagination worked obstinately, for he could not picture it to himself in intelligible images. And in his soul he did not believe that those relations were really so simple and rude, as he had been told. When they had laughed at him and assured him that they were such, and, indeed, could not be otherwise, he smiled stupidly and confusedly, but thought nevertheless that the relations with women did not have to be in such a shameful form for everyone, and that, in all probability, there was something purer, less rude and abusive to a human being.

Now looking at the dark-eyed working woman with admiration, Foma distinctly felt just that rude inclination toward her, and he was ashamed and afraid of something. And Yefim, standing beside him, said admonitively:

"There you are staring at the woman, so that I cannot keep silence any longer. You do not know her, but when she winks at you, you may, because of your youth—and with a nature like yours—you may do such a thing that we'll have to go home on foot by the shore. And we'll have to thank God if our trousers at least remain with us."

"What do you want?" asked Foma, red with confusion.

"I want nothing. And you had better mind me. In regard to affairs with women I may perfectly well be a teacher. You must deal with a woman very plainly—give her a bottle of vodka, something to eat after it, then a couple of bottles of beer and after everything give her twenty kopecks in cash. For this price she will show you all her love in the best way possible."

"You are lying," said Foma, softly.

"I am lying? Why shall I lie to you since I have observed that same policy perhaps a hundred times? Just charge me to have dealings with her. Eh? I'll make you acquainted with her in a moment."

"Very well," said Foma, feeling that he could hardly breathe and that something was choking his throat.

"Well, then, I'll bring her up in the evening."

And Yefim smiled approvingly into Foma's face and walked off. Until evening Foma walked about as though lost in mist, not noticing the respectful and beseeching glances with which the peasants greeted him at the receiver's instigation. Dread fell on him, he felt himself guilty before somebody, and to all those that addressed him he replied humbly and gently, as though excusing himself for something. Some of the working people went home toward evening, others gathered on the shore near a big, bright bonfire and began cooking their supper. Fragments of their conversation floated about in the stillness of the evening. The reflection of the fire fell on the river in red and yellow stripes, which trembled on the calm water and on the window panes of the cabin where Foma was s itting. He sat in the corner on a lounge, which was covered with oilcloth— and waited. On the table before him were a few bottles of vodka and beer, and plates with bread and dessert. He covered the windows and did not light the lamp; the faint light from the bonfire, penetrating through the curtains, fell on the table, on the bottles and on the wall, and trembled, now growing brighter, now fainter. It was quiet on the steamer and on the barges, only from the shore came indistinct sounds of conversation, and the river was splashing, scarcely audible, against the sides of the steamer. It seemed to Foma that somebody was hiding in the dark near by, listening to him and spying upon him. Now somebody is walking over the gang-plank of the barges with quick and heavy steps—the gang-plank strikes against the water clangously and angrily. Foma hears the muffled laughter of the captain and his lowered voice. Yefim stands by the cabin door and speaks softly, but somewhat reprimandingly, as though instructing. Foma suddenly felt like crying out:

"It is not necessary!"

And he arose from the lounge—but at this moment the cabin door was opened, the tall form of a woman appeared on the threshold, and, noiselessly closing the door behind her, she said in a low voice:

"Oh dear! How dark it is! Is there a living soul somewhere around here?"

"Yes," answered Foma, softly.

"Well, then, good evening."

And the woman moved forward carefully.

"I'll light the lamp," said Foma in a broken voice, and, sinking on the lounge, he curled himself up in the corner.

"It is good enough this way. When you get used to it you can see everything in the dark as well."

"Be seated," said Foma.

"I will."

She sat down on the lounge about two steps away from him. Foma saw the glitter of her eyes, he saw a smile on her full lips. It seemed to him that this smile of hers was not at all like that other smile before— this smile seemed plaintive, sad. This smile encouraged him; he breathed with less difficulty at the sight of these eyes, which, on meeting his own, suddenly glanced down on the floor. But he did not know what to say to this woman and for about two minutes both were silent. It was a heavy, awkward silence. She began to speak:

"You must be feeling lonesome here all alone?"

"Yes," answered Foma.

"And do you like our place here?" asked the woman in a low voice.

"It is nice. There are many woods here."

And again they became silent.

"The river, if you like, is more beautiful than the Volga," uttered Foma, with an effort.

"I was on the Volga."

"Where?"

"In the city of Simbirsk."

"Simbirsk?" repeated Foma like an echo, feeling that he was again unable to say a word.

But she evidently understood with whom she had to deal, and she suddenly asked him in a bold whisper:

"Why don't you treat me to something?"

"Here!" Foma gave a start. "Indeed, how queer I am? Well, then, come up to the table."

He bustled about in the dark, pushed the table, took up one bottle, then another, and again returned them to their place, laughing guiltily and confusedly as he did so. She came up close to him and stood by his side, and, smiling, looked at his face and at his trembling hands.

"Are you bashful?" she suddenly whispered.

He felt her breath on his cheek and replied just as softly:

"Yes."

Then she placed her hands on his shoulders and quietly drew him to her breast, saying in a soothing whisper:

"Never mind, don't be bashful, my young, handsome darling. How I pity you!"

And he felt like crying because of her whisper, his heart was melting in sweet fatigue; pressing his head close to her breast, he clasped her with his hands, mumbling to her some inarticulate words, which were unknown to himself.

"Be gone!" said Foma in a heavy voice, staring at the wall with his eyes wide open.

Having kissed him on the cheek she walked out of the cabin, saying to him:

"Well, good-bye."

Foma felt intolerably ashamed in her presence; but no sooner did she disappear behind the door than he jumped up and seated himself on the lounge. Then he arose, staggering, and at once he was seized with the feeling of having lost something very valuable, something whose presence he did not seem to have noticed in himself until the moment it was lost. But immediately a new, manly feeling of self-pride took possession of him. It drowned his shame, and, instead of the shame, pity for the woman sprang up within him—for the half-clad woman, who went out alone into the dark of the chilly May night. He hastily came out on the deck—it was a starlit, but moonless night; the coolness and the darkness embraced him. On the shore the golden-red pile of coals was still glimmering. Foma listened—an oppressive stillness filled the air, only the water was murmuring, breaking against the anchor chains. There was not a sound of footsteps to be heard. Foma now longed to call the woman, but he did not know her name. Eagerly inhaling the fresh air into his broad chest, he stood on deck for a few minutes. Suddenly, from beyond the roundhouse— from the prow—a moan reached his ears— a deep, loud moan, resembling a wail. He shuddered and went thither carefully, understanding that she was there.

She sat on the deck close to the side of the steamer, and, leaning her head against a heap of ropes, she wept. Foma saw that her bare white shoulders were trembling, he heard her pitiful moans, and began to feel depressed. Bending over her, he asked her timidly:

"What is it?"

She nodded her head and said nothing in reply.

"Have I offended you?"

"Go away," she said.

"But, how?" said Foma, alarmed and confused, touching her head with his hand. "Don't be angry. You came of your own free will."

"I am not angry!" she replied in a loud whisper. "Why should I be angry at you? You are not a seducer. You are a pure soul! Eh, my darling! Be seated here by my side."

And taking Foma by the hand, she made him sit down, like a child, in her lap, pressed his head close to her breast, and, bending over him, pressed her lips to his for a long time.

"What are you crying about?" asked Foma, caressing her cheek with one hand, while the other clasped the woman's neck.

"I am crying about myself. Why have you sent me away?" she asked plaintively.

"I began to feel ashamed of myself," said Foma, lowering his head.

"My darling! Tell me the truth—haven't you been pleased with me?" she asked with a smile, but her big, hot tears were still trickling down on Foma's breast.

"Why should you speak like this?" exclaimed the youth, almost frightened, and hotly began to mumble to her some words about her beauty, about her kindness, telling her how sorry he was for her and how bashful in her presence. And she listened and kept on kissing his cheeks, his neck, his head and his uncovered breast.

He became silent—then she began to speak—softly and mournfully as though speaking of the dead:

"And I thought it was something else. When you said, 'Be gone!' I got up and went away. And your words made me feel sad, very sad. There was a time, I remembered, when they caressed me and fondled me unceasingly, without growing tired; for a single kind smile they used to do for me anything I pleased. I recalled all this and began to cry! I felt sorry for my youth, for I am now thirty years old, the last days for a woman! Eh, Foma Ignatyevich!" she exclaimed, lifting her voice louder, and reiterating the rhythm of her harmonious speech, whose accents rose and fell in unison with the melodious murmuring of the water.

"Listen to me—preserve your youth! There is nothing in the world better than that. There is nothing more precious than youth. With youth, as with gold, you can accomplish anything you please. Live so that you shall have in old age something to remind you of your youth. Here I recalled myself, and though I cried, yet my heart blazed up at the very recollection of my past life. And again I was young, as though I drank of the water of life! My sweet child I'll have a good time with you, if I please you, we'll enjoy ourselves as much as we can. Eh! I'll burn to ashes, now that I have blazed up!"

And pressing the youth close to herself, she greedily began to kiss him on the lips.

"Lo-o-ok o-u-u-u-t!" the watch on the barge wailed mournfully, and, cutting short the last syllable, began to strike his mallet against the cast-iron board.

The shrill, trembling sounds harshly broke the solemn quiet of the night.

A few days later, when the barges had discharged their cargo and the steamer was ready to leave for Perm, Yefim noticed, to his great sorrow, that a cart came up to the shore and that the dark-eyed Pelageya, with a trunk and with some bundles, was in it.

"Send a sailor to bring her things," ordered Foma, nodding his head toward the shore.

With a reproachful shake of his head, Yefim carried out the order angrily, and then asked in a lowered voice:

"So she, too, is coming with us?"

"She is going with me," Foma announced shortly.

"It is understood. Not with all of us. Oh, Lord!"

"Why are you sighing?"

"Yes. Foma Ignatyich! We are going to a big city. Are there not plenty of women of her kind?"

"Well, keep quiet!" said Foma, sternly.

"I will keep quiet, but this isn't right!"

"What?"

"This very wantonness of ours. Our steamer is perfect, clean—and suddenly there is a woman there! And if it were at least the right sort of a woman! But as it is, she merely bears the name of woman."

Foma frowned insinuatingly and addressed the captain, imperiously emphasizing his words:

"Yefim, I want you to bear it in mind, and to tell it to everybody here, that if anyone will utter an obscene word about her, I'll strike him on the head with a log of wood!"

"How terrible!" said Yefim, incredulously, looking into the master's face with curiosity. But he immediately made a step backward. Ignat's son, like a wolf, showed his teeth, the apples of his eyes became wider, and he roared:

"Laugh! I'll show you how to laugh!"

Though Yefim lost courage, he nevertheless said with dignity:

"Although you, Foma Ignatyich, are the master, yet as I was told, 'Watch, Yefim,' and then I am the captain here."

"The captain?" cried Foma, shuddering in every limb and turning pale. "And who am I?"

"Well, don't bawl! On account of such a trifle as a woman."

Red spots came out on Foma's pale face, he shifted from one foot to the other, thrust his hands into the pockets of his jacket with a convulsive motion and said in a firm and even voice:

"You! Captain! See here, say another word against me—and you go to the devil! I'll put you ashore! I'll get along as well with the pilot! Understand? You cannot command me. Do you see?"

Yefim was dumfounded. He looked at his master and comically winked his eyes, finding no reply to his words.

"Do you understand, I say?"

"Yes. I understand!" drawled Yefim. "But what is all this noise about? On account of—"

"Silence!"

Foma's eyes, which flashed wildly, and his face distorted with wrath, suggested to the captain the happy thought to leave his master as soon as possible and, turning around quickly, he walked off.

"Pshaw! How terrible! As it seems the apple did not fall too far from the tree," he muttered sneeringly, walking on the deck. He was angry at Foma, and considered himself offended for nothing, but at the same time he began to feel over himself the real, firm hand of a master. For years accustomed to being subordinate, he rather liked this manifestation of power over him, and, entering the cabin of the old pilot, he related to him the scene between himself and his master, with a shade of satisfaction in his voice.

183

"See?" he concluded his story. "A pup coming from a good breed is an excellent dog at the very first chase. From his exterior he is so-so. A man of rather heavy mind as yet. Well, never mind, let him have his fun. It seems now as though nothing wrong will come out of this. With a character like his, no. How he bawled at me! A regular trumpet, I tell you! And he appointed himself master at once. As though he had sipped power and strictness out of a ladle."

Yefim spoke the truth: during these few days Foma underwent a striking transformation. The passion now kindled in him made him master of the soul and body of a woman; he eagerly absorbed the fiery sweetness of this power, and this burned out all that was awkward in him, all that gave him the appearance of a somewhat stupid, gloomy fellow, and, destroying it, filled his heart with youthful pride, with the consciousness of his human personality. Love for a woman is always fruitful to the man, be the love whatever it may; even though it were to cause but sufferings there is always much that is rich in it. Working as a powerful poison on those whose souls are afflicted, it is for the healthy man as fire for iron, which is to be transformed into steel.

Foma's passion for the thirty-year-old woman, who lamented in his embraces her dead youth, did not tear him away from his affairs; he was never lost in the caresses, or in his affairs, bringing into both his whole self. The woman, like good wine, provoked in him alike a thirst for labour and for love, and she, too, became younger from the kisses of the youth.

In Perm, Foma found a letter waiting for him. It was from his godfather, who notified him that Ignat, out of anxiety for his son, had begun to drink heavily, and that it was harmful to drink thus, for a man of his age. The letter concluded with advice to hurry up matters in order to return home the sooner. Foma felt alarmed over this advice, and it clouded the clear holiday of his heart. But this shadow soon melted in his worries over his affairs, and in the caresses of Pelageya. His life streamed on with the swiftness of a river wave, and each day brought to him new sensations, awakening in him new thoughts. Pelageya's relations with him contained all the passion of a mistress, all that power of feeling which women of her age put into their passion when drinking the last drops from the cup of life. But at times a different feeling awoke in her, a feeling not less powerful, and by which Foma became still more attached to her—something similar to a mother's yearning to guard her beloved son from errors, to teach him the wisdom of life. Oftentimes at night, sitting in his embraces on the deck, she spoke to him tenderly and sadly:

"Mind me as an older sister of yours. I have lived, I know men. I have seen a great deal in my life! Choose your companions with care, for there are people just as contagious as a disease. At first you cannot tell them even when you see them; he looks to be a man like everybody else, and, suddenly, without being aware of it yourself, you will start to imitate him in life. You look around—and you find that you have contracted his scabs. I myself have lost everything on account of a friend. I had a husband and two children. We lived well. My husband was a clerk at a volost." She became silent and looked for a long time at the water, which was stirred by the vessel. Then she heaved a sigh and spoke to him again:

"May the Holy Virgin guard you from women of my kind—be careful. You are tender as yet, your heart has not become properly hardened. And women are fond of such as you—strong, handsome, rich. And most of all beware of the quiet women. They stick to a man like blood-suckers, and suck and suck. And at the same time they are always so kind, so gentle. They will keep on sucking your juice, but will preserve themselves. They'll only break your heart in vain. You had better have dealings with those that are bold, like myself. These live not for the sake of gain."

And she was indeed disinterested. In Perm Foma purchased for her different new things and what-not. She was delighted, but later, having examined them, she said sadly:

"Don't squander your money too freely. See that your father does not get angry. I love you anyway, without all this."

She had already told him that she would go with him only as far as Kazan, where she had a married sister. Foma could not believe that she would leave him, and when, on the eve of their arrival at Kazan, she repeated her words, he became gloomy and began to implore her not to forsake him.

"Do not feel sorry in advance," she said. "We have a whole night before us. You will have time to feel sorry when I bid you good-bye, if you will feel sorry at all."

But he still tried to persuade her not to forsake him, and, finally—which was to be expected—announced his desire to marry her.

"So, so!" and she began to laugh. "Shall I marry you while my husband is still alive? My darling, my queer fellow! You have a desire to marry, eh? But do they marry such women as I am? You will have many, many mistresses. Marry then, when you have overflowed, when you have had your fill of all sweets and feel like having rye bread. Then you may marry! I have noticed that a healthy man, for his own peace, must not marry early. One woman will not be enough to satisfy him, and he'll go to other women. And for your own happiness, you should take a wife only when you know that she alone will suffice for you."

But the more she spoke, the more persistent Foma became in his desire not to part with her.

"Just listen to what I'll tell you," said the woman, calmly. "A splinter of wood is burning in your hand, and you can see well even without its light—you had better dip it into water, so that there will be no smell of smoke and your hand will not be burned."

"I do not understand your words."

"Do understand. You have done me no wrong, and I do not wish to do you any. And, therefore, I am going away."

It is hard to say what might have been the result of this dispute if an accident had not interfered with it. In Kazan Foma received a telegram from Mayakin, who wrote to his godson briefly: "Come immediately on the passenger steamer." Foma's heart contracted nervously, and a few hours later, gloomy and pale, his teeth set together, he stood on the deck of the steamer, which was leaving the harbour, and clinging to the rail with his hands, he stared motionlessly into the face of his love, who was floating far away from him together with the harbour and the shore. Pelageya waved her handkerchief and smiled, but he knew that she was crying, shedding many painful tears. From her tears the entire front of Foma's shirt was wet, and from her tears, his heart, full of gloomy alarm, was sad and cold. The figure of the woman was growing smaller and smaller, as though melting away, and Foma, without lifting his eyes, stared at her and felt that aside from fear for his father and sorrow for the woman, some new, powerful and caustic sensation was awakening in his soul. He could not name it, but it seemed to him as something like a grudge against someone.

The crowd in the harbour blended into a close, dark and dead spot, faceless, formless, motionless. Foma went away from the rail and began to pace the deck gloomily.

The passengers, conversing aloud, seated themselves to drink tea; the porters bustled about on the gallery, setting the tables; somewhere below, on the stern, in the third class, a child was crying, a harmonica was wailing, the cook was chopping something with knives, the dishes were jarring—producing a rather harsh noise. Cutting the waves and making foam, shuddering under the strain and sighing heavily, the enormous steamer moved rapidly against the current. Foma looked at the wide strip of broken, struggling, and enraged waves at the stern of the steamer, and began to feel a wild desire to break or tear something; also to go, breast foremost, against the current and to mass its pressure against himself, against his breast and his shoulders.

"Fate!" said someone beside him in a hoarse and weary voice.

This word was familiar to him: his Aunt Anfisa had often used it as an answer to his questions, and he had invested in this brief word a conception of a power, similar to the power of God. He glanced at the speakers: one of them was a gray little old man, with a kind face; the other

187

was younger, with big, weary eyes and with a little black wedge-shaped beard. His big gristly nose and his yellow, sunken cheeks reminded Foma of his godfather.

"Fate!" The old man repeated the exclamation of his interlocutor with confidence, and began to smile. "Fate in life is like a fisherman on the river: it throws a baited hook toward us into the tumult of our life and we dart at it with greedy mouths. Then fate pulls up the rod—and the man is struggling, flopping on the ground, and then you see his heart is broken. That's how it is, my dear man."

Foma closed his eyes, as if a ray of the sun had fallen full on them, and shaking his head, he said aloud:

"True! That is true!"

The companions looked at him fixedly: the old man, with a fine, wise smile; the large-eyed man, unfriendly, askance. This confused Foma; he blushed and walked away, thinking of Fate and wondering why it had first treated him kindly by giving him a woman, and then took back the gift from him, so simply and abusively? And he now understood that the vague, caustic feeling which he carried within him was a grudge against Fate for thus sporting with him. He had been too much spoiled by life, to regard more plainly the first drop of poison from the cup which was just started, and he passed all the time of the journey without sleep, pondering over the old man's words and fondling his grudge. This grudge, however, did not awaken in him despondency and sorrow, but rather a feeling of anger and revenge.

Foma was met by his godfather, and to his hasty and agitated question, Mayakin, his greenish little eyes flashing excitedly, said when he seated himself in the carriage beside his godson:

"Your father has grown childish."

"Drinking?"

"Worse—he has lost his mind completely."

"Really? Oh Lord! Tell me."

"Don't you understand? A certain lady is always around him."

188

"What about her?" exclaimed Foma, recalling his Pelageya, and for some reason or other his heart was filled with joy.

"She sticks to him and—bleeds him."

"Is she a quiet one?"

"She? Quiet as a fire. Seventy-five thousand roubles she blew out of his pocket like a feather!"

"Oh! Who is she?"

"Sonka Medinskaya, the architect's wife."

"Great God! Is it possible that she—Did my father—Is it possible that he took her as his sweetheart?" asked Foma, with astonishment, in a low voice.

His godfather drew back from him, and comically opening his eyes wide, said convincedly:

"You are out of your mind, too! By God, you're out of your mind! Come to your senses! A sweetheart at the age of sixty-three! And at such a price as this. What are you talking about? Well, I'll tell this to Ignat."

And Mayakin filled the air with a jarring, hasty laughter, at which his goat-like beard began to tremble in an uncomely manner. It took Foma a long time to obtain a categorical answer; the old man, contrary to his habit, was restless and irritated; his speech, usually fluent, was now interrupted; he was swearing and expectorating as he spoke, and it was with difficulty that Foma learned what the matter was. Sophya Pavlovna Medinskaya, the wealthy architect's wife, who was well known in the city for her tireless efforts in the line of arranging various charitable projects, persuaded Ignat to endow seventy-five thousand roubles for the erection of a lodging-house in the city and of a public library with a reading-room. Ignat had given the money, and already the newspapers lauded him for his generosity. Foma had seen the woman more than once on the streets; she was short; he knew that she was considered as one of the most beautiful women in the city, and that bad rumours were afoot as to her behaviour.

"Is that all?" exclaimed Foma, when his godfather concluded the story. "And I thought God knows what!"

"You? You thought?" cried Mayakin, suddenly grown angry. "You thought nothing, you beardless youngster!"

"Why do you abuse me?" Foma said.

"Tell me, in your opinion, is seventy-five thousand roubles a big sum or not?"

"Yes, a big sum," said Foma, after a moment's thought.

"Ah, ha!"

"But my father has much money. Why do you make such a fuss about it?"

Yakov Tarasovich was taken aback. He looked into the youth's face with contempt and asked him in a faint voice:

"And you speak like this?"

"I? Who then?"

"You lie! It is your young foolishness that speaks. Yes! And my old foolishness—brought to test a million times by life—says that you are a young dog as yet, and it is too early for you to bark in a basso."

Foma hearing this, had often been quite provoked by his godfather's too picturesque language.

Mayakin always spoke to him more roughly than his father, but now the youth felt very much offended by the old man and said to him reservedly, but firmly:

"You had better not abuse me without reflection, for I am no longer a small child."

"Come, come!" exclaimed Mayakin, mockingly lifting his eyebrows and squinting.

This roused Foma's indignation. He looked full into the old man's eyes and articulated with emphasis:

"And I am telling you that I don't want to hear any more of that undeserved abuse of yours. Enough!"

"Mm! So-o! Pardon me."

190

Yakov Tarasovich closed his eyes, chewed a little with his lips, and, turning aside from his godson, kept silent for awhile. The carriage turned into a narrow street, and, noticing from afar the roof of his house, Foma involuntarily moved forward. At the same time Mayakin asked him with a roguish and gentle smile:

"Foma! Tell me—on whom you have sharpened your teeth? Eh?"

"Why, are they sharp?" asked Foma, pleased with the manner in which Mayakin now regarded him.

"Pretty good. That's good, dear. That's very good! Your father and I were afraid lest you should be a laggard. Well, have you learned to drink vodka?"

"I drank it."

"Rather too soon! Did you drink much of it?"

"Why much?"

"Does it taste good?"

"Not very."

"So. Never mind, all this is not so bad. Only you are too outspoken. You are ready to confess all your sins to each and every pope that comes along. You must consider it isn't always necessary to do that. Sometimes by keeping silent you both please people and commit no sins. Yes. A man's tongue is very seldom sober. Here we are. See, your father does not know that you have arrived. Is he home yet, I wonder?"

He was at home: his loud, somewhat hoarse laughter was heard from the open windows of the rooms. The noise of the carriage, which stopped at the house, caused Ignat to look out of the window, and at the sight of his son he cried out with joy:

"Ah! You've come."

After a while he pressed Foma to his breast with one hand, and, pressing the palm of his other hand against his son's forehead, thus bending his head back, he looked into his face with beaming eyes and spoke contentedly:

"You are sunburnt. You've grown strong. You're a fine fellow! Madame! How's my son? Isn't he fine?"

"Not bad looking," a gentle, silver voice was heard. Foma glanced from behind his father's shoulder and noticed that a slender woman with magnificent fair hair was sitting in the front corner of the room, resting her elbows on the table; her dark eyes, her thin eyebrows and plump, red lips strikingly defined on her pale face. Behind her armchair stood a large philodendron-plant whose big, figured leaves were hanging down in the air over her little golden head.

"How do you do, Sophya Pavlovna," said Mayakin, tenderly, approaching her with his hand outstretched. "What, are you still collecting contributions from poor people like us?"

Foma bowed to her mutely, not hearing her answer to Mayakin, nor what his father was saying to him. The lady stared at him steadfastly and smiled to him affably and serenely. Her childlike figure, clothed in some kind of dark fabric, was almost blended with the crimson stuff of the armchair, while her wavy, golden hair and her pale face shone against the dark background. Sitting there in the corner, beneath the green leaves, she looked at once like a flower, and like an ikon.

"See, Sophya Pavlovna, how he is staring at you. An eagle, eh?" said Ignat.

Her eyes became narrower, a faint blush leaped to her cheeks, and she burst into laughter. It sounded like the tinkling of a little silver bell. And she immediately arose, saying:

"I wouldn't disturb you. Good-bye!"

When she went past Foma noiselessly, the scent of perfume came to him, and he noticed that her eyes were dark blue, and her eyebrows almost black.

"The sly rogue glided away," said Mayakin in a low voice, angrily looking after her.

"Well, tell us how was the trip? Have you squandered much money?" roared Ignat, pushing his son into the same armchair where Medinskaya had been sitting awhile before. Foma looked at him askance and seated himself in another chair.

"Isn't she a beautiful young woman, eh?" said Mayakin, smiling, feeling Foma with his cunning eyes. "If you keep on gaping at her she will eat away all your insides."

Foma shuddered for some reason or other, and, saying nothing in reply, began to tell his father about the journey in a matter-of-fact tone. But Ignat interrupted him:

"Wait, I'll ask for some cognac."

"And you are keeping on drinking all the time, they say," said Foma, disapprovingly.

Ignat glanced at his son with surprise and curiosity, and asked:

"Is this the way to speak to your father?"

Foma became confused and lowered his head.

"That's it!" said Ignat, kind-heartedly, and ordered cognac to be brought to him.

Mayakin, winking his eyes, looked at the Gordyeeffs, sighed, bid them good-bye, and, after inviting them to have tea with him in his raspberry garden in the evening, went away.

"Where is Aunt Anfisa?" asked Foma, feeling that now, being alone with his father, he was somewhat ill at ease.

"She went to the cloister. Well, tell me, and I will have some cognac."

Foma told his father all about his affairs in a few minutes and he concluded his story with a frank confession:

"I have spent much money on myself."

"How much?"

"About six hundred roubles."

"In six weeks! That's a good deal. I see as a clerk you're too expensive for me. Where have you squandered it all?"

"I gave away three hundred puds of grain."

"To whom? How?"

Foma told him all about it.

"Hm! Well, that's all right!" Ignat approved. "That's to show what stuff we are made of. That's clear enough—for the father's honour—for the honour of the firm. And there is no loss either, because that gives a good reputation. And that, my dear, is the very best signboard for a business. Well, what else?"

"And then, I somehow spent more."

"Speak frankly. It's not the money that I am asking you about—I just want to know how you lived there," insisted Ignat, regarding his son attentively and sternly.

"I was eating, drinking." Foma did not give in, bending his head morosely and confusedly.

"Drinking vodka?"

"Vodka, too."

"Ah! So. Isn't it rather too soon?"

"Ask Yefim whether I ever drank enough to be intoxicated."

"Why should I ask Yefim? You must tell me everything yourself. So you are drinking? I don't like it."

"But I can get along without drinking."

"Come, come! Do you want some cognac?"

Foma looked at his father and smiled broadly. And his father answered him with a kindly smile:

"Eh, you. Devil! Drink, but look out—know your business. What can you do? A drunkard will sleep himself sober, a fool—never. Let us understand this much at least, for our own consolation. And did you have a good time with girls, too? Be frank! Are you afraid that I will beat you, or what?"

"Yes. There was one on the steamer. I had her there from Perm to Kazan."

"So," Ignat sighed heavily and said, frowning: "You've become defiled rather too soon."

"I am twenty years old. And you yourself told me that in your days fellows married at the age of fifteen," replied Foma, confused.

"Then they married. Very well, then, let us drop the subject. Well, you've had dealings with a woman. What of it? A woman is like vaccination, you cannot pass your life without her. As for myself, I cannot play the hypocrite. I began to go around with women when I was younger than you are now. But you must be on your guard with them."

Ignat became pensive and was silent for a long time, sitting motionless, his head bent low on his breast.

"Listen, Foma," he started again, sternly and firmly. "I shall die before long. I am old. Something oppresses my breast. I breathe with difficulty. I'll die. Then all my affairs will fall on your shoulders. At first your godfather will assist you—mind him! You started quite well; you attended to everything properly; you held the reins firmly in your hands. And though you did squander a big sum of money, it is evident that you did not lose your head. God grant the same in the future. You should know this: business is a living, strong beast; you must manage it ably; you must put a strong bridle on it or it will conquer you. Try to stand above your business. Place yourself so that it will all be under your feet; that each little tack shall be visible to you."

Foma looked at his father's broad chest, heard his heavy voice and thought to himself:

"Oh, but you won't die so soon!"

This thought pleased him and awakened in him a kind, warm feeling for his father.

"Rely upon your godfather. He has enough common sense in his head to supply the whole town with it. All he lacks is courage, or he would have risen high. Yes, I tell you my days on earth are numbered. Indeed, it is high time to prepare myself for death; to cast everything aside; to fast, and see to it that people bear me good-will."

"They will!" said Foma with confidence.

"If there were but a reason why they should."

"And the lodging-house?"

Ignat looked at his son and began to laugh.

"Yakov has had time to tell it to you already! The old miser. He must have abused me?"

"A little." Foma smiled.

"Of course! Don't I know him?"

"He spoke of it as though it were his own money."

Ignat leaned back in his chair and burst into still louder laughter.

"The old raven, eh? That's quite true. Whether it be his own money or mine, it is all the same to him. There he is trembling now. He has an aim in view, the bald-headed fellow. Can you tell me what it is?"

Foma thought awhile and said:

"I don't know."

"Eh, you're stupid. He wants to tell our fortunes."

How is that?"

"Come now, guess!"

Foma looked at his father and—guessed it. His face became gloomy, he slightly raised himself from the armchair and said resolutely:

"No, I don't want to. I shall not marry her!"

"Oh? Why so? She is a strong girl; she is not foolish; she's his only child."

"And Taras? The lost one? But I—I don't want to at all!"

"The lost one is gone, consequently it is not worthwhile speaking of him. There is a will, dear, which says: 'All my movable and real estates shall go to my daughter, Lubov.' And as to the fact that she is your godfather's daughter, we'll set this right."

"It is all the same," said Foma, firmly. "I shall not marry her!"

"Well, it is rather early to speak of it now! But why do you dislike her so much?"

I do not like such as she is."

"So-o! Just think of it! And which women are more to your liking, sir, may I ask?"

196

"Those that are more simple. She's always busy with her Gymnasium students and with her books. She's become learned. She'll be laughing at my expense," said Foma, emotionally.

"That is quite true. She is too bold. But that is a trifle. All sorts of rust can be removed if you try to do it. That's a matter for the future. And your godfather is a clever old man. His was a peaceful, sedentary life; sitting in one place he gave a thought to everything. It is worthwhile listening to him, for he can see the wrong side of each and every worldly affair. He is our aristocrat—descending from Mother Yekaterina—ha, ha! He understands a great deal about himself. And as his stem was cut off by Taras, he decided to put you in Taras's place, do you see?"

"No, I'd rather select my place myself," said Foma, stubbornly.

"You are foolish as yet." Ignat smiled in reply to his son's words.

Their conversation was interrupted by the arrival of Aunt Anfisa.

"Foma! You've come," she cried out, somewhere behind the doors. Foma rose and went to meet her, with a gentle smile.

Again his life streamed on slowly, calmly, monotonously. Again the Exchange and his father's instructions. Retaining a kindly sarcastic and encouraging tone in his relation toward his son, Ignat began to treat him more strictly. He censured him for each and every trifle and constantly reminded him that he brought him up freely; that he was never in his way and that he never beat him.

"Other fathers beat fellows like yourself with logs of wood. And I never even touched you with a finger."

"Evidently I didn't deserve it," said Foma one day, calmly.

Ignat became angry at his son for these words and for the tone.

"Don't talk so much!" he roared. "You've picked up courage because of the softness of my hand. You find an answer to every word I say. Beware; though my hand was soft, it can nevertheless still squeeze you so that tears will gush forth from your heels. You've grown up too soon, like a toad-stool, just sprung up from the ground. You have a bad smell already."

"Why are you so angry at me?" asked Foma, perplexed and offended, when his father chanced to be in a happy frame of mind.

"Because you cannot tolerate it when your father grumbles at you. You're ready to quarrel immediately."

"But it is offensive. I have not grown worse than I was before. Don't I see how others live at my age?"

"Your head wouldn't fall off from my scolding you. And I scold you because I see there is something in you that is not mine. What it is, I do not know, but I see it is there. And that something is harmful to you."

These words of Ignat made the son very thoughtful. Foma also felt something strange in himself, something which distinguished him from the youth of his age, but he, too, could not understand what it was. And he looked at himself with suspicion.

Foma liked to be on the Exchange amid the bustle and talk of the sedate people who were making deals amounting to thousands of roubles; the respect with which the less well-to-do tradesmen greeted and spoke to him—to Foma, the son of the millionaire—flattered him greatly. He felt happy and proud whenever he successfully managed some part of his father's business, assuming all responsibility on his own shoulders, and received a smile of approval from his father for it. There was in him a great deal of ambition, yearning to appear as a grown-up man of business, but—just as before his trip to Perm—he lived as in solitude; he still felt no longing for friends, although he now came in contact everyday with the merchants' sons of his age. They had invited him more than once to join them in their sprees, but he rather rudely and disdainfully declined their invitations and even laughed at them.

"I am afraid. Your fathers may learn of your sprees, and as they'll give you a drubbing, I might also come in for a share."

What he did not like in them was that they were leading a dissipated and depraved life, without their fathers' knowledge, and that the money they were spending was either stolen from their parents or borrowed on long-termed promissory notes, to be paid with exorbitant interest.

They in turn did not like him for this very reserve and aversion, which contained the pride so offensive to them. He was timid about speaking to people older than himself, fearing lest he should appear in their eyes stupid and thick-headed.

He often recalled Pelageya, and at first he felt melancholy whenever her image flashed before his imagination. But time went on, and little by little rubbed off the bright colours of this woman; and before he was aware of it his thoughts were occupied by the slender, angel-like Medinskaya. She used to come up to Ignat almost every Sunday with various requests, all of which generally had but one aim—to hasten the building of the lodging-asylum. In her presence Foma felt awkward, huge, heavy; this pained him, and he blushed deeply under the endearing look of Sophya Pavlovna's large eyes. He noticed that every time she looked at him, her eyes would grow darker, while her upper lip would tremble and raise itself slightly, thus displaying very small white teeth. This always frightened him. When his father noticed how steadfastly he was staring at Medinskaya he told him one day:

"Don't be staring so much at that face. Look out, she is like a birch ember: from the outside it is just as modest, smooth and dark—altogether cold to all appearances—but take it into your hand and it will burn you."

Medinskaya did not kindle in the youth any sensual passion, for there was nothing in her that resembled Pelageya, and altogether she was not at all like other women. He knew that shameful rumours about her were in the air, but he did not believe any of them. But his relations to her were changed when he noticed her one day in a carriage beside a stout man in a gray hat and with long hair falling over his shoulders. His face was like a bladder—red and bloated; he had neither moustache nor beard, and altogether he looked like a woman in disguise. Foma was told that this was her husband. Then dark and contradicting feelings sprang up within him: he felt like insulting the architect, and at the same time he envied and respected him. Medinskaya now seemed to him less beautiful and more accessible; he began to feel sorry for her, and yet he thought malignantly:

"She must surely feel disgusted when he kisses her."

And after all this he sometimes perceived in himself some bottomless and oppressive emptiness, which could not be filled up by anything—neither by the impressions of the day just gone by nor by the recollection of the past; and the Exchange, and his affairs, and his thoughts of Medinskaya—all were swallowed up by this emptiness. It alarmed him: in the dark depth of this emptiness he suspected some hidden existence of a hostile power, as yet formless but already carefully and persistently striving to become incarnate.

In the meantime Ignat, changing but little outwardly, was growing ever more restless and querulous and was complaining more often of being ill.

"I lost my sleep. It used to be so sound that even though you had torn off my skin, I would not have felt it. While now I toss about from side to side, and I fall asleep only toward morning. And every now and then I awaken. My heart beats unevenly, now, though tired out; often thus: tuk-tuk-tuk. And sometimes it sinks of a sudden—and it seems as though it would soon tear itself away and fall somewhere into the deep; into the bosom. Oh Lord, have pity upon me through Thy great mercy." And heaving a penitent sigh, he would lift heavenward his stern eyes, grown dim now, devoid of their bright, sparkling glitter.

"Death keeps an eye on me somewhere close by," he said one day morosely, but humbly. And indeed, it soon felled his big, sturdy body to the ground.

This happened in August, early in the morning. Foma was sound asleep when suddenly he felt somebody shaking him by the shoulder, and a hoarse voice called at his ear:

"Get up."

He opened his eyes and saw that his father was seated in a chair near his bed, monotonously repeating in a dull voice:

"Get up, get up."

The sun had just risen, and its light, falling on Ignat's white linen shirt, had not yet lost its rosy tints.

"It's early," said Foma, stretching himself.

"Well, you'll sleep enough later."

Lazily muffling himself in the blanket, Foma asked:

"Why do you need me?"

"Get up, dear, will you, please?" exclaimed Ignat, adding, somewhat offended: "It must be necessary, since I am waking you."

When Foma looked closely at his father's face, he noticed that it was gray and weary.

"Are you ill? "

"Slightly."

"Shall we send for a doctor?"

"The devil take him!" Ignat waved his hand. "I am not a young man any longer. I know it as well without him."

"What?"

"Oh, I know it!" said the old man, mysteriously, casting a strange glance around the room. Foma was dressing himself, and his father, with lowered head, spoke slowly:

"I am afraid to breathe. Something tells me that if I should now heave a deep sigh, my heart would burst. Today is Sunday! After the morning mass is over, send for the priest."

"What are you talking about, papa?" Foma smiled.

"Nothing. Wash yourself and go into the garden. I ordered the samovar to be brought there. We'll drink our tea in the morning coolness. I feel like drinking now hot, strong tea. Be quicker."

The old man rose with difficulty from the chair, and, bent and barefooted, left the room in a staggering gait. Foma looked at his father, and a shooting chill of fear made his heart shrink. He washed himself in haste, and hurried out into the garden.

There, under an old, spreading apple-tree sat Ignat in a big oaken armchair. The light of the sun fell in thin stripes through the branches of the trees upon the white figure of the old man clad in his night-garments. There was such a profound silence in the garden that even the rustle of a branch, accidentally touched by Foma's clothes, seemed to him like a loud sound and he shuddered. On the table, before his father, stood the samovar, purring like a well-fed tom-cat and exhaling a stream of steam into the air. Amid the silence and the fresh verdure of the garden, which had been washed by abundant rains the day before, this bright spot of the boldly shining, loud brass seemed to Foma as something unnecessary, as something which suited neither the time nor the place—nor the feeling that sprang up within him at the sight of the sickly, bent old man, who was dressed in white, and who sat alone underneath the mute, motionless, dark-green foliage, wherein red apples were modestly peeping.

"Be seated," said Ignat.

"We ought to send for a doctor." Foma advised him irresolutely, seating himself opposite him.

"It isn't necessary. It's a little better now in the open air. And now I'll sip some tea and perhaps that will do me more good," said Ignat, pouring out tea into the glasses, and Foma noticed that the teapot was trembling in his father's hand.

"Drink."

Silently moving up one glass for himself, Foma bent over it, blowing the foam off the surface of the tea, and with pain in his heart, hearing the loud, heavy breathing of his father. Suddenly something struck against the table with such force that the dishes began to rattle.

Foma shuddered, threw up his head and met the frightened, almost senseless look of his father's eyes. Ignat stared at his son and whispered hoarsely:

"An apple fell down (the devil take it!). It sounded like the firing of a gun."

"Won't you have some cognac in your tea?" Foma suggested.

"It is good enough without it."

They became silent. A flight of finches winged past over the garden, scattering a provokingly cheerful twittering in the air. And again the ripe beauty of the garden was bathed in solemn silence. The fright was still in Ignat's eyes.

"Oh Lord, Jesus Christ!" said he in a low voice, making the sign of the cross. "Yes. There it is—the last hour of my life."

"Stop, papa!" whispered Foma.

"Why stop? We'll have our tea, and then send for the priest, and for Mayakin."

"I'd rather send for them now."

"They'll soon toll for the mass—the priest isn't home—and then there's no hurry, it may pass soon."

And he noisily started to sip the tea out of the saucer.

"I should live another year or two. You are young, and I am very much afraid for you. Live honestly and firmly; do not covet what belongs to other people, take good care of your own."

It was hard for him to speak, he stopped short and rubbed his chest with his hand.

"Do not rely upon others; expect but little from them. We all live in order to take, not to give. Oh Lord! Have mercy on the sinner!"

Somewhere in the distance the deep sound of the bell fell on the silence of the morning. Ignat and Foma crossed themselves three times.

After the first sound of the bell-tone came another, then a third, and soon the air was filled with sounds of the church-bells, coming from all sides—flowing, measured, calling aloud.

"There, they are tolling for the mass," said Ignat, listening to the echo of the bell-metal. "Can you tell the bells by their sounds?"

"No," answered Foma.

"Just listen. This one now—do you hear? the bass—this is from the Nikola Church. It was presented by Peter Mitrich Vyagin—and this, the hoarse one—this is at the church of Praskeva Pyatnitza."

203

The singing waves of the bell-tones agitated the air, which was filled with them, and they died away in the clear blue of the sky. Foma stared thoughtfully at his father's face and saw that the alarm was disappearing from his eyes, and that they were now brighter.

But suddenly the old man's face turned very red, his eyes distended and rolled out of their orbits, his mouth opened with fright, and from it issued a strange, hissing sound:

"F-F-A-A-ch."

Immediately after this Ignat's head fell back on his shoulder, and his heavy body slowly slipped down from the chair to the ground as if the earth had dragged him imperiously unto itself. Foma was motionless and silent for awhile, then he rushed up to Ignat, lifted his head from the ground and looked into his face. The face was dark, motionless, and the wide-open eyes expressed nothing—neither pain, nor fear, nor joy. Foma looked around him. As before, nobody was in the garden, and the resounding chatter of the bells was still roaring in the air. Foma's hands began to tremble, he let go his father's head, and it struck heavily against the ground. Dark, thick blood began to gush in a narrow stream from his open mouth across his blue cheek.

Foma struck his breast with both hands, and kneeling before the dead body, he wildly cried aloud. He was trembling with fright, and with eyes like those of a madman he was searching for someone in the verdure of the garden.

CHAPTER IV

HIS father's death stupefied Foma and filled him with a strange sensation; quiet was poured into his soul—a painful, immovable quiet, which absorbed all the sounds of life without accounting for it. All sorts of acquaintances were bustling about him; they appeared, disappeared, said something to him—his replies to them were untimely, and their words called forth no images in him, drowning, without leaving any trace, in the bottomless depths of the death-like silence which filled his soul. He neither cried, nor grieved, nor thought of anything; pale and gloomy, with knitted brow, he was attentively listening to this quiet, which had forced out all his feelings, benumbed his heart and tightly clutched his brains. He was conscious but of the purely physical sensation of heaviness in all his frame and particularly in his breast, and then it also seemed to him that it was always twilight, and even though the sun was still high in the sky—everything on earth looked dark and melancholy.

The funeral was arranged by Mayakin. Hastily and briskly he was bustling about in the rooms, making much clatter with the heels of his boots; he cried at the household help imperiously, clapped his godson on the shoulder, consoling him:

"And why are you petrified? Roar and you will feel relieved. Your father was old—old in body. Death is prepared for all of us, you cannot escape it—consequently you must not be prematurely torpid. You cannot bring him to life again with your sorrow, and your grief is unnecessary to him, for it is said: 'When the body is robbed of the soul by the terrible angels, the soul forgets all relatives and acquaintances,' which means that you are of no consequence to him now, whether you cry or laugh. But the living must care for the living. You had better cry, for this is human. It brings much relief to the heart."

But neither did these words provoke anything in Foma's head or in his heart. He came to himself, however, on the day of the funeral, thanks to the persistence of his godfather, who was assiduously and oddly trying to rouse his sad soul.

The day of the funeral was cloudy and dreary. Amid a heavy cloud of dust an enormous crowd of people, winding like a black ribbon, followed the coffin of Ignat Gordyeeff. Here and there flashed the gold of the priest's robes, and the dull noise of the slow movement of the crowd blended in harmony with the solemn music of the choir, composed of the bishop's choristers. Foma was pushed from behind and from the sides; he walked, seeing nothing but the gray head of his father, and the mournful singing resounded in his heart like a melancholy echo. And Mayakin, walking beside him, kept on intrusively whispering in his ears:

"Look, what a crowd—thousands! The governor himself came out to accompany your father to the church, the mayor, and almost the entire city council. And behind you—just turn around! There goes Sophya Pavlovna. The town pays its respects to Ignat."

At first Foma did not listen to his godfather's whisper, but when he mentioned Medinskaya, he involuntarily looked back and noticed the governor. A little drop of something pleasant fell into his heart at the sight of this important personage, with a bright ribbon across his shoulder, with orders on his breast, pacing after the coffin, an expression of sorrow on his stern countenance.

Blessed is the road where this soul goeth today," Yakov Tarasovich hummed softly, moving his nose, and he again whispered in his godson's ear:

"Seventy-five thousand roubles is such a sum that you can demand so many escorts for it. Have you heard that Sonka is making arrangements for the laying of the corner-stone on the fifteenth? Just forty days after the death of your father."

206

Foma again turned back, and his eyes met the eyes of Medinskaya. He heaved a deep sigh at her caressing glance, and felt relieved at once, as if a warm ray of light penetrated his soul and something melted there. And then and there he considered that it was unbecoming him to turn his head from side to side.

At church Foma's head began to ache, and it seemed to him that everything around and underneath him was shaking. In the stifling air, filled with dust, with the breathing of the people and the smoke of the incense, the flames of the candles were timidly trembling. The meek image of Christ looked down at him from the big ikon, and the flames of the candles, reflected in the tarnished gold of the crown over the Saviour's brow, reminded him of drops of blood.

Foma's awakened soul was greedily feeding itself on the solemn, gloomy poetry of the liturgy, and when the touching citation was heard, "Come, let us give him the last kiss," a loud, wailing sob escaped from Foma's chest, and the crowd in church was stirred to agitation by this outburst of grief.

Having uttered the sob, Foma staggered. His godfather immediately caught him by his arms and began to push him forward to the coffin, singing quite loudly and with some anger:

Kiss him who was but lately with us. Kiss, Foma, kiss him—he is given over to the grave, covered with a stone. He is settling down in darkness, and is buried with the dead."

Foma touched his father's forehead with his lips and sprang back from the coffin with horror.

"Hold your peace! You nearly knocked me down," Mayakin remarked to him, in a low voice, and these simple, calm words supported Foma better than his godfather's hands.

"Ye that behold me mute and lifeless before you, weep for me, brethren and friends," begged Ignat through the mouth of the Church. But his son was not crying any longer; his horror was called forth by the black, swollen face of his father, and this horror somewhat sobered his soul, which had been intoxicated by the mournful music of the Church's lament for its sinful son. He was surrounded by acquaintances, who were kindly consoling him; he listened to them and understood that they all felt sorry for him and that he became dear to them. And his godfather whispered in his ear:

"See, how they all fawn upon you. The tom-cats have smelt the fat."

These words were unpleasant to Foma, but they were useful to him, as they caused him to answer at all events.

At the cemetery, when they sang for Ignat's eternal memory, he cried again bitterly and loud. His godfather immediately seized him by the arms and led him away from the grave, speaking to him earnestly:

"What a faint-hearted fellow you are! Do I not feel sorry for him? I have known his real value, while you were but his son. And yet, I do not cry. For more than thirty years we lived together in perfect harmony—how much had been spoken, how much thought—how much sorrow drunk. You are young; it is not for you to grieve! Your life is before you, and you will be rich in all sorts of friendship; while I am old, and now that I buried my only friend, I am like a pauper. I can no longer make a bosom friend!"

The old man's voice began to jar and squeak queerly. His face was distorted, his lips were stretched into a big grimace and were quivering, and from his small eyes frequent tears were running over the now contracted wrinkles of his face. He looked so pitiful and so unlike himself, that Foma stopped short, pressed him close to his body with the tenderness of a strong man and cried with alarm:

"Don't cry, father—darling! Don't cry."

"There you have it!" said Mayakin, faintly, and, heaving a deep sigh, he suddenly turned again into a firm and clever old man.

"You must not cry," said he, mysteriously, seating himself in the carriage beside his godson. "You are now the commander-in-chief in the war and you must command your soldiers bravely. Your soldiers are the roubles, and you have a great army of these. Make war incessantly!"

Surprised at the quickness of his transformation, Foma listened to his words and for some reason or other they reminded him of those clods of earth, which the people threw into Ignat's grave upon his coffin.

"On whom am I to make war?" said Foma with a sigh.

"I'll teach you that! Did your father tell you that I was a clever old man and that you should mind me?"

"He did."

"Then do mind me! If my mind should be added to your youthful strength, a good victory might be won. Your father was a great man, but he did not look far before him and he could not take my advice. He gained success in life not with his mind, but more with his head. Oh, what will become of you? You had better move into my house, for you will feel lonesome in yours."

"Aunt is there."

"Aunt? She is sick. She will not live long."

"Do not speak of it," begged Foma in a low voice.

"And I will speak of it. You need not fear death—you are not an old woman on the oven. Live fearlessly and do what you were appointed to do. Man is appointed for the organisation of life on earth. Man is capital—like a rouble, he is made up of trashy copper groshes and copecks. From the dust of the earth, as it is said; and even as he has intercourse with the world, he absorbs grease and oil, sweat and tears—a soul and a mind form themselves in him. And from this he starts to grow upward and downward. Now, you see his price is a grosh, now a fifteen copeck silver piece, now a hundred roubles, and sometimes he is above any price. He is put into circulation and he must bring interests to life. Life knows the value of each of us and will not check our course before time. Nobody, dear, works to his own detriment, if he is wise. And life has saved up much wisdom. Are you listening?"

"I am."

"And what do you understand?"

"Everything."

"You are probably lying?" Mayakin doubted.

"But, why must we die?" asked Foma in a low voice.

Mayakin looked into his face with regret, smacked his lips and said:

"A wise man would never ask such a question. A wise man knows for himself that if it is a river, it must be flowing somewhere, and if it were standing in one place, it would be a swamp."

"You're simply mocking me at random," said Foma, sternly. "The sea is not flowing anywhere."

"The sea receives all rivers into itself, and then, powerful storms rage in it at times. Then the sea of life also submits on agitation, stirred up by men, and death renovates the waters of the sea of life, that they might not become spoiled. No matter how many people are dying, they are nevertheless forever growing in number."

"What of it? But my father is dead."

"You will die as well."

"Then what have I to do with the fact that people are growing in number?" Foma smiled sadly.

"Eh, he, he!" sighed Mayakin. "That, indeed, concerns none of us. There, your trousers probably reason in the same way: what have we to do with the fact that there are all sorts of stuff in the world? But you do not mind them—you wear them out and throw them away."

Foma glanced at his godfather reproachfully, and noticing that the old man was smiling, he was astonished and he asked respectfully:

"Can it be true, father, that you do not fear death?"

"Most of all I fear foolishness, my child," replied Mayakin with humble bitterness. "My opinion is this: if a fool give you honey, spit upon it; if a wise man give you poison, drink it! And I will tell you that the perch has a weak soul since his fins do not stand on end."

The old man's mocking words offended and angered Foma. He turned aside and said:

"You can never speak without these subterfuges."

"I cannot!" exclaimed Mayakin, and his eyes began to sparkle with alarm. "Each man uses the very same tongue he has. Do I seem to be stern? Do I?"

Foma was silent.

"Eh, you. Know this—he loves who teaches. Remember this well. And as to death, do not think of it. It is foolish, dear, for a live man to think of death. 'Ecclesiastes' reflected on death better than anybody else reflected on it, and said that a living dog is better than a dead lion."

They came home. The street near the house was crowded with carriages, and from the open windows came loud sounds of talk. As soon as Foma appeared in the hall, he was seized by the arms and led away to the table and there was urged to drink and eat something. A marketplace noise smote the air; the hall was crowded and suffocating. Silently, Foma drank a glass of vodka, then another, and a third. Around him they were munching and smacking their lips; the vodka poured out from the bottles was gurgling, the wine-glasses were tinkling. They were speaking of dried sturgeon and of the bass of the soloist of the bishop's choir, and then again of the dried sturgeon, and then they said that the mayor also wished to make a speech, but did not venture to do so after the bishop had spoken, fearing lest he should not speak so well as the bishop. Someone was telling with feeling:

"The deceased one used to do thus: he would cut off a slice of salmon, pepper it thickly, cover it with another slice of salmon, and then send it down immediately after a drink."

"Let us follow his example," roared a thick basso. Offended to the quick, Foma looked with a frown at the fat lips and at the jaws chewing the tasty food, and he felt like crying out and driving away all these people, whose sedateness had but lately inspired him with respect for them.

"You had better be more kind, more sociable," said Mayakin in a low voice, coming up to him.

"Why are they gobbling here? Is this a tavern?" cried Foma, angrily.

"Hush," Mayakin remarked with fright and hastily turned to look around with a kind smile on his face.

But it was too late; his smile was of no avail. Foma's words had been overheard, the noise and the talk was subsiding, some of the guests began to bustle about hurriedly, others, offended, frowned, put down their forks and knives and walked away from the table, all looking at Foma askance.

Silent and angry, he met these glances without lowering his eyes.

"I ask you to come up to the table! "cried Mayakin, gleaming amid the crowd of people like an ember amid ashes. "Be seated, pray! They're soon serving pancakes."

Foma shrugged his shoulders and walked off toward the door, saying aloud:

"I shall not eat."

He heard a hostile rumbling behind him and his godfather's wheedling voice saying to somebody:

"It's for grief. Ignat was at once father and mother to him."

Foma came out in the garden and sat down on the same place where his father had died. The feeling of loneliness and grief oppressed his heart. He unbuttoned the collar of his shirt to make his breathing easier, rested his elbows on the table, and with his head tightly pressed between his hands, he sat motionless. It was drizzling and the leaves of the apple-tree were rustling mournfully under the drops of the rain. He sat there for a long time alone, motionless, watching how the small drops were falling from the apple-tree. His head was heavy from the vodka, and in his heart there was a growing grudge against men. Some indefinite, impersonal feelings and thoughts were springing up and vanishing within him; before him flashed the bald skull of his godfather with a little crown of silver hair and with a dark face, which resembled the faces of the ancient ikons. This face with the toothless mouth and the malicious smile, rousing in Foma hatred and fear, augmented in him the consciousness of solitude. Then he recalled the kind eyes of Medinskaya and her small, graceful figure; and beside her arose the tall, robust, and rosy-cheeked Lubov

212

Mayakina with smiling eyes and with a big light golden-coloured braid. "Do not rely upon men, expect but little at their hands"—his father's words began to ring in his memory. He sighed sadly and cast a glance around him. The tree leaves were fluttering from the rain, and the air was full of mournful sounds. The gray sky seemed as though weeping, and on the trees cold tears were trembling. And Foma's soul was dry, dark; it was filled with a painful feeling of orphanhood. But this feeling gave birth to the question:

"How shall I live now that I am alone?"

The rain drenched his clothes, and when he felt that he was shivering with cold he arose and went into the house.

Life was tugging him from all sides, giving him no chance to be concentrated in thinking of and grieving for his father, and on the fortieth day after Ignat's death Foma, attired in holiday clothes, with a pleasant feeling in his heart, went to the ceremony of the corner-stone laying of the lodging-asylum. Medinskaya notified him in a letter the day before, that he had been elected as a member of the building committee and also as honorary member of the society of which she was president. This pleased him and he was greatly agitated by the part he was to play today at the laying of the corner-stone. On his way he thought of how everything would be and how he should behave in order not to be confused before the people.

"Eh, eh! Hold on!"

He turned around. Mayakin came hastening to him from the sidewalk. He was in a frock-coat that reached his heels, in a high cap, and he carried a huge umbrella in his hand.

"Come on, take me up there," said the old man, cleverly jumping into the carriage like a monkey. "To tell the truth, I was waiting for you. I was looking around, thinking it was time for you to go."

"Are you going there?" asked Foma.

"Of course! I must see how they will bury my friend's money in the ground."

Foma looked at him askance and was silent. "Why do you frown upon me? Don't fear, you will also start out as a benefactor among men."

"What do you mean?" asked Foma, reservedly. "I've read in the newspaper this morning that you were elected as a member of the building committee and also as an honorary member of Sophya's society."

"Yes."

"This membership will eat into your pocket!" sighed Mayakin.

"That wouldn't ruin me."

"I don't know it," observed the old man, maliciously.

"I speak of this more because there is altogether very little wisdom in this charity business, and I may even say that it isn't a business at all, but simply harmful nonsense."

"Is it harmful to aid people?" asked Foma, hotly.

"Eh, you cabbage head!" said Mayakin with a smile. "You had better come up to my house, I'll open your eyes in regard to this. I must teach you! Will you come?"

"Very well, I will come!" replied Foma.

"So. And in the meantime, hold yourself proud at the laying of the corner-stone. Stand in view of everybody. If I don't tell this to you, you might hide yourself behind somebody's back."

"Why should I hide myself?" said Foma, displeased.

"That's just what I say: there is no reason why. For the money was donated by your father and you are entitled to the honour as his heir. Honour is just the same as money. With honour a business man will get credit everywhere, and everywhere there is a way open to him. Then come forward, so that everybody may see you and that if you do five copecks' worth of work, you should get a rouble in return for it. And if you will hide yourself—nothing but foolishness will be the result."

They arrived at their destination, where all the important people had gathered already, and an enormous crowd of people surrounded the piles of wood, bricks and earth. The bishop, the governor, the representatives of the city's aristocracy and the administration formed, together with

214

the splendidly dressed ladies, a big bright group and looked at the efforts of the two stonemasons, who were preparing the bricks and the lime. Mayakin and his godson wended their way toward this group. He whispered to Foma:

"Lose no courage, these people have robbed their bellies to cover themselves with silk."

And he greeted the governor before the bishop, in a respectfully cheerful voice.

"How do you do, your Excellency? Give me your blessing, your Holiness!"

"Ah, Yakov Tarasovich!" exclaimed the governor with a friendly smile, shaking and squeezing Mayakin's hand, while the old man was at the same time kissing the bishop's hand. "How are you, deathless old man?"

"I thank you humbly, your Excellency! My respects to Sophya Pavlovna!" Mayakin spoke fast, whirling like a peg-top amid the crowd of people. In a minute he managed to shake hands with the presiding justice of the court, with the prosecutor, with the mayor—in a word, with all those people whom he considered it necessary to greet first; such as these, however, were few. He jested, smiled and at once attracted everybody's attention to his little figure, and Foma with downcast head stood behind him, looking askance at these people wrapped in costly stuffs, embroidered with gold; he envied the old man's adroitness and lost his courage, and feeling that he was losing his courage—he grew still more timid. But now Mayakin seized him by the hand and drew him up to himself.

"There, your Excellency, this is my godson, Foma, the late Ignat's only son."

"Ah!" said the governor in his basso, "I'm very pleased. I sympathise with you in your misfortune, young man!" he said, shaking Foma's hand, and became silent; then he added resolutely and confidently: "To lose a father, that is a very painful misfortune."

215

And, having waited about two seconds for Foma's answer, he turned away from him, addressing Mayakin approvingly:

"I am delighted with the speech you made yesterday in the city hall! Beautiful, clever, Yakov Tarasovich. Proposing to use the money for this public club, they do not understand the real needs of the population."

"And then, your Excellency, a small capital means that the city will have to add its own money."

"Perfectly true! Perfectly true!"

"Temperance, I say, is good! Would to God that all were sober! I don't drink, either, but what is the use of these performances, libraries and all that, since the people cannot even read?"

The governor replied approvingly.

"Here, I say, you better use this money for a technical institution. If it should be established on a small plan, this money alone will suffice, and in case it shouldn't, we can ask for more in St. Petersburg—they'll give it to us. Then the city wouldn't have to add of its own money, and the whole affair would be more sensible."

"Precisely! I fully agree with you! But how the liberals began to cry at you! Eh? Ha, ha!"

"That has always been their business, to cry."

The deep cough of the archdeacon of the cathedral announced the beginning of the divine service.

Sophya Pavlovna came up to Foma, greeted him and said in a sad, low voice:

"I looked at your face on the day of the funeral, and my heart saddened. My God, I thought, how he must suffer!"

And Foma listened to her and felt as though he was drinking honey.

"These cries of yours, they shook my soul, my poor child! I may speak to you this way, for I am an old woman already."

"You!" exclaimed Foma, softly.

"Isn't that so?" she asked, naively looking into his face.

Foma was silent, his head bent on his breast.

"Don't you believe that I am an old woman?"

"I believe you; that is, I believe everything you may say; only this is not true!" said Foma, feelingly, in a low voice.

"What is not true? What do you believe me?"

"No! not this, but that. I—excuse me! I cannot speak!" said Foma, sadly, all aflush with confusion. "I am not cultured."

"You need not trouble yourself on this account," said Medinskaya, patronisingly. "You are so young, and education is accessible to everybody. But there are people to whom education is not only unnecessary, but who can also be harmed by it. Those that are pure of heart, sanguine, sincere, like children, and you are of those people. You are, are you not?"

What could Foma say in answer to this question? He said sincerely:

"I thank you humbly!"

And noticing that his words called forth a gay gleam in Medinskaya's eyes, Foma appeared ridiculous and stupid in his own eyes; he immediately became angry at himself and said in a muffled voice:

"Yes, I am such. I always speak my mind. I cannot deceive. If I see something to laugh at, I laugh openly. I am stupid!"

"What makes you speak that way?" said the woman, reproachfully, and adjusting her dress, she accidentally stroked Foma's hand, in which he held his hat. This made him look at his wrist and smile joyously and confusedly.

"You will surely be present at the dinner, won't you?" asked Medinskaya.

"Yes."

"And tomorrow at the meeting in my house?"

"Without fail!"

"And perhaps sometime you will drop in, simply on a visit, wouldn't you?"

"I—I thank you! I'll come!"

"I must thank you for the promise."

They became silent. In the air soared the reverently soft voice of the bishop, who recited the prayer expressively, outstretching his hand over the place where the corner-stone of the house was laid:

"May neither the wind, nor water, nor anything else bring harm unto it; may it be completed in thy benevolence, and free all those that are to live in it from all kinds of calumny."

"How rich and beautiful our prayers are, are they not?" asked Medinskaya.

"Yes," said Foma, shortly, without understanding her words and feeling that he was blushing again.

"They will always be opponents of our commercial interests," Mayakin whispered loudly and convincingly, standing beside the city mayor, not far from Foma. "What is it to them? All they want is somehow to deserve the approval of the newspaper. But they cannot reach the main point. They live for mere display, not for the organisation of life; these are their only measures: the newspapers and Sweden! [Mayakin speaks of Sweden, meaning Switzerland.—Translator's note.] The doctor scoffed at me all day yesterday with this Sweden. The public education, says he, in Sweden, and everything else there is first-class! But what is Sweden, anyway? It may be that Sweden is but a fib, is but used as an example, and that there is no education whatever or any of the other things there. And then, we don't live for the sake of Sweden, and Sweden cannot put us to test. We have to make our lip according to our own last. Isn't it so?

And the archdeacon droned, his head thrown back:

"Eternal me-emo-ory to the founder of this ho-ouse!"

Foma shuddered, but Mayakin was already by his side, and pulling him by the sleeve, asked:

"Are you going to the dinner?"

And Medinskaya's velvet-like, warm little hand glided once more over Foma's hand.

The dinner was to Foma a real torture. For the first time in his life among these uniformed people, he saw that they were eating and speaking—doing everything better than he, and he felt that between him and Medinskaya, who was seated just opposite him, was a high mountain, not a table. Beside him sat the secretary of the society of which Foma had been made an honorary member; he was a young court officer, bearing the odd name of Ookhtishchev. As if to make his name appear more absurd than it really was, he spoke in a loud, ringing tenor, and altogether—plump, short, round-faced and a lively talker—he looked like a brand new bell.

"The very best thing in our society is the patroness; the most reasonable is what we are doing—courting the patroness; the most difficult is to tell the patroness such a compliment as would satisfy her; and the most sensible thing is to admire the patroness silently and hopelessly. So that in reality, you are a member not of 'the Society of Solicitude,' and so on, but of the Society of Tantaluses, which is composed of persons bent on pleasing Sophya Medinskaya."

Foma listened to his chatter, now and then looking at the patroness, who was absorbed in a conversation with the chief of the police; Foma roared in reply to his interlocutor, pretending to be busy eating, and he wished that all this would end the sooner. He felt that he was wretched, stupid, ridiculous and he was certain that everybody was watching and censuring him. This tied him with invisible shackles, thus checking his words and his thoughts. At last he went so far, that the line of various physiognomies, stretched out by the table opposite him, seemed to him a long and wavy white strip besprinkled with laughing eyes, and all these eyes were pricking him unpleasantly and painfully.

Mayakin sat near the city mayor, waved his fork in the air quickly, and kept on talking all the time, now contracting, now expanding the wrinkles of his face. The mayor, a gray-headed, red-faced, short-necked man, stared at him like a bull, with obstinate attention and at times he rapped on the edge of the table with his big finger affirmatively. The animated talk and laughter drowned his godfather's bold speech, and

Foma was unable to hear a single word of it, much more so that the tenor of the secretary was unceasingly ringing in his ears:

"Look, there, the archdeacon arose; he is filling his lungs with air; he will soon proclaim an eternal memory for Ignat Matveyich."

"May I not go away?" asked Foma in a low voice.

"Why not? Everybody will understand this."

The deacon's resounding voice drowned and seemed to have crushed the noise in the hail; the eminent merchants fixed their eyes on the big, wide-open mouth, from which a deep sound was streaming forth, and availing himself of this moment, Foma arose from his seat and left the hall.

After awhile he breathed freely and, sitting in his cab, thought sadly that there was no place for him amid these people. Inwardly, he called them polished. He did not like their brilliancy, their faces, their smiles or their words, but the freedom and the cleverness of their movements, their ability to speak much and on any subject, their pretty costumes—all this aroused in him a mixture of envy and respect for them. He felt sad and oppressed at the consciousness of being unable to talk so much and so fluently as all these people, and here he recalled that Luba Mayakina had more than once scoffed at him on this account.

Foma did not like Mayakin's daughter, and since he had learned from his father of Mayakin's intention to marry him to Luba, the young Gordyeeff began to shun her. But after his father's death he was almost every day at the Mayakins, and somehow Luba said to him one day:

"I am looking at you, and, do you know?—you do not resemble a merchant at all."

"Nor do you look like a merchant's daughter," said Foma, and looked at her suspiciously. He did not understand the meaning of her words; did she mean to offend him, or did she say these words without any kind thoughts?

"Thank God for this!" said she and smiled to him a kind, friendly smile.

"What makes you so glad?" he asked.

"The fact that we don't resemble our fathers."

Foma glanced at her in astonishment and kept silent.

"Tell me frankly," said she, lowering her voice, "you do not love my father, do you? You don't like him?"

"Not very much," said Foma, slowly.

"And I dislike him very much."

"What for?"

"For everything. When you grow wiser, you will know it yourself. Your father was a better man."

"Of course!" said Foma, proudly.

After this conversation an attachment sprang up between them almost immediately, and growing stronger from day to day, it soon developed into friendship, though a somewhat odd friendship it was.

Though Luba was not older than her god-brother, she nevertheless treated him as an older person would treat a little boy. She spoke to him condescendingly, often jesting at his expense; her talk was always full of words which were unfamiliar to Foma; and she pronounced these words with particular emphasis and with evident satisfaction. She was especially fond of speaking about her brother Taras, whom she had never seen, but of whom she was telling such stories as would make him look like Aunt Anfisa's brave and noble robbers. Often, when complaining of her father, she said to Foma:

"You will also be just such a skinflint."

All this was unpleasant to the youth and stung his vanity. But at times she was straightforward, simple-minded, and particularly kind and friendly to him; then he would unburden his heart before her, and for a long time they would share each other's thoughts and feelings.

Both spoke a great deal and spoke sincerely, but neither one understood the other; it seemed to Foma that whatever Luba had to say was foreign to him and unnecessary to her, and at the same time he clearly saw that his awkward words did not at all interest her, and that she did not care to

221

understand them. No matter how long these conversations lasted, they gave both of them the sensation of discomfort and dissatisfaction. As if an invisible wall of perplexity had suddenly arisen and stood between them. They did not venture to touch this wall, or to tell each other that they felt it was there—they resumed their conversations, dimly conscious that there was something in each of them that might bind and unite them.

When Foma arrived at his godfather's house, he found Luba alone. She came out to meet him, and it was evident that she was either ill or out of humour; her eyes were flashing feverishly and were surrounded with black circles. Feeling cold, she muffled herself in a warm shawl and said with a smile:

"It is good that you've come! For I was sitting here alone; it is lonesome—I don't feel like going anywhere. Will you drink tea?"

"I will. What is the matter with you, are you ill?"

"Go to the dining-room, and I'll tell them to bring the samovar," she said, not answering his question.

He went into one of the small rooms of the house, whose two windows overlooked the garden. In the middle of the room stood an oval table, surrounded with old-fashioned, leather-covered chairs; on one partition hung a clock in a long case with a glass door, in the corner was a cupboard for dishes, and opposite the windows, by the walls, was an oaken sideboard as big as a fair-sized room.

"Are you coming from the banquet?" asked Luba, entering.

Foma nodded his head mutely.

"Well, how was it? Grand?"

"It was terrible!" Foma smiled. "I sat there as if on hot coals. They all looked there like peacocks, while I looked like a barn-owl."

Luba was taking out dishes from the cupboard and said nothing to Foma.

"Really, why are you so sad?" asked Foma again, glancing at her gloomy face.

She turned to him and said with enthusiasm and anxiety:

"Ah, Foma! What a book I've read! If you could only understand it!"

"It must be a good book, since it worked you up in this way," said Foma, smiling.

"I did not sleep. I read all night long. Just think of it: you read—and it seems to you that the gates of another kingdom are thrown open before you. And the people there are different, and their language is different, everything different! Life itself is different there."

"I don't like this," said Foma, dissatisfied. "That's all fiction, deceit; so is the theatre. The merchants are ridiculed there. Are they really so stupid? Of course! Take your father, for example."

"The theatre and the school are one and the same, Foma," said Luba, instructively. "The merchants used to be like this. And what deceit can there be in books?"

"Just as in fairy—tales, nothing is real."

"You are wrong! You have read no books; how can you judge? Books are precisely real. They teach you how to live."

"Come, come!" Foma waved his hand. "Drop it; no good will come out of your books! There, take your father, for example, does he read books? And yet he is clever! I looked at him today and envied him. His relations with everybody are so free, so clever, he has a word for each and every one. You can see at once that whatever he should desire he is sure to attain."

"What is he striving for?" exclaimed Luba. "Nothing but money. But there are people that want happiness for all on earth, and to gain this end they work without sparing themselves; they suffer and perish! How can my father be compared with these?"

"You need not compare them. They evidently like one thing, while your father likes another."

"They do not like anything!"

How's that?

"They want to change everything."

"So they do strive for something?" said Foma, thoughtfully. "They do wish for something?"

"They wish for happiness for all!" cried Luba, hotly. "I can't understand this," said Foma, nodding his head. "Who cares there for my happiness? And then again, what happiness can they give me, since I, myself, do not know as yet what I want? No, you should have rather looked at those that were at the banquet."

"Those are not men!" announced Luba, categorically.

"I do not know what they are in your eyes, but you can see at once that they know their place. A clever, easy-going lot."

"Ah, Foma!" exclaimed Luba, vexed. "You understand nothing! Nothing agitates you! You are an idler."

"Now, that's going too far! I've simply not had time enough to see where I am."

"You are simply an empty man," said Luba, resolutely and firmly.

"You were not within my soul," replied Foma, calmly. "You cannot know my thoughts."

"What is there that you should think of?" said Luba, shrugging her shoulders.

"So? First of all, I am alone. Secondly, I must live. Don't I understand that it is altogether impossible for me to live as I am now? I do not care to be made the laughing-stock of others. I cannot even speak to people. No, nor can I think." Foma concluded his words and smiled confusedly.

"It is necessary to read, to study," Luba advised him convincingly, pacing up and down the room.

"Something is stirring within my soul," Foma went on, not looking at her, as though speaking to himself; "but I cannot tell what it is. I see, for instance, that whatever my godfather says is clever and reasonable. But that does not attract me. The other people are by far more interesting to me."

"You mean the aristocrats?" asked Luba.

"Yes."

"That's just the place for you!" said Luba, with a smile of contempt. "Eh, you! Are they men? Do they have souls?"

"How do you know them? You are not acquainted with them."

"And the books? Have I not read books about them?"

The maid brought in the samovar, and the conversation was interrupted. Luba made tea in silence while Foma looked at her and thought of Medinskaya. He was wishing to have a talk with her.

"Yes," said the girl, thoughtfully, "I am growing more and more convinced everyday that it is hard to live. What shall I do? Marry? Whom? Shall I marry a merchant who will do nothing but rob people all his life, nothing but drink and play cards? A savage? I do not want it! I want to be an individual. I am such, for I know how wrong the construction of life is. Shall I study? My father will not allow this. 0h Lord! Shall I run away? I have not enough courage. What am I to do?"

She clasped her hands and bowed her head over the table.

"If you knew but how repulsive everything is. There is not a living soul around here. Since my mother died, my father drove everyone away. Some went off to study. Lipa, too, left us. She writes me:

'Read.' Ah, I am reading! I am reading!" she exclaimed, with despair in her voice, and after a moment's silence she went on sadly:

"Books do not contain what the heart needs most, and there's much I cannot understand in them. And then, I feel weary to be reading all the time alone, alone! I want to speak to a man, but there is none to speak to! I feel disgusted. We live but once, and it is high time for me to live, and yet there is not a soul! Wherefore shall I live? Lipa tells me: 'Read and you will understand it.' I want bread and she gives me a stone. I understand what one must do—one must stand up for what he loves and believes. He must fight for it."

And she concluded, uttering something like a moan:

"But I am alone! Whom shall I fight? There are no enemies here. There are no men! I live here in a prison!"

Foma listened to her words, fixedly examining the fingers of his hand; he felt that in her words was some great distress, but he could not understand her. And when she became silent, depressed and sad, he found nothing to tell her save a few words that were like a reproach:

"There, you yourself say that books are worthless to you, and yet you instruct me to read."

She looked into his face, and anger flashed in her eyes.

"Oh, how I wish that all these torments would awaken within you, the torments that constantly oppress me. That your thoughts, like mine, would rob you of your sleep, that you, too, would be disgusted with everything, and with yourself as well! I despise every one of you. I hate you!"

All aflush, she looked at him so angrily and spoke with so much spitefulness, that in his astonishment he did not even feel offended by her. She had never before spoken to him in such manner.

"What's the matter with you?" he asked her.

"I hate you, too! You, what are you? Dead, empty; how will you live? What will you give to mankind?" she said with malice, in a low voice.

"I'll give nothing; let them strive for it themselves," answered Foma, knowing that these words would augment her anger.

"Unfortunate creature!" exclaimed the girl with contempt.

The assurance and the power of her reproaches involuntarily compelled Foma to listen attentively to her spiteful words; he felt there was common sense in them. He even came nearer to her, but she, enraged and exasperated, turned away from him and became silent.

It was still light outside, and the reflection of the setting sun lay still on the branches of the linden-trees before the windows, but the room was already filled with twilight, and the sideboard, the clock and the cupboard seemed to have grown in size. The huge pendulum peeped out every moment from beneath the glass of the clock-case, and flashing dimly, was hiding with a weary sound now on the right side, now on the left. Foma looked at the pendulum and he began to feel awkward and

226

lonesome. Luba arose and lighted the lamp which was hanging over the table. The girl's face was pale and stern.

"You went for me," said Foma, reservedly. "What for? I can't understand."

"I don't want to speak to you!" replied Luba, angrily.

"That's your affair. But nevertheless, what wrong have I done to you?"

"You?

"I."

"Understand me, I am suffocating! It is close here. Is this life? Is this the way how to live? What am I? I am a hanger-on in my father's house. They keep me here as a housekeeper. Then they'll marry me! Again housekeeping. It's a swamp. I am drowning, suffocating."

"And what have I to do with it?" asked Foma.

"You are no better than the others."

"And therefore I am guilty before you?"

"Yes, guilty! You must desire to be better."

"But do I not wish it?" exclaimed Foma.

The girl was about to tell him something, but at this time the bell began to ring somewhere, and she said in a low voice, leaning back in her chair:

"It's father."

"I would not feel sorry if he stayed away a little longer," said Foma. "I wish I could listen to you some more. You speak so very oddly."

"Ah! my children, my doves!" exclaimed Yakov Tarasovich, appearing in the doorway. "You're drinking tea? Pour out some tea for me, Lugava!"

Sweetly smiling, and rubbing his hands, he sat down near Foma and asked, playfully jostling him in the side:

"What have you been cooing about?"

"So—about different trifles," answered Luba.

"I haven't asked you, have I?" said her father to her, with a grimace. "You just sit there, hold your tongue, and mind your woman's affairs."

"I've been telling her about the dinner," Foma interrupted his godfather's words.

"Aha! So-o-o. Well, then, I'll also speak about the dinner. I have been watching you of late. You don't behave yourself sensibly!"

"What do you mean?" asked Foma, knitting his brow, ill pleased.

"I just mean that your behaviour is preposterous, and that's all. When the governor, for instance, speaks to you, you keep quiet."

"What should I tell him? He says that it is a misfortune to lose a father. Well, I know it. What could I tell him?"

"But as the Lord willed it so, I do not grumble, your Excellency. That's what you should have said, or something in this spirit. Governors, my dear, are very fond of meekness in a man."

"Was I to look at him like a lamb?" said Foma, with a smile.

"You did look like a lamb, and that was unnecessary. You must look neither like a lamb, nor like a wolf, but just play off before him as though saying: 'You are our father, we are your children,' and he will immediately soften."

"And what is this for?"

"For any event. A governor, my dear, can always be of use somewhere."

"What do you teach him, papa?" said Luba, indignantly, in a low voice.

"Well, what?"

"To dance attendance."

"You lie, you learned fool! I teach him politics, not dancing attendance; I teach him the politics of life. You had better leave us alone! Depart from evil, and prepare some lunch for us. Go ahead!"

Luba rose quickly and throwing the towel across the back of the chair, left the room. Mayakin, winking his eyes, looked after her, tapped the table with his fingers and said:

"I shall instruct you, Foma. I shall teach you the most genuine, true knowledge and philosophy, and if you understand them, your life will be faultless."

Foma saw how the wrinkles on the old man's forehead were twitching, and they seemed to him like lines of Slavonic letters.

"First of all, Foma, since you live on this earth, it is your duty to think over everything that takes place about you. Why? That you may not suffer for your own senselessness, and may not harm others by your folly. Now, every act of man is double-faced, Foma. One is visible to all—this is the wrong side; the other is concealed—and that is the real one. It is that one that you must be able to find in order to understand the sense of the thing. Take for example the lodging-asylums, the work-houses, the poor-houses and other similar institutions. Just consider, what are they for?"

"What is there to consider here?" said Foma, wearily "Everybody knows what they are for—for the poor and feeble."

"Eh, dear! Sometimes everybody knows that a certain man is a rascal and a scoundrel, and yet all call him Ivan or Peter, and instead of abusing him they respectfully add his father's name to his own."

"What has this to do with it?"

"It's all to the point. So you say that these houses are for the poor, for beggars, consequently, in accordance with Christ's commandment. Very well! But who is the beggar? The beggar is a man, forced by fate to remind us of Christ; he is a brother of Christ; he is the bell of the Lord and he rings in life to rouse our conscience, to arouse the satiety of the flesh of man. He stands by the window and sings out: 'For the sake of Christ!' and by his singing he reminds us of Christ, of His holy commandment to help the neighbour. But men have so arranged their life that it is impossible for them to act according to the teachings of Christ, and Jesus Christ has become altogether unnecessary to us. Not one time, but perhaps a hundred thousand times have we turned Him over to the cross, and yet we cannot drive Him altogether out of life,

229

because His poor brethren sing His Holy name on the streets and thus remind us of Him. And now we have arranged to lock up these beggars in separate houses that they should not walk around on the streets and should not rouse our conscience.

"Cle-ver!" whispered Foma, amazed, staring fixedly at his godfather.

"Aha!" exclaimed Mayakin, his eyes beaming with triumph.

"How is it that my father did not think of this?" asked Foma, uneasily.

"Just wait! Listen further, it is still worse. So you see, we have arranged to lock them up in all sorts of houses and that they might be kept there cheaply, we have compelled those old and feeble beggars to work and we need give no alms now, and since our streets have been cleared of the various ragged beggars, we do not see their terrible distress and poverty, and we may, therefore, think that all men on earth are well-fed, shod and clothed. That's what all these different houses are for, for the concealment of the truth, for the banishment of Christ from our life! Is this clear to you?"

"Yes!" said Foma, confused by the old man's clever words.

"And this is not all. The pool is not yet baled out to the bottom!" exclaimed Mayakin, swinging his hand in the air with animation.

The wrinkles of his face were in motion; his long, ravenous nose was stirring, and in his voice rang notes of irritability and emotion.

"Now, let us look at this thing from the other side. Who contributes most in favour of the poor, for the support of these houses, asylums, poor-houses? The rich people, the merchants, our body of merchants. Very well! And who commands our life and regulates it? The nobles, the functionaries and all sorts of other people, not belonging to our class. From them come the laws, the newspapers, science—everything from them. Before, they were land-owners, now their land was snatched away from them—and they started out in service. Very well! But who are the most powerful people today? The merchant is the supreme power in an empire, because he has the millions on his side! Isn't that so?"

"True!" assented Foma, eager to hear the sooner that which was to follow, and which was already sparkling in the eyes of his godfather.

"Just mark this," the old man went on distinctly and impressively. "We merchants had no hand in the arrangement of life, nor do we have a voice or a hand in it today. Life was arranged by others, and it is they that multiplied all sorts of scabs in life—idlers and poor unfortunates; and since by multiplying them they obstructed life and spoilt it—it is, justly judging, now their duty to purify it. But we are purifying it, we contribute money for the poor, we look after them—we, judge it for yourself, why should we mend another's rags, since we did not tear them? Why should we repair a house, since others have lived in it and since it belongs to others? Were it not wiser for us to step aside and watch until a certain time how rottenness is multiplying and choking those that are strangers to us? They cannot conquer it, they have not the means to do it. Then they will turn to us and say: 'Pray, help us, gentlemen!' and we'll tell them: 'Let us have room for our work! Rank us among the builders of this same life!' And as soon as they do this we, too, will have to clear life at one sweep of all sorts of filth and chaff. Then the Emperor will see with his clear eyes who are really his faithful servants, and how much wisdom they have saved up while their hands were idle. Do you understand?"

"Of course, I do!" exclaimed Foma.

When his godfather spoke of the functionaries, Foma reminded himself of the people that were present at the dinner; he recalled the brisk secretary, and a thought flashed through his mind that this stout little man has in all probability an income of no more than a thousand roubles a year, while he, Foma, has a million. But that man lives so easily and freely, while he, Foma, does not know how to live, is indeed abashed to live. This comparison and his godfather's speech roused in him a whirl of thoughts, but he had time to grasp and express only one of them:

"Indeed, do we work for the sake of money only? What's the use of money if it can give us no power?"

"Aha!" said Mayakin, winking his eyes.

"Eh!" exclaimed Foma, offended. "How about my father? Have you spoken to him?"

"I spoke to him for twenty years."

"Well, how about him?"

"My words did not reach him. The crown of your father's head was rather thick. His soul was open to all, while his mind was hidden away far within him. Yes, he made a blunder, and I am very sorry about the money."

"I am not sorry for the money."

"You should have tried to earn even a tenth part of it, then speak."

"May I come in?" came Luba's voice from behind the door.

"Yes, step right in," said the father.

"Will you have lunch now?" she asked, entering.

"Let us have it."

She walked up to the sideboard and soon the dishes were rattling. Yakov Tarasovich looked at her, moved his lips, and suddenly striking Foma's knee with his hand, he said to him:

"That's the way, my godson! Think."

Foma responded with a smile and thought: "But he's clever—cleverer than my father."

But another voice within him immediately replied:

"Cleverer, but worse."

CHAPTER V

FOMA'S dual relation toward Mayakin grew stronger and stronger as time went on; listening to his words attentively and with eager curiosity, he felt that each meeting with his godfather was strengthening in him the feeling of hostility toward the old man. Sometimes Yakov Tarasovich roused in his godson a feeling akin to fear, sometimes even physical aversion. The latter usually came to Foma whenever the old man was pleased with something and laughed. From laughter the old man's wrinkles would tremble, thus changing the expression of his face every now and then; his dry, thin lips would stretch out and move nervously, displaying black broken teeth, and his red little beard was as though aflame. His laughter sounded like the squeaking of rusty hinges, and altogether the old man looked like a lizard at play. Unable to conceal his feelings, Foma often expressed them to Mayakin rather rudely, both in words and in gesture, but the old man, pretending not to notice it, kept a vigilant eye on him, directing his each and every step. Wholly absorbed by the steamship affairs of the young Gordyeeff, he even neglected his own little shop, and allowed Foma considerable leisure time. Thanks to Mayakin's important position in town and to his extensive acquaintance on the Volga, business was splendid, but Mayakin's zealous interest in his affairs strengthened Foma's suspicions that his godfather was firmly resolved to marry him to Luba, and this made the old man more repulsive to him.

He liked Luba, but at the same time she seemed suspicious and dangerous for him. She did not marry, and Mayakin never said a word about it; he gave no evening parties, invited none of the youths to his house and did not allow Luba to leave the house. And all her girl friends were married already. Foma admired her words and listened to her just as eagerly as to her father; but whenever she started to speak of Taras with love and anguish, it seemed to him that she was hiding another man under that name, perhaps that same Yozhov, who according to her words, had to leave the university for some reason or other, and go to Moscow. There was a great deal of simplemindedness and kindness in her, which pleased Foma, and ofttimes her words awakened in him a feeling of pity for her; it seemed to him that she was not alive, that she was dreaming though awake.

His conduct at the funeral feast for his father became known to all the merchants and gave him a bad reputation. On the Exchange, he noticed, everybody looked at him sneeringly, malevolently, and spoke to him in some peculiar way. One day he heard behind him a low exclamation, full of contempt:

"Gordyeeff! Milksop!"

He felt that this was said of him, but he did not turn around to see who it was that flung those words at him. The rich people, who had inspired him with timidity before, were now losing in his eyes the witchery of their wealth and wisdom. They had more than once snatched out of his hands this or that profitable contract; he clearly saw that they would do it again, and they all seemed to him alike—greedy for money, always ready to cheat one another. When he imparted to his godfather his observation, the old man said:

"How then? Business is just the same as war—a hazardous affair. There they fight for the purse, and in the purse is the soul."

"I don't like this," announced Foma.

"Neither do I like everything—there's too much fraud.

But to be fair in business matters is utterly impossible; you must be shrewd! In business, dear, on approaching a man you must hold honey in your left hand, and clutch a knife in your right. Everybody would like to buy five copecks' worth for a half a copeck."

234

"Well, this isn't too good," said Foma, thoughtfully. "But it will be good later. When you have taken the upper hand, then it will be good. Life, dear Foma, is very simple: either bite everybody, or lie in the gutter.

The old man smiled, and the broken teeth in his mouth roused in Foma the keen thought:

"You have bitten many, it seems."

"There's but one word—battle!" repeated the old man.

"Is this the real one?" asked Foma, looking at Mayakin searchingly.

"That is, what do you mean—the real?"

"Is there nothing better than this? Does this contain everything?"

"Where else should it be? Everybody lives for himself. Each of us wishes the best for himself. And what is the best? To go in front of others, to stand above them. So that everybody is trying to attain the first place in life—one by this means, another by that means. But everyone is positively anxious to be seen from afar, like a tower. And man was indeed appointed to go upward. Even the Book of Job says: 'Man is born unto trouble, as the sparks, to fly upward.' Just see: even children at play always wish to surpass one another. And each and every game has its climax, which makes it interesting. Do you understand?"

"I understand this!" said Foma, firmly and confidently.

"But you must also feel this. With understanding alone you cannot go far, and you must desire, and desire so that a big mountain should seem to you but a hillock, and the sea but a puddle. Eh! When I was of your age I had an easy life, while you are only taking aim. But then, good fruit does not ripen early."

The old man's monotonous speeches soon accomplished what they were intended to do. Foma listened to them and made clear to himself the aim of life. He must be better than others, he resolved, and the ambition, kindled by the old man, took deep root in his heart. It took root within his heart, but did not fill it up, for Foma's relations toward Medinskaya assumed that character, which they were bound to assume. He longed for her, he always yearned to see her; while in her presence he became timid, awkward and stupid; he knew it and suffered on this account. He frequently visited her, but it was hard to find her at home alone; perfumed dandies like flies over a piece of sugar—were always flitting about her. They spoke to her in French, sang and laughed, while he looked at them in silence, tortured by anger and jealousy. His legs crossed, he sat somewhere in a corner of her richly furnished drawing-room, where it was extremely difficult to walk without overturning or at least striking against something—Foma sat and watched them sternly.

Over the soft rugs she was noiselessly passing hither and thither, casting to him kind glances and smiles, while her admirers were fawning upon her, and they all, like serpents, were cleverly gliding by the various little tables, chairs, screens, flower-stands—a storehouse full of beautiful and frail things, scattered about the room with a carelessness equally dangerous to them and to Foma. But when he walked there, the rugs did not drown his footsteps, and all these things caught at his coat, trembled and fell. Beside the piano stood a sailor made of bronze, whose hand was lifted, ready to throw the life-saving ring; on this ring were ropes of wire, and these always pulled Foma by the hair. All this provoked laughter among Sophya Pavlovna and her admirers, and Foma suffered greatly, changing from heat to cold.

But he felt no less uncomfortable even when alone with her. Greeting him with a kindly smile, she would take a seat beside him in one of the cosy corners of her drawing-room and would usually start her conversation by complaining to him of everybody:

"You wouldn't believe how glad I am to see you!" Bending like a cat, she would gaze into his eyes with her dark glance, in which something avidious would now flash up.

"I love to speak to you," she said, musically drawling her words. "I've grown tired of all the rest of them. They're all so boring, ordinary and worn-out, while you are fresh, sincere. You don't like those people either, do you?"

"I can't bear them!" replied Foma, firmly.

236

"And me?" she asked softly.

Foma turned his eyes away from her and said, with a sigh:

"How many times have you asked me that?"

"Is it hard for you to tell me?"

"It isn't hard, but what for?"

"I must know it."

"You are making sport of me," said Foma, sternly. And she opened her eyes wide and inquired in a tone of great astonishment:

"How do I make sport of you? What does it mean to make sport?"

And her face looked so angelic that he could not help believing her.

"I love you! I love you! It is impossible not to love you!" said he hotly, and immediately added sadly, lowering his voice: "But you don't need it!"

"There you have it!" sighed Medinskaya, satisfied, drawing back from him. "I am always extremely pleased to hear you say this, with so much youthfulness and originality. Would you like to kiss my hand?"

Without saying a word he seized her thin, white little hand and carefully bending down to it, he passionately kissed it for a long time. Smiling and graceful, not in the least moved by his passion, she freed her hand from his. Pensively, she looked at him with that strange glitter in her eyes, which always confused Foma; she examined him as something rare and extremely curious, and said:

"How much strength and power and freshness of soul you possess! Do you know? You merchants are an altogether new race, an entire race with original traditions, with an enormous energy of body and soul. Take you, for instance—you are a precious stone, and you should be polished. Oh!"

Whenever she told him: "You," or "according to your merchant fashion," it seemed to Foma that she was pushing him away from her with these words. This at once saddened and offended him. He was silent, looking at her small maidenly figure, which was always somehow particularly well dressed, always sweet-scented like a flower. Sometimes he was seized with a wild, coarse desire to embrace and kiss her. But her beauty and the fragility of her thin, supple body awakened in him a fear of breaking and disfiguring her, and her calm, caressing voice and the clear, but somewhat cautious look of her eyes chilled his passion; it seemed to him as though she were looking straight into his soul, divining all his thoughts. But these bursts of emotion were rare. Generally the youth regarded Medinskaya with adoration, admiring everything in her—her beauty, her words, her dresses. And beside this adoration there was in him a painfully keen consciousness of his remoteness from her, of her supremacy over him.

These relations were established between them within a short time; after two or three meetings Medinskaya was in full possession of the youth and she slowly began to torture him. Evidently she liked to have a healthy, strong youth at her mercy; she liked to rouse and tame the animal in him merely with her voice and glance, and confident of the power of her superiority, she found pleasure in thus playing with him. On leaving her, he was usually half-sick from excitement, bearing her a grudge, angry with himself, filled with many painful and intoxicating sensations. And about two days later he would come to undergo the same torture again.

One day he asked her timidly:

"Sophya Pavlovna! Have you ever had any children?"

"No."

"I thought not!" exclaimed Foma with delight.

She cast at him the look of a very naive little girl, and said:

"What made you think so? And why do you want to know whether I had any children or not?"

Foma blushed, and, bending his head, began to speak to her in a heavy voice, as though he was lifting every word from the ground and as though each word weighed a few puds.

"You see—a woman who—has given birth to children—such a woman has altogether different eyes."

"So? What kind are they then?"

238

"Shameless!" Foma blurted out.

Medinskaya broke into her silver laughter, and Foma, looking at her, also began to laugh.

"Excuse me!" said he, at length. "Perhaps I've said something wrong, improper."

"Oh, no, no! You cannot say anything improper. You are a pure, amiable boy. And so, my eyes are not shameless?"

"Yours are like an angel's!" announced Foma with enthusiasm, looking at her with beaming eyes. And she glanced at him, as she had never done before; her look was that of a mother, a sad look of love mingled with fear for the beloved.

"Go, dear one. I am tired; I need a rest," she said to him, as she rose without looking at him. He went away submissively.

For some time after this incident her attitude toward him was stricter and more sincere, as though she pitied him, but later their relations assumed the old form of the cat-and-mouse play.

Foma's relation toward Medinskaya could not escape his godfather's notice, and one day the old man asked him, with a malicious grimace:

"Foma! You had better feel your head more often so that you may not lose it by accident."

"What do you mean?" asked Foma.

"I speak of Sonka. You are going to see her too often."

"What has that to do with you?" said Foma, rather rudely. "And why do you call her Sonka?"

"It's nothing to me. I would lose nothing if you should be fleeced. And as to calling her Sonka—everybody knows that is her name. So does everybody know that she likes to rake up the fire with other people's hands."

"She is clever!" announced Foma, firmly, frowning and hiding his hands in his pockets. "She is intelligent."

"Clever, that's true! How cleverly she arranged that entertainment; there was an income of two thousand four hundred roubles, the

239

expenses—one thousand nine hundred; the expenses really did not even amount to a thousand roubles, for everybody does everything for her for nothing. Intelligent! She will educate you, and especially will those idlers that run around her."

"They're not idlers, they are clever people!" replied Foma, angrily, contradicting himself now. "And I learn from them. What am I? I know nothing. What was I taught? While there they speak of everything—and each one has his word to say. Do not hinder me from being like a man."

"Pooh! How you've learned to speak! With so much anger, like the hail striking against the roof! Very well, be like a man, but in order to be like a man it might be less dangerous for you to go to the tavern; the people there are after all better than Sophya's people. And you, young man, you should have learned to discriminate one person from another. Take Sophya, for instance: What does she represent? An insect for the adornment of nature and nothing more!"

Intensely agitated, Foma set his teeth together and walked away from Mayakin, thrusting his hands still deeper into his pockets. But the old man soon started again a conversation about Medinskaya.

They were on their way back from the bay after an inspection of the steamers, and seated in a big and commodious sledge, they were enthusiastically discussing business matters in a friendly way. It was in March. The water under the sledge-runners was bubbling, the snow was already covered with a rather dirty fleece, and the sun shone warmly and merrily in the clear sky.

"Will you go to your lady as soon as we arrive?" asked Mayakin, unexpectedly, interrupting their business talk.

"I will," said Foma, shortly, and with displeasure,

"Mm. Tell me, how often do you give her presents?" asked Mayakin, plainly and somewhat intimately.

"What presents? What for?" Foma wondered.

"You make her no presents? You don't say. Does she live with you then merely so, for love's sake?"

Foma boiled up with anger and shame, turned abruptly toward the old man and said reproachfully:

"Eh! You are an old man, and yet you speak so that it is a shame to listen to you! To say such a thing! Do you think she would come down to this?"

Mayakin smacked his lips and sang out in a mournful voice:

"What a blockhead you are! What a fool!" and suddenly grown angry, he spat out: "Shame upon you! All sorts of brutes drank out of the pot, nothing but the dregs remained, and now a fool has made a god unto himself of this dirty pot. Devil! You just go up to her and tell her plainly: 'I want to be your lover. I am a young man, don't charge me much for it.'"

"Godfather!" said Foma, sternly, in a threatening voice, "I cannot bear to hear such words. If it were someone else."

"But who except myself would caution you? Good God!" Mayakin cried out, clasping his hands. "So she has led you by the nose all winter long! What a nose! What a beast she is!"

The old man was agitated; in his voice rang vexation, anger, even tears Foma had never before seen him in such a state, and looking at him, he was involuntarily silent.

"She will ruin you! Oh Lord! The Babylonian prostitute!"

Mayakin's eyes were blinking, his lips were trembling, and in rude, cynical words he began to speak of Medinskaya, irritated, with a wrathful jar in his voice.

Foma felt that the old man spoke the truth. He now began to breathe with difficulty and he felt that his mouth had a dry, bitter taste.

"Very well, father, enough," he begged softly and sadly, turning aside from Mayakin.

"Eh, you ought to get married as soon as possible!" exclaimed the old man with alarm.

"For Christ's sake, do not speak," uttered Foma in a dull voice.

Mayakin glanced at his godson and became silent. Foma's face looked drawn; he grew pale, and there was a great deal of painful, bitter stupor in his half-open lips and in his sad look. On the right and on the left of the road a field stretched itself, covered here and there with patches of winter-raiment. Rooks were hopping busily about over the black spots, where the snow had melted. The water under the sledge-runners was splashing, the muddy snow was kicked up by the hoofs of the horses.

"How foolish man is in his youth!" exclaimed Mayakin, in a low voice. Foma did not look at him.

"Before him stands the stump of a tree, and yet he sees the snout of a beast—that's how he frightens himself. Oh, oh!"

"Speak more plainly," said Foma, sternly.

"What is there to say? The thing is clear: girls are cream; women are milk; women are near, girls are far. Consequently, go to Sonka, if you cannot do without it, and tell her plainly. That's how the matter stands. Fool! If she is a sinner, you can get her more easily. Why are you so angry, then? Why so bristled up?"

"You don't understand," said Foma, in a low voice.

"What is it I do not understand? I understand everything!"

"The heart. Man has a heart," sighed the youth.

Mayakin winked his eyes and said:

"Then he has no mind."

CHAPTER VI

WHEN Foma arrived in the city he was seized with sad, revengeful anger. He was burning with a passionate desire to insult Medinskaya, to abuse her. His teeth firmly set together, his hands thrust deep into his pockets, he walked for a few hours in succession about the deserted rooms of his house, he sternly knitted his brow, and constantly threw his chest forward. His breast was too narrow to hold his heart, which was filled with wrath. He stamped the floor with heavy and measured steps, as though he were forging his anger.

"The vile wretch—disguised herself as an angel!" Pelageya vividly arose in his memory, and he whispered malignantly and bitterly:

"Though a fallen woman, she is better. She did not play the hypocrite. She at once unfolded her soul and her body, and her heart is surely just as her breast—white and sound."

Sometimes Hope would whisper timidly in his ear:

"Perhaps all that was said of her was a lie."

But he recalled the eager certainty of his godfather, and the power of his words, and this thought perished. He set his teeth more firmly together and threw his chest still more forward. Evil thoughts like splinters of wood stuck into his heart, and his heart was shattered by the acute pain they caused.

By disparaging Medinskaya, Mayakin made her more accessible to his godson, and Foma soon understood this. A few days passed, and Foma's agitated feelings became calm, absorbed by the spring business cares. The sorrow for the loss of the individual deadened the spite he owed the woman, and the thought of the woman's accessibility increased his passion for her. And somehow, without perceiving it himself, he suddenly understood and resolved that he ought to go up to Sophya Pavlovna and tell her plainly, openly, just what he wanted of her—that's all! He even felt a certain joy at this resolution, and he boldly started off to Medinskaya, thinking on the way only how to tell her best all that was necessary.

The servants of Medinskaya were accustomed to his visits, and to his question whether the lady was at home the maid replied:

"Please go into the drawing-room. She is there alone."

He became somewhat frightened, but noticing in the mirror his stately figure neatly clad with a frock-coat, and his swarthy, serious face in a frame of a downy black beard, set with large dark eyes—he raised his shoulders and confidently stepped forward through the parlour. Strange sounds of a string instrument were calmly floating to meet him; they seemed to burst into quiet, cheerless laughter, complaining of something, tenderly stirring the heart, as though imploring it for attention and having no hopes of getting it. Foma did not like to hear music—it always filled him with sadness. Even when the "machine" in the tavern played some sad tune, his heart filled with melancholy anguish, and he would either ask them to stop the "machine" or would go away some little distance feeling that he could not listen calmly to these tunes without words, but full of lamentation and tears. And now he involuntarily stopped short at the door of the drawing-room.

A curtain of long strings of parti-coloured glass beads hung over the door. The beads had been strung so as to form a fantastic figure of some kind of plants; the strings were quietly shaking and it seemed that pale shadows of flowers were soaring in the air. This transparent curtain did not hide the inside of the drawing-room from Foma's eyes. Seated on a couch in her favourite corner, Medinskaya played the mandolin. A large Japanese umbrella, fastened up to the wall, shaded the little woman in black by its mixture of colours; the high bronze lamp under a red lamp-shade cast on her the light of sunset. The mild sounds of the slender strings were trembling sadly in the narrow room, which was filled with

244

soft and fragrant twilight. Now the woman lowered the mandolin on her knees and began running her fingers over the strings, also to examine fixedly something before her. Foma heaved a sigh.

A soft sound of music soared about Medinskaya, and her face was forever changing as though shadows were falling on it, falling and melting away under the flash of her eyes.

Foma looked at her and saw that when alone she was not quite so good-looking as in the presence of people—now her face looked older, more serious—her eyes had not the expression of kindness and gentleness, they had a rather tired and weary look. And her pose, too, was weary, as if the woman were about to stir but could not. Foma noticed that the feeling which prompted him to come to her was now changing in his heart into some other feeling. He scraped with his foot along the floor and coughed.

"Who is that?" asked the woman, starting with alarm. And the strings trembled, issuing an alarmed sound.

"It is I," said Foma, pushing aside the strings of the beads.

"Ah! But how quietly you've entered. I am glad to see you. Be seated! Why didn't you come for such a long time?"

Holding out her hand to him, she pointed with the other at a small armchair beside her, and her eyes were gaily smiling.

"I was out on the bay inspecting my steamers," said Foma, with exaggerated ease, moving his armchair nearer to the couch.

"Is there much snow yet on the fields?"

"As much as one may want. But it is already melting considerably. There is water on the roads everywhere."

He looked at her and smiled. Evidently Medinskaya noticed the ease of his behaviour and something new in his smile, for she adjusted her dress and drew farther away from him. Their eyes met—and Medinskaya lowered her head.

"Melting!" said she, thoughtfully, examining the ring on her little finger.

"Ye-es, streams everywhere." Foma informed her, admiring his boots.

"That's good. Spring is coming."

Now it won't be delayed long."

"Spring is coming," repeated Medinskaya, softly, as if listening to the sounds of her words.

"People will start to fall in love," said Foma, with a smile, and for some reason or other firmly rubbed his hands.

"Are you preparing yourself?" asked Medinskaya, drily.

"I have no need for it. I have been ready long ago. I am already in love for all my life."

She cast a glance at him, and started to play again, looking at the strings and saying pensively:

"Spring. How good it is that you are but beginning to live. The heart is full of power, and there is nothing dark in it."

"Sophya Pavlovna!" exclaimed Foma, softly.She interrupted him with a caressing gesture.

"Wait, dearest! Today I can tell you something good. Do you know, a person who has lived long has such moments that when he looks into his heart he unexpectedly finds there something long forgotten. For years it lay somewhere in the depth of his heart, but lost none of the fragrance of youth, and when memory touches it, then spring comes over that person, breathing upon him the vivifying freshness of the morning of his life. This is good, though it is very sad."

The strings trembled and wept under the touch of her fingers, and it seemed to Foma that their sounds and the soft voice of the woman were touching his heart gently and caressingly. But, still firm in his decision, he listened to her words and, not knowing their meaning, thought:

"You may speak! And I won't believe anything you may say."

This thought irritated him. And he felt sorry that he could not listen to her words as attentively and trustfully as before.

"Are you thinking of how it is necessary to live?" asked the woman.

"Sometimes I think of it, and then I forget again. I have no time for it!" said Foma and smiled. "And then, what is there to think of? It is simple. You see how others live. Well, consequently, you must imitate them."

"Ah, don't do this! Spare yourself. You are so good! There is something peculiar in you; what—I do not know. But it can be felt. And it seems to me, it will be very hard for you to get along in life. I am sure, you will not go along the usual way of the people of your circle. No! You cannot be pleased with a life which is wholly devoted to gain, to hunts after the rouble, to this business of yours. Oh, no! I know, you will have a desire for something else, will you not?"

She spoke quickly, with a look of alarm in her eyes. Looking at her, Foma thought:

"What is she driving at?"

And he answered her slowly:

"Perhaps I will have a desire for something else. Perhaps I have it already."

Drawing up closer to him, she looked into his face and spoke convincingly:

"Listen! Do not live like all other people! Arrange your life somehow differently. You are strong, young. You are good!"

"And if I am good then there must be good for me!" exclaimed Foma, feeling that he was seized with agitation, and that his heart was beginning to beat with anxiety.

"Ah, but that is not the case! Here on earth it is worse for the good people than for the bad ones!" said Medinskaya, sadly.

And again the trembling notes of music began to dance at the touch of her fingers. Foma felt that if he did not start to say at once what was necessary, he would tell her nothing later.

"God bless me!" he said to himself, and in a lowered voice, strengthening his heart, began:

"Sophya Pavlovna! Enough! I have something to say. I have come to tell you: 'Enough!' We must deal fairly, openly. At first you have attracted me to yourself, and now you are fencing away from me. I cannot understand what you say. My mind is dull, but I can feel that you wish to hide yourself. I can see it—do you understand now what brought me here?"

His eyes began to flash and with each word his voice became warmer and louder. She moved her body forward and said with alarm:

"Oh, cease."

"No, I won't, I will speak!"

"I know what you want to say."

"You don't know it all!" said Foma, threateningly, rising to his feet. "But I know everything about you—everything."

"Yes? Then the better it is for me," said Medinskaya, calmly.

She also arose from the couch, as though about to go away somewhere, but after a few seconds she again seated herself on the couch. Her face was serious, her lips were tightly compressed, but her eyes were lowered, and Foma could not see their expression. He thought that when he told her, "I know everything about you!" she would be frightened, she would feel ashamed and confused, would ask his forgiveness for having made sport of him. Then he would embrace her and forgive her. But that was not the case; it was he who was confused by her calmness. He looked at her, searching for words to resume his speech, but found them not.

"It is better," she repeated firmly and drily. "So you have learned everything, have you? And, of course, you've censured me, as I deserve. I understand. I am guilty before you. But no, I cannot justify myself."

She became silent and suddenly, lifting her hands with a nervous gesture, clasped her head, and began to adjust her hair.

Foma heaved a deep sigh. Her words had killed in him a certain hope—a hope, whose presence in his heart he only felt now that it was dead. And shaking his head, he said, with bitter reproach:

"There was a time when I looked at you and thought, 'How beautiful she is, how good, the dove!' And now you say yourself, 'I am guilty.' Ah!"

The voice of the youth broke down. And the woman began to laugh softly.

"How fine and how ridiculous you are, and what a pity that you cannot understand all this!"

The youth looked at her, feeling himself disarmed by her caressing words and melancholy smile. That cold, harsh something, which he had in his heart against her, was now melting before the warm light of her eyes. The woman now seemed to him small, defenseless, like a child. She was saying something in a gentle voice as though imploring, and forever smiling, but he paid no attention to her words.

"I've come to you," said he, interrupting her words, "without pity. I meant to tell you everything. And yet I said nothing. I don't feel like doing it. My heart sank. You are breathing upon me so strangely. Eh, I should not have seen you! What are you to me? It would be better for me to go away, it seems."

"Wait, dearest, don't go away!" said the woman, hastily, holding out her hand to him. "Why so severe? Do not be angry at me! What am I to you? You need a different friend, a woman just as simple-minded and sound-souled as you are. She must be gay, healthy. I—I am already an old woman. I am forever worrying. My life is so empty and so weary, so empty! Do you know, when a person has grown accustomed to live merrily, and then cannot be merry, he feels bad! He desires to live cheerfully, he desires to laugh, yet he does not laugh—it is life that is laughing at him. And as to men. Listen! Like a mother, I advise you, I beg and implore you—obey no one except your own heart! Live in accordance with its promptings. Men know nothing, they cannot tell you anything that is true. Do not heed them."

Trying to speak as plainly and intelligibly as possible, she was agitated, and her words came incoherently hurriedly one after another. A pitiful smile played on her lips all the time, and her face was not beautiful.

"Life is very strict. It wants all people to submit to its requests, and only the very strong ones can resist it with impunity. It is yet questionable whether they can do it! Oh, if you knew how hard it is to live. Man goes so far that he begins to fear his own self. He is split into judge and criminal—he judges his own self and seeks justification before himself. And he is willing to pass days and nights with those that despise him, and that are repulsive to him—just to avoid being alone with himself."

Foma lifted his head and said distrustfully, with surprise:

"I cannot understand what it is! Lubov also says the same."

"Which Lubov? What does she say?"

"My foster-sister. She says the same,—she is forever complaining of life. It is impossible to live, she says."

"Oh, she is yet young! And it is a great happiness that she already speaks of this."

"Happiness!" Foma drawled out mockingly. "It must be a fine happiness that makes people sigh and complain."

"You'd better listen to complaints. There is always much wisdom in these complaints of men. Oh! There is more wisdom in these complaints than anywhere else. You listen to these,—they will teach you to find your way."

Foma heard the woman's voice, which sounded convincing; and perplexed, looked about him. Everything had long been familiar to him, but today it looked somewhat new to him. A mass of trifles filled the room, all the walls were covered with pictures and shelves, bright and beautiful objects were staring from every corner. The reddish light of the lamp filled one with melancholy. Twilight wrapped everything in the room, and only here and there the gold of the frames, or the white spots of marble flashed dimly. Heavy fabrics were motionlessly hanging before the doors. All this embarrassed and almost choked Foma; he felt as though he had lost his way. He was sorry for the woman. But she also irritated him.

"Do you hear how I speak to you? I wish I were your mother, or your sister. Never before did anybody awaken in me so warm and kindred a feeling as you have done. And you, you look at me in such an unfriendly way. Do you believe me? Yes? No?"

He looked at her and said with a sigh:

"I don't know. I used to believe you."

"And now?" she asked hastily.

"And now—it is best for me to go! I don't understand anything, and yet I long to understand. I do not even understand myself. On my way to you I knew what to say, and here all is confused. You have put me up on the rack, you have set me on edge. And then you tell me—'I am as a mother to you'—which means—begone!"

"Understand me, I feel sorry for you!" the woman exclaimed softly.

Foma's irritation against her was growing stronger and stronger, and as he went on speaking to her, his words became absurd. While he spoke, he kept on moving his shoulders as though tearing something that entangled him.

"Sorry? What for? I do not need it. Eh, I cannot speak well! It is bad to be dumb. But—I would have told you! You did not treat me properly—indeed, why have you so enticed a man? Am I a plaything for you?"

"I only wanted to see you by my side," said the woman simply, in a guilty voice.

He did not hear these words.

"And when it came to the point, you were frightened and you shut yourself off from me. You began to repent. Ha, ha! Life is bad! And why are you always complaining of some life? What life? Man is life, and except man there is no life. You have invented some other monster. You have done this to deceive the eye, to justify yourself. You do some mischief, you lose yourself in different inventions and foolishnesses and

251

then you sigh! Ah, life! Oh, life! And have you not done it yourself? And covering yourself with complaints, you confuse others. You have lost your way, very well, but why do you want to lead me astray? Is it wickedness that speaks in you: 'I feel bad,' you say, 'let him also feel bad—there, I'll besprinkle his heart with my poisonous tears!' Isn't that so? Eh! God has given you the beauty of an angel, but your heart—where is it?"

Standing before her, he trembled in every limb, and examined her from head to foot with reproachful looks. Now his words came freely from his heart, he spoke not loud, but with power and pleasure. Her head raised, the woman stared into his face, with wide-open eyes. Her lips were trembling and deep wrinkles appeared at the corners of her mouth.

"A beautiful person should lead a good life. While of you they say things." Foma's voice broke down; he raised his hand and concluded in a dull voice:

"Goodbye!"

"Goodbye!" said Medinskaya, softly.

He did not give her his hand, but, turning abruptly, he walked away from her. But already at the door he felt that he was sorry for her, and he glanced at her across his shoulder. There, in the corner, she stood alone, her head bent, her hands hanging motionless.

Understanding that he could not leave her thus, he became confused, and said softly, but without repenting:

"Perhaps I said something offensive—forgive me! For after all I love you," and he heaved a deep sigh.

The woman burst into soft, nervous laughter.

"No, you have not offended me. God speed you."

"Well, then goodbye!" repeated Foma in a still lower voice.

"Yes," replied the woman, also in a low voice.

Foma pushed aside the strings of beads with his hand; they swung back noisily and touched his cheeks. He shuddered at this cold touch and went out, carrying away a heavy, perplexed feeling in his breast, with his heart beating as though a soft but strong net were cast over it.

252

It was night by this time; the moon was shining and the frost covered the puddles with coatings of dull silver. Foma walked along the sidewalk, he broke these with his cane, and they cracked mournfully. The shadows of the houses fell on the road in black squares, and the shadows of the trees—in wonderful patterns. And some of them looked like thin hands, helplessly clutching the ground.

"What is she doing now?" thought Foma, picturing to himself the woman, alone, in the corner of a narrow room, in the reddish half-light.

"It is best for me to forget her," he decided. But he could not forget her; she stood before him, provoking in him now intense pity, now irritation and even anger. And her image was so clear, and the thoughts of her were so painful, as though he was carrying this woman in his breast. A cab was coming from the opposite side, filling the silence of the night with the jarring of the wheels on the cobble-stones and with their creaking on the ice. When the cab was passing across a moonlit strip, the noise was louder and more brisk, and in the shadows it was heavier and duller. The driver and the passenger in it were shaking and hopping about; for some reason or other they both bent forward and together with the horse formed one big, black mass. The street was speckled with spots of light and shade, but in the distance the darkness seemed thick as though the street were fenced off by a wall, rising from earth to the skies. Somehow it occurred to Foma that these people did not know whither they were going. And he, too, did not know whither he was going. His house rose before his imagination—six big rooms, where he lived alone. Aunt Anfisa had gone to the cloister, perhaps never to return—she might die there. At home were Ivan, the old deaf dvornik, the old maid, Sekleteya, his cook and servant, and a black, shaggy dog, with a snout as blunt as that of a sheat-fish. And the dog, too, was old.

"Perhaps I really ought to get married," thought Foma, with a sigh.

But the very thought of how easy it was for him to get married made him ill at ease, and even ridiculous in his own eyes. It were but necessary to ask his godfather tomorrow for a bride,—and before a month would

253

pass, a woman would live with him in his house. And she would be near him day and night. He would say to her: "Let's go for a walk!" and she would go. He would tell her: "Let's go to sleep!" and again she would go. Should she desire to kiss him, she would kiss him, even though he did not like it. And if he should tell her: "Go away, I don't want it," she would feel offended. What would he speak to her about? What would she tell him? He thought and pictured to himself young ladies of his acquaintance, daughters of merchants. Some of them were very pretty, and he knew that any one of them would marry him willingly. But he did not care to have any of them as his wife. How awkward and shameful it must be when a girl becomes a wife. And what does the newly-married couple say to each other after the wedding, in the bedroom? Foma tried to think what he would say in such a case, and confused, he began to laugh, finding no appropriate words. Then he recalled Luba Mayakin. She would surely be first to say something, uttering some unintelligible words, which were foreign to herself. Somehow it seemed to him that all her words were foreign, and she did not speak as was proper for a girl of her age, appearance and descent.

And here his thoughts rested on Lubov's complaints. His gait became slower; he was now astounded by the fact that all the people that were near to him and with whom he talked a great deal, always spoke to him of life. His father, his aunt, his godfather, Lubov, Sophya Pavlovna, all these either taught him to understand life, or complained of it. He recalled the words said by the old man on the steamer about Fate, and many other remarks on life, reproaches and bitter complaints against it, which he happened to hear from all sorts of people.

"What does it mean?" he thought, "what is life, if it is not man? And man always speaks as if life were something else, something outside of man, and that something hinders him from living. Perhaps it is the devil?"

A painful feeling of fear fell on the youth; he shuddered and hastily looked around. The street was deserted and quiet; the dark windows of the houses stared dimly into the dark of night, and along the walls and fences Foma's shadow followed him.

"Driver!" he cried out aloud, quickening his steps. The shadow started and crawled after him, frightened, black, silent. It seemed to Foma that there was a cold breath behind him, and that something huge, invisible, and terrible was overtaking him. Frightened, he almost ran to meet the cab, which appeared noisily from the darkness, and when he seated himself in the cab, he dared not look back, though he wished to do so.

CHAPTER VII

ABOUT a week passed since Foma spoke to Medinskaya. And her image stood fixedly before Foma by night and by day, awakening in his heart a gnawing feeling of anxiety. He longed to go to her, and was so much afflicted over her that even his bones were aching from the desire of his heart to be near her again. But he was sternly silent; he frowned and did not care to yield to this desire, industriously occupying himself with his affairs and provoking in himself a feeling of anger against the woman. He felt that if he went up to her, he would no longer find her to be the same as he had left her; something must have changed within her after that conversation, and she would no longer receive him as cordially as before, would not smile at him the clear smile that used to awaken in him strange thoughts and hopes. Fearing that all this was lost and that something else must have taken its place, he restrained himself and suffered.

His work and his longing for the woman did not hinder him from thinking of life. He did not philosophize about this enigma, which was already stirring a feeling of alarm in his heart; he was not able to argue, but he began to listen attentively to everything that men said of life, and he tried to remember their words. They did not make anything clear to him; nay, they increased his perplexity and prompted him to regard them suspiciously. They were clever, cunning and sensible—he saw it; in dealings with them it was always necessary to be on one's guard; he knew already that in important matters none of them spoke as they thought. And watching them carefully, he felt that their sighs and their complaints of life awakened in him distrust. Silently he looked at everybody with suspicion, and a thin wrinkle masked his forehead.

One morning his godfather said to him on the Exchange:

"Anany has arrived. He would like to see you. Go up to him toward evening, and see that you hold your tongue. Anany will try to loosen it in order to make you talk on business matters. He is cunning, the old devil; he is a holy fox; he'll lift his eyes toward heaven, and meanwhile will put his paw into your pocket and grab your purse. Be on your guard."

"Do we owe him anything?" asked Foma.

"Of course! We haven't paid yet for the barge, and then fifty five-fathom beams were taken from him not long ago. If he wants everything at once—don't give. A rouble is a sticky thing; the longer it turns about in your hand, the more copecks will stick to it. A rouble is like a good pigeon—it goes up in the air, you turn around and see—it has brought a whole flock with it into the pigeon-house."

"But how can we help paying it now, if he demands it?"

"Let him cry and ask for it—and you roar—but don't give it to him."

I'll go up there soon."

Anany Savvich Shchurov was a rich lumber-dealer, had a big saw-mill, built barges and ran rafts. He had had dealings with Ignat, and Foma had more than once seen this tall, heavily-bearded, long-armed, white-haired old man, who kept himself as erect as a pine-tree. His big, handsome figure, his open face and his clear eyes called forth in Foma a feeling of respect for Shchurov, although he heard it rumoured that this lumber-dealer had gained his wealth not by honest toil and that he was leading an evil life at home, in an obscure village of the forest district; and Ignat had told Foma that when Shchurov was young and was but a poor peasant, he sheltered a convict in the bath-house, in his garden, and that there the convict made counterfeit money for him. Since that time Anany began to grow rich. One day his bathhouse burned down, and in the ashes they discovered the corpse of a man with a fractured skull. There was a rumour in the village that Shchurov himself had killed his workman—killed and then burned him. Such things had happened more than once with the good-looking old man; but similar rumours were on foot with reference to many a rich man in town—they had all, it was said, hoarded up their millions by way of robberies, murders and, mainly, by passing counterfeit money. Foma had heard such stories in his childhood and he never before considered whether they were true or not.

He also knew that Shchurov had got rid of two wives—one of them died during the first night of the wedding, in Anany's embraces. Then he took his son's wife away from him, and his son took to drink for grief and would have perished in drunkenness had he not come to himself in time and gone off to save himself in a hermitage, in Irgiz. And when his mistress-daughter-in-law had passed away, Shchurov took into his house a dumb beggar-girl, who was living with him to this day, and who had recently borne him a dead child. On his way to the hotel, where Anany stayed, Foma involuntarily recalled all this, and felt that Shchurov had become strangely interesting to him.

When Foma opened the door and stopped respectfully on the threshold of the small room, whose only window overlooked the rusty roof of the neighbouring house, he noticed that the old Shchurov had just risen from sleep, and sitting on his bed, leaning his hands against it, he stared at the ground; and he was so bent that his long, white beard fell over his knees. But even bent, he was large.

"Who entered?" asked Anany in a hoarse and angry voice, without lifting his head.

"I. How do you do, Anany Savvich?"

The old man raised his head slowly and, winking his large eyes, looked at Foma.

"Ignat's son, is that right?"

"The same."

"Well, come over here, sit down by the window. Let me see how you've grown up. Will you not have a glass of tea with me?"

"I wouldn't mind."

"Waiter!" cried the old man, expanding his chest, and, taking his beard in his hand, he began to examine Foma in silence. Foma also looked at him stealthily.

The old man's lofty forehead was all covered with wrinkles, and its skin was dark. Gray, curly locks covered his temples and his sharp-pointed ears; his calm blue eyes lent the upper part of his face a wise and good expression. But his cheeks and his lips were thick and red, and seemed out of place on his face. His thin, long nose was turned downward as though it wished to hide itself in his white moustache; the old man moved his lips, and from beneath them small, yellow teeth were gleaming. He had on a pink calico shirt, a silk belt around his waist, and black, loose trousers, which were tucked into his boots. Foma stared at his lips and thought that the old man was surely such as he was said to be.

"As a boy you looked more like your father," said Shchurov suddenly, and sighed. Then, after a moment's silence, he asked: "Do you remember your father? Do you ever pray for him? You must, you must pray!" he went on, after he heard Foma's brief answer. "Ignat was a terrible sinner, and he died without repentance, taken unawares. He was a great sinner!"

"He was not more sinful than others," replied Foma, angrily, offended in his father's behalf.

"Than who, for instance?" demanded Shchurov, strictly.

"Are there not plenty of sinners?"

"There is but one man on earth more sinful than was the late Ignat— and that is that cursed heathen, your godfather Yashka," ejaculated the old man.

"Are you sure of it?" inquired Foma, smiling.

"I? Of course, I am!" said Shchurov, confidently, nodding his head, and his eyes became somewhat darker. "I will also appear before the Lord, and that not sinless. I shall bring with me a heavy burden before His holy countenance. I have been pleasing the devil myself, only I trust to God for His mercy, while Yashka believes in nothing, neither in dreams, nor in the singing of birds. Yashka does not believe in God, this I know! And for his non-belief he will yet receive his punishment on earth."

"Are you sure of this, too?"

"Yes, I am. And don't you think I also know that you consider it ludicrous to listen to me. What a sagacious fellow, indeed! But he who has committed many sins is always wise. Sin is a teacher. That's why Yashka Mayakin is extraordinarily clever."

Listening to the old man's hoarse and confident voice, Foma thought:

"He is scenting death, it seems."

The waiter, a small man, with a face which was pale and characterless, brought in the samovar and quickly hastened out of the room, with short steps. The old man was undoing some bundles on the window-sill and said, without looking at Foma:

"You are bold, and the look of your eyes is dark. Before, there used to be more light-eyed people, because then the souls used to be brighter. Before, everything was simpler—both the people and the sins, and now everything has become complicated. Eh, eh!"

He made tea, seated himself opposite Foma and went on again:

"Your father at your age was a water-pumper and stayed with the fleet near our village. At your age Ignat was as clear to me as glass. At a single glance you could tell what sort of a man he was. While you—here I am looking at you, but cannot see what you are. Who are you? You don't know it yourself, my lad, and that's why you'll suffer. Everybody nowadays must suffer, because they do not know themselves. Life is a mass of wind-fallen trees, and you must know how to find your way through it. Where is it? All are going astray, and the devil is delighted. Are you married?"

"Not yet," said Foma.

"There again, you are not married, and yet, I'm quite sure, you are not pure any longer. Well, are you working hard in your business?"

"Sometimes. Meanwhile I am with my godfather."

"What sort of work is it you have nowadays?" said the old man, shaking his head, and his eyes were constantly twinkling, now turning dark, now brightening up again. "You have no labour now! In former years the merchant travelled with horses on business. Even at night, in snowstorms, he used to go! Murderers used to wait for him on the road and kill him. And he died a martyr, washing his sins away with blood. Now they travel by rail; they are sending telegrams, or they've even invented something that a man may speak in his office and you can hear him five miles away. There the devil surely has a hand in it! A man sits, without motion, and commits sins merely because he feels lonesome, because he has nothing to do: the machine does all his work. He has no work, and without toil man is ruined! He has provided himself with machines and thinks it is good! While the machine is the devil's trap for you. He thus catches you in it. While toiling, you find no time for sin, but having a machine—you have freedom. Freedom kills a man, even as the sunbeams kill the worm, the dweller of the depth of earth. Freedom kills man!"

And pronouncing his words distinctly and positively, the old Anany struck the table four times with his finger. His face beamed triumphantly, his chest rose high, and over it the silver hair of his beard shook noiselessly. Dread fell on Foma as he looked at him and listened to his words, for there was a ring of firm faith in them, and it was the power of this faith that confused Foma. He had already forgotten all he knew about the old man, all of which he had but a while ago believed to be true.

"Whoever gives freedom to his body, kills his soul!" said Anany, looking at Foma so strangely as if he saw behind him somebody, who was grieved and frightened by his words; and whose fear and pain delighted him. "All you people of today will perish through freedom. The devil has captured you—he has taken toil away from you, and slipped machines and telegrams into your hands. How freedom eats into the souls of men! Just tell me, why are the children worse than their fathers? Because of their freedom, yes. That's why they drink and lead depraved lives with women. They have less strength because they have less work, and they have not the spirit of cheerfulness because they have no worries. Cheerfulness comes in time of rest, while nowadays no one is getting tired."

"Well," said Foma, softly, "they were leading depraved lives and drinking just as much in former days as now, I suppose."

"Do you know it? You should keep silence!" cried Anany, flashing his eyes sternly. "In former days man had more strength, and the sins were according to his strength. While you, of today, have less strength, and more sins, and your sins are more disgusting. Then men were like oak-trees. And God's judgment will also be in accordance with their strength. Their bodies will be weighed, and angels will measure their blood, and the angels of God will see that the weight of the sins does not exceed the weight of the body and the blood. Do you understand? God will not condemn the wolf for devouring a sheep, but if a miserable rat should be guilty of the sheep's death, God will condemn the rat!"

"How can a man tell how God will judge man?" asked Foma, thoughtfully. "A visible trial is necessary."

"Why a visible trial?"

"That people might understand."

"Who, but the Lord, is my judge?"

Foma glanced at the old man and lowering his head, became silent. He again recalled the fugitive convict, who was killed and burnt by Shchurov, and again he believed that it really was so. And the women—his wives and his mistresses—had surely been hastened toward their graves by this old man's caresses; he had crushed them with his bony chest, drunk the sap of their life with these thick lips of his which were scarlet yet from the clotted blood of the women, who died in the embraces of his long sinewy arms. And now, awaiting death, which was already somewhere beside him, he counts his sins, judges others, and perhaps judges himself, and says:

"Who, but the Lord, is my judge?"

"Is he afraid or not?" Foma asked himself and became pensive, stealthily scrutinising the old man.

262

"Yes, my lad! Think," spoke Shchurov, shaking his head, "think, how you are to live. The capital in your heart is small, and your habits are great, see that you are not reduced to bankruptcy before your own self! Ho-ho-ho!"

"How can you tell what and how much I have within my heart?" said Foma, gloomily, offended by his laughter.

"I can see it! I know everything, because I have lived long! Oh-ho-ho! How long I have lived! Trees have grown up and been cut down, and houses built out of them, and even the houses have grown old. While I have seen all this and am still alive, and when, at times, I recall my life, I think, 'Is it possible that one man could accomplish so much? Is it possible that I have witnessed all this?'" The old man glanced at Foma sternly, shook his head and became silent.

It became quiet. Outside the window something was softly rustling on the roof of the house; the rattle of wheels and the muffled sounds of conversation were heard from below, from the street. The samovar on the table sang a sad tune. Shchurov was fixedly staring into his glass of tea, stroking his beard, and one could hear that something rattled in his breast, as if some burden was turning about in it.

"It's hard for you to live without your father, isn't it?" said he.

"I am getting used to it," replied Foma.

"You are rich, and when Yakov dies, you will be richer still. He'll leave everything to you."

"I don't need it."

"To whom else should he leave it? He has but one daughter, and you ought to marry that daughter, and that she is your godsister and foster-sister—no matter! That can be arranged—and then you would be married. What good is there in the life you are now leading? I suppose you are forever running about with the girls?"

"No."

"You don't say! Eh, eh, eh! the merchant is passing away. A certain forester told me—I don't know whether he lied or not—that in former days the dogs were wolves, and then degenerated into dogs. It is the same with our calling; we will soon also be dogs. We will take up science, put stylish hats on our heads, we'll do everything that is necessary in order to lose our features, and there will be nothing by which to distinguish us from other people. It has become a custom to make Gymnasium students of all children. The merchants, the nobles, the commoners—all are adjusted to match the same colour. They dress them in gray and teach them all the same subjects. They grow man even as they grow a tree. Why do they do it? No one knows. Even a log could be told from another by its knot at least, while here they want to plane the people over so that all of them should look alike. The coffin is already waiting for us old people. Ye-es! It may be that about fifty years hence, no one will believe that I lived in this world. I, Anany, the son of Savva, by the surname of Shchurov. So! And that I, Anany, feared no one, save God. And that in my youth I was a peasant, that all the land I possessed then was two desyatins and a quarter; while toward my old age I have hoarded up eleven thousand desyatins, all forests, and perhaps two millions in cash."

"There, they always speak of money!" said Foma, with dissatisfaction. "What joy does man derive from money?" "Mm," bellowed Shchurov. "You will make a poor merchant, if you do not understand the power of money."

"Who does understand it?" asked Foma.

"I!" said Shchurov, with confidence. "And every clever man. Yashka understands it. Money? That is a great deal, my lad! Just spread it out before you and think, 'What does it contain?' Then will you know that all this is human strength, human mind. Thousands of people have put their life into your money and thousands more will do it. And you can throw it all into the fire and see how the money is burning, and at that moment you will consider yourself master."

"But nobody does this."

"Because fools have no money. Money is invested in business. Business gives bread to the masses. And you are master over all those masses.

Wherefore did God create man? That man should pray to Him. He was alone and He felt lonesome, so He began to desire power, and as man was created in the image of the Lord, man also desires power. And what, save money, can give power? That's the way. Well, and you—have you brought me money?"

"No," answered Foma. From the words of the old man Foma's head was heavy and troubled, and he was glad that the conversation had, at last, turned to business matters.

"That isn't right," said Shchurov, sternly knitting his brow. "It is overdue—you must pay.

"You'll get a half of it tomorrow."

"Why a half? Why not all?"

"We are badly in need of money now."

"And haven't you any? But I also need it."

"Wait a little."

"Eh, my lad, I will not wait! You are not your father. Youngsters like you, milksops, are an unreliable lot. In a month you may break up the whole business. And I would be the loser for it. You give me all the money tomorrow, or I'll protest the notes. It wouldn't take me long to do it!"

Foma looked at Shchurov, with astonishment. It was not at all that same old man, who but a moment ago spoke so sagaciously about the devil. Then his face and his eyes seemed different, and now he looked fierce, his lips smiled pitilessly, and the veins on his cheeks, near his nostrils, were eagerly trembling. Foma saw that if he did not pay him at once, Shchurov would indeed not spare him and would dishonour the firm by protesting the notes.

"Evidently business is poor?" grinned Shchurov. "Well, tell the truth—where have you squandered your father's money?"

Foma wanted to test the old man:

"Business is none too brisk," said he, with a frown. "We have no contracts. We have received no earnest money, and so it is rather hard."

"So-o! Shall I help you out?"

"Be so kind. Postpone the day of payment," begged Foma, modestly lowering his eyes.

"Mm. Shall I assist you out of my friendship for your father? Well, be it so, I'll do it."

"And for how long will you postpone it?" inquired Foma.

"For six months."

"I thank you humbly."

"Don't mention it. You owe me eleven thousand six hundred roubles. Now listen: rewrite the notes for the amount of fifteen thousand, pay me the interest on this sum in advance. And as security I'll take a mortgage on your two barges."

Foma rose from the chair and said, with a smile:

"Send me the notes tomorrow. I'll pay you in full."

Shchurov also rose from his chair and, without lowering his eyes at Foma's sarcastic look, said, calmly scratching his chest:

"That's all right."

"Thank you for your kindness."

"That's nothing! You don't give me a chance, or I would have shown you my kindness!" said the old man lazily, showing his teeth.

"Yes! If one should fall into your hands—"

"He'd find it warm—"

"I am sure you'd make it warm for him."

"Well, my lad, that will do!" said Shchurov, sternly. "Though you consider yourself quite clever, it is rather too soon. You've gained nothing, and already you began to boast! But you just win from me—then you may shout for joy. Goodbye. Have all the money for tomorrow."

"Don't let that trouble you. Goodbye!"

"God be with you!"

When Foma came out of the room he heard that the old man gave a slow, loud yawn, and then began to hum in a rather hoarse bass:

"Open for us the doors of mercy. Oh blessed Virgin Mary!"

Foma carried away with him from the old man a double feeling. Shchurov pleased him and at the same time was repulsive to him.

He recalled the old man's words about sin, thought of the power of his faith in the mercy of the Lord, and the old man aroused in Foma a feeling akin to respect.

"He, too, speaks of life; he knows his sins; but does not weep over them, does not complain of them. He has sinned—and he is willing to stand the consequences. Yes. And she?" He recalled Medinskaya, and his heart contracted with pain.

"And she is repenting. It is hard to tell whether she does it purposely, in order to hide from justice, or whether her heart is really aching. 'Who, but the Lord,' says he, 'is to judge me?' That's how it is."

It seemed to Foma that he envied Anany, and the youth hastened to recall Shchurov's attempts to swindle him. This called forth in him an aversion for the old man He could not reconcile his feelings and, perplexed, he smiled.

"Well, I have just been at Shchurov's," he said, coming to Mayakin and seating himself by the table.

Mayakin, in a greasy morning-gown, a counting-board in his hand, began to move about in his leather-covered arm-chair impatiently, and said with animation:

"Pour out some tea for him, Lubava! Tell me, Foma, I must be in the City Council at nine o'clock; tell me all about it, make haste!"

Smiling, Foma related to him how Shchurov suggested to rewrite the notes.

"Eh!" exclaimed Yakov Tarasovich regretfully, with a shake of the head. "You've spoilt the whole mass for me, dear! How could you be so straightforward in your dealings with the man? Psha! The devil drove me to send you there! I should have gone myself. I would have turned him around my finger!"

"Hardly! He says, 'I am an oak.'"

"An oak? And I am a saw. An oak! An oak is a good tree, but its fruits are good for swine only. So it comes out that an oak is simply a blockhead."

"But it's all the same, we have to pay, anyway."

"Clever people are in no hurry about this; while you are ready to run as fast as you can to pay the money. What a merchant you are!"

Yakov Tarasovich was positively dissatisfied with his godson. He frowned and in an angry manner ordered his daughter, who was silently pouring out tea:

"Push the sugar nearer to me. Don't you see that I can't reach it?"

Lubov's face was pale, her eyes seemed troubled, and her hands moved lazily and awkwardly. Foma looked at her and thought:

"How meek she is in the presence of her father."

"What did he speak to you about?" asked Mayakin.

"About sins."

"Well, of course! His own affair is dearest to each and every man. And he is a manufacturer of sins. Both in the galleys and in hell they have long been weeping and longing for him, waiting for him impatiently."

"He speaks with weight," said Foma, thoughtfully, stirring his tea.

"Did he abuse me?" inquired Mayakin, with a malicious grimace.

"Somewhat."

"And what did you do?"

"I listened."

"Mm! And what did you hear?"

"'The strong,' he says, 'will be forgiven; but there is no forgiveness for the weak.'"

"Just think of it! What wisdom! Even the fleas know that."

For some reason or another, the contempt with which Mayakin regarded Shchurov, irritated Foma, and, looking into the old man's face, he said with a grin:

"But he doesn't like you."

"Nobody likes me, my dear," said Mayakin, proudly. "There is no reason why they should like me. I am no girl. But they respect me. And they respect only those they fear." And the old man winked at his godson boastfully.

"He speaks with weight," repeated Foma. "He is complaining. 'The real merchant,' says he, 'is passing away. All people are taught the same thing,' he says: 'so that all may be equal, looking alike.'"

"Does he consider it wrong?"

"Evidently so."

"Fo-o-o-l!" Mayakin drawled out, with contempt.

"Why? Is it good?" asked Foma, looking at his godfather suspiciously.

"We do not know what is good; but we can see what is wise. When we see that all sorts of people are driven together in one place and are all inspired there with one and the same idea—then must we acknowledge that it is wise. Because—what is a man in the empire? Nothing more than a simple brick, and all bricks must be of the same size. Do you understand? And those people that are of equal height and weight—I can place in any position I like."

"And whom does it please to be a brick?" said Foma, morosely.

"It is not a question of pleasing, it is a matter of fact. If you are made of hard material, they cannot plane you. It is not everybody's phiz that you can rub off. But some people, when beaten with a hammer, turn into gold. And if the head happens to crack—what can you do? It merely shows it was weak."

"He also spoke about toil. 'Everything,' he says, 'is done by machinery, and thus are men spoiled.'"

"He is out of his wits!" Mayakin waved his hand disdainfully. "I am surprised, what an appetite you have for all sorts of nonsense! What does it come from?"

"Isn't that true, either?" asked Foma, breaking into stern laughter.

"What true thing can he know? A machine! The old blockhead should have thought—'what is the machine made of?' Of iron! Consequently, it need not be pitied; it is wound up—and it forges roubles for you. Without any words, without trouble, you set it into motion and it revolves. While a man, he is uneasy and wretched; he is often very wretched. He wails, grieves, weeps, begs. Sometimes he gets drunk. Ah, how much there is in him that is superfluous to me! While a machine is like an arshin (yardstick), it contains exactly so much as the work required. Well, I am going to dress. It is time."

He rose and went away, loudly scraping with his slippers along the floor. Foma glanced after him and said softly, with a frown:

"The devil himself could not see through all this. One says this, the other, that."

"It is precisely the same with books," said Lubov in a low voice.

Foma looked at her, smiling good-naturedly. And she answered him with a vague smile.

Her eyes looked fatigued and sad.

"You still keep on reading?" asked Foma.

"Yes," the girl answered sadly.

"And are you still lonesome?"

"I feel disgusted, because I am alone. There's no one here to say a word to."

"That's bad."

She said nothing to this, but, lowering her head, she slowly began to finger the fringes of the towel.

"You ought to get married," said Foma, feeling that he pitied her.

"Leave me alone, please," answered Lubov, wrinkling her forehead.

"Why leave you alone? You will get married, I am sure."

"There!" exclaimed the girl softly, with a sigh. "That's just what I am thinking of—it is necessary. That is, I'll have to get married. But how? Do you know, I feel now as though a mist stood between other people and myself—a thick, thick mist!"

270

"That's from your books," Foma interposed confidently.

"Wait! And I cease to understand what is going on about me. Nothing pleases me. Everything has become strange to me. Nothing is as it should be. Everything is wrong. I see it. I understand it, yet I cannot say that it is wrong, and why it is so."

"It is not so, not so," muttered Foma. "That's from your books. Yes. Although I also feel that it's wrong. Perhaps that is because we are so young and foolish."

"At first it seemed to me," said Lubov, not listening to him, "that everything in the books was clear to me. But now—"

"Drop your books," suggested Foma, with contempt.

"Ah, don't say that! How can I drop them? You know how many different ideas there are in the world! O Lord! They're such ideas that set your head afire. According to a certain book everything that exists on earth is rational."

"Everything?" asked Foma.

"Everything! While another book says the contrary is true."

"Wait! Now isn't this nonsense?"

"What were you discussing?" asked Mayakin, appearing at the door, in a long frock-coat and with several medals on his collar and his breast.

"Just so," said Lubov, morosely.

"We spoke about books," added Foma.

"What kind of books?"

"The books she is reading. She read that everything on earth is rational."

"Really!"

"Well, and I say it is a lie!"

"Yes." Yakov Tarasovich became thoughtful, he pinched his beard and winked his eyes a little.

"What kind of a book is it?" he asked his daughter, after a pause.

"A little yellow-covered book," said Lubov, unwillingly.

"Just put that book on my table. That is said not without reflection—everything on earth is rational! See someone thought of it. Yes. It is even very cleverly expressed. And were it not for the fools, it might have been perfectly correct. But as fools are always in the wrong place, it cannot be said that everything on earth is rational. And yet, I'll look at the book. Maybe there is common sense in it. Goodbye, Foma! Will you stay here, or do you want to drive with me?"

"I'll stay here a little longer."

"Very well."

Lubov and Foma again remained alone.

"What a man your father is," said Foma, nodding his head toward the direction of his godfather.

"Well, what kind of a man do you think he is?"

"He retorts every call, and wants to cover everything with his words."

"Yes, he is clever. And yet he does not understand how painful my life is," said Lubov, sadly.

"Neither do I understand it. You imagine too much."

"What do I imagine?" cried the girl, irritated.

"Why, all these are not your own ideas. They are someone else's."

"Someone else's. Someone else's."

She felt like saying something harsh; but broke down and became silent. Foma looked at her and, setting Medinskaya by her side, thought sadly:

"How different everything is—both men and women—and you never feel alike."

They sat opposite each other; both were lost in thought, and neither one looked at the other. It was getting dark outside, and in the room it was quite dark already. The wind was shaking the linden-trees, and their branches seemed to clutch at the walls of the house, as though they felt cold and implored for shelter in the rooms.

"Luba!" said Foma, softly.

She raised her head and looked at him.

"Do you know, I have quarrelled with Medinskaya."

"Why?" asked Luba, brightening up.

"So. It came about that she offended me. Yes, she offended me."

"Well, it's good that you've quarrelled with her," said the girl, approvingly, "for she would have turned your head. She is a vile creature; she is a coquette, even worse than that. Oh, what things I know about her!"

"She's not at all a vile creature," said Foma, morosely. "And you don't know anything about her. You are all lying!"

"Oh, I beg your pardon!"

"No. See here, Luba," said Foma, softly, in a beseeching tone, "don't speak ill of her in my presence. It isn't necessary. I know everything. By God! She told me everything herself."

"Herself!" exclaimed Luba, in astonishment. "What a strange woman she is! What did she tell you?"

"That she is guilty," Foma ejaculated with difficulty, with a wry smile.

"Is that all?" There was a ring of disappointment in the girl's question; Foma heard it and asked hopefully:

"Isn't that enough?"

"What will you do now?"

"That's just what I am thinking about."

"Do you love her very much?"

Foma was silent. He looked into the window and answered confusedly:

"I don't know. But it seems to me that now I love her more than before."

"Than before the quarrel?"

"Yes."

"I wonder how one can love such a woman!" said the girl, shrugging her shoulders.

"Love such a woman? Of course! Why not?" exclaimed Foma.

"I can't understand it. I think, you have become attached to her just because you have not met a better woman."

"No, I have not met a better one!" Foma assented, and after a moment's silence said shyly, "Perhaps there is none better."

"Among our people," Lubov interposed.

"I need her very badly! Because, you see, I feel ashamed before her."

"Why so?"

"Oh, in general, I fear her; that is, I would not want her to think ill of me, as of others. Sometimes I feel disgusted. I think—wouldn't it be a great idea to go out on such a spree that all my veins would start tingling. And then I recall her and I do not venture. And so everything else, I think of her, 'What if she finds it out?' and I am afraid to do it."

"Yes," the girl drawled out thoughtfully, "that shows that you love her. I would also be like this. If I loved, I would think of him—of what he might say . . ."

"And everything about her is so peculiar," Foma related softly. "She speaks in a way all her own. And, God! How beautiful she is! And then she is so small, like a child."

"And what took place between you?" asked Lubov.

Foma moved his chair closer to her, and stooping, he lowered his voice for some reason or other, and began to relate to her all that had taken place between him and Medinskaya. He spoke, and as he recalled the words he said to Medinskaya, the sentiments that called forth the words were also awakened in him.

"I told her, 'Oh, you! why did you make sport of me?'" he said angrily and with reproach.

And Luba, her cheeks aflame with animation, spurred him on, nodding her head approvingly:

"That's it! That's good! Well, and she?"

"She was silent!" said Foma, sadly, with a shrug of the shoulders. "That is, she said different things; but what's the use?"

274

He waved his hand and became silent. Luba, playing with her braid, was also silent. The samovar had already become cold. And the dimness in the room was growing thicker and thicker, outside the window it was heavy with darkness, and the black branches of the linden-trees were shaking pensively.

"You might light the lamp," Foma went on.

"How unhappy we both are," said Luba, with a sigh.

Foma did not like this.

"I am not unhappy," he objected in a firm voice. "I am simply—not yet accustomed to life."

"He who knows not what he is going to do tomorrow, is unhappy," said Luba, sadly. "I do not know it, neither do you. Whither go? Yet go we must, Why is it that my heart is never at ease? Some kind of a longing is always quivering within it."

"It is the same with me," said Foma. "I start to reflect, but on what? I cannot make it clear to myself. There is also a painful gnawing in my heart. Eh! But I must go up to the club."

"Don't go away," Luba entreated.

"I must. Somebody is waiting there for me. I am going. Goodbye!"

"Till we meet again!" She held out her hand to him and sadly looked into his eyes.

"Will you go to sleep now?" asked Foma, firmly shaking her hand.

"I'll read a little."

"You're to your books as the drunkard to his whisky," said the youth, with pity.

"What is there that is better?"

Walking along the street he looked at the windows of the house and in one of them he noticed Luba's face. It was just as vague as everything that the girl told him, even as vague as her longings. Foma nodded his head toward her and with a consciousness of his superiority over her, thought:

"She has also lost her way, like the other one."

At this recollection he shook his head, as though he wanted to frighten away the thought of Medinskaya, and quickened his steps.

Night was coming on, and the air was fresh. A cold, invigorating wind was violently raging in the street, driving the dust along the sidewalks and throwing it into the faces of the passers-by. It was dark, and people were hastily striding along in the darkness. Foma wrinkled his face, for the dust filled his eyes, and thought:

"If it is a woman I meet now—then it will mean that Sophya Pavlovna will receive me in a friendly way, as before. I am going to see her tomorrow. And if it is a man—I won't go tomorrow, I'll wait."

But it was a dog that came to meet him, and this irritated Foma to such an extent that he felt like striking him with his cane.

In the refreshment-room of the club, Foma was met by the jovial Ookhtishchev. He stood at the door, and chatted with a certain stout, whiskered man; but, noticing Gordyeeff, he came forward to meet him, saying, with a smile:

"How do you do, modest millionaire!" Foma rather liked him for his jolly mood, and was always pleased to meet him.

Firmly and kind-heartedly shaking Ookhtishchev's hand, Foma asked him:

"And what makes you think that I am modest?"

"What a question! A man, who lives like a hermit, who neither drinks, nor plays, nor likes any women. By the way, do you know, Foma Ignatyevich, that peerless patroness of ours is going abroad tomorrow for the whole summer?"

"Sophya Pavlovna?" asked Foma, slowly. "Of course! The sun of my life is setting. And, perhaps, of yours as well?"

Ookhtishchev made a comical, sly grimace and looked into Foma's face.

And Foma stood before him, feeling that his head was lowering on his breast, and that he was unable to hinder it.

"Yes, the radiant Aurora."

276

"Is Medinskaya going away?" a deep bass voice asked. "That's fine! I am glad."

"May I know why?" exclaimed Ookhtishchev. Foma smiled sheepishly and stared in confusion at the whiskered man, Ookhtishchev's interlocutor.

That man was stroking his moustache with an air of importance, and deep, heavy, repulsive words fell from his lips on Foma's ears.

"Because, you see, there will be one co-cot-te less in town."

"Shame, Martin Nikitich!" said Ookhtishchev, reproachfully, knitting his brow.

"How do you know that she is a coquette?" asked Foma, sternly, coming closer to the whiskered man. The man measured him with a scornful look, turned aside and moving his thigh, drawled out:

"I didn't say—coquette."

"Martin Nikitich, you mustn't speak that way about a woman who—" began Ookhtishchev in a convincing tone, but Foma interrupted him:

"Excuse me, just a moment! I wish to ask the gentleman, what is the meaning of the word he said?"

And as he articulated this firmly and calmly, Foma thrust his hands deep into his trousers-pockets, threw his chest forward, which at once gave his figure an attitude of defiance. The whiskered gentleman again eyed Foma with a sarcastic smile.

"Gentlemen!" exclaimed Ookhtishchev, softly.

"I said, co-cot-te," pronounced the whiskered man, moving his lips as if he tasted the word. "And if you don't understand it, I can explain it to you."

"You had better explain it," said Foma, with a deep sigh, not lifting his eyes off the man.

Ookhtishchev clasped his hands and rushed aside.

"A cocotte, if you want to know it, is a prostitute," said the whiskered man in a low voice, moving his big, fat face closer to Foma.

Foma gave a soft growl and, before the whiskered man had time to move away, he clutched with his right hand his curly, grayish hair. With a convulsive movement of the hand, Foma began to shake the man's head and his big, solid body; lifting up his left hand, he spoke in a dull voice, keeping time to the punishment:

"Don't abuse a person—in his absence. Abuse him—right in his face—straight in his eyes."

He experienced a burning delight, seeing how comically the stout arms were swinging in the air, and how the legs of the man, whom he was shaking, were bending under him, scraping against the floor. His gold watch fell out of the pocket and dangled on the chain, over his round paunch. Intoxicated with his own strength and with the degradation of the sedate man, filled with the burning feeling of malignancy, trembling with the happiness of revenge, Foma dragged him along the floor and in a dull voice, growled wickedly, in wild joy. In these moments he experienced a great feeling—the feeling of emancipation from the wearisome burden which had long oppressed his heart with grief and morbidness. He felt that he was seized by the waist and shoulders from behind, that someone seized his hand and bent it, trying to break it; that someone was crushing his toes; but he saw nothing, following with his bloodshot eyes the dark, heavy mass moaning and wriggling in his hand. Finally, they tore him away and downed him, and, as through a reddish mist, he noticed before him on the floor, at his feet, the man he had thrashed. Dishevelled, he was moving his legs over the floor, attempting to rise; two dark men were holding him by the arms, his hands were dangling in the air like broken wings, and, in a voice that was choking with sobs, he cried to Foma:

"You mustn't beat me! You mustn't! I have an . . .

Order. You rascal! Oh, rascal! I have children.

Everybody knows me! Scoundrel! Savage, 0—0—0! You may expect a duel!"

And Ookhtishchev spoke loudly in Foma's ear:

"Come, my dear boy, for God's sake!"

"Wait, I'll give him a kick in the face," begged Foma. But he was dragged off. There was a buzzing in his ears, his heart beat fast, but he felt relieved and well. At the entrance of the club he heaved a deep sigh of relief and said to Ookhtishchev, with a good-natured smile:

"I gave him a sound drubbing, didn't I?"

"Listen! "exclaimed the gay secretary, indignantly. "You must pardon me but that was the act of a savage! The devil take it. I never witnessed such a thing before!"

"My dear man!" said Foma, friendly, "did he not deserve the drubbing? Is he not a scoundrel? How can he speak like that behind a person's back? No! Let him go to her and tell it plainly to her alone."

"Excuse me. The devil take you! But it wasn't for her alone that you gave him the drubbing?"

"That is, what do you mea,—not for her alone? For whom then?" asked Foma, amazed.

"For whom? I don't know. Evidently you had old accounts to settle! Oh Lord! That was a scene! I shall not forget it in all my life!"

"He—that man—who is he?" asked Foma, and suddenly burst out laughing. "How he roared, the fool!"

Ookhtishchev looked fixedly into his face and asked:

"Tell me, is it true, that you don't know whom you've thrashed? And is it really only for Sophya Pavlovna?"

"It is, by God!" avowed Foma.

"So, the devil knows what the result may be!" He stopped short, shrugged his shoulders perplexedly, waved his hand, and again began to pace the sidewalk, looking at Foma askance. "You'll pay for this, Foma Ignatyevich."

"Will he take me to court?"

"Would to God he does. He is the Vice-Governor's son-in-law,"

"Is that so?" said Foma, slowly, and made a long face.

"Yes. To tell the truth, he is a scoundrel and a rascal. According to this fact I must admit, that he deserves a drubbing. But taking into consideration the fact that the lady you defended is also—"

"Sir!" said Foma, firmly, placing his hand on Ookhtishchev's shoulder, "I have always liked you, and you are now walking with me. I understand it and can appreciate it. But do not speak ill of her in my presence. Whatever she may be in your opinion, in my opinion, she is dear to me. To me she is the best woman. So I am telling you frankly. Since you are going with me, do not touch her. I consider her good, therefore she is good."

There was great emotion in Foma's voice. Ookhtishchev looked at him and said thoughtfully:

"You are a queer man, I must confess."

"I am a simple man—a savage. I have given him a thrashing and now I feel jolly, and as to the result, let come what will.'

"I am afraid that it will result in something bad. Do you know—to be frank, in return for your frankness—I also like you, although—Mm! It is rather dangerous to be with you. Such a knightly temper may come over you and one may get a thrashing at your hands."

"How so? This was but the first time. I am not going to beat people every day, am I?" said Foma, confused. His companion began to laugh.

"What a monster you are! Listen to me—it is savage to fight—you must excuse me, but it is abominable. Yet, I must tell you, in this case you made a happy selection. You have thrashed a rake, a cynic, a parasite—a man who robbed his nephews with impunity."

"Well, thank God for that!" said Foma with satisfaction. "Now I have punished him a little."

"A little? Very well, let us suppose it was a little. But listen to me, my child, permit me to give you advice. I am a man of the law. He, that Kayazev, is a rascal! True! But you must not thrash even a rascal, for he is a social being, under the paternal custody of the law. You cannot touch him until he transgresses the limits of the penal code. But even then, not you, but we, the judges, will give him his due. While you must have patience."

"And will he soon fall into your hands?" inquired Foma, naively.

"It is hard to tell. Being far from stupid, he will probably never be caught, and to the end of his days he will live with you and me in the same degree of equality before the law. Oh God, what I am telling you!" said Ookhtishchev, with a comical sigh.

"Betraying secrets?" grinned Foma.

"It isn't secrets; but I ought not to be frivolous. De-e-evil! But then, this affair enlivened me. Indeed, Nemesis is even then true to herself when she simply kicks like a horse."

Foma stopped suddenly, as though he had met an obstacle on his way.

"Nemesis—the goddess of Justice," babbled Ookhtishchev. "What's the matter with you?"

"And it all came about," said Foma, slowly, in a dull voice, "because you said that she was going away."

"Who?

"Sophya Pavlovna."

"Yes, she is going away. Well?"

He stood opposite Foma and stared at him, with a smile in his eyes. Gordyeeff was silent, with lowered head, tapping the stone of the sidewalk with his cane.

"Come," said Ookhtishchev.

Foma started, saying indifferently:

"Well, let her go. And I am alone." Ookhtishchev, waving his cane, began to whistle, looking at his companion.

"Sha'n't I be able to get along without her?" asked Foma, looking somewhere in front of him and then, after a pause, he answered himself softly and irresolutely:

"Of course, I shall."

"Listen to me!" exclaimed Ookhtishchev. "I'll give you some good advice. A man must be himself. While you, you are an epic man, so to say, and the lyrical is not becoming to you. It isn't your genre."

"Speak to me more simply, sir," said Foma, having listened attentively to his words.

"More simply? Very well. I want to say, give up thinking of this little lady. She is poisonous food for you."

"She told me the same," put in Foma, gloomily.

"She told you?" Ookhtishchev asked and became thoughtful. "Now, I'll tell you, shouldn't we perhaps go and have supper?"

"Let's go," Foma assented. And he suddenly roared obdurately, clinching his fists and waving them in the air: "Well, let us go, and I'll get wound up; I'll break loose, after all this, so you can't hold me back!"

"What for? We'll do it modestly."

"No! wait!" said Foma, anxiously, seizing him by the shoulder. "What's that? Am I worse than other people? Everybody lives, whirls, hustles about, has his own point. While I am weary. Everybody is satisfied with himself. And as to their complaining, they lie, the rascals! They are simply pretending for beauty's sake. I have no reason to pretend. I am a fool. I don't understand anything, my dear fellow. I simply wish to live! I am unable to think. I feel disgusted; one says this, another that! Pshaw! But she, eh! If you knew. My hope was in her. I expected of her—just what I expected, I cannot tell; but she is the best of women! And I had so much faith in her—when sometimes she spoke such peculiar words, all her own. Her eyes, my dear boy, are so beautiful! Oh Lord! I was ashamed to look upon them, and as I am telling you, she would say a few words, and everything would become clear to me. For I did not come to her with love alone—I came to her with all my soul! I sought—I thought that since she was so beautiful, consequently, I might become a man by her side!"

Ookhtishchev listened to the painful, unconnected words that burst from his companion's lips. He saw how the muscles of his face contracted with the effort to express his thoughts, and he felt that behind this bombast there was a great, serious grief. There was something intensely pathetic in the powerlessness of this strong and savage youth, who suddenly started to pace the sidewalk with big, uneven steps. Skipping along after him with his short legs, Ookhtishchev felt it his duty somehow to calm Foma. Everything Foma had said and done that evening awakened in the jolly secretary a feeling of lively curiosity toward Foma, and then he felt flattered by the frankness of the young millionaire. This frankness confused him with its dark power; he was disconcerted by its pressure, and though, in spite of his youth, he had a stock of words ready for all occasions in life, it took him quite awhile to recall them.

"I feel that everything is dark and narrow about me," said Gordyeeff. "I feel that a burden is falling on my shoulders, but what it is I cannot understand! It puts a restraint on me, and it checks the freedom of my movements along the road of life. Listening to people, you hear that each says a different thing. But she could have said—"

"Eh, my dear boy!" Ookhtishchev interrupted Foma, gently taking his arm. "That isn't right! You have just started to live and already you are philosophizing! No, that is not right! Life is given us to live! Which means—live and let others live. That's the philosophy! And that woman. Bah! Is she then the only one in the world? The world is large enough. If you wish, I'll introduce you to such a virile woman, that even the slightest trace of your philosophy would at once vanish from your soul! Oh, a remarkable woman! And how well she knows how to avail herself of life! Do you know, there's also something epic about her? She is beautiful; a Phryne, I may say, and what a match she would be to you! Ah, devil! It is really a splendid idea. I'll make you acquainted with her! We must drive one nail out with another."

"My conscience does not allow it," said Foma, sadly and sternly. "So long as she is alive, I cannot even look at women."

"Such a robust and healthy young man. Ho, ho!" exclaimed Ookhtishchev, and in the tone of a teacher began to argue with Foma that it was essential for him to give his passion an outlet in a good spree, in the company of women.

"This will be magnificent, and it is indispensable to you. You may believe me. And as to conscience, you must excuse me. You don't define it quite properly. It is not conscience that interferes with you, but timidity, I believe. You live outside of society. You are bashful, and awkward. Youare dimly conscious of all this, and it is this consciousness that you mistake for conscience. In this case there can be no question about conscience. What has conscience to do here, since it is natural for man to enjoy himself, since it is his necessity and his right?"

Foma walked on, regulating his steps to those of his companion, and staring along the road, which lay between two rows of buildings, resembled an enormous ditch, and was filled with darkness. It seemed that there was no end to the road and that something dark, inexhaustible and suffocating was slowly flowing along it in the distance. Ookhtishchev's kind, suasive voice rang monotonously in Foma's ears, and though he was not listening to his words, he felt that they were tenacious in their way; that they adhered to him, and that he was involuntarily memorizing them. Notwithstanding that a man walked beside him, he felt as though he were alone, straying in the dark. And the darkness seized him and slowly drew him along, and he felt that he was drawn somewhere, and yet had no desire to stop. Some sort of fatigue hindered his thinking; there was no desire in him to resist the admonitions of his companion—and why should he resist them?

"It isn't for everyone to philosophize," said Ookhtishchev, swinging his cane in the air, and somewhat carried away by his wisdom. "For if everybody were to philosophize, who would live? And we live but once! And therefore it were best to make haste to live. By God! That's true! But what's the use of talking? Would you permit me to give you a shaking up? Let's go immediately to a pleasure-house I know. Two sisters live there. Ah, how they live! You will come?"

"Well, I'll go," said Foma, calmly, and yawned. "Isn't it rather late?" he asked, looking up at the sky which was covered with clouds.

"It's never too late to go to see them!" exclaimed Ookhtishchev, merrily.

CHAPTER VIII

ON the third day after the scene in the club, Foma found himself about seven versts from the town, on the timber-wharf of the merchant Zvantzev, in the company of the merchant's son of Ookhtishchev—a sedate, bald-headed and red-nosed gentleman with side whiskers—and four ladies. The young Zvantzev wore eyeglasses, was thin and pale, and when he stood, the calves of his legs were forever trembling as though they were disgusted at supporting the feeble body, clad in a long, checked top-coat with a cape, in whose folds a small head in a jockey cap was comically shaking. The gentleman with the side whiskers called him Jean and pronounced this name as though he was suffering from an inveterate cold. Jean's lady was a tall, stout woman with a showy bust. Her head was compressed on the sides, her low forehead receded, her long, sharp-pointed nose gave her face an expression somewhat bird-like. And this ugly face was perfectly motionless, and the eyes alone, small, round and cold, were forever smiling a penetrating and cunning smile. Ookhtishchev's lady's name was Vera; she was a tall, pale woman with red hair. She had so much hair, that it seemed as though the woman had put on her head an enormous cap which was coming down over her ears, her cheeks and her high forehead, from under which her large blue eyes looked forth calmly and lazily.

The gentleman with the side whiskers sat beside a young, plump, buxom girl, who constantly giggled in a ringing voice at something which he whispered in her ear as he leaned over her shoulder.

And Foma's lady was a stately brunette, clad all in black. Dark-complexioned, with wavy locks, she kept her head so erect and high and looked at everything about her with such condescending haughtiness, that it was at once evident that she considered herself the most important person there.

The company were seated on the extreme link of the raft, extending far into the smooth expanse of the river. Boards were spread out on the raft and in the centre stood a crudely constructed table; empty bottles, provision baskets, candy-wrappers and orange peels were scattered about everywhere. In the corner of the raft was a pile of earth, upon which a bonfire was burning, and a peasant in a short fur coat, squatting, warmed his hands over the fire, and cast furtive glances at the people seated around the table. They had just finished eating their sturgeon soup, and now wines and fruits were before them on the table.

Fatigued with a two-days' spree and with the dinner that had just been finished, the company was in a weary frame of mind. They all gazed at the river, chatting, but their conversation was now and again interrupted by long pauses.

The day was clear and bright and young, as in spring. The cold, clear sky stretched itself majestically over the turbid water of the gigantically-wide, overflowing river, which was as calm as the sky and as vast as the sea. The distant, mountainous shore was tenderly bathed in bluish mist. Through it, there, on the mountain tops, the crosses of churches were flashing like big stars. The river was animated at the mountainous shore; steamers were going hither and thither, and their noise came in deep moans toward the rafts and into the meadows, where the calm flow of the waves filled the air with soft and faint sounds. Gigantic barges stretched themselves one after another against the current, like huge pigs, tearing asunder the smooth expanse of the river. Black smoke came in ponderous puffs from the chimneys of the steamers, slowly melting in the fresh air, which was full of bright sunshine. At times a whistle resounded—it was like the roar of some huge, enraged animal, embittered by toil. And on the meadows near the rafts, all was calm and silent. Solitary trees that had been drowned by the flood, were now already covered with light-green spangles of foliage. Covering their roots and reflecting their tops, the water gave them the appearance of globes, and it seemed as though the slightest breeze would send them floating, fantastically beautiful, down the mirror-like bosom of the river.

The red-haired woman, pensively gazing into the distance, began to sing softly and sadly:

> "Along the Volga river
> A little boat is flo-o-oating."

The brunette, snapping her large, stern eyes with contempt, said, without looking at her: "We feel gloomy enough without this."

"Don't touch her. Let her sing!" entreated Foma, kindly, looking into his lady's face. He was pale some spark seemed to flash up in his eyes now and then, and an indefinite, indolent smile played about his lips.

"Let us sing in chorus!" suggested the man with the side whiskers.

"No, let these two sing!" exclaimed Ookhtishchev with enthusiasm. "Vera, sing that song! You know, 'I will go at dawn.' How is it? Sing, Pavlinka!"

The giggling girl glanced at the brunette and asked her respectfully: "Shall I sing, Sasha?"

"I shall sing myself," announced Foma's companion, and turning toward the lady with the birdlike face, she ordered:

"Vassa, sing with me!"

Vassa immediately broke off her conversation with Zvantzev, stroked her throat a little with her hand and fixed her round eyes on the face of her sister. Sasha rose to her feet, leaned her hand against the table, and her head lifted haughtily, began to declaim in a powerful, almost masculine voice:

> "Life on earth is bright to him,
> Who knows no cares or woe,

And whose heart is not consumed
By passion's ardent glow!"

Her sister nodded her head and slowly, plaintively began to moan in a deep contralto:

"Ah me! Of me the maiden fair."

Flashing her eyes at her sister, Sasha exclaimed in her low-pitched notes:

"Like a blade of grass my heart has withered."

The two voices mingled and floated over the water in melodious, full sounds, which quivered from excess of power. One of them was complaining of the unbearable pain in the heart, and intoxicated by the poison of its plaint, it sobbed with melancholy and impotent grief; sobbed, quenching with tears the fire of the suffering. The other—the lower, more masculine voice—rolled powerfully through the air, full of the feeling of bloody mortification and of readiness to avenge. Pronouncing the words distinctly, the voice came from her breast in a deep stream, and each word reeked with boiling blood, stirred up by outrage, poisoned by offence and mightily demanding vengeance.

"I will requite him,"

sang Vassa, plaintively, closing her eyes.

"I will inflame him,
I'll dry him up,"

Sasha promised sternly and confidently, wafting into the air strong, powerful tones, which sounded like blows. And suddenly, changing the tempo of the song and striking a higher pitch, she began to sing, as slowly as her sister, voluptuous and exultant threats:

"Drier than the raging wind,
Drier than the mown-down grass,
Oi, the mown and dried-up grass."

Resting his elbows on the table, Foma bent his head, and with knitted brow, gazed into the face of the woman, into her black, half-shut eyes Staring fixedly into the distance, her eyes flashed so brightly and malignantly that, because of their light, the velvety voice, that burst from the woman's chest, seemed to him also black and flashing, like her eyes. He recalled her caresses and thought:

"How does she come to be such as she is? It is even fearful to be with her."

Ookhtishchev, sitting close to his lady, an expression of happiness on his face, listened to the song and was radiant with satisfaction. The gentleman with the side whiskers and Zvantzev were drinking wine, softly whispering something as they leaned toward each other. The red-headed woman was thoughtfully examining the palm of Ookhtishchev's hand, holding it in her own, and the jolly girl became sad. She drooped her head low and listened to the song, motionless, as though bewitched by it. From the fire came the peasant. He stepped carefully over the boards, on tiptoe; his hands were clasped behind his back, and his broad, bearded face was now transformed into a smile of astonishment and of a naive delight.

"Eh! but feel, my kind, brave man!"

entreated Vassa, plaintively, nodding her head. And her sister, her chest bent forward, her hand still higher, wound up the song in powerful triumphant notes:

"The yearning and the pangs of love!"

When she finished singing, she looked haughtily about her, and seating herself by Foma's side, clasped his neck with a firm and powerful hand.

"Well, was it a nice song?"

"It's capital!" said Foma with a sigh, as he smiled at her.

The song filled his heart with thirst for tenderness and, still full of charming sounds, it quivered, but at the touch of her arm he felt awkward and ashamed before the other people.

"Bravo-o! Bravo, Aleksandra Sarelyevna!" shouted Ookhtishchev, and the others were clapping their hands. But she paid no attention to them, and embracing Foma authoritatively, said:

"Well, make me a present of something for the song."

"Very well, I will," Foma assented.

"What?"

"You tell me."

"I'll tell you when we come to town. And if you'll give me what I like—Oh, how I will love you!"

"For the present?" asked Foma, smiling suspiciously. "You ought to love me anyway."

She looked at him calmly and, after a moment's thought, said resolutely:

"It's too soon to love you anyway. I will not lie. Why should I lie to you? I am telling you frankly. I love you for money, for presents. Because aside from money, men have nothing. They cannot give anything more than money. Nothing of worth. I know it well already. One can love merely so. Yes, wait a little—I'll know you better and then, perhaps, I may love you free of charge. And meanwhile, you mustn't take me amiss. I need much money in my mode of life."

Foma listened to her, smiled and now and then quivered from the nearness of her sound, well-shaped body. Zvantzev's sour, cracked and boring voice was falling on his ears. "I don't like it. I cannot understand the beauty of this renowned Russian song. What is it that sounds in it? Eh? The howl of a wolf. Something hungry, wild. Eh! it's the groan of a sick dog—altogether something beastly. There's nothing cheerful, there's no chic to it; there are no live and vivifying sounds in it. No, you ought to hear what and how the French peasant sings. Ah! or the Italian."

"Excuse me, Ivan Nikolayevich," cried Ookhtishchev, agitated.

"I must agree with you, the Russian song is monotonous and gloomy. It has not, you know, that brilliancy of culture," said the man with the side whiskers wearily, as he sipped some wine out of his glass.

"But nevertheless, there is always a warm heart in it," put in the red-haired lady, as she peeled an orange.

The sun was setting. Sinking somewhere far beyond the forest, on the meadow shore, it painted the entire forest with purple tints and cast rosy and golden spots over the dark cold water. Foma gazed in that direction at this play of the sunbeams, watched how they quivered as they were transposed over the placid and vast expanse of waters, and catching fragments of conversation, he pictured to himself the words as a swarm of dark butterflies, busily fluttering in the air. Sasha, her head resting on his shoulder, was softly whispering into his ear something at which he blushed and was confused, for he felt that she was kindling in him the desire to embrace this woman and kiss her unceasingly. Aside from her, none of those assembled there interested him—while Zvantzev and the gentleman with the side whiskers were actually repulsive to him.

"What are you staring at? Eh?" he heard Ookhtishchev's jestingly-stern voice.

The peasant, at whom Ookhtishchev shouted, drew the cap from his head, clapped it against his knee and answered, with a smile:

"I came over to listen to the lady's song."

"Well, does she sing well?"

"What a question! Of course," said the peasant, looking at Sasha, with admiration in his eyes.

"That's right!" exclaimed Ookhtishchev.

"There is a great power of voice in that lady's breast," said the peasant, nodding his head.

At his words, the ladies burst out laughing and the men made some double-meaning remarks about Sasha.

After she had calmly listened to these and said nothing in reply, Sasha asked the peasant:

"Do you sing?"

"We sing a little!" and he waved his hand, "What songs do you know?"

"All kinds. I love singing." And he smiled apologetically.

"Come, let's sing something together, you and I."

"How can we? Am I a match for you?"

"Well, strike up!"

"May I sit down?"

"Come over here, to the table."

"How lively this is!" exclaimed Zvantzev, wrinkling his face.

"If you find it tedious, go and drown yourself," said Sasha, angrily flashing her eyes at him.

"No, the water is cold," replied Zvantzev, shrinking at her glance.

"As you please!" The woman shrugged her shoulders. "But it is about time you did it, and then, there's also plenty of water now, so that you wouldn't spoil it all with your rotten body."

"Fie, how witty!" hissed the youth, turning away from her, and added with contempt: "In Russia even the prostitutes are rude."

He addressed himself to his neighbour, but the latter gave him only an intoxicated smile in return. Ookhtishchev was also drunk. Staring into the face of his companion, with his eyes grown dim, he muttered something and heard nothing. The lady with the bird-like face was pecking candy, holding the box under her very nose. Pavlinka went away to the edge of the raft and, standing there, threw orange peels into the water.

"I never before participated in such an absurd outing and—company," said Zvantzev, to his neighbour, plaintively.

And Foma watched him with a smile, delighted that this feeble and ugly-looking man felt bored, and that Sasha had insulted him. Now and then he cast at her a kind glance of approval. He was pleased with the fact that she was so frank with everybody and that she bore herself proudly, like a real gentlewoman.

The peasant seated himself on the boards at her feet, clasped his knees in his hands, lifted his face to her and seriously listened to her words.

"You must raise your voice, when I lower mine, understand?"

"I understand; but, Madam, you ought to hand me some just to give me courage!"

"Foma, give him a glass of brandy!"

And when the peasant emptied it, cleared his throat with pleasure, licked his lips and said: "Now, I can do it," she ordered, knitting her brow:

"Begin!"

The peasant made a wry mouth, lifted his eyes to her face, and started in a high-pitched tenor:

"I cannot drink, I cannot eat."

Trembling in every limb, the woman sobbed out tremulously, with strange sadness:

"Wine cannot gladden my soul."

The peasant smiled sweetly, tossed his head to and fro, and closing his eyes, poured out into the air a tremulous wave of high-pitched notes:

"Oh, time has come for me to bid goodbye!"

And the woman, shuddering and writhing, moaned and wailed:

"Oi, from my kindred I must part."

Lowering his voice and swaying to and fro, the peasant declaimed in a sing-song with a remarkably intense expression of anguish:

"Alas, to foreign lands I must depart."

When the two voices, yearning and sobbing, poured forth into the silence and freshness of the evening, everything about them seemed warmer and better; everything seemed to smile the sorrowful smile of sympathy on the anguish of the man whom an obscure power is tearing away from his native soil into some foreign place, where hard labour and degradation are in store for him. It seemed as though not the sounds, nor the song, but the burning tears of the human heart in which the plaint had surged up—it seemed as though these tears moistened the air. Wild grief and pain from the sores of body and soul, which were wearied in the struggle with stern life; intense sufferings from the wounds dealt to man by the iron hand of want—all this was invested in the simple, crude words and was tossed in ineffably melancholy sounds toward the distant, empty sky, which has no echo for anybody or anything.

Foma had stepped aside from the singers, and stared at them with a feeling akin to fright, and the song, in a huge wave, poured forth into his breast, and the wild power of grief, with which it had been invested, clutched his heart painfully. He felt that tears would soon gush from his breast, something was clogging his throat and his face was quivering. He dimly saw Sasha's black eyes; immobile and flashing gloomily, they seemed to him enormous and still growing larger and larger. And it seemed to him that it was not two persons who were singing—that everything about him was singing and sobbing, quivering and palpitating in torrents of sorrow, madly striving somewhere, shedding burning tears, and all—and all things living seemed clasped in one powerful embrace of despair. And it seemed to him that he, too, was singing in unison with all of them—with the people, the river and the distant shore, whence came plaintive moans that mingled with the song.

Now the peasant went down on his knees, and gazing at Sasha, waved his hands, and she bent down toward him and shook her head, keeping time to the motions of his hands. Both were now singing without words, with sounds only, and Foma still could not believe that only two voices were pouring into the air these moans and sobs with such mighty power.

When they had finished singing, Foma, trembling with excitement, with a tear-stained face, gazed at them and smiled sadly.

"Well, did it move you?" asked Sasha. Pale with fatigue, she breathed quickly and heavily.

Foma glanced at the peasant. The latter was wiping the sweat off his brow and looking around him with such a wandering look as though he could not make out what had taken place.

All was silence. All were motionless and speechless.

"0h Lord!" sighed Foma, rising to his feet. "Eh, Sasha! Peasant! Who are you?" he almost shouted.

"I am—Stepan," said the peasant, smiling confusedly, and also rose to his feet. "I'm Stepan. Of course!"

"How you sing! Ah!" Foma exclaimed in astonishment, uneasily shifting from foot to foot.

"Eh, your Honour!" sighed the peasant and added softly and convincingly: "Sorrow can compel an ox to sing like a nightingale. And what makes the lady sing like this, only God knows. And she sings, with all her veins—that is to say, so you might just lie down and die with sorrow! Well, that's a lady."

"That was sung very well!" said Ookhtishchev in a drunken voice.

No, the devil knows what this is!" Zvantzev suddenly shouted, almost crying, irritated as he jumped up from the table. "I've come out here for a good time. I want to enjoy myself, and here they perform a funeral service for me! What an outrage! I can't stand this any longer. I'm going away!"

"Jean, I am also going. I'm weary, too," announced the gentleman with the side whiskers.

"Vassa," cried Zvantzev to his lady, "dress yourself!"

"Yes, it's time to go," said the red-haired lady to Ookhtishchev. "It is cold, and it will soon be dark."

"Stepan! Clear everything away!" commanded Vassa.

All began to bustle about, all began to speak of something. Foma stared at them in suspense and shuddered. Staggering, the crowd walked along the rafts. Pale and fatigued, they said to one another stupid, disconnected things. Sasha jostled them unceremoniously, as she was getting her things together.

"Stepan! Call for the horses!"

"And I'll drink some more cognac. Who wants some more cognac with me?" drawled the gentleman with the side whiskers in a beatific voice, holding a bottle in his hands.

Vassa was muffling Zvantzev's neck with a scarf. He stood in front of her, frowning, dissatisfied, his lips curled capriciously, the calves of his legs shivering. Foma became disgusted as he looked at them, and he went off to the other raft. He was astonished that all these people behaved as though they had not heard the song at all. In his breast the song was alive and there it called to life a restless desire to do something, to say something. But he had no one there to speak to.

The sun had set and the distance was enveloped in blue mist. Foma glanced thither and turned away. He did not feel like going to town with these people, neither did he care to stay here with them. And they were still pacing the raft with uneven steps, shaking from side to side and muttering disconnected words. The women were not quite as drunk as the men, and only the red-haired one could not lift herself from the bench for a long time, and finally, when she rose, she declared:

"Well, I'm drunk."

Foma sat down on a log of wood, and lifting the axe, with which the peasant had chopped wood for the fire, he began to play with it, tossing it up in the air and catching it.

"Oh, my God! How mean this is!" Zvantzev's capricious voice was heard.

Foma began to feel that he hated it, and him, and everybody, except Sasha, who awakened in him a certain uneasy feeling, which contained at once admiration for her and a fear lest she might do something unexpected and terrible.

"Brute!" shouted Zvantzev in a shrill voice, and Foma noticed that he struck the peasant on the chest, after which the peasant removed his cap humbly and stepped aside.

"Fo-o-ol!" cried Zvantzev, walking after him and lifting his hand.

Foma jumped to his feet and said threateningly, in a loud voice:

"Eh, you! Don't touch him!"

"Wha-a-at?" Zvantzev turned around toward him.

"Stepan, come over here," called Foma.

"Peasant!" Zvantzev hurled with contempt, looking at Foma.

Foma shrugged his shoulders and made a step toward him; but suddenly a thought flashed vividly through his mind! He smiled maliciously and inquired of Stepan, softly:

"The string of rafts is moored in three places, isn't it?

"In three, of course!"

"Cut the connections!"

"And they?"

"Keep quiet! Cut!"

"But—"

"Cut! Quietly, so they don't notice it!"

The peasant took the axe in his hands, slowly walked up to the place where one link was well fastened to another link, struck a few times with his axe, and returned to Foma.

"I'm not responsible, your Honour," he said.

"Don't be afraid."

"They've started off," whispered the peasant with fright, and hastily made the sign of the cross. And Foma gazed, laughing softly, and experienced a painful sensation that keenly and sharply stung his heart with a certain strange, pleasant and sweet fear.

The people on the raft were still pacing to and fro, moving about slowly, jostling one another, assisting the ladies with their wraps, laughing and talking, and the raft was meanwhile turning slowly and irresolutely in the water.

"If the current carries them against the fleet," whispered the peasant, "they'll strike against the bows—and they'll be smashed into splinters."

"Keep quiet!"

"They'll drown!"

"You'll get a boat, and overtake them."

"That's it! Thank you. What then? They're after all human beings. And we'll be held responsible for them." Satisfied now, laughing with delight, the peasant dashed in bounds across the rafts to the shore. And Foma stood by the water and felt a passionate desire to shout something, but he controlled himself, in order to give time for the raft to float off farther, so that those drunken people would not be able to jump across to the moored links. He experienced a pleasant caressing sensation as he saw the raft softly rocking upon the water and floating off farther and farther from him every moment. The heavy and dark feeling, with which his heart had been filled during this time, now seemed to float away together with the people on the raft. Calmly he inhaled the fresh air and with it something sound that cleared his brain. At the very edge of the floating raft stood Sasha, with her back toward Foma; he looked at her beautiful figure and involuntarily recalled Medinskaya. The latter was smaller in size. The recollection of her stung him, and he cried out in a loud, mocking voice:

"Eh, there! Good-bye! Ha! ha! ha!"

Suddenly the dark figures of the people moved toward him and crowded together in one group, in the centre of the raft. But by this time a clear strip of water, about three yards wide, was flashing between them and Foma.

There was a silence lasting for a few seconds.

Then suddenly a hurricane of shrill, repulsively pitiful sounds, which were full of animal fright, was hurled at Foma, and louder than all and more repulsive than all, Zvantzev's shrill, jarring cry pierced the ear:

"He-e-elp!"

Some one—in all probability, the sedate gentleman with the side whiskers—roared in his basso:

"Drowning! They're drowning people!"

"Are you people?" cried Foma, angrily, irritated by their screams which seemed to bite him. And the people ran about on the raft in the madness of fright; the raft rocked under their feet, floated faster on account of this, and the agitated water was loudly splashing against and under it. The screams rent the air, the people jumped about, waving their hands, and the stately figure of Sasha alone stood motionless and speechless on the edge of the raft.

"Give my regards to the crabs!" cried Foma. Foma felt more and more cheerful and relieved in proportion as the raft was floating away from him.

"Foma Ignatyevich!" said Ookhtishchev in a faint, but sober voice, "look out, this is a dangerous joke. I'll make a complaint."

"When you are drowned? You may complain!" answered Foma, cheerfully.

"You are a murderer!" exclaimed Zvantzev, sobbing. But at this time a ringing splash of water was heard as though it groaned with fright or with astonishment. Foma shuddered and became as though petrified. Then rang out the wild, deafening shrieks of the women, and the terror-stricken screams of men, and all the figures on the raft remained petrified in their places. And Foma, staring at the water, felt as though he really were petrified. In the water something black, surrounded with splashes, was floating toward him.

Rather instinctively than consciously, Foma threw himself with his chest on the beams of the raft, and stretched out his hands, his head hanging down over the water. Several incredibly long seconds passed. Cold, wet arms clasped his neck and dark eyes flashed before him. Then he understood that it was Sasha.

The dull horror, which had suddenly seized him, vanished, replaced now by wild, rebellious joy. Having dragged the woman out of the water, he grasped her by the waist, clasped her to his breast, and, not knowing what to say to her, he stared into her eyes with astonishment. She smiled at him caressingly.

"I am cold," said Sasha, softly, and quivered in every limb.

Foma laughed gaily at the sound of her voice, lifted her into his arms and quickly, almost running, dashed across the rafts to the shore. She was wet and cold, but her breathing was hot, it burned Foma's cheek and filled his breast with wild joy.

"You wanted to drown me?" said she, firmly, pressing close to him. "It was rather too early. Wait!"

"How well you have done it," muttered Foma, as he ran.

"You're a fine, brave fellow! And your device wasn't bad, either, though you seem to be so peaceable."

"And they are still roaring there, ha! ha!"

"The devil take them! If they are drowned, we'll be sent to Siberia," said the woman, as though she wanted to console and encourage him by this. She began to shiver, and the shudder of her body, felt by Foma, made him hasten his pace.

Sobs and cries for help followed them from the river. There, on the placid water, floated in the twilight a small island, withdrawing from the shore toward the stream of the main current of the river, and on that little island dark human figures were running about.

Night was closing down upon them.

CHAPTER IX

ONE Sunday afternoon, Yakov Tarasovich Mayakin was drinking tea in his garden and talking to his daughter. The collar of his shirt unbuttoned, a towel wound round his neck, he sat on a bench under a canopy of verdant cherry-trees, waved his hands in the air, wiped the perspiration off his face, and incessantly poured forth into the air his brisk speech.

"The man who permits his belly to have the upper hand over him is a fool and a rogue! Is there nothing better in the world than eating and drinking? Upon what will you pride yourself before people, if you are like a hog?"

The old man's eyes sparkled irritably and angrily, his lips twisted with contempt, and the wrinkles of his gloomy face quivered.

"If Foma were my own son, I would have made a man of him!"

Playing with an acacia branch, Lubov mutely listened to her father's words, now and then casting a close and searching look in his agitated, quivering face. Growing older, she changed, without noticing it, her suspicious and cold relation toward the old man. In his words she now began to find the same ideas that were in her books, and this won her over on her father's side, involuntarily causing the girl to prefer his live words to the cold letters of the book. Always overwhelmed with business affairs, always alert and clever, he went his own way alone, and she perceived his solitude, knew how painful it was, and her relations toward her father grew in warmth. At times she even entered into arguments with the old man; he always regarded her remarks contemptuously and sarcastically; but more tenderly and attentively from time to time.

"If the deceased Ignat could read in the newspapers of the indecent life his son is leading, he would have killed Foma!" said Mayakin, striking the table with his fists. "How they have written it up! It's a disgrace!"

"He deserves it," said Lubov.

"I don't say it was done at random! They've barked at him, as was necessary. And who was it that got into such a fit of anger?"

"What difference does it make to you?" asked the girl.

"It's interesting to know. How cleverly the rascal described Foma's behaviour. Evidently he must have been with him and witnessed all the indecency himself."

"Oh, no, he wouldn't go with Foma on a spree!' said Lubov, confidently, and blushed deeply at her father's searching look.

"So! You have fine acquaintances, Lubka! "said Mayakin with humorous bitterness. "Well, who wrote it?"

"What do you wish to know it for, papa?"

"Come, tell me!"

She had no desire to tell, but the old man persisted, and his voice was growing more and more dry and angry. Then she asked him uneasily:

"And you will not do him any ill for it?"

"I? I will—bite his head off! Fool! What can I do to him? They, these writers, are not a foolish lot and are therefore a power—a power, the devils! And I am not the governor, and even he cannot put one's hand out of joint or tie one's tongue. Like mice, they gnaw us little by little. And we have to poison them not with matches, but with roubles. Yes! Well, who is it?"

"Do you remember, when I was going to school, a Gymnasium student used to come up to us. Yozhov? Such a dark little fellow!"

"Mm! Of course, I saw him. I know him. So it's he?"

"Yes."

"The little mouse! Even at that time one could see already that something wrong would come out of him. Even then he stood in the way of other people. A bold boy he was. I should have looked after him then. Perhaps, I might have made a man of him."

Lubov looked at her father, smiled inimically, and asked hotly:

"And isn't he who writes for newspapers a man?"

For a long while, the old man did not answer his daughter. Thoughtfully, he drummed with his fingers against the table and examined his face, which was reflected in the brightly polished brass of the samovar. Then he raised his head, winked his eyes and said impressively and irritably:

"They are not men, they are sores! The blood of the Russian people has become mixed, it has become mixed and spoiled, and from the bad blood have come all these book and newspaper-writers, these terrible Pharisees. They have broken out everywhere, and they are still breaking out, more and more. Whence comes this spoiling of the blood? From slowness of motion. Whence the mosquitoes, for instance? From the swamp. All sorts of uncleanliness multiply in stagnant waters. The same is true of a disordered life."

"That isn't right, papa!" said Lubov, softly.

"What do you mean by—not right?"

"Writers are the most unselfish people, they are noble personalities! They don't want anything—all they strive for is justice—truth! They're not mosquitoes."

Lubov grew excited as she lauded her beloved people; her face was flushed, and her eyes looked at her father with so much feeling, as though imploring him to believe her, being unable to convince him.

"Eh, you!" said the old man, with a sigh, interrupting her. "You've read too much! You've been poisoned! Tell me—who are they? No one knows! That Yozhov—what is he? Only God knows. All they want is the truth, you say? What modest people they are! And suppose truth is the very dearest thing there is? Perhaps everybody is seeking it in silence? Believe me—man cannot be unselfish. Man will not fight for what belongs not to him, and if he does fight—his name is 'fool,' and he is of no use to anybody. A man must be able to stand up for himself, for his own, then will he attain something! Here you have it! Truth! Here I have been reading the same newspaper for almost forty years, and I can see well—here is my face before you, and before me, there on the samovar is again my face, but it is another face. You see, these newspapers give a samovar face to everything, and do not see the real one. And yet you believe them. But I know that my face on the samovar is distorted. No one can tell the real truth; man's throat is too delicate for this. And then, the real truth is known to nobody."

"Papa!" exclaimed Lubov, sadly, "But in books and in newspapers they defend the general interests of all the people."

"And in what paper is it written that you are weary of life, and that it was time for you to get married? So, there your interest is not defended! Eh! You! Neither is mine defended. Who knows what I need? Who, but myself, understands my interests?"

"No, papa, that isn't right, that isn't right! I cannot refute you, but I feel that this isn't right!" said Lubov almost with despair.

"It is right!" said the old man, firmly. "Russia is confused, and there is nothing steadfast in it; everything is staggering! Everybody lives awry, everybody walks on one side, there's no harmony in life. All are yelling out of tune, in different voices. And not one understands what the other is in need of! There is a mist over everything—everybody inhales that mist, and that's why the blood of the people has become spoiled—hence the sores. Man is given great liberty to reason, but is not permitted to do anything—that's why man does not live; but rots and stinks."

"What ought one to do, then?" asked Lubov, resting her elbows on the table and bending toward her father.

"Everything!" cried the old man, passionately. "Do everything. Go ahead! Let each man do whatever he knows best! But for that liberty must be given to man—complete freedom! Since there has come a time, when everyraw youth believes that he knows everything and was created for the complete arrangement of life—give him, give the rogue freedom! Here, Carrion, live! Come, come, live! Ah! Then such a comedy will

305

follow; feeling that his bridle is off, man will then rush up higher than his ears, and like a feather will fly hither and thither. He'll believe himself to be a miracle worker, and then he'll start to show his spirit."

The old man paused awhile and, lowering his voice, went on, with a malicious smile:

"But there is very little of that creative spirit in him! He'll bristle up for a day or two, stretch himself on all sides—and the poor fellow will soon grow weak. For his heart is rotten—he, he, he! Here, he, he, he! The dear fellow will be caught by the real, worthy people, by those real people who are competent to be the actual civil masters, who will manage life not with a rod nor with a pen, but with a finger and with brains.

"What, they will say. Have you grown tired, gentlemen? What, they will say, your spleens cannot stand a real fire, can they? So—"and, raising his voice, the old man concluded his speech in an authoritative tone:

"Well, then, now, you rabble, hold your tongues, and don't squeak! Or we'll shake you off the earth, like worms from a tree! Silence, dear fellows! Ha, ha, ha! That's how it's going to happen, Lubavka! He, he, he!"

The old man was in a merry mood. His wrinkles quivered, and carried away by his words, he trembled, closed his eyes now and then, and smacked his lips as though tasting his own wisdom.

"And then those who will take the upper hand in the confusion will arrange life wisely, after their own fashion. Then things won't go at random, but as if by rote. It's a pity that we shall not live to see it!"

The old man's words fell one after another upon Lubov like meshes of a big strong net—they fell and enmeshed her, and the girl, unable to free herself from them, maintained silence, dizzied by her father's words. Staring into his face with an intense look, she sought support for herself in his words and heard in them something similar to what she had read in books, and which seemed to her the real truth. But the malignant, triumphant laughter of her father stung her heart, and the wrinkles, which seemed to creep about on his face like so many dark little snakes, inspired her with a certain fear for herself in his presence. She felt that he was turning her aside from what had seemed so simple and so easy in her dreams.

"Papa!" she suddenly asked the old man, in obedience to a thought and a desire that unexpectedly flashed through her mind. "Papa! and what sort of a man—what in your opinion is Taras?"

Mayakin shuddered. His eyebrows began to move angrily, he fixed his keen, small eyes on his daughter's face and asked her drily:

"What sort of talk is this?"

"Must he not even be mentioned?" said Lubov, softly and confusedly.

I don't want to speak of him—and I also advise you not to speak of him! "—the old man threatened her with his finger and lowered his head with a gloomy frown. But when he said that he did not want to speak of his son, he evidently did not understand himself correctly, for after a minute's silence he said sternly and angrily:

"Taraska, too, is a sore. Life is breathing upon you, milksops, and you cannot discriminate its genuine scents, and you swallow all sorts of filth, wherefore there is trouble in your heads. That's why you are not competent to do anything, and you are unhappy because of this incompetence. Taraska. Yes. He must be about forty now. He is lost to me! A galley-slave—is that my son? A blunt-snouted young pig. He would not speak to his father, and—he stumbled."

"What did he do?" asked Lubov, eagerly listening to the old man's words.

"Who knows? It may be that now he cannot understand himself, if he became sensible, and he must have become a sensible man; he's the son of a father who's not stupid, and then he must have suffered not a little. They coddle them, the nihilists! They should have turned them over to me. I'd show them what to do. Into the desert! Into the isolated places—march! Come, now, my wise fellows, arrange life there according to your own will! Go ahead! And as authorities over them I'd station the robust peasants. Well, now, honourable gentlemen, you were given to eat and to drink, you were given an education—what have you learned? Pay your debts, pray. Yes, I would not spend a broken grosh on them. I would squeeze all the price out of them—give it up! You must not set a man at naught. It is not enough to imprison him! You transgressed the law, and are a gentleman? Never mind, you must work. Out of a single seed comes an ear of corn, and a man ought not be permitted to perish without being of use! An economical carpenter finds a place for each and every chip of wood—just so must every man be profitably used up, and used up entire, to the very last vein. All sorts of trash have a place in life, and man is never trash. Eh! it is bad when power lives without reason, nor is it good when reason lives without power. Take Foma now. Who is coming there—give a look."

Turning around, Lubov noticed the captain of the "Yermak," Yefim, coming along the garden path. He had respectfully removed his cap and bowed to her. There was a hopelessly guilty expression on his face and he seemed abashed. Yakov Tarasovich recognized him and, instantly grown alarmed, he cried:

"Where are you coming from? What has happened?"

"I—I have come to you!" said Yefim, stopping short at the table, with a low bow.

"Well, I see, you've come to me. What's the matter? Where's the steamer?"

"The steamer is there!" Yefim thrust his hand somewhere into the air and heavily shifted from one foot to the other.

"Where is it, devil? Speak coherently—what has happened?" cried the old man, enraged.

"So—a misfortune, Yakov."

"Have you been wrecked?"

"No, God saved us."

"Burned up? Well, speak more quickly."

Yefim drew air into his chest and said slowly:

"Barge No. 9 was sunk—smashed up. One man's back was broken, and one is altogether missing, so that he must have drowned. About five more were injured, but not so very badly, though some were disabled."

"So-o!" drawled out Mayakin, measuring the captain with an ill-omened look.

"Well, Yefimushka, I'll strip your skin off"

"It wasn't I who did it!" said Yefim, quickly.

"Not you?" cried the old man, shaking with rage. "Who then?"

"The master himself."

"Foma? And you. Where were you?"

"I was lying in the hatchway."

"Ah! You were lying."

"I was bound there."

"Wha-at?" screamed the old man in a shrill voice.

"Allow me to tell you everything as it happened. He was drunk and he shouted: '"Get away! I'll take command myself!' I said 'I can't! I am the captain.' 'Bind him!' said he. And when they had bound me, they lowered me into the hatchway, with the sailors. And as the master was drunk, he wanted to have some fun. A fleet of boats was coming toward us. Six empty barges towed by 'Cheruigorez.' So Foma Ignatyich blocked their way. They whistled. More than once. I must tell the truth—they whistled!"

"Well?"

"Well, and they couldn't manage it—the two barges in front crashed into us. And as they struck the side of our ninth, we were smashed to pieces. And the two barges were also smashed. But we fared much worse."

Mayakin rose from the chair and burst into jarring, angry laughter. And Yefim sighed, and, outstretching his hands, said:xxx"He has a very violent character. When he is sober he is silent most of the time, and walks around thoughtfully, but when he wets his springs with wine—then he breaks loose. Then he is not master of himself and of his business—

but their wild enemy—you must excuse me! And I want to leave, Yakov Tarasovich! I am not used to being without a master, I cannot live without a master!"

"Keep quiet!" said Mayakin, sternly. "Where's Foma?"

"There; at the same place. Immediately after the accident, he came to himself and at once sent for workmen. They'll lift the barge. They may have started by this time."

"Is he there alone?" asked Mayakin, lowering his head.

"Not quite," replied Yefim, softly, glancing stealthily at Lubov.

"Really?"

"There's a lady with him. A dark one."

"So."

"It looks as though the woman is out of her wits," said Yefim, with a sigh. "She's forever singing. She sings very well. It's very captivating."

"I am not asking you about her!" cried Mayakin, angrily. The wrinkles of his face were painfully quivering, and it seemed to Lubov that her father was about to weep.

"Calm yourself, papa!" she entreated caressingly. "Maybe the loss isn't so great."

"Not great?" cried Yakov Tarasovich in a ringing voice. "What do you understand, you fool? Is it only that the barge was smashed? Eh, you! A man is lost! That's what it is! And he is essential to me! I need him, dull devils that you are!" The old man shook his head angrily and with brisk steps walked off along the garden path leading toward the house.

And Foma was at this time about four hundred versts away from his godfather, in a village hut, on the shore of the Volga. He had just awakened from sleep, and lying on the floor, on a bed of fresh hay, in the middle of the hut, he gazed gloomily out of the window at the sky, which was covered with gray, scattered clouds.

The wind was tearing them asunder and driving them somewhere; heavy and weary, one overtaking another, they were passing across the sky in an enormous flock. Now forming a solid mass, now breaking into fragments, now falling low over the earth, in silent confusion, now again rising upward, one swallowed by another.

Without moving his head, which was heavy from intoxication, Foma looked long at the clouds and finally began to feel as though silent clouds were also passing through his breast,—passing, breathing a damp coldness upon his heart and oppressing him. There was something impotent in the motion of the clouds across the sky. And he felt the same within him. Without thinking, he pictured to himself all he had gone through during the past months. It seemed to him as though he had fallen into a turbid, boiling stream, and now he had been seized by dark waves, that resembled these clouds in the sky; had been seized and carried away somewhere, even as the clouds were carried by the wind. In the darkness and the tumult which surrounded him, he saw as though through a mist that certain other people were hastening together with him—to-day not those of yesterday, new ones each day, yet all looking alike—equally pitiful and repulsive. Intoxicated, noisy, greedy, they flew about him as in a whirlwind, caroused at his expense, abused him, fought, screamed, and even wept more than once. And he beat them. He remembered that one day he had struck somebody on the face, torn someone's coat off and thrown it into the water and that some one had kissed his hands with wet, cold lips as disgusting as frogs. Had kissed and wept, imploring him not to kill. Certain faces flashed through his memory, certain sounds and words rang in it. A woman in a yellow silk waist, unfastened at the breast, had sung in a loud, sobbing voice:

"And so let us live while we canAnd then—e'en grass may cease to grow."

All these people, like himself, grown wild and beastlike, were seized by the same dark wave and carried away like rubbish. All these people, like himself, must have been afraid to look forward to see whither this powerful, wild wave was carrying them. And drowning their fear in wine, they were rushing forward down the current struggling, shouting, doing something absurd, playing the fool, clamouring, clamouring, without ever being cheerful. He was doing the same, whirling in their midst. And now it seemed to him, that he was doing all this for fear of himself, in order to pass the sooner this strip of life, or in order not to think of what would be afterward.

Amid the burning turmoil of carouses, in the crowd of people, seized by debauchery, perplexed by violent passions, half-crazy in their longing to forget themselves—only Sasha was calm and contained. She never drank to intoxication, always addressed people in a firm, authoritative voice, and all her movements were equally confident, as though this stream had not taken possession of her, but she was herself mastering its violent course. She seemed to Foma the cleverest person of all those that surrounded him, and the most eager for noise and carouse; she held them all in her sway, forever inventing something new and speaking in one and the same manner to everybody; for the driver, the lackey and the sailor she had the same tone and the same words as for her friends and for Foma. She was younger and prettier than Pelageya, but her caresses were silent, cold. Foma imagined that deep in her heart she was concealing from everybody something terrible, that she would never love anyone, never reveal herself entire. This secrecy in the woman attracted him toward her with a feeling of timorous curiosity, of a great, strained interest in her calm, cold soul, which seemed even as dark as her eyes.

Somehow Foma said to her one day:

"But what piles of money you and I have squandered!"

She glanced at him, and asked:

"And why should we save it?"

"Indeed, why?" thought Foma, astonished by the fact that she reasoned so simply.

"Who are you?" he asked her at another occasion.

"Why, have you forgotten my name?"

"Well, the idea!"

"What do you wish to know then?"

"I am asking you about your origin."

"Ah! I am a native of the province of Yaroslavl. I'm from Ooglich. I was a harpist. Well, shall I taste sweeter to you, now that you know who I am?"

"Do I know it?" asked Foma, laughing.

"Isn't that enough for you? I shall tell you nothing more about it. What for? We all come from the same place, both people and beasts. And what is there that I can tell you about myself? And what for? All this talk is nonsense. Let's rather think a little as to how we shall pass the day."

On that day they took a trip on a steamer, with an orchestra of music, drank champagne, and every one of them got terribly drunk. Sasha sang a peculiar, wonderfully sad song, and Foma, moved by her singing, wept like a child. Then he danced with her the "Russian dance," and finally, perspiring and fatigued, threw himself overboard in his clothes and was nearly drowned.

Now, recalling all this and a great deal more, he felt ashamed of himself and dissatisfied with Sasha. He looked at her well-shaped figure, heard her even breathing and felt that he did not love this woman, and that she was unnecessary to him. Certain gray, oppressive thoughts were slowly springing up in his heavy, aching head. It seemed to him as though everything he had lived through during this time was twisted within him into a heavy and moist ball, and that now this ball was rolling about in his breast, unwinding itself slowly, and the thin gray cords were binding him.

"What is going on in me?" he thought. "I've begun to carouse. Why? I don't know how to live. I don't understand myself. Who am I?"

He was astonished by this question, and he paused over it, attempting to make it clear to himself—why he was unable to live as firmly and confidently as other people do. He was now still more tortured. by conscience. More uneasy at this thought, he tossed about on the hay and irritated, pushed Sasha with his elbow.

"Be careful!" said she, although nearly asleep.

"It's all right. You're not such a lady of quality!" muttered Foma.

"What's the matter with you?"

"Nothing."

She turned her back to him, and said lazily, with a lazy yawn:

"I dreamed that I became a harpist again. It seemed to me that I was singing a solo, and opposite me stood a big, dirty dog, snarling and waiting for me to finish the song. And I was afraid of the dog. And I knew that it would devour me, as soon as I stopped singing. So I kept singing, singing. And suddenly it seemed my voice failed me. Horrible! And the dog is gnashing his teeth. 0h Lord, have mercy on me! What does it mean?"

"Stop your idle talk!" Foma interrupted her sternly. "You better tell me what you know about me."

"I know, for instance, that you are awake now," she answered, without turning to him.

"Awake? That's true. I've awakened," said Foma, thoughtfully and, throwing his arm behind his head, went on: "That's why I am asking you. What sort of man do you think I am?"

"A man with a drunken headache," answered Sasha, yawning.

"Aleksandra!" exclaimed Foma, beseechingly, "don't talk nonsense! Tell me conscientiously, what do you think of me?"

"I don't think anything!" she said drily. "Why are you bothering me with nonsense?"

"Is this nonsense?" said Foma, sadly. "Eh, you devils! This is the principal thing. The most essential thing to me."

He heaved a deep sigh and became silent. After a minute's silence, Sasha began to speak in her usual, indifferent voice:

"Tell him who he is, and why he is such as he is? Did you ever see! Is it proper to ask such questions of our kind of women? And on what ground should I think about each and every man? I have not even time to think about myself, and, perhaps, I don't feel like doing it at all."

Foma laughed drily and said:

"I wish I were like this—and had no desires for anything."

Then the woman raised her head from the pillow, looked into Foma's face and lay down again, saying:

"You are musing too much. Look out—no good will come of it to you. I cannot tell you anything about yourself. It is impossible to say anything true about a man. Who can understand him? Man does not know himself. Well, here, I'll tell you—you are better than others. But what of it?"

"And in what way am I better?" asked Foma, thoughtfully.

"So! When one sings a good song—you weep. When one does some mean thing—you beat him. With women you are simple, you are not impudent to them. You are peaceable. And you can also be daring, sometimes."

Yet all this did not satisfy Foma.

"You're not telling me the right thing!" said he, softly.

"Well, I don't know what you want. But see here, what are we going to do after they have raised the barge?"

"What can we do?" asked Foma.

"Shall we go to Nizhni or to Kazan?"

"What for?"

To carouse."

"1 don't want to carouse any more."

"What else are you going to do?"

"What? Nothing."

And both were silent for a long time, without looking at each other.

"You have a disagreeable character," said Sasha, "a wearisome character."

"But nevertheless I won't get drunk any more!" said Foma, firmly and confidently.

"You are lying!" retorted Sasha, calmly.

"You'll see! What do you think—is it good to lead such a life as this?"

"I'll see."

"No, just tell me—is it good?"

"But what is better?"

Foma looked at her askance and, irritated, said:

"What repulsive words you speak."

"Well, here again I haven't pleased him!" said Sasha, laughing.

"What a fine crowd!" said Foma, painfully wrinkling his face. "They're like trees. They also live, but how? No one understands. They are crawling somewhere. And can give no account either to themselves or to others. When the cockroach crawls, he knows whither and wherefore he wants to go? And you? Whither are you going?"

"Hold on!" Sasha interrupted him, and asked him calmly: "What have you to do with me? You may take from me all that you want, but don't you creep into my soul!"

"Into your so-o-ul!" Foma drawled out, with contempt. "Into what soul? He, he!"

She began to pace the room, gathering together the clothes that were scattered everywhere. Foma watched her and was displeased because she did not get angry at him for his words about her soul. Her face looked calm and indifferent, as usual, but he wished to see her angry or offended; he wished for something human from the woman.

"The soul!" he exclaimed, persisting in his aim. "Can one who has a soul live as you live? A soul has fire burning in it, there is a sense of shame in it."

By this time she was sitting on a bench, putting on her stockings, but at his words she raised her head and sternly fixed her eyes upon his face.

"What are you staring at?" asked Foma.

"Why do you speak that way?" said she, without lifting her eyes from him.

"Because I must."

"Look out—must you really?"

There was something threatening in her question. Foma felt intimidated and said, this time without provocation in his voice:

"How could I help speaking?"

"Oh, you!" sighed Sasha and resumed dressing herself

"And what about me?"

"Merely so. You seem as though you were born of two fathers. Do you know what I have observed among people?"

"Well?"

"If a man cannot answer for himself, it means that he is afraid of himself, that his price is a grosh!"

"Do you refer to me?" asked Foma, after a pause.

"To you, too."

She threw a pink morning gown over her shoulders and, standing in the centre of the room, stretched out her hand toward Foma, who lay at her feet, and said to him in a low, dull voice:

"You have no right to speak about my soul. You have nothing to do with it! And therefore hold your tongue! I may speak! If I please, I could tell something to all of you. Eh, how I could tell it! Only,—who will dare to listen to me, if I should speak at the top of my voice? And I have some words about you,—they're like hammers! And I could knock you all on your heads so that you would lose your wits. And although you are all rascals—you cannot be cured by words. You should be burned in the fire—just as frying-pans are burned out on the first Monday of Lent."

Raising her hands she abruptly loosened her hair, and when it fell over her shoulders in heavy, black locks—the woman shook her head haughtily and said, with contempt:

"Never mind that I am leading a loose life! It often happens, that the man who lives in filth is purer than he who goes about in silks. If you only knew what I think of you, you dogs, what wrath I bear against you! And because of this wrath—I am silent! For I fear that if I should sing it to you—my soul would become empty. I would have nothing to live on."

Foma looked at her, and now he was pleased with her. In her words there was something akin to his frame of mind. Laughing, he said to her, with satisfaction on his face and in his voice:

"And I also feel that something is growing within my soul. Eh, I too shall have my say, when the time comes."

"Against whom?" asked Sasha, carelessly.

"I—against everybody!" exclaimed Foma, jumping to his feet. "Against falsehood. I shall ask—"

"Ask whether the samovar is ready," Sasha ordered indifferently.

Foma glanced at her and cried, enraged:

"Go to the devil! Ask yourself."

"Well, all right, I shall. What are you snarling about?"

And she stepped out of the hut.

In piercing gusts the wind blew across the river, striking against its bosom, and covered with troubled dark waves, the river was spasmodically rushing toward the wind with a noisy splash, and all in the froth of wrath. The willow bushes on the shore bent low to the ground—trembling, they now were about to lie down on the ground, now, frightened, they thrust themselves away from it, driven by the blows of the wind. In the air rang a whistling, a howling, and a deep groaning sound, that burst from dozens of human breasts:

"It goes—it goes—it goes!"

This exclamation, abrupt as a blow, and heavy as the breath from an enormous breast, which is suffocating from exertion, was soaring over the river, falling upon the waves, as if encouraging their mad play with the wind, and they struck the shores with might.

Two empty barges lay anchored by the mountainous shore, and their tall masts, rising skyward, rocked in commotion from side to side, as though describing some invisible pattern in the air. The decks of both barges were encumbered with scaffolds, built of thick brown beams; huge sheaves were hanging everywhere; chains and ropes were fastened to them, and rocking in the air; the links of the chains were faintly clanging.

A throng of peasants in blue and in red blouses pulled a large beam across the dock and, heavily stamping their feet, groaned with full chest:

"It goes—it goes—it goes!"

Here and there human figures clung to the scaffoldings, like big lumps of blue and red; the wind, blowing their blouses and their trousers, gave the men odd forms, making them appear now hump-backed, now round and puffed up like bladders. The people on the scaffolds and on the decks of the barges were making fast, hewing, sawing, driving in nails; and big arms, with shirt sleeves rolled up to the elbows were seen everywhere. The wind scattered splinters of wood, and a varied, lively, brisk noise in the air; the saw gnawed the wood, choking with wicked joy; the beams, wounded by the axes, moaned and groaned drily; the boards cracked sickly as they split from the blows they received; the jointer squeaked maliciously. The iron clinking of the chains and the groaning creaking of the sheaves joined the wrathful roaring of the waves, and the wind howled loudly, scattering over the river the noise of toil and drove the clouds across the sky.

"Mishka-a! The deuce take you!" cried someone from the top of the scaffolding. And from the deck, a large-formed peasant, with his head thrown upward, answered:

"Wh-a-at?" And the wind, playing with his long, flaxen beard, flung it into his face.

"Hand us the end."

A resounding basso shouted as through a speaking-trumpet:

"See how you've fastened this board, you blind devil? Can't you see? I'll rub your eyes for you!"

"Pull, my boys, come on!"

"Once more—brave—boys!" cried out some one in a loud, beseeching voice.

Handsome and stately, in a short cloth jacket and high boots, Foma stood, leaning his back against a mast, and stroking his beard with his trembling hand, admired the daring work of the peasants. The noise about him called forth in him a persistent desire to shout, to work together with the peasants, to hew wood, to carry burdens, to command—to compel everybody to pay attention to him, and to show them his strength, his skill, and the live soul within him. But he restrained himself. And standing speechless, motionless, he felt ashamed and afraid of something. He was embarrassed by the fact that he was master over everybody there, and that if he were to start to work himself, no one would believe that he was working merely to satisfy his desire, and not to spur them on in their work; to set them an example. And then, the peasants might laugh at him, in all probability.

A fair and curly-headed fellow, with his shirt collar unbuttoned, was now and again running past him, now carrying a log on his shoulder, now an axe in his hands; he was skipping along, like a frolicsome goat, scattering about him cheerful, ringing laughter, jests, violent oaths, and working unceasingly, now assisting one, now another, as he was cleverly and quickly running across the deck, which was obstructed with timber and shavings. Foma watched him closely, and envied this merry fellow, who was radiant with something healthy and inspiring.

"Evidently he is happy," thought Foma, and this thought provoked in him a keen, piercing desire to insult him somehow, to embarrass him. All those about him were seized with the zest of pressing work, all were unanimously and hastily fastening the scaffoldings, arranging the pulleys, preparing to raise the sunken barge from the bottom of the river; all were sound and merry—they all lived. While he stood alone, aside from them, not knowing what to do, not knowing how to do anything, feeling himself superfluous to this great toil. It vexed him to feel that he was superfluous among men, and the more closely he watched them, the more intense was this vexation. And he was stung most by the thought that all this was being done for him. And yet he was out of place there.

"Where is my place, then?" he thought gloomily. "Where is my work? Am I, then, some deformed being? I have just as much strength as any of them. But of what use is it to me?" The chains clanged, the pulleys groaned, the blows of the axes resounded loud over the river, and the barges rocked from the shocks of the waves, but to Foma it seemed that he was rocking not because the barge was rocking under his feet, but rather because he was not able to stand firmly anywhere, he was not destined to do so.

The contractor, a small-sized peasant with a small pointed gray beard, and with narrow little eyes on his gray wrinkled face, came up to him and said, not loud, but pronouncing his words with a certain m the bottom of the river. He wished that they might not succeed, that they might feel embarrassed in his presence, and a wicked thought flashed through his mind:

"Perhaps the chains will break."

"Boys! Attention!" shouted the contractor. "Start all together. God bless us!" And suddenly, clasping his hands in the air, he cried in a shrill voice:

"Let—her—go-o-o!"

The labourers took up his shout, and all cried out in one voice, with excitement and exertion:

"Let her go! She moves."

The pulleys squeaked and creaked, the chains clanked, strained under the heavy weight that suddenly fell upon them; and the labourers, bracing their chests against the handle of the windlasses, roared and tramped heavily. The waves splashed noisily between the barges as though unwilling to give up their prize to the men. Everywhere about Foma, chains and ropes were stretched and they quivered from the strain—they were creeping somewhere across the deck, past his feet, like huge gray worms; they were lifted upward, link after link, falling back with a rattling noise, and all these sounds were drowned by the deafening roaring of the labourers.

"It goes, it goes, it goes," they all sang in unison, triumphantly. But the ringing voice of the contractor pierced the deep wave of their voices, and cut it even as a knife cuts bread.

"My boys! Go ahead, all at once, all at once."

Foma was seized with a strange emotion; passionately he now longed to mingle with this excited roaring of the labourers, which was as broad and as powerful as the river—to blend with this irritating, creaking, squeaking, clanging of iron and turbulent splashing of waves. Perspiration came out on his face from the intensity of his desire, and suddenly pale from agitation, he tore himself away from the mast, and rushed toward the windlasses with big strides.

"All at once! At once!" he cried in a fierce voice. When he reached the lever of the windlass, he dashed his chest against it with all his might, and not feeling the pain, he began to go around the windlass, roaring, and firmly stamping his feet against the deck. Something powerful and burning rushed into his breast, replacing the efforts which he spent while turning the windlass-lever! Inexpressible joy raged within him and forced itself outside in an agitated cry. It seemed to him that he alone, that only his strength was turning the lever, thus raising the weight, and that his strength was growing and growing. Stooping, and lowering his head, like a bull he massed the power of the weight, which threw him back, but yielded to him, nevertheless. Each step forward excited him the more, each expended effort was immediately replaced in him by a flood of burning and vehement pride. His head reeled, his eyes were blood-shot, he saw nothing, he only felt that they were yielding to him, that he would soon conquer, that he would overthrow with his strength something huge which obstructed his way—would overthrow, conquer and then breathe easily and freely, full of proud delight. For the first time in his life he experienced such a powerful, spiritualizing sensation, and he drank it with all the strength of a hungry, thirsty soul; he was intoxicated by it and he gave vent to his joy in loud, exulting cries in unison with the workers:

"It goes—it goes—it goes."

"Hold on! Fasten! Hold on, boys!"

Something dashed against Foma's chest, and he was hurled backward.

"I congratulate you on a successful result, Foma Ignatyich!" the contractor congratulated him and the wrinkles quivered on his face in cheerful beams.

"Thank God! You must be quite tired now?"

Cold wind blew in Foma's face. A contented, boastful bustle was in the air about him; swearing at one another in a friendly way, merry, with smiles on their perspiring brows, the peasants approached him and surrounded him closely. He smiled in embarrassment: the excitement within him had not yet calmed down and this hindered him from understanding what had happened and why all those who surrounded him were so merry and contented.

"We've raised a hundred and seventy thousand puds as if we plucked a radish from a garden-bed!" said some one.

"We ought to get a vedro of whisky from our master."

Foma, standing on a heap of cable, looked over the heads of the workers and saw; between the barges, side by side with them, stood a third barge, black, slippery, damaged, wrapped in chains. It was warped all over, it seemed as though it swelled from some terrible disease and, impotent, clumsy, it was suspended between its companions, leaning against them. Its broken mast stood out mournfully in the centre; reddish streams of water, like blood, were running across the deck, which was covered with stains of rust. Everywhere on the deck lay heaps of iron, of black, wet stumps of wood, and of ropes.

"Raised?" asked Foma, not knowing what to say at the sight of this ugly, heavy mass, and again feeling offended at the thought that merely for the sake of raising this dirty, bruised monster from the water, his soul had foamed up with such joy.

"How's the barge?" asked Foma, indefinitely, addressing the contractor.

"It's pretty good! We must unload right away, and put a company of about twenty carpenters to work on it—they'll bring it quickly into shape I "said the contractor in a consoling tone.

And the light-haired fellow, gaily and broadly smiling into Foma's face, asked:

"Are we going to have any vodka?"

"Can't you wait? You have time!" said the contractor, sternly. "Don't you see—the man is tired."

Then the peasants began to speak:

"Of course, he is tired!

"That wasn't easy work!"

"Of course, one gets tired if he isn't used to work."

"It is even hard to eat gruel if you are not used to it."

"I am not tired," said Foma, gloomily, and again were heard the respectful exclamations of the peasants, as they surrounded him more closely.

"Work, if one likes it, is a pleasant thing."

"It's just like play."

"It's like playing with a woman."

But the light-haired fellow persisted in his request:

"Your Honour! You ought to treat us to a vedro of vodka, eh?" he said, smiling and sighing.

Foma looked at the bearded faces before him and felt like saying something offensive to them. But somehow everything became confused in his brain, he found no thoughts in it and, finally, without giving himself an account of his words, said angrily:

"All you want is to drink all the time! It makes no difference to you what you do! You should have thought—why? to what purpose? Eh, you!"

There was an expression of perplexity on the faces of those that surrounded him, blue and red, bearded figures began to sigh, scratch themselves, shift themselves from one foot to another. Others cast a hopeless glance at Foma and turned away.

"Yes, yes!" said the contractor, with a sigh. "That wouldn't harm! That is—to think—why and how. These are words of wisdom."

The light-haired fellow had a different opinion on the matter; smiling kind-heartedly, he waved his hand and said:

"We don't have to think over our work! If we have it—we do it! Our business is simple! When a rouble is earned—thank God! we can do everything."

"And do you know what's necessary to do?" questioned Foma, irritated by the contradiction.

"Everything is necessary—this and that."

"But where's the sense?"

"There's but one and the same sense in everything for our class—when you have earned for bread and taxes—live! And when there's something to drink, into the bargain."

"Eh, you!" exclaimed Foma, with contempt. "You're also talking! What do you understand?"

"Is it our business to understand?" said the light-haired fellow, with a nod of the head. It now bored him to speak to Foma. He suspected that he was unwilling to treat them to vodka and he was somewhat angry.

"That's it!" said Foma, instructively, pleased that the fellow yielded to him, and not noticing the cross, sarcastic glances. "And he who understands feels that it is necessary to do everlasting work!"

"That is, for God!" explained the contractor, eyeing the peasants, and added, with a devout sigh:

"That's true. Oh, how true that is!"

And Foma was inspired with the desire to say something correct and important, after which these people might regard him in a different light, for he was displeased with the fact that all, save the light-haired fellow, kept silent and looked at him askance, surlily, with such weary, gloomy eyes.

"It is necessary to do such work," he said, moving his eyebrows. "Such work that people may say a thousand years hence: 'This was done by the peasants of Bogorodsk—yes!

The light-haired fellow glanced at Foma with astonishment and asked:

"Are we, perhaps, to drink the Volga dry?" Then he sniffed and, nodding his head, announced: "We can't do that—we should all burst."

Foma became confused at his words and looked about him; the peasants were smiling morosely, disdainfully, sarcastically. And these smiles stung him like needles. A serious-looking peasant, with a big gray beard, who had not yet opened his mouth up to that time, suddenly opened it now, came closer to Foma and said slowly:

"And even if we were to drink the Volga dry, and eat up that mountain, into the bargain—that too would be forgotten, your Honour. Everything will be forgotten. Life is long. It is not for us to do such deeds as would stand out above everything else. But we can put up scaffoldings—that we can!"

He spoke and sceptically spitting at his feet, indifferently walked off from Foma, and slipped into the crowd, as a wedge into a tree. His words crushed Foma completely; he felt, that the peasants considered him stupid and ridiculous. And in order to save his importance as master in their eyes, to attract again the now exhausted attention of the peasants to himself, he bristled up, comically puffed up his cheeks and blurted out in an impressive voice:

"I make you a present of three buckets of vodka."

Brief speeches have always the most meaning and are always apt to produce a strong impression. The peasants respectfully made way for Foma, making low bows to him, and, smiling merrily and gratefully, thanked him for his generosity in a unanimous roar of approval.

"Take me over to the shore," said Foma, feeling that the excitement that had just been aroused in him would not last long. A worm was gnawing his heart, and he was weary.

326

"I feel disgusted!" he said, entering the hut where Sasha, in a smart, pink gown, was bustling about the table, arranging wines and refreshments. "I feel disgusted, Aleksandra! If you could only do something with me, eh?"

She looked at him attentively and, seating herself on the bench, shoulder to shoulder with him, said:

"Since you feel disgusted—it means that you want something. What is it you want?"

"I don't know!" replied Foma, nodding his head mournfully.

"Think of it—search."

"I am unable to think. Nothing comes out of my thinking."

"Eh, you, my child!" said Sasha, softly and disdainfully, moving away from him. "Your head is superfluous to you."

Foma neither caught her tone nor noticed her movement. Leaning his hands against the bench, he bent forward, looked at the floor, and, swaying his body to and fro, said:

"Sometimes I think and think—and the whole soul is stuck round with thoughts as with tar. And suddenly everything disappears, without leaving any trace. Then it is dark in the soul as in a cellar—dark, damp and empty—there is nothing at all in it! It is even terrible—I feel then as though I were not a man, but a bottomless ravine. You ask me what I want?"

Sasha looked at him askance and pensively began to sing softly:

"Eh, when the wind blows—mist comes from the sea."

"I don't want to carouse—it is repulsive! Always the same—the people, the amusements, the wine. When I grow malicious—I'd thrash everybody. I am not pleased with men—what are they? It is impossible to understand them—why do they keep on living? And when they speak the truth—to whom are we to listen? One says this, another that. While I—I cannot say anything."

"Eh, without thee, dear, my life is weary,"

sang Sasha, staring at the wall before her. And Foma kept on rocking and said:

"There are times when I feel guilty before men. Everybody lives, makes noise, while I am frightened, staggered—as if I did not feel the earth under me. Was it, perhaps, my mother that endowed me with apathy? My godfather says that she was as cold as ice—that she was forever yearning towards something. I am also yearning. Toward men I am yearning. I'd like to go to them and say: 'Brethren, help me! Teach me! I know not how to live!. And if I am guilty—forgive me!' But looking about, I see there's no one to speak to. No one wants it—they are all rascals! And it seems they are even worse than I am. For I am, at least, ashamed of living as I am, while they are not! They go on."

Foma uttered some violent, unbecoming invectives and became silent. Sasha broke off her song and moved still farther away from him. The wind was raging outside the window, hurling dust against the window-panes. Cockroaches were rustling on the oven as they crawled over a bunch of pine wood splinters. Somewhere in the yard a calf was lowing pitifully.

Sasha glanced at Foma, with a sarcastic smile, and said:

"There's another unfortunate creature lowing. You ought to go to him; perhaps you could sing in unison. And placing her hand on his curly head she jestingly pushed it on the side.

"What are people like yourself good for? That's what you ought to think of. What are you groaning about? You are disgusted with being idle—occupy yourself, then, with business."

"0h Lord!" Foma nodded his head. "It is hard for one to make himself understood. Yes, it is hard!" And irritated, he almost cried out: "What business? I have no yearning toward business! What is business? Business is merely a name—and if you should look into the depth, into the root of it—you'll find it is nothing but absurdity! Do I not understand it? I understand everything, I see everything, I feel everything! Only my tongue is dumb. What aim is there in business? Money? I have plenty of it! I could choke you to death with it, cover you with it. All this business is nothing but fraud. I meet business people—well, and what about them? Their greediness is immense, and yet they purposely whirl about in business that they might not see themselves. They hide themselves, the devils. Try to free them from this bustle—what will happen? Like blind men they will grope about hither and thither; they'll lose their mind—they'll go mad! I know it! Do you think that business brings happiness into man? No, that's not so—something else is missing here. This is not everything yet! The river flows that men may sail on it; the tree grows—to be useful; the dog—to guard the house. There is justification for everything in the world! And men, like cockroaches, are altogether superfluous on earth. Everything is for them, and they—what are they for? Aha! Wherein is their justification? Ha, ha, ha!"

Foma was triumphant. It seemed to him that he had found something good for himself, something severe against men. And feeling that, because of this, there was great joy in him, he laughed loudly.

"Does not your head ache?" inquired Sasha, anxiously, scrutinizing his face.

"My soul aches!" exclaimed Foma, passionately. "And it aches because it is upright—because it is not to be satisfied with trifles. Answer it, how to live? To what purpose? There—take my godfather—he is wise! He says—create life! But he's the only one like this. Well, I'll ask him, wait! And everybody says—life has usurped us! Life has choked us. I shall ask these, too. And how can we create life? You must keep it in your hands to do this, you must be master over it. You cannot make even a pot, without taking the clay into your hands."

"Listen!" said Sasha, seriously. "I think you ought to get married, that's all!"

"What for?" asked Foma, shrugging his shoulders.

"You need a bridle."

"All right! I am living with you—you are all of a kind, are you not? One is not sweeter than the other. I had one before you, of the same kind as you. No, but that one did it for love's sake. She had taken a liking to me—and consented; she was good—but, otherwise, she was in every way the same as you—though you are prettier than she. But I took a liking to a certain lady—a lady of noble birth! They said she led a loose life, but I did not get her. Yes, she was clever, intelligent; she lived in luxury. I used to think—that's where I'll taste the real thing! I did not get her—and, it may be, if I had succeeded, all would have taken a different turn. I yearned toward her. I thought—I could not tear myself away. While now that I have given myself to drink, I've drowned her in wine—I am forgetting her—and that also is wrong. 0 man! You are a rascal, to be frank."

Foma became silent and sank into meditation. And Sasha rose from the bench and paced the hut to and fro, biting her lips. Then she stopped short before him, and, clasping her hands to her head, said:

"Do you know what? I'll leave you."

"Where will you go?" asked Foma, without lifting his head.

"I don't know—it's all the same!"

"But why?"

"You're always saying unnecessary things. It is lonesome with you. You make me sad."

Foma lifted his head, looked at her and burst into mournful laughter.

"Really? Is it possible?"

"You do make me sad! Do you know? If I should reflect on it, I would understand what you say and why you say it—for I am also of that sort—when the time comes, I shall also think of all this. And then I shall be lost. But now it is too early for me. No, I want to live yet, and then, later, come what will!"

"And I—will I, too, be lost?" asked Foma, indifferently, already fatigued by his words.

"Of course!" replied Sasha, calmly and confidently. "All such people are lost. He, whose character is inflexible, and who has no brains—what sort of a life is his? We are like this."

"I have no character at all," said Foma, stretching himself. Then after a moment's silence he added:

"And I have no brains, either."

They were silent for a minute, eyeing each other.

"What are we going to do?" asked Foma.

"We must have dinner."

"No, I mean, in general? Afterward?"

"Afterward? I don't know?"

"So you are leaving me?"

"I am. Come, let's carouse some more before we part. Let's go to Kazan, and there we'll have a spree—smoke and flame! I'll sing your farewell song."

"Very well," assented Foma. "It's quite proper at leave taking. Eh, you devil! That's a merry life! Listen, Sasha. They say that women of your kind are greedy for money; are even thieves."

"Let them say," said Sasha, calmly.

"Don't you feel offended?" asked Foma, with curiosity. "But you are not greedy. It's advantageous to you to be with me. I am rich, and yet you are going away; that shows you're not greedy."

"I?" Sasha thought awhile and said with a wave of the hand: "Perhaps I am not greedy—what of it? I am not of the very lowest of the street women. And against whom shall I feel a grudge? Let them say whatever they please. It will be only human talk, not the bellowing of bulls. And human holiness and honesty are quite familiar to me! Eh, how well I know them! If I were chosen as a judge, I would acquit the dead only l" and bursting into malicious laughter, Sasha said: "Well, that will do, we've spoken enough nonsense. Sit down at the table!"

On the morning of the next day Foma and Sasha stood side by side on the gangway of a steamer which was approaching a harbour on the Ustye.

Sasha's big black hat attracted everybody's attention by its deftly bent brim, and its white feathers, and Foma was ill at ease as he stood beside her, and felt as though inquisitive glances crawled over his perplexed face. The steamer hissed and quivered as it neared the landing-bridge, which was sprinkled by a waiting crowd of people attired in bright summer clothes, and it seemed to Foma that he noticed among the crowd of various faces and figures a person he knew, who now seemed to be hiding behind other people's backs, and yet lifted not his eye from him.

"Let's go into the cabin!" said he to his companion uneasily.

"Don't acquire the habit of hiding your sins from people," replied Sasha, with a smile. "Have you perhaps noticed an acquaintance there?"

"Mm. Yes. Somebody is watching me."

"A nurse with a milk bottle? Ha, ha, ha!"

"Well, there you're neighing!" said Foma, enraged, looking at her askance. "Do you think I am afraid?"

"I can see how brave you are."

"You'll see. I'll face anybody," said Foma, angrily, but after a close look at the crowd in the harbour his face suddenly assumed another expression, and he added softly:

"Oh, it's my godfather."

At the very edge of the landing-stage stood Yakov Tarasovich, squeezed between two stout women, with his iron-like face lifted upward, and he waved his cap in the air with malicious politeness. His beard shook, his bald crown flashed, and his small eye pierced Foma like borers.

"What a vulture!" muttered Foma, raising his cap and nodding his head to his godfather.

His bow evidently afforded great pleasure to Mayakin. The old man somehow coiled himself up, stamped his feet, and his face seemed beaming with a malicious smile.

"The little boy will get money for nuts, it seems!" Sasha teased Foma. Her words together with his godfather's smile seemed to have kindled a fire in Foma's breast.

"We shall see what is going to happen," hissed Foma, and suddenly he became as petrified in malicious calm. The steamer made fast, and the people rushed in a wave to the landing-place. Pressed by the crowd, Mayakin disappeared for awhile from the sight of his godson and appeared again with a maliciously triumphant smile. Foma stared at him fixedly, with knitted brow, and came toward him slowly pacing the gang planks. They jostled him in the back, they leaned on him, they squeezed him, and this provoked Foma still more. Now he came face to face with the old man, and the latter greeted him with a polite bow, and asked:

"Whither are you travelling, Foma Ignatyich?"

"About my affairs," replied Foma, firmly, without greeting his godfather.

"That's praiseworthy, my dear sir!" said Yakov Tarasovich, all beaming with a smile. "The lady with the feathers—what is she to you, may I ask?"

"She's my mistress," said Foma, loud, without lowering his eyes at the keen look of his godfather.

Sasha stood behind him calmly examining over his shoulder the little old man, whose head hardly reached Foma's chin. Attracted by Foma's loud words, the public looked at them, scenting a scandal. And Mayakin, too, perceived immediately the possibility of a scandal and instantly estimated correctly the quarrelsome mood of his godson. He contracted his wrinkles, bit his lips, and said to Foma, peaceably:

"I have something to speak to you about. Will you come with me to the hotel?"

"Yes; for a little while."

"You have no time, then? It's a plain thing, you must be making haste to wreck another barge, eh?" said the old man, unable to contain himself any longer.

"And why not wreck them, since they can be wrecked?" retorted Foma, passionately and firmly.

"Of course, you did not earn them yourself; why should you spare them? Well, come. And couldn't we drown that lady in the water for awhile?" said Mayakin, softly.

"Drive to the town, Sasha, and engage a room at the Siberian Inn. I'll be there shortly!" said Foma and turning to Mayakin, he announced boldly:

"I am ready! Let us go!"

Neither of them spoke on their way to the hotel. Foma, seeing that his godfather had to skip as he went in order to keep up with him, purposely took longer strides, and the fact that the old man could not keep step with him supported and strengthened in him the turbulent feeling of protest which he was by this time scarcely able to master.

"Waiter!" said Mayakin, gently, on entering the hall of the hotel, and turning toward a remote corner, "let us have a bottle of moorberry kvass."

"And I want some cognac," ordered Foma.

"So-o! When you have poor cards you had better always play the lowest trump first!" Mayakin advised him sarcastically.

"You don't know my game!" said Foma, seating himself by the table.

"Really? Come, come! Many play like that."

"How?"

"I mean as you do—boldly, but foolishly."

"I play so that either the head is smashed to pieces, or the wall broken in half," said Foma, hotly, and struck the table with his fist.

"Haven't you recovered from your drunkenness yet?" asked Mayakin with a smile.

Foma seated himself more firmly in his chair, and, his face distorted with wrathful agitation, he said:

"Godfather, you are a sensible man. I respect you for your common sense."

"Thank you, my son!" and Mayakin bowed, rising slightly, and leaning his hands against the table.

"Don't mention it. I want to tell you that I am no longer twenty. I am not a child any longer."

"Of course not!" assented Mayakin. "You've lived a good while, that goes without saying! If a mosquito had lived as long it might have grown as big as a hen."

"Stop your joking!" Foma warned him, and he did it so calmly that Mayakin started back, and the wrinkles on his face quivered with alarm.

"What did you come here for?" asked Foma.

"Ah! you've done some nasty work here. So I want to find out whether there's much damage in it! You see, I am a relative of yours. And then, I am the only one you have."

"You are troubling yourself in vain. Do you know, papa, what I'll tell you? Either give me full freedom, or take all my business into your own hands. Take everything! Everything—to the last rouble!"

This proposition burst forth from Foma altogether unexpectedly to himself; he had never before thought of anything like it. But now that he uttered such words to his godfather it suddenly became clear to him that if his godfather were to take from him all his property he would become a perfectly free man, he could go wherever he pleased, do whatever he pleased. Until this moment he had been bound and enmeshed with something, but he knew not his fetters and was unable to break them, while now they were falling off of themselves so simply, so easily. Both an alarming and a joyous hope blazed up within his breast, as though he noticed that suddenly light had begun to flash upon his turbid life, that a wide, spacious road lay open now before him. Certain images sprang up in his mind, and, watching their shiftings, he muttered incoherently:

"Here, this is better than anything! Take everything, and be done with it! And—as for me—I shall be free to go anywhere in the wide world! I cannot live like this. I feel as though weights were hanging on me, as though I were all bound. There—I must not go, this I must not do.

335

I want to live in freedom, that I may know everything myself. I shall search life for myself. For, otherwise, what am I? A prisoner! Be kind, take everything. The devil take it all! Give me freedom, pray! What kind of a merchant am I? I do not like anything. And so—I would forsake men—everything. I would find a place for myself, I would find some kind of work, and would work. By God! Father! set me at liberty! For now, you see, I am drinking. I'm entangled with that woman."

Mayakin looked at him, listened attentively to his words, and his face was stern, immobile as though petrified. A dull, tavern noise smote the air, some people went past them, they greeted Mayakin, but he saw nothing, staring fixedly at the agitated face of his godson, who smiled distractedly, both joyously and pitifully.

"Eh, my sour blackberry!" said Mayakin, with a sigh, interrupting Foma's speech. "I see you've lost your way. And you're prating nonsense. I would like to know whether the cognac is to blame for it, or is it your foolishness?"

"Papa!" exclaimed Foma, "this can surely be done. There were cases where people have cast away all their possessions and thus saved themselves."

"That wasn't in my time. Not people that are near to me!" said Mayakin, sternly, "or else I would have shown them how to go away!"

"Many have become saints when they went away."

"Mm! They couldn't have gone away from me! The matter is simple—you know how to play at draughts, don't you? Move from one place to another until you are beaten, and if you're not beaten then you have the queen. Then all ways are open to you. Do you understand? And why am I talking to you seriously? Psha!"

"Papa! why don't you want it?" exclaimed Foma, angrily.

"Listen to me! If you are a chimney-sweep, go, carrion, on the roof! If you are a fireman, stand on the watch-tower! And each and every sort of men must have its own mode of life. Calves cannot roar like bears! If you live your own life; go on, live it! And don't talk nonsense, and don't

336

creep where you don't belong. Arrange your life after your pattern." And from the dark lips of the old man gushed forth in a trembling, glittering stream the jarring, but confident and bold words so familiar to Foma. Seized with the thought of freedom, which seemed to him so easily possible, Foma did not listen to his words. This idea had eaten into his brains, and in his heart the desire grew stronger and stronger to sever all his connections with this empty and wearisome life, with his godfather, with the steamers, the barges and the carouses, with everything amidst which it was narrow and stifling for him to live.

The old man's words seemed to fall on him from afar; they were blended with the clatter of the dishes, with the scraping of the lackey's feet along the floor, with some one's drunken shouting. Not far from them sat four merchants at a table and argued loudly:

"Two and a quarter—and thank God!"

"Luka Mitrich! How can I?"

"Give him two and a half!"

"That's right! You ought to give it, it's a good steamer, it tows briskly."

"My dear fellows, I can't. Two and a quarter!"

"And all this nonsense came to your head from your youthful passion!" said Mayakin, importantly, accompanying his words with a rap on the table. "Your boldness is stupidity; all these words of yours are nonsense. Would you perhaps go to the cloister? or have you perhaps a longing to go on the highways?"

Foma listened in silence. The buzzing noise about him now seemed to move farther away from him. He pictured himself amid a vast restless crowd of people; without knowing why they bustled about hither and thither, jumped on one another; their eyes were greedily opened wide; they were shouting, cursing, falling, crushing one another, and they were all jostling about on one place. He felt bad among them because he did not understand what they wanted, because he had no faith in their words, and he felt that they had no faith in themselves, that they understood nothing.

And if one were to tear himself away from their midst to freedom, to the edge of life, and thence behold them—then all would become clear to him. Then he would also understand what they wanted, and would find his own place among them.

"Don't I understand," said Mayakin, more gently, seeing Foma lost in thought, and assuming that he was reflecting on his words—"I understand that you want happiness for yourself. Well, my friend, it is not to be easily seized. You must seek happiness even as they search for mushrooms in the wood, you must bend your back in search of it, and finding it, see whether it isn't a toad-stool."

"So you will set me free?" asked Foma, suddenly lifting his head, and Mayakin turned his eyes away from his fiery look.

"Father! at least for a short time! Let me breathe, let me step aside from everything!" entreated Foma. "I will watch how everything goes on. And then—if not—I shall become a drunkard."

"Don't talk nonsense. Why do you play the fool?" cried Mayakin, angrily.

"Very well, then!" replied Foma, calmly. "Very well! You do not want it? Then there will be nothing! I'll squander it all! And there is nothing more for us to speak of. Goodbye! I'll set out to work, you'll see! It will afford you joy. Everything will go up in smoke!" Foma was calm, he spoke with confidence; it seemed to him that since he had thus decided, his godfather could not hinder him. But Mayakin straightened himself in his chair and said, also plainly and calmly:

"And do you know how I can deal with you?"

"As you like!" said Foma, with a wave of the hand. "Well then. Now I like the following: I'll return to town and will see to it that you are declared insane, and put into a lunatic asylum."

"Can this be done?" asked Foma, distrustfully, but with a tone of fright in his voice.

"We can do everything, my dear."

Foma lowered his head, and casting a furtive glance at his godfather's face, shuddered, thinking:

"He'll do it; he won't spare me."

"If you play the fool seriously I must also deal with you seriously. I promised your father to make a man of you, and I will do it; if you cannot stand on your feet, I'll put you in irons. Then you will stand. Though I know all these holy words of yours are but ugly caprices that come from excessive drinking. But if you do not give that up, if you keep on behaving indecently, if you ruin, out of wantonness, the property accumulated by your father, I'll cover you all up. I'll have a bell forged over you. It is very inconvenient to fool with me."

Mayakin spoke gently. The wrinkles of his cheeks all rose upward, and his small eyes in their dark sockets were smiling sarcastically, coldly. And the wrinkles on his forehead formed an odd pattern, rising up to his bald crown. His face was stern and merciless, and breathed melancholy and coldness upon Foma's soul.

"So there's no way out for me?" asked Foma, gloomily. "You are blocking all my ways?"

"There is a way. Go there! I shall guide you. Don't worry, it will be right! You will come just to your proper place."

This self-confidence, this unshakable boastfulness aroused Foma's indignation. Thrusting his hands into his pockets in order not to strike the old man, he straightened himself in his chair and clinching his teeth, said, facing Mayakin closely:

"Why are you boasting? What are you boasting of? Your own son, where is he? Your daughter, what is she? Eh, you—you life-builder! Well, you are clever. You know everything. Tell me, what for do you live? What for are you accumulating money? Do you think you are not going to die? Well, what then? You've captured me. You've taken hold of me, you've conquered me. But wait, I may yet tear myself away from you! It isn't the end yet! Eh, you! What have you done for life? By what will you be remembered? My father, for instance, donated a lodging-house, and you—what have you done?"

Mayakin's wrinkles quivered and sank downward, wherefore his face assumed a sickly, weeping expression.

"How will you justify yourself?" asked Foma, softly, without lifting his eyes from him.

"Hold your tongue, you puppy!" said the old man in a low voice, casting a glance of alarm about the room.

"I've said everything! And now I'm going! Hold me back!"

Foma rose from his chair, thrust his cap on his head, and measured the old man with abhorrence.

"You may go; but I'll—I'll catch you! It will come out as I say!" said Yakov Tarasovich in a broken voice.

"And I'll go on a spree! I'll squander all!"

"Very well, we'll see!"

"Goodbye! you hero," Foma laughed.

"Goodbye, for a short while! I'll not go back on my own. I love it. I love you, too. Never mind, you're a good fellow!" said Mayakin, softly, and as though out of breath.

"Do not love me, but teach me. But then, you cannot teach me the right thing!" said Foma, as he turned his back on the old man and left the hall.

Yakov Tarasovich Mayakin remained in the tavern alone. He sat by the table, and, bending over it, made drawings of patterns on the tray, dipping his trembling finger in the spilt kvass, and his sharp-pointed head was sinking lower and lower over the table, as though he did not decipher, and could not make out what his bony finger was drawing on the tray.

Beads of perspiration glistened on his bald crown, and as usual the wrinkles on his cheeks quivered with frequent, irritable starts.

In the tavern a resounding tumult smote the air so that the window-panes were rattling. From the Volga were wafted the whistlings of steamers, the dull beating of the wheels upon the water, the shouting of the loaders—life was moving onward unceasingly and unquestionably.

Summoning the waiter with a nod Yakov Tarasovich asked him with peculiar intensity and impressiveness

"How much do I owe for all this?"

CHAPTER X

PREVIOUS to his quarrel with Mayakin, Foma had caroused because of the weariness of life, out of curiosity, and half indifferently; now he led a dissipated life out of spite, almost in despair; now he was filled with a feeling of vengeance and with a certain insolence toward men, an insolence which astonished even himself at times. He saw that the people about him, like himself, lacked support and reason, only they did not understand this, or purposely would not understand it, so as not to hinder themselves from living blindly, and from giving themselves completely, without a thought, to their dissolute life. He found nothing firm in them, nothing steadfast; when sober, they seemed to him miserable and stupid; when intoxicated, they were repulsive to him, and still more stupid. None of them inspired him with respect, with deep, hearty interest; he did not even ask them what their names were; he forgot where and when he made their acquaintance, and regarding them with contemptuous curiosity, always longed to say and do something that would offend them. He passed days and nights with them in different places of amusement, and his acquaintances always depended just upon the category of each of these places. In the expensive and elegant restaurants certain sharpers of the better class of society surrounded him—gamblers, couplet singers, jugglers, actors, and property-holders who were ruined by leading depraved lives. At first these people treated him with a patronizing air, and boasted before him of their refined tastes, of their knowledge of the merits of wine and food, and then they courted favours of him, fawned upon him, borrowed of him money which he scattered about without counting, drawing it from the banks, and already borrowing it on promissory notes. In the cheap taverns hair-dressers, markers, clerks, functionaries and choristers surrounded him like vultures; and among these people he always felt better—freer. In these he saw plain people, not so monstrously deformed and distorted as that "clean society" of the elegant restaurants; these were less depraved, cleverer, better understood by him. At times they evinced wholesome, strong emotions, and there was always something more human in them. But, like the "clean society," these were also eager for money, and shamelessly fleeced him, and he saw it and rudely mocked them.

To be sure, there were women. Physically healthy, but not sensual, Foma bought them, the dear ones and the cheap ones, the beautiful and the ugly, gave them large sums of money, changed them almost every week, and in general, he treated the women better than the men. He laughed at them, said to them disgraceful and offensive words, but he could never, even when half-drunk, rid himself of a certain bashfulness in their presence. They all, even the most brazen-faced, the strongest and the most shameless, seemed to him weak and defenseless, like small children. Always ready to thrash any man, he never laid a hand on women, although when irritated by something he sometimes abused them indecently. He felt that he was immeasurably stronger than any woman, and every woman seemed to him immeasurably more miserable than he was. Those of the women who led their dissolute lives audaciously, boasting of their depravity, called forth in Foma a feeling of bashfulness, which made him timid and awkward. One evening, during supper hour, one of these women, intoxicated and impudent, struck Foma on the cheek with a melon-rind. Foma was half-drunk. He turned pale with rage, rose from his chair, and thrusting his hands into his pockets, said in a fierce voice which trembled with indignation:

"You carrion, get out. Begone! Someone else would have broken your head for this. And you know that I am forbearing with you, and that my arm is never raised against any of your kind. Drive her away to the devil!"

A few days after her arrival in Kazan, Sasha became the mistress of a certain vodka-distiller's son, who was carousing together with Foma. Going away with her new master to some place on the Kama, she said to Foma:

"Goodbye, dear man! Perhaps we may meet again. We're both going the same way! But I advise you not to give your heart free rein. Enjoy yourself without looking back at anything. And then, when the gruel is eaten up, smash the bowl on the ground. Goodbye!"

And she impressed a hot kiss upon his lips, at which her eyes looked still darker.

Foma was glad that she was leaving him, he had grown tired of her and her cold indifference frightened him. But now something trembled within him, he turned aside from her and said in a low voice:

"Perhaps you will not live well together, then come back to me."

"Thank you!" she replied, and for some reason or other burst into hoarse laughter, which was uncommon with her.

Thus lived Foma, day in and day out, always turning around on one and the same place, amid people who were always alike, and who never inspired him with any noble feelings. And then he considered himself superior to them, because the thoughts of the possibility of freeing himself from this life was taking deeper and deeper root in his mind, because the yearning for freedom held him in an ever firmer embrace, because ever brighter were the pictures as he imagined himself drifting away to the border of life, away from this tumult and confusion. More than once, by night, remaining all by himself, he would firmly close his eyes and picture to himself a dark throng of people, innumerably great and even terrible in its immenseness. Crowded together somewhere in a deep valley, which was surrounded by hillocks, and filled with a dusty mist, this throng jostled one another on the same place in noisy confusion, and looked like grain in a hopper. It was as though an invisible millstone, hidden beneath the feet of the crowd, were grinding it, and people moved about it like waves—now rushing downward to be ground the sooner and disappear, now bursting upward in the effort to escape the merciless millstone. There were also people who resembled crabs just caught and thrown into a huge basket—clutching at one another, they twined about heavily, crawled somewhere and interfered with one another, and could do nothing to free themselves from captivity.

Foma saw familiar faces amid the crowd: there his father is walking boldly, sturdily pushing aside and overthrowing everybody on his way; he is working with his long paws, massing everything with his chest, and laughing in thundering tones. And then he disappears, sinking somewhere in the depth, beneath the feet of the people. There, wriggling like a snake, now jumping on people's shoulders, now gliding between their feet, his godfather is working with his lean, but supple and sinewy body. Here Lubov is crying and struggling, following her father, with abrupt but faint movements, now remaining behind him, now nearing him again. Striding softly with a kind smile on her face, stepping aside from everybody, and making way for everyone, Aunt Anfisa is slowly moving along. Her image quivers in the darkness before Foma, like the modest flame of a wax candle. And it dies out and disappears in the darkness. Pelagaya is quickly going somewhere along a straight road. There Sophya Pavlovna Medinskaya is standing, her hands hanging impotently, just as she stood in her drawing-room when he saw her last. Her eyes were large, but some great fright gleams in them. Sasha, too, is here. Indifferent, paying no attention to the jostling, she is stoutly going straight into the very dregs of life, singing her songs at the top of her voice, her dark eyes fixed in the distance before her. Foma hears tumult, howls, laughter, drunken shouts, irritable disputes about copecks—songs and sobs hover over this enormous restless heap of living human bodies crowded into a pit. They jump, fall, crawl, crush one another, leap on one another's shoulders, grope everywhere like blind people, stumbling everywhere over others like themselves, struggle, and, falling, disappear from sight. Money rustles, soaring like bats over the heads of the people, and the people greedily stretch out their hands toward it, the gold and silver jingles, bottles rattle, corks pop, someone sobs, and a melancholy female voice sings:

"And so let us live while we can,
And then—e'en grass may cease to grow!"

This wild picture fastened itself firmly in Foma's mind, and growing clearer, larger and more vivid with each time it arose before him, rousing in his breast something chaotic, one great indefinite feeling into which fell, like streams into a river, fear and revolt and compassion and wrath and many another thing. All this boiled up within his breast into strained desire, which was thrusting it asunder into a desire whose power was choking him, and his eyes were filled with tears; he longed to shout, to howl like a beast, to frighten all the people, to check their senseless bustle, to pour into the tumult and vanity of their life something new, his own—to tell them certain loud firm words, to guide them all into one direction, and not one against another. He desired to seize them by their heads, to tear them apart one from another, to thrash some, to fondle others, to reproach them all, to illumine them with a certain fire.

There was nothing in him, neither the necessary words, nor the fire; all he had was the longing which was clear to him, but impossible of fulfillment. He pictured himself above life outside of the deep valley, wherein people were bustling about; he saw himself standing firmly on his feet and—speechless. He might have cried to the people:

"See how you live! Aren't you ashamed?"

And he might have abused them. But if they were to ask on hearing his voice:

"And how ought we to live?"

It was perfectly clear to him that after such a question he would have to fly down head foremost from the heights there, beneath the feet of the throng, upon the millstone. And laughter would accompany him to his destruction.

Sometimes he was delirious under the pressure of this nightmare. Certain meaningless and unconnected words burst from his lips; he even perspired from this painful struggle within him. At times it occurred to him that he was going mad from intoxication, and that that was the reason why this terrible and gloomy picture was forcing itself into his mind. With a great effort of will he brushed aside these pictures and excitements; but as soon as he was alone and not very drunk, he was again seized by his delirium and again grew faint under its weight. And his thirst for freedom was growing more and more intense, torturing him by its force. But tear himself away from the shackles of his wealth he could not. Mayakin, who had Foma's full power of attorney to manage his affairs, acted now in such a way that Foma was bound to feel almost every day the burden of the obligations which rested upon him. People were constantly applying to him for payments, proposing to him terms for the transportation of freight. His employees overwhelmed him in person and by letter with trifles with which he had never before concerned himself, as they used to settle these trifles at their own risk. They looked for him and found him in the taverns, questioned him as to what and how it should be done; he would tell them sometimes without at all understanding in what way this or that should be done. He noticed their concealed contempt for him, and almost always saw that they did not do the work as he had ordered, but did it in a different and better way. In this he felt the clever hand of his godfather, and understood that the old man was thus pressing him in order to turn him to his way. And at the same time he noticed that he was not the master of his business, but only a component part of it, and an insignificant part at that. This irritated him and moved him farther away from the old man, it augumented his longing to tear himself away from his business, even at the cost of his own ruin. Infuriated, he flung money about the taverns and dives, but this did not last long. Yakov Tarasovich closed his accounts in the banks, withdrawing all deposits. Soon Foma began to feel that even on promissory notes, they now gave him the money not quite as willingly as before. This stung his vanity; and his indignation was roused, and he was frightened when he learned that his godfather had circulated a rumour in the business world that he, Foma, was out of his mind, and that, perhaps, it might become necessary to appoint a guardian for him. Foma did not know the limits of his godfather's power, and did not venture to take anyone's counsel in this matter. He was convinced that in the business world the old man was a power, and that he could do anything he pleased. At first it was painful for him to feel Mayakin's hand over him, but later he became reconciled to this, renounced everything, and resumed his restless, drunken life, wherein there was only one consolation—the people. With each succeeding day he became more and more convinced that they were more irrational and altogether worse than he—that they were not the masters of life, but its slaves, and that it was turning them around, bending and breaking them at its will, while they succumbed to it unfeelingly and resignedly, and none of them but he desired freedom. But he wanted it, and therefore proudly elevated himself above his drinking companions, not desiring to see in them anything but wrong.

One day in a tavern a certain half-intoxicated man complained to him of his life. This was a small-sized, meagre man, with dim, frightened eyes, unshaven, in a short frock coat, and with a bright necktie. He blinked pitifully, his ears quivered spasmodically, and his soft little voice also trembled.

"I've struggled hard to make my way among men; I've tried everything, I've worked like a bull. But life jostled me aside, crushed me under foot, gave me no chance. All my patience gave way. Eh! and so I've taken to drink. I feel that I'll be ruined. Well, that's the only way open to me!"

"Fool!" said Foma with contempt. "Why did you want to make your way among men? You should have kept away from them, to the right. Standing aside, you might have seen where your place was among them, and then gone right to the point!"

"I don't understand your words." The little man shook his close-cropped, angular head.

Foma laughed, self-satisfied.

"Is it for you to understand it?""No; do you know, I think that he whom God decreed—"

"Not God, but man arranges life!" Foma blurted out, and was even himself astonished at the audacity of his words. And the little man glancing at him askance also shrank timidly.

"Has God given you reason?" asked Foma, recovering from his embarrassment.

"Of course; that is to say, as much as is the share of a small man," said Foma's interlocutor irresolutely.

"Well, and you have no right to ask of Him a single grain more! Make your own life by your own reason. And God will judge you. We are all in His service. And in His eyes we are all of equal value. Understand?"

It happened very often that Foma would suddenly say something which seemed audacious even to himself, and which, at the same time, elevated him in his own eyes. There were certain unexpected, daring thoughts and words, which suddenly flashed like sparks, as though an impression produced them from Foma's brains. And he noticed more than once that whatever he had carefully thought out beforehand was expressed by him not quite so well, and more obscure, than that which suddenly flashed up in his heart.

Foma lived as though walking in a swamp, in danger of sinking at each step in the mire and slime, while his godfather, like a river loach, wriggled himself on a dry, firm little spot, vigilantly watching the life of his godson from afar.

After his quarrel with Foma, Yakov Tarasovich returned home, gloomy and pensive. His eyes flashed drily, and he straightened himself like a tightly-stretched string. His wrinkles shrank painfully, his face seemed to have become smaller and darker, and when Lubov saw him in this state it appeared to her that he was seriously ill, but that he was forcing and restraining himself. Mutely and nervously the old man flung himself about the room, casting in reply to his daughter's questions, dry curt words, and finally shouted to her:

"Leave me alone! You see it has nothing to do with you."

She felt sorry for him when she noticed the gloomy and melancholy expression of his keen, green eyes; she made it her duty to question him as to what had happened to him, and when he seated himself at the dinner-table she suddenly approached him, placed her hands on his shoulders, and looking down into his face, asked him tenderly and anxiously:

"Papa, are you ill? tell me!"

Her caresses were extremely rare; they always softened the lonely old man, and though he did not respond to them for some reason or other he nevertheless could not help appreciating them. And now he shrugged his shoulders, thus throwing off her hands and said:

"Go, go to your place. How the itching curiosity of Eve gives you no rest."

But Lubov did not go away; persistingly looking into his eyes, she asked, with an offended tone in her voice:

"Papa, why do you always speak to me in such a way as though I were a small child, or very stupid?"

"Because you are grown up and yet not very clever. Yes! That's the whole story! Go, sit down and eat!"

She walked away and silently seated herself opposite her father, compressing her lips for affront. Contrary to his habits Mayakin ate slowly, stirring his spoon in his plate of cabbage-soup for a long time, and examining the soup closely.

"If your obstructed mind could but comprehend your father's thoughts!" said he, suddenly, as he sighed with a sort of whistling sound.

Lubov threw her spoon aside and almost with tears in her voice, said:

"Why do you insult me, papa? You see that I am alone, always alone! You understand how difficult my life is, and you never say a single kind

350

word to me. You never say anything to me! And you are also lonely; life is difficult for you too, I can see it. You find it very hard to live, but you alone are to blame for it! You alone!

"Now Balaam's she-ass has also started to talk!" said the old man, laughing. "Well! what will be next?"

"You are very proud of your wisdom, papa."

"And what else?"

"That isn't good; and it pains me greatly. Why do you repulse me? You know that, save you, I have no one."

Tears leaped to her eyes; her father noticed them, and his face quivered.

"If you were not a girl!" he exclaimed. "If you had as much brains as Marfa Poosadnitza, for instance. Eh, Lubov? Then I'd laugh at everybody, and at Foma. Come now, don't cry!"

She wiped her eyes and asked:

"What about Foma?"

"He's rebellious. Ha! ha! he says: 'Take away my property, give me freedom!' He wants to save his soul in the kabak. That's what entered Foma's head."

"Well, what is this?" asked Lubov, irresolutely. She wanted to say that Foma's desire was good, that it was a noble desire if it were earnest, but she feared to irritate her father with her words, and she only gazed at him questioningly.

"What is it?" said Mayakin, excitedly, trembling. "That either comes to him from excessive drinking, or else—Heaven forbid—from his mother, the orthodox spirit. And if this heathenish leaven is going to rise in him I'll have to struggle hard with him! There will be a great conflict between us. He has come out, breast foremost, against me; he has at once displayed great audacity. He's young—there's not much cunning in him as yet. He says: 'I'll drink away everything, everything will go up in smoke! I'll show you how to drink!

Mayakin lifted his hand over his head, and, clenching his fist, threatened furiously.

"How dare you? Who established the business? Who built it up? You? Your father. Forty years of labour were put into it, and you wish to destroy it? We must all go to our places here all together as one man, there cautiously, one by one. We merchants, tradesmen, have for centuries carried Russia on our shoulders, and we are still carrying it. Peter the Great was a Czar of divine wisdom, he knew our value. How he supported us! He had printed books for the express purpose of teaching us business. There I have a book which was printed at his order by Polidor Virgily Oorbansky, about inventory, printed in 1720. Yes, one must understand this. He understood it, and cleared the way for us. And now we stand on our own feet, and we feel our place. Clear the way for us! We have laid the foundation of life, instead of bricks we have laid ourselves in the earth. Now we must build the stories. Give us freedom of action! That's where we must hold our course. That's where the problem lies; but Foma does not comprehend this. But he must understand it, must resume the work. He has his father's means. When I die mine will be added to his. Work, you puppy! And he is raving. No, wait! I'll lift you up to the proper point!"

The old man was choking with agitation and with flashing eyes looked at his daughter so furiously as though Foma were sitting in her place. His agitation frightened Lubov, but she lacked the courage to interrupt her father, and she looked at his stern and gloomy face in silence.

"The road has been paved by our fathers, and you must walk on it. I have worked for fifty years to what purpose? That my children may resume it after I am gone. My children! Where are my children?"

The old man drooped his head mournfully, his voice broke down, and he said sadly, as if he were speaking unto himself:

"One is a convict, utterly ruined; the other, a drunkard. I have little hope in him. My daughter, to whom, then, shall I leave my labour before my death? If I had but a son-in-law. I thought Foma would become a man and would be sharpened up, then I would give you unto him, and with you all I have—there! But Foma is good for nothing, and I see no one else in his stead. What sort of people we have now! In former days the people were as of iron, while now they are of india-rubber. They are all bending now. And nothing—they have no firmness in them. What is it? Why is it so?"

Mayakin looked at his daughter with alarm. She was silent.

"Tell me," he asked her, "what do you need? How, in your opinion, is it proper to live? What do you want? You have studied, read, tell me what is it that you need?"

The questions fell on Lubov's head quite unexpectedly to her, and she was embarrassed. She was pleased that her father asked her about this matter, and was at the same time afraid to reply, lest she should be lowered in his estimation. And then, gathering courage, as though preparing to jump across the table, she said irresolutely and in a trembling voice:

"That all the people should be happy and contented; that all the people should be equal, all the people have an equal right to life, to the bliss of life, all must have freedom, even as they have air. And equality ineverything!"

At the beginning of her agitated speech her father looked at her face with anxious curiosity in his eyes, but as she went on hastily hurling her words at him his eyes assumed an altogether different expression, and finally he said to her with calm contempt:

"I knew it before—you are a gilded fool!"

She lowered her head, but immediately raised it and exclaimed sadly:

"You have said so yourself—freedom."

"You had better hold your tongue!" the old man shouted at her rudely. "You cannot see even that which is visibly forced outside of each man. How can all the people be happy and equal, since each one wants to be above the other? Even the beggar has his pride and always boasts of something or other before other people. A small child, even he wants to be first among his playmates. And one man will never yield to another;

only fools believe in it. Each man has his own soul, and his own face; only those who love not their souls and care not for their faces can be planed down to the same size. Eh, you! You've read much trash, and you've devoured it!"

Bitter reproach and biting contempt were expressed on the old man's face. He noisily pushed his chair away from the table, jumped up, and folding his hands behind his back, began to dart about in the room with short steps, shaking his head and saying something to himself in an angry, hissing whisper. Lubov, pale with emotion and anger, feeling herself stupid and powerless before him, listening to his whisper, and her heart palpitated wildly.

"I am left alone, alone, like Job. 0h Lord! What shall I do? Oh, alone! Am I not wise? Am I not clever? But life has outwitted me also. What does it love? Whom does it fondle? It beats the good, and suffers not the bad to go unpunished, and no one understands life's justice."

The girl began to feel painfully sorry for the old man; she was seized with an intense yearning to help him; she longed to be of use to him.

Following him with burning eyes, she suddenly said in a low voice:

"Papa, dear! do not grieve. Taras is still alive. Perhaps he—"

Mayakin stopped suddenly as though nailed to the spot, and he slowly lifted his head.

"The tree that grew crooked in its youth and could not hold out will certainly break when it's old. But nevertheless, even Taras is a straw to me now. Though I doubt whether he is better than Foma. Gordyeeff has a character, he has his father's daring. He can take a great deal on himself. But Taraska, you recalled him just in time. Yes!"

And the old man, who a moment ago had lost his courage to the point of complaining, and, grief-stricken had run about the room like a mouse in a trap, now calmly and firmly walked up with a careworn face to the table, carefully adjusted his chair, and seated himself, saying:

354

"We'll have to sound Taraska. He lives in Usolye at some factory. I was told by some merchants—they're making soda there, I believe. I'll find out the particulars. I'll write to him."

"Allow me to write to him, papa!" begged Lubov, softly, flushing, trembling with joy.

"You?" asked Mayakin, casting a brief glance at her; he then became silent, thought awhile and said:

"That's all right. That's even better! Write to him. Ask him whether he isn't married, how he lives, what he thinks. But then I'll tell you what to write when the time has come."

"Do it at once, papa," said the girl.

"It is necessary to marry you off the sooner. I am keeping an eye on a certain red-haired fellow. He doesn't seem to be stupid. He's been polished abroad, by the way.

"Is it Smolin, papa?" asked Lubov, inquisitively and anxiously.

"And supposing it is he, what of it?" inquired Yakov Tarasovich in a business-like tone.

"Nothing, I don't know him," replied Lubov, indefinitely.

"We'll make you acquainted. It's time, Lubov, it's time. Our hopes for Foma are poor, although I do not give him up."

"I did not reckon on Foma—what is he to me?"

"That's wrong. If you had been cleverer perhaps he wouldn't have gone astray! Whenever I used to see you together, I thought: 'My girl will attract the fellow to herself! That will be a fine affair!' But I was wrong. I thought that you would know what is to your advantage without being told of it. That's the way, my girl!" said the father, instructively.

She became thoughtful as she listened to his impressive speech. Robust and strong, Lubov was thinking of marriage more and more frequently of late, for she saw no other way out of her loneliness. The desire to forsake her father and go away somewhere in order to study something, to do something. This desire she had long since overcome, even as she conquered in herself many another longing just as keen, but shallow and indefinite. From the various books she had read a thick sediment remained within her, and though it was something live it had the life of a protoplasm. This sediment developed in the girl a feeling of dis-satisfaction with her life, a yearning toward personal independence, a longing to be freed from the heavy guardianship of her father, but she had neither the power to realize these desires, nor the clear conception of their realization. But nature had its influence on her, and at the sight of young mothers with children in their arms Lubov often felt a sad and mournful languor within her. At times stopping before the mirror she sadly scrutinized in it her plump, fresh face with dark circles around her eyes, and she felt sorry for herself. She felt that life was going past her, forgetting her somewhere on the side. Now listening to her father's words she pictured to herself what sort of man Smolin might be. She had met him when he was yet a Gymnasium student, his face was covered with freckles, he was snub-nosed, always clean, sedate and tiresome. He danced heavily, awkwardly, he talked uninterestingly. A long time had passed since then, he had been abroad, had studied something there, how was he now? From Smolin her thoughts darted to her brother, and with a sinking heart she thought: what would he say in reply to her letter? What sort of a man was he? The image of her brother as she had pictured it to herself prevented her from seeing both her father and Smolin, and she had already made up her mind not to consent to marry before meeting Taras, when suddenly her father shouted to her:

"Eh, Lubovka! Why are you thoughtful? What are you thinking of mostly?"

"So, everything goes so swiftly," replied Luba, with a smile.

"What goes swiftly?"

"Everything. A week ago it was impossible to speak with you about Taras, while now—"

"'Tis need, my girl! Need is a power, it bends a steel rod into a spring. And steel is stubborn. Taras, we'll see what he is! Man is to be appreciated by his resistance to the power of life; if it isn't life that wrings him, but he that wrings life to suit himself, my respects to that man! Allow me to shake your hand, let's run our business together. Eh, I am old. And how very brisk life has become now! With each succeeding year there is more and more interest in it, more and more relish to it! I wish I could live forever, I wish I could act all the time!" The old man smacked his lips, rubbed his hands, and his small eyes gleamed greedily.

"But you are a thin-blooded lot! Ere you have grown up you are already overgrown and withered. You live like an old radish. And the fact that life is growing fairer and fairer is incomprehensible to you. I have lived sixty-seven years on this earth, and though I am now standing close to my grave I can see that in former years, when I was young, there were fewer flowers on earth, and the flowers were not quite as beautiful as they are now. Everything is growing more beautiful! What buildings we have now! What different trade implements. What huge steamers! A world of brains has been put into everything! You look and think; what clever fellows you are—0h people! You merit reward and respect! You've arranged life cleverly. Everything is good, everything is pleasant. Only you, our successors, you are devoid of all live feelings! Any little charlatan from among the commoners is cleverer than you! Take that Yozhov, for instance, what is he? And yet he represents himself as judge over us, and even over life itself—he has courage. But you, pshaw! You live like beggars! In your joy you are beasts, in your misfortune vermin! You are rotten! They ought to inject fire into your veins, they ought to take your skin off and strew salt upon your raw flesh, then you would have jumped!"

Yakov Tarasovich, small-sized, wrinkled and bony, with black, broken teeth in his mouth, bald-headed and dark, as though burned by the heat of life and smoked in it, trembled in vehement agitation, showering jarring words of contempt upon his daughter, who was young, well-grown and plump. She looked at him with a guilty expression in her eyes, smiled confusedly, and in her heart grew a greater and greater respect for the live old man who was so steadfast in his desires.

And Foma went on straying and raving, passing his days and nights in taverns and dens, and mastering more and more firmly his contemptuously-hateful bearing toward the people that surrounded him. At times they awakened in him a sad yearning to find among them some sort of resistance to his wicked feeling, to meet a worthy and courageous man who would cause him to blush with shame by his burning reproach. This yearning became clearer—each time it sprang up in him it was a longing for assistance on the part of a man who felt that he had lost his way and was perishing.

"Brethren!" he cried one day, sitting by the table in a tavern, half-intoxicated, and surrounded by certain obscure and greedy people, who ate and drank as though they had not had a piece of bread in their mouths for many a long day before.

"Brethren! I feel disgusted. I am tired of you! Beat me unmercifully, drive me away! You are rascals, but you are nearer to one another than to me. Why? Am I not a drunkard and a rascal as well? And yet I am a stranger to you! I can see I am a stranger. You drink out of me and secretly you spit upon me. I can feel it! Why do you do it?"

To be sure, they could treat him in a different way. In the depth of his soul perhaps not one of them considered himself lower than Foma, but he was rich, and this hindered them from treating him more as a companion, and then he always spoke certain comically wrathful, conscience-rending words, and this embarrassed them. Moreover, he was strong and ready to fight, and they dared not say a word against him. And that was just what he wanted. He wished more and more intensely that one of these people he despised would stand up against him, face to face, and would tell him something strong, which, like a lever, would turn him aside from the sloping road, whose danger he felt, and whose filth he saw, being filled with helpless aversion for it.

And Foma found what he needed.

One day, irritated by the lack of attention for him, he cried to his drinking-companions:

"You boys, keep quiet, every one of you! Who gives you to drink and to eat? Have you forgotten it? I'll bring you in order! I'll show you how to respect me! Convicts! When I speak you must all keep quiet!"

And, indeed, all became silent; either for fear lest they might lose his good will, or, perhaps, afraid that he, that healthy and strong beast, might beat them. They sat in silence about a minute, concealing their anger at him, bending over the plates and attempting to hide from him their fright and embarrassment. Foma measured them with a self-satisfied look, and gratified by their slavish submissiveness, said boastfully:

"Ah! You've grown dumb now, that's the way! I am strict! I—"

"You sluggard!" came some one's calm, loud exclamation.

"Wha-at?" roared Foma, jumping up from his chair. "Who said that?"

Then a certain, strange, shabby-looking man arose at the end of the table; he was tall, in a long frock-coat, with a heap of grayish hair on his large head. His hair was stiff, standing out in all directions in thick locks, his face was yellow, unshaven, with a long, crooked nose. To Foma it seemed that he resembled a swab with which the steamer decks are washed, and this amused the half-intoxicated fellow.

"How fine!" said he, sarcastically. "What are you snarling at, eh? Do you know who I am?"

With the gesture of a tragic actor the man stretched out to Foma his hand, with its long, pliant fingers like those of a juggler, and he said in a deep hoarse basso:

"You are the rotten disease of your father, who, though he was a plunderer, was nevertheless a worthy man in comparison with you."

Because of the unexpectedness of this, and because of his wrath, Foma's heart shrank. He fiercely opened his eyes wide and kept silent, finding no words to reply to this insolence. And the man, standing before him, went on hoarsely, with animation, beastlike rolling his large, but dim and swollen, eyes:

"You demand of us respect for you, you fool! How have you merited it? Who are you? A drunkard, drinking away the fortune of your father. You savage! You ought to be proud that I, a renowned artist, a disinterested and faithful worshipper at the shrine of art, drink from the same bottle with you! This bottle contains sandal and molasses, infused with snuff-tobacco, while you think it is port wine. It is your license for the name of savage and ass."

"Eh, you jailbird!" roared Foma, rushing toward the artist. But he was seized and held back. Struggling in the arms of those that seized him, he was compelled to listen without replying, to the thundering, deep and heavy bass of the man who resembled a swab.

"You have thrown to men a few copecks out of the stolen roubles, and you consider yourself a hero! You are twice a thief. You have stolen the roubles and now you are stealing gratitude for your few copecks! But I shall not give it to you! I, who have devoted all my life to the condemnation of vice, I stand before you and say openly: 'You are a fool and a beggar because you are too rich! Here lies the wisdom: all the rich are beggars.' That's how the famous coupletist, Rimsky-Kannibalsky, serves Truth!"

Foma was now standing meekly among the people that had closely surrounded him, and he eagerly listened to the coupletist's thundering words, which now aroused in him a sensation as though somebody was scratching a sore spot, and thus soothing the acute itching of the pain. The people were excited; some attempted to check the coupletist's flow of eloquence, others wanted to lead Foma away somewhere. Without saying a word he pushed them aside and listened, more and more absorbed by the intense pleasure of humiliation which he felt in the presence of these people. The pain irritated by the words of the coupletist, caressed Foma's soul more and more passionately, and the coupletist went on thundering, intoxicated with the impurity of his accusation:

"You think that you are the master of life? You are the low slave of the rouble."

Someone in the crowd hiccoughed, and, evidently displeased with himself for this, cursed each time he hiccoughed:

"Oh devil."

And a certain, unshaven, fat-faced man took pity on Foma, or, perhaps, became tired of witnessing that scene, and, waving his hands, he drawled out plaintively:

"Gentlemen, drop that! It isn't good! For we are all sinners! Decidedly all, believe me!"

"Well, speak on!" muttered Foma. "Say everything! I won't touch you."

The mirrors on the walls reflected this drunken confusion, and the people, as reflected in the mirrors, seemed more disgusting and hideous than they were in reality.

"I do not want to speak! "exclaimed the coupletist, "I do not want to cast the pearls of truth and of my wrath before you."

He rushed forward, and raising his head majestically, turned toward the door with tragic footsteps.

"You lie!" said Foma, attempting to follow him. "Hold on! you have made me agitated, now calm me."

They seized him, surrounded him and shouted something to him while he was rushing forward, overturning everybody. When he met tactile obstacles on his way the struggle with them gave him ease, uniting all his riotous feelings into one yearning to overthrow that which hindered him. And now, after he had jostled them all aside and rushed out into the street, he was already less agitated. Standing on the sidewalk he looked about the street and thought with shame:

"How could I permit that swab to mock me and abuse my father as a thief?"

It was dark and quiet about him, the moon was shining brightly, and a light refreshing breeze was blowing. Foma held his face to the cool breeze as he walked against the wind with rapid strides, timidly looking about on all sides, and wishing that none of the company from the tavern would follow him. He understood that he had lowered himself in the eyes of all these people. As he walked he thought of what he had come to: a sharper had publicly abused him in disgraceful terms, while he, the son of a well-known merchant, had not been able to repay him for his mocking.

"It serves me right!" thought Foma, sadly and bitterly. "That serves me right! Don't lose your head, understand. And then again, I wanted it myself. I interfered with everybody, so now, take your share!" These thoughts made him feel painfully sorry for himself. Seized and sobered by them he kept on strolling along the streets, and searching for something strong and firm in himself. But everything within him was confused; it merely oppressed his heart, without assuming any definite forms. As in a painful dream he reached the river, seated himself on the beams by the shore, and began to look at the calm dark water, which was covered with tiny ripples. Calmly and almost noiselessly flowed on the broad, mighty river, carrying enormous weights upon its bosom. The river was all covered with black vessels, the signal lights and the stars were reflected in its water; the tiny ripples, murmuring softly, were gently breaking against the shore at the very feet of Foma. Sadness was breathed down from the sky, the feeling of loneliness oppressed Foma.

"Oh Lord Jesus Christ!" thought he, sadly gazing at the sky. "What a failure I am. There is nothing in me. God has put nothing into me. Of what use am I? Oh Lord Jesus!"

At the recollection of Christ Foma felt somewhat better—his loneliness seemed alleviated, and heaving a deep sigh, he began to address God in silence:

"Oh Lord Jesus Christ! Other people do not understand anything either, but they think that all is known to them, and therefore it is easier for them to live. While I—I have no justification. Here it is night, and I am alone, I have no place to go, I am unable to say anything to anybody. I love no one—only my godfather, and he is soulless. If Thou hadst but punished him somehow! He thinks there is none cleverer and better on earth than himself. While Thou sufferest it. And the same with me. If some misfortune were but sent to me. If some illness were to overtake me. But here I am as strong as iron. I am drinking, leading a gay life. I live in filth, but the body does not even rust, and only my soul aches. Oh Lord! To what purpose is such a life?"

Vague thoughts of protest flashed one after another through the mind of the lonely, straying man, while the silence about him was growing deeper, and night ever darker and darker. Not far from the shore lay a boat at anchor; it rocked from side to side, and something was creaking in it as though moaning.

"How am I to free myself from such a life as this?" reflected Foma, staring at the boat. "And what occupation is destined to be mine? Everybody is working."

And suddenly he was struck by a thought which appeared great to him:

"And hard work is cheaper than easy work! Some man will give himself up entire to his work for a rouble, while another takes a thousand with one finger."

He was pleasantly roused by this thought. It seemed to him that he discovered another falsehood in the life of man, another fraud which they conceal. He recalled one of his stokers, the old man Ilya, who, for ten copecks, used to be on watch at the fireplace out of his turn, working for a comrade eight hours in succession, amid suffocating heat. One day, when he had fallen sick on account of overwork, he was lying on the bow of the steamer, and when Foma asked him why he was thus ruining himself, Ilya replied roughly and sternly:

"Because every copeck is more necessary to me than a hundred roubles to you. That's why!"

And, saying this, the old man turned his body, which was burning with pain, with its back to Foma.

Reflecting on the stoker his thoughts suddenly and without any effort, embraced all those petty people that were doing hard work. He wondered, Why do they live? What pleasure is it for them to live on earth? They constantly do but their dirty, hard work, they eat poorly, are poorly clad, they drink. One man is sixty years old, and yet he keeps on toiling side by side with the young fellows. And they all appeared to Foma as a huge pile of worms, which battled about on earth just to get something to eat. In his memory sprang up his meetings with these people, one after another—their remarks about life—now sarcastic and mournful, now hopelessly gloomy remarks—their wailing songs. And now he also recalled how one day in the office Yefim had said to the clerk who hired the sailors:

"Some Lopukhin peasants have come here to hire themselves out, so don't give them more than ten roubles a month. Their place was burned down to ashes last summer, and they are now in dire need—they'll work for ten roubles."

Sitting on the beams, Foma rocked his whole body to and fro, and out of the darkness, from the river, various human figures appeared silently before him—sailors, stokers, clerks, waiters, half-intoxicated painted women, and tavern-loungers. They floated in the air like shadows; something damp and brackish came from them, and the dark, dense throng moved on slowly, noiselessly and swiftly, like clouds in an autumn sky. The soft splashing of the waves poured into his soul like sadly sighing music. Far away, somewhere on the other bank of the river, burned a wood-pile; embraced by the darkness on all sides, it was at times almost absorbed by it, and in the darkness it trembled, a reddish spot scarcely visible to the eye. But now the fire flamed up again, the darkness receded, and it was evident that the flame was striving upward. And then it sank again.

"0h Lord, 0h Lord!" thought Foma, painfully and bitterly, feeling that grief was oppressing his heart with ever greater power. "Here I am, alone, even as that fire. Only no light comes from me, nothing but fumes and smoke. If I could only meet a wise man! Someone to speak to. It is utterly impossible for me to live alone. I cannot do anything. I wish I might meet a man."

Far away, on the river, two large purple fires appeared, and high above them was a third. A dull noise resounded in the distance, something black was moving toward Foma.

"A steamer going up stream," he thought. "There may be more than a hundred people aboard, and none of them give a single thought to me. They all know whither they are sailing. Every one of them has something that is his own. Every one, I believe, understands what he wants. But what do I want? And who will tell it to me? Where is such a man?"

The lights of the steamer were reflected in the river, quivering in it; the illumined water rushed away from it with a dull murmur, and the steamer looked like a huge black fish with fins of fire.

A few days elapsed after this painful night, and Foma caroused again. It came about by accident and against his will. He had made up his mind to restrain himself from drinking, and so went to dinner in one of the most expensive hotels in town, hoping to find there none of his familiar drinking-companions, who always selected the cheaper and less respectable places for their drinking bouts. But his calculation proved to be wrong; he at once came into the friendly joyous embrace of the brandy-distiller's son, who had taken Sasha as mistress.

He ran up to Foma, embraced him and burst into merry laughter.

"Here's a meeting! This is the third day I have eaten here, and I am wearied by this terrible lonesomeness. There is not a decent man in the whole town, so I have had to strike up an acquaintance with newspaper men. They're a gay lot, although at first they played the aristocrat and kept sneering at me. After awhile we all got dead drunk. They'll be here again today—I swear by the fortune of my father! I'll introduce you to them. There is one writer of feuilletons here; you know, that some one who always lauded you, what's his name? An amusing fellow, the devil take him! Do you know it would be a good thing to hire one like that for personal use! Give him a certain sum of money and order him to amuse! How's that? I had a certain coupletist in my employ,—it was rather entertaining to be with him. I used to say to him sometimes: 'Rimsky! give us some couplets!' He would start, I tell you, and he'd make you split your sides with laughter. It's a pity, he ran off somewhere. Have you had dinner?"

"Not yet. And how's Aleksandra?" asked Foma, somewhat deafened by the loud speech of this tall, frank, red-faced fellow clad in a motley costume.

"Well, do you know," said the latter with a frown, "that Aleksandra of yours is a nasty woman! She's so obscure, it's tiresome to be with her, the devil take her! She's as cold as a frog,—brrr! I guess I'll send her away."

"Cold—that's true," said Foma and became pensive. "Every person must do his work in a first class manner," said the distiller's son, instructively. "And if you become some one's s mistress you must perform your duty in the best way possible, if you are a decent woman. Well, shall we have a drink?"

They had a drink. And naturally they got drunk. A large and noisy company gathered in the hotel toward evening. And Foma, intoxicated, but sad and calm, spoke to them with heavy voice:

"That's the way I understand it: some people are worms, others sparrows. The sparrows are the merchants. They peck the worms. Such is their destined lot. They are necessary But I and you—all of you—are to no purpose. We live so that we cannot be compared to anything—without justification, merely at random. And we are utterly unnecessary. But even these here, and everybody else, to what purpose are they? You must understand that. Brethren! We shall all burst! By God! And why shall we burst? Because there is always something superfluous in us, there is something superfluous in our souls. And all our life is superfluous! Comrades! I weep. To what purpose am I? I am unnecessary! Kill me, that I may die; I want to die."

And he wept, shedding many drunken tears. A drunken, small-sized, swarthy man sat down close to him, began to remind him of something, tried to kiss him, and striking a knife against the table, shouted:

"True! Silence! These are powerful words! Let the elephants and the mammoths of the disorder of life speak! The raw Russian conscience speaks holy words! Roar on, Gordyeeff! Roar at everything!" And again he clutched at Foma's shoulders, flung himself on his breast, raising to Foma's face his round, black, closely-cropped head, which was ceaselessly turning about on his shoulders on all sides, so that Foma was unable to see his face, and he was angry at him for this, and kept on pushing him aside, crying excitedly:

"Get away! Where is your face? Go on!"

A deafening, drunken laughter smote the air about them, and choking with laughter, the son of the brandy-distiller roared to someone hoarsely:

"Come to me! A hundred roubles a month with board and lodging! Throw the paper to the dogs. I'll give you more!"

And everything rocked from side to side in rhythmic, wave-like movement. Now the people moved farther away from Foma, now they came nearer to him, the ceiling descended, the floor rose, and it seemed to Foma that he would soon be flattened and crushed. Then he began to feel that he was floating somewhere over an immensely wide and stormy river, and, staggering, he cried out in fright:

"Where are we floating? Where is the captain?"

He was answered by the loud, senseless laughter of the drunken crowd, and by the shrill, repulsive shout of the swarthy little man:

"True! we are all without helm and sails. Where is the captain? What? Ha, ha, ha!"

Foma awakened from this nightmare in a small room with two windows, and the first thing his eyes fell upon was a withered tree. It stood near the window; its thick trunk, barkless, with a rotten heart, prevented the light from entering the room; the bent, black branches, devoid of leaves, stretched themselves mournfully and helplessly in the air, and shaking to and fro, they creaked softly, plaintively. A rain was falling; streams of water were beating against the window-panes, and one could hear how the water was falling to the ground from the roof, sobbing there. This sobbing sound was joined by another sound—a shrill, often interrupted, hasty scratching of a pen over paper, and then by a certain spasmodic grumbling.

When he turned with difficulty his aching, heavy head on the pillow, Foma noticed a small, swarthy man, who sat by the table hastily scratching with his pen over the paper, shaking his round head approvingly, wagging it from side to side, shrugging his shoulders, and, with all his small body clothed in night garments only, constantly moving about in his chair, as though he were sitting on fire, and could not get up for some reason or other. His left hand, lean and thin, was now firmly rubbing his forehead, now making certain incomprehensible signs in the air; his bare feet scraped along the floor, a certain vein quivered on his neck, and even his ears were moving. When he turned toward Foma, Foma saw his thin lips whispering something, his sharp-pointed nose turned down to his thin moustache, which twitched upward each time the little man smiled. His face was yellow, bloated, wrinkled, and his black, vivacious small sparkling eyes did not seem to belong to him.

Having grown tired of looking at him, Foma slowly began to examine the room with his eyes. On the large nails, driven into the walls, hung piles of newspapers, which made the walls look as though covered with swellings. The ceiling was pasted with paper which had been white once upon a time; now it was puffed up like bladders, torn here and there, peeled off and hanging in dirty scraps; clothing, boots, books, torn pieces of paper lay scattered on the floor. Altogether the room gave one the impression that it had been scalded with boiling water.

The little man dropped the pen, bent over the table, drummed briskly on its edge with his fingers and began to sing softly in a faint voice:

"Take the drum and fear not,—
And kiss the sutler girl aloud—
That's the sense of learning—
And that's philosophy."

Foma heaved a deed sigh and said:

"May I have some seltzer?"

"Ah!" exclaimed the little man, and jumping up from his chair, appeared at the wide oilcloth-covered lounge, where Foma lay. "How do you do, comrade! Seltzer? Of course! With cognac or plain?"

"Better with cognac," said Foma, shaking the lean, burning hand which was outstretched to him, and staring fixedly into the face of the little man.

"Yegorovna!" cried the latter at the door, and turning to Foma, asked: "Don't you recognise me, Foma Ignatyevich?"

"I remember something. It seems to me we had met somewhere before."

"That meeting lasted for four years, but that was long ago! Yozhov."

"0h Lord!" exclaimed Foma, in astonishment, slightly rising from the lounge. "Is it possible that it is you?"

"There are times, dear, when I don't believe it myself, but a real fact is something from which doubt jumps back as a rubber ball from iron."

Yozhov's face was comically distorted, and for some reason or other his hands began to feel his breast.

"Well, well!" drawled out Foma. "But how old you have grown! Ah-ah! How old are you?"

"Thirty."

"And you look as though you were fifty, lean, yellow. Life isn't sweet to you, it seems? And you are drinking, too, I see."

Foma felt sorry to see his jolly and brisk schoolmate so worn out, and living in this dog-hole, which seemed to be swollen from burns. He looked at him, winked his eyes mournfully and saw that Yozhov's face was for ever twitching, and his small eyes were burning with irritation. Yozhov was trying to uncork the bottle of water, and thus occupied, was silent; he pressed the bottle between his knees and made vain efforts to take out the cork. And his impotence moved Foma.

"Yes; life has sucked you dry. And you have studied. Even science seems to help man but little," said Gordyeeff plaintively.

"Drink!" said Yozhov, turning pale with fatigue, and handing him the glass. Then he wiped his forehead, seated himself on the lounge beside Foma, and said:

"Leave science alone! Science is a drink of the gods; but it has not yet fermented sufficiently, and, therefore is not fit for use, like vodka which has not yet been purified from empyreumatic oil. Science is not ready for man's happiness, my friend. And those living people that use it get nothing but headaches. Like those you and I have at present. Why do you drink so rashly?"

"I? What else am I to do?" asked Foma, laughing. Yozhov looked at Foma searchingly with his eyes half closed, and he said:

"Connecting your question with everything you jabbered last night, I feel within my troubled soul that you, too, my friend, do not amuse yourself because life is cheerful to you."

"Eh!" sighed Foma, heavily, rising from the lounge. "What is my life? It is something meaningless. I live alone. I understand nothing. And yet there is something I long for. I yearn to spit on all and then disappear somewhere! I would like to run away from everything. I am so weary!"

"That's interesting!" said Yozhov, rubbing his hands and turning about in all directions. "This is interesting, if it is true and deep, for it shows that the holy spirit of dissatisfaction with life has already penetrated into the bed chambers of the merchants, into the death chambers of souls drowned in fat cabbage soup, in lakes of tea and other liquids. Give me a circumstantial account of it. Then, my dear, I shall write a novel."

"I have been told that you have already written something about me?" inquired Foma, with curiosity, and once more attentively scrutinized his old friend unable to understand what so wretched a creature could write.

"Of course I have! Did you read it?"

"No, I did not have the chance."

"And what have they told you?"

"That you gave me a clever scolding."

"Hm! And doesn't it interest you to read it yourself?" inquired Yozhov, scrutinizing Gordyeeff closely.

"I'll read it!" Foma assured him, feeling embarrassed before Yozhov, and that Yozhov was offended by such regard for his writings. "Indeed, it is interesting since it is about myself," he added, smiling kindheartedly at his comrade.

In saying this he was not at all interested, and he said it merely out of pity for Yozhov. There was quite another feeling in him; he wished to know what sort of a man Yozhov was, and why he had become so worn out. This meeting with Yozhov gave rise in him to a tranquil and kind feeling; it called forth recollections of his childhood, and these flashed now in his memory,—flashed like modest little lights, timidly shining at him from the distance of the past. Yozhov walked up to the table on which stood a boiling samovar, silently poured out two glasses of tea as strong as tar, and said to Foma:

"Come and drink tea. And tell me about yourself."

"I have nothing to tell you. I have not seen anything in life. Mine is an empty life! You had better tell me about yourself. I am sure you know more than I do, at any rate."

Yozhov became thoughtful, not ceasing to turn his whole body and to waggle his head. In thoughtfulness his face became motionless, all its wrinkles gathered near his eyes and seemed to surround them with rays, and because of this his eyes receded deeper under his forehead.

"Yes, my dear, I have seen a thing or two, and I know a great deal," he began, with a shake of the head. "And perhaps I know even more than it is necessary for me to know, and to know more than it is necessary is just as harmful to man as it is to be ignorant of what it is essential to know. Shall I tell you how I have lived? Very well; that is, I'll try. I have never told any one about myself, because I have never aroused interest in anyone. It is most offensive to live on earth without arousing people's interest in you!"

"I can see by your face and by everything else that your life has not been a smooth one!" said Foma, feeling pleased with the fact that, to all appearances, life was not sweet to his comrade as well. Yozhov drank his tea at one draught, thrust the glass on the saucer, placed his feet on the edge of the chair, and clasping his knees in his hands, rested his chin upon them. In this pose, small sized and flexible as rubber, he began:

"The student Sachkov, my former teacher, who is now a doctor of medicine, a whist-player and a mean fellow all around, used to tell me whenever I knew my lesson well: 'You're a fine fellow, Kolya! You are an able boy. We proletariats, plain and poor people, coming from the backyard of life, we must study and study, in order to come to the front, ahead of everybody. Russia is in need of wise and honest people. Try to be such, and you will be master of your fate and a useful member of society. On us commoners rest the best hopes of the country. We are destined to bring into it light, truth,' and so on. I believed him, the brute. And since then about twenty years have elapsed. We proletariats have grown up, but have neither appropriated any wisdom, nor brought light into life. As before, Russia is still suffering from its chronic disease—a superabundance of rascals; while we, the proletariats, take pleasure in filling their dense throngs. My teacher, I repeat, is a lackey, a characterless and dumb creature, who must obey the orders of the mayor. While 1 am a clown in the employ of society. Fame pursues me here in town, dear. I walk along the street and I hear one driver say to another: 'There goes Yozhov! How cleverly he barks, the deuce take him!' Yes! Even this cannot be so easily attained."

Yozhov's face wrinkled into a bitter grimace, and he began to laugh, noiselessly, with his lips only. Foma did not understand his words, and, just to say something, he remarked at random:

"You didn't hit, then, what you aimed at?"

"Yes, I thought I would grow up higher. And so I should! So I should, I say!"

He jumped up from his chair and began to run about in the room, exclaiming briskly in a shrill voice:

"But to preserve one's self pure for life and to be a free man in it, one must have vast powers! I had them. I had elasticity, cleverness. I have spent all these in order to learn something which is absolutely unnecessary to me now. I have wasted the whole of myself in order to preserve something within myself. Oh devil! I myself and many others with me, we have all robbed ourselves for the sake of saving up something for life. Just think of it: desiring to make of myself a valuable man, I have underrated my individuality in every way possible. In order to study, and not die of starvation, I have for six years in succession taught blockheads how to read and write, and had to bear a mass of abominations at the hands of various papas and mammas, who humiliated me without any constraint. Earning my bread and tea, I could not, I had not the time to earn my shoes, and I had to turn to charitable institutions with humble petitions for loans on the strength of my poverty. If the philanthropists could only reckon up how much of the spirit they kill in man while supporting the life of his body! If they only knew that each rouble they give for bread contains ninety-nine copecks' worth of poison for the soul! If they could only burst from excess of their kindness and pride, which they draw from their holy activity! There is none on earth more disgusting and repulsive than he who gives alms, even as there is none more miserable than he who accepts it!"

Yozhov staggered about in the room like a drunken man, seized with madness, and the paper under his feet was rustling, tearing, flying in scraps. He gnashed his teeth, shook his head, his hands waved in the air like broken wings of a bird, and altogether it seemed as though he were being boiled in a kettle of hot water. Foma looked at him with a strange, mixed sensation; he pitied Yozhov, and at the same time he was pleased to see him suffering.

"I am not alone, he is suffering, too," thought Foma, as Yozhov spoke. And something clashed in Yozhov's throat, like broken glass, and creaked like an unoiled hinge.

"Poisoned by the kindness of men, I was ruined through the fatal capacity of every poor fellow during the making of his career, through the capacity of being reconciled with little in the expectation of much. Oh! Do you know, more people perish through lack of proper self-appreciation than from consumption, and perhaps that is why the leaders of the masses serve as district inspectors!"

"The devil take the district inspectors!" said Foma, with a wave of the hand. "Tell me about yourself."

"About myself! I am here entire!" exclaimed Yozhov, stopping short in the middle of the room, and striking his chest with his hands. "I have already accomplished all I could accomplish. I have attained the rank of the public's entertainer—and that is all I can do! To know what should be done, and not to be able to do it, not to have the strength for your work—that is torture!"

"That's it! Wait awhile! "said Foma, enthusiastically. "Now tell me what one should do in order to live calmly; that is, in order to be satisfied with one's self."

To Foma these words sounded loud, but empty, and their sounds died away without stirring any emotion in his heart, without giving rise to a single thought in his mind.

"You must always be in love with something unattainable to you. A man grows in height by stretching himself upwards."

Now that he had ceased speaking of himself, Yozhov began to talk more calmly, in a different voice. His voice was firm and resolute, and his face assumed an expression of importance and sternness. He stood in the centre of the room, his hand with outstretched fingers uplifted, and spoke as though he were reading:

"Men are base because they strive for satiety. The well-fed man is an animal because satiety is the self-contentedness of the body. And the self-contentedness of the spirit also turns man into animal."

Again he started as though all his veins and muscles were suddenly strained, and again he began to run about the room in seething agitation.

"A self-contented man is the hardened swelling on the breast of society. He is my sworn enemy. He fills himself up with cheap truths, with gnawed morsels of musty wisdom, and he exists like a storeroom where a stingy housewife keeps all sorts of rubbish which is absolutely unnecessary to her, and worthless. If you touch such a man, if you open the door into him, the stench of decay will be breathed upon you, and a stream of some musty trash will be poured into the air you breathe. These unfortunate people call themselves men of firm character, men of principles and convictions. And no one cares to see that convictions are to them but the clothes with which they cover the beggarly nakedness of their souls. On the narrow brows of such people there always shines the inscription so familiar to all: calmness and confidence. What a false inscription! Just rub their foreheads with firm hand and then you will see the real sign-board, which reads: 'Narrow mindedness and weakness of soul!'"

Foma watched Yozhov bustling about the room, and thought mournfully:

"Whom is he abusing? I can't understand; but I can see that he has been terribly wounded."

"How many such people have I seen!" exclaimed Yozhov, with wrath and terror. "How these little retail shops have multiplied in life! In them you will find calico for shrouds, and tar, candy and borax for the extermination of cockroaches, but you will not find anything fresh, hot, wholesome! You come to them with an aching soul exhausted by loneliness; you come, thirsting to hear something that has life in it. And they offer to you some worm cud, ruminated book-thoughts, grown sour with age. And these dry, stale thoughts are always so poor that, in order to give them expression, it is necessary to use a vast number of high-sounding and empty words. When such a man speaks I say to myself: 'There goes a well-fed, but over-watered mare, all decorated with bells; she's carting a load of rubbish out of the town, and the miserable wretch is content with her fate.'"

"They are superfluous people, then," said Foma. Yozhov stopped short in front of him and said with a biting smile on his lips:

"No, they are not superfluous, oh no! They exist as an example, to show what man ought not to be. Speaking frankly, their proper place is the anatomical museums, where they preserve all sorts of monsters and various sickly deviations from the normal. In life there is nothing that is superfluous, dear. Even I am necessary! Only those people, in whose souls dwells a slavish cowardice before life, in whose bosoms there are enormous ulcers of the most abominable self-adoration, taking the places of their dead hearts—only those people are superfluous; but even they are necessary, if only for the sake of enabling me to pour my hatred upon them."

All day long, until evening, Yozhov was excited, venting his blasphemy on men he hated, and his words, though their contents were obscure to Foma, infected him with their evil heat, and infecting called forth in him an eager desire for combat. At times there sprang up in him distrust of Yozhov, and in one of these moments he asked him plainly:

"Well! And can you speak like that in the face of men?"

"I do it at every convenient occasion. And every Sunday in the newspaper. I'll read some to you if you like."

Without waiting for Foma's reply, he tore down from the wall a few sheets of paper, and still continuing to run about the room, began to read to him. He roared, squeaked, laughed, showed his teeth and looked like an angry dog trying to break the chain in powerless rage. Not grasping

376

the ideals in his friend's creations, Foma felt their daring audacity, their biting sarcasm, their passionate malice, and he was as well pleased with them as though he had been scourged with besoms in a hot bath.

"Clever!" he exclaimed, catching some separate phrase. "That's cleverly aimed!"

Every now and again there flashed before him the familiar names of merchants and well-known citizens, whom Yozhov had stung, now stoutly and sharply, now respectfully and with a fine needle-like sting.

Foma's approbation, his eyes burning with satisfaction, and his excited face gave Yozhov still more inspiration, and he cried and roared ever louder and louder, now falling on the lounge from exhaustion, now jumping up again and rushing toward Foma.

"Come, now, read about me!" exclaimed Foma, longing to hear it. Yozhov rummaged among a pile of papers, tore out one sheet, and holding it in both hands, stopped in front of Foma, with his legs straddled wide apart, while Foma leaned back in the broken-seated armchair and listened with a smile.

The notice about Foma started with a description of the spree on the rafts, and during the reading of the notice Foma felt that certain particular words stung him like mosquitoes. His face became more serious, and he bent his head in gloomy silence. And the mosquitoes went on multiplying.

"Now that's too much! "said he, at length, confused and dissatisfied. "Surely you cannot gain the favour of God merely because you know how to disgrace a man."

"Keep quiet! Wait awhile!" said Yozhov, curtly, and went on reading.

Having established in his article that the merchant rises beyond doubt above the representatives of other classes of society in the matter of nuisance and scandal-making, Yozhov asked: "Why is this so?" and replied:

"It seems to me that this predilection for wild pranks comes from the lack of culture in so far as it is dependent upon the excess of energy and upon idleness. There cannot be any doubt that our merchant class, with but few exceptions, is the healthiest and, at the same time, most inactive class."

"That's true!" exclaimed Foma, striking the table with his fist. "That's true! I have the strength of a bull and do the work of a sparrow."

"Where is the merchant to spend his energy? He cannot spend much of it on the Exchange, so he squanders the excess of his muscular capital in drinking-bouts in kabaky; for he has no conception of other applications of his strength, which are more productive, more valuable to life. He is still a beast, and life has already become to him a cage, and it is too narrow for him with his splendid health and predilection for licentiousness. Hampered by culture he at once starts to lead a dissolute life. The debauch of a merchant is always the revolt of a captive beast. Of course this is bad. But, ah! it will be worse yet, when this beast, in addition to his strength, shall have gathered some sense and shall have disciplined it. Believe me, even then he will not cease to create scandals, but they will be historical events. Heaven deliver us from such events! For they will emanate from the merchant's thirst for power; their aim will be the omnipotence of one class, and the merchant will not be particular about the means toward the attainment of this aim.

"Well, what do you say, is it true?" asked Yozhov, when he had finished reading the newspaper, and thrown it aside.

"I don't understand the end," replied Foma. "And as to strength, that is true! Where am I to make use of my strength since there is no demand for it! I ought to fight with robbers, or turn a robber myself. In general I ought to do something big. And that should be done not with the head, but with the arms and the breast. While here we have to go to the Exchange and try to aim well to make a rouble. What do we need it for? And what is it, anyway? Has life been arranged in this form forever? What sort of life is it, if everyone is grieved and finds it too narrow for him? Life ought to be according to the taste of man. If it is narrow for me, I must move it asunder that I may have more room. I must break it and reconstruct it. But nod? That's where the trouble lies! What ought to be done that life may be freer? That I do not understand, and that's all there is to it."

"Yes!" drawled out Yozhov. "So that's where you've gone! That, dear, is a good thing! Ah, you ought to study a little! How are you about books? Do you read any?"

"No, I don't care for them. I haven't read any."

"That's just why you don't care for them.""I am even afraid to read them. I know one—a certain girl—it's worse than drinking with her! And what sense is there in books? One man imagines something and prints it, and others read it. If it is interesting, it's all right. But learn from a book how to live!—that is something absurd. It was written by man, not by God, and what laws and examples can man establish for himself?"

"And how about the Gospels? Were they not written by men?"

"Those were apostles. Now there are none."

"Good, your refutation is sound! It is true, dear, there are no apostles. Only the Judases remained, and miserable ones at that."

Foma felt very well, for he saw that Yozhov was attentively listening to his words and seemed to be weighing each and every word he uttered. Meeting such bearing toward him for the first time in his life, Foma unburdened himself boldly and freely before his friend, caring nothing for the choice of words, and feeling that he would be understood because Yozhov wanted to understand him.

"You are a curious fellow!" said Yozhov, about two days after their meeting. "And though you speak with difficulty, one feels that there is a great deal in you—great daring of heart! If you only knew a little about the order of life! Then you would speak loud enough, I think. Yes!"

"But you cannot wash yourself clean with words, nor can you then free yourself," remarked Foma, with a sigh. "You have said something about people who pretend that they know everything, and can do everything. I also know such people. My godfather, for instance. It would be a good thing to set out against them, to convict them; they're a pretty dangerous set!"

"I cannot imagine, Foma, how you will get along in life if you preserve within you that which you now have," said Yozhov, thoughtfully.

"It's very hard. I lack steadfastness. Of a sudden I could perhaps do something. I understand very well that life is difficult and narrow for every one of us. I know that my godfather sees that, too! But he profits by this narrowness. He feels well in it; he is sharp as a needle, and he'll make his way wherever he pleases. But I am a big, heavy man, that's why I am suffocating! That's why I live in fetters. I could free myself from everything with a single effort: just to move my body with all my strength, and then all the fetters will burst!"

"And what then?" asked Yozhov.

"Then?" Foma became pensive, and, after a moment's thought, waved his hand. "I don't know what will be then. I shall see!"

"We shall see!" assented Yozhov.

He was given to drink, this little man who was scalded by life. His day began thus: in the morning at his tea he looked over the local newspapers and drew from the news notices material for his feuilleton, which he wrote right then and there on the corner of the table. Then he ran to the editorial office, where he made up "Provincial Pictures" out of clippings from country newspapers. On Friday he had to write his Sunday feuilleton. For all they paid him a hundred and twenty-five roubles a month; he worked fast, and devoted all his leisure time to the "survey and study of charitable institutions." Together with Foma he strolled about the clubs, hotels and taverns till late at night, drawing material everywhere for his articles, which he called "brushes for the cleansing of the conscience of society." The censor he styled as superintendent of the diffusion of truth and righteousness in life," the newspaper he called "the go-between, engaged in introducing the reader to dangerous ideas," and his own work, "the sale of a soul in retail," and "an inclination to audacity against holy institutions."

Foma could hardly make out when Yozhov jested and when he was in earnest. He spoke of everything enthusiastically and passionately, he condemned everything harshly, and Foma liked it. But often, beginning to argue enthusiastically, he refuted and contradicted himself with equal enthusiasm or wound up his speech with some ridiculous turn. Then it appeared to Foma that that man loved nothing, that nothing was firmly rooted within him, that nothing guided him. Only when speaking of himself he talked in a rather peculiar voice, and the more impassioned he was in speaking of himself, the more merciless and enraged was he in reviling everything and everybody. And his relation toward Foma was dual; sometimes he gave him courage and spoke to him hotly, quivering in every limb.

"Go ahead! Refute and overthrow everything you can! Push forward with all your might. There is nothing more valuable than man, know this! Cry at the top of your voice: 'Freedom! Freedom!'"

But when Foma, warmed up by the glowing sparks of these words, began to dream of how he should start to refute and overthrow people who, for the sake of personal profit, do not want to broaden life, Yozhov would often cut him short:

"Drop it! You cannot do anything! People like you are not needed. Your time, the time of the strong but not clever, is past, my dear! You are too late! There is no place for you in life."

"No? You are lying!" cried Foma, irritated by contradiction.

"Well, what can you accomplish?"

"I?"

"You!"

"Why, I can kill you!" said Foma, angrily, clenching his fist.

"Eh, you scarecrow!" said Yozhov, convincingly and pitifully, with a shrug of the shoulder. "Is there anything in that? Why, I am anyway half dead already from my wounds."

And suddenly inflamed with melancholy malice, he stretched himself and said:

"My fate has wronged me. Why have I lowered myself, accepting the sops of the public? Why have I worked like a machine for twelve years in succession in order to study? Why have I swallowed for twelve long years in the Gymnasium and the University the dry and tedious trash and the contradictory nonsense which is absolutely useless to me? In order to become feuilleton-writer, to play the clown from day to day, entertaining the public and convincing myself that that is necessary and useful to them. Where is the powder of my youth? I have fired off all the charge of my soul at three copecks a shot. What faith have I acquired for myself? Only faith in the fact that everything in this life is worthless, that everything must be broken, destroyed. What do I love? Myself. And I feel that the object of my love does not deserve my love. What can I accomplish?"

He almost wept, and kept on scratching his breast and his neck with his thin, feeble hands.

But sometimes he was seized with a flow of courage, and then he spoke in a different spirit:

"I? Oh, no, my song is not yet sung to the end! My breast has imbibed something, and I'll hiss like a whip! Wait, I'll drop the newspaper, I'll start to do serious work, and write one small book, which I will entitle 'The Passing of the Soul'; there is a prayer by that name, it is read for the dying. And before its death this society, cursed by the anathema of inward impotence, will receive my book like incense."

Listening to each and every word of his, watching him and comparing his remarks, Foma saw that Yozhov was just as weak as he was, that he, too, had lost his way. But Yozhov's mood still infected Foma, his speeches enriched Foma's vocabulary, and sometimes he noticed with joyous delight how cleverly and forcibly he had himself expressed this or that idea. He often met in Yozhov's house certain peculiar people, who, it seemed to him, knew everything, understood everything, contradicted everything, and saw deceit and falsehood in everything. He watched them in silence, listened to their words; their audacity pleased him, but he was embarrassed and repelled by their condescending and haughty bearing toward him. And then he clearly saw that in Yozhov's room they were all cleverer and better than they were in the street and in the hotels. They held peculiar conversations, words and gestures for use in the room, and all this was changed outside the room, into the most commonplace and human. Sometimes, in the room, they all blazed up like a huge woodpile, and Yozhov was the brightest firebrand among them; but the light of this bonfire illuminated but faintly the obscurity of Foma Gordyeeff's soul.

One day Yozhov said to him:

"Today we will carouse! Our compositors have formed a union, and they are going to take all the work from the publisher on a contract. There will be some drinking on this account, and I am invited. It was I who advised them to do it. Let us go? You will give them a good treat."

"Very well!" said Foma, to whom it was immaterial with whom he passed the time, which was a burden to him.

In the evening of that day Foma and Yozhov sat in the company of rough-faced people, on the outskirts of a grove, outside the town. There were twelve compositors there, neatly dressed; they treated Yozhov simply, as a comrade, and this somewhat surprised and embarrassed Foma, in whose eyes Yozhov was after all something of a master or superior to them, while they were really only his servants. They did not seem to notice Gordyeeff, although, when Yozhov introduced Foma to them, they shook hands with him and said that they were glad to see him. He lay down under a hazel-bush, and watched them all, feeling himself a stranger in this company, and noticing that even Yozhov seemed to have got away from him deliberately, and was paying but little attention to him. He perceived something strange about Yozhov; the little feuilleton-writer seemed to imitate the tone and the speech of the compositors. He bustled about with them at the woodpile, uncorked bottles of beer, cursed, laughed loudly and tried his best to resemble them. He was even dressed more simply than usual.

"Eh, brethren!" he exclaimed, with enthusiasm. "I feel well with you! I'm not a big bird, either. I am only the son of the courthouse guard, and noncommissioned officer, Matvey Yozhov!"

"Why does he say that?" thought Foma. "What difference does it make whose son a man is? A man is not respected on account of his father, but for his brains."

The sun was setting like a huge bonfire in the sky, tinting the clouds with hues of gold and of blood. Dampness and silence were breathed from the forest, while at its outskirts dark human figures bustled about noisily. One of them, short and lean, in a broad-brimmed straw hat, played the accordion; another one, with dark moustache and with his cap on the back of his head, sang an accompaniment softly. Two others tugged at a stick, testing their strength. Several busied themselves with the basket containing beer and provisions; a tall man with a grayish beard threw branches on the fire, which was enveloped in thick, whitish smoke. The damp branches, falling on the fire, crackled and rustled plaintively, and the accordion teasingly played a lively tune, while the falsetto of the singer reinforced and completed its loud tones.

Apart from them all, on the brink of a small ravine, lay three young fellows, and before them stood Yozhov, who spoke in a ringing voice:

"You bear the sacred banner of labour. And I, like yourselves, am a private soldier in the same army. We all serve Her Majesty, the Press. And we must live in firm, solid friendship."

"That's true, Nikolay Matveyich!" some one's thick voice interrupted him. "And we want to ask you to use your influence with the publisher! Use your influence with him! Illness and drunkenness cannot be treated as one and the same thing. And, according to his system, it comes out thus; if one of us gets drunk he is fined to the amount of his day's earnings; if he takes sick the same is done. We ought to be permitted to present the doctor's certificate, in case of sickness, to make it certain; and he, to be just, ought to pay the substitute at least half the wages of the sick man. Otherwise, it is hard for us. What if three of us should suddenly be taken sick at once?"

"Yes; that is certainly reasonable," assented Yozhov. "But, my friends, the principle of cooperation—"

Foma ceased listening to the speech of his friend, for his attention was diverted by the conversation of others. Two men were talking; one was a tall consumptive, poorly dressed and angry-looking man; the other a fair-haired and fair-bearded young man.

"In my opinion," said the tall man sternly, and coughing, "it is foolish! How can men like us marry? There will be children. Do we have enough to support them? The wife must be clothed—and then you can't tell what sort of a woman you may strike."

"She's a fine girl," said the fair-haired man, softly. "Well, it's now that she is fine. A betrothed girl is one thing, a wife quite another. But that isn't the main point. You can try—perhaps she will really be good. But then you'll be short of means. You will kill yourself with work, and you will ruin her, too. Marriage is an impossible thing for us. Do you mean to say that we can support a family on such earnings? Here, you see, I have only been married four years, and my end is near. I have seen no joy—nothing but worry and care."

He began to cough, coughed for a long time, with a groan, and when he had ceased, he said to his comrade in a choking voice:

"Drop it, nothing will come of it!"

His interlocutor bent his head mournfully, while Foma thought:

"He speaks sensibly. It's evident he can reason well."

The lack of attention shown to Foma somewhat offended him and aroused in him at the same time a feeling of respect for these men with dark faces impregnated with lead-dust. Almost all of them were engaged in practical serious conversation, and their remarks were studded with certain peculiar words. None of them fawned upon him, none bothered him with ov, with his back to the fire, and he saw before him a row of brightly illuminated, cheerful and simple faces. They were all excited from drinking, but were not yet intoxicated; they laughed, jested, tried to sing, drank, and ate cucumbers, white bread and sausages. All this had for

Foma a particularly pleasant flavour; he grew bolder, seized by the general good feeling, and he longed to say something good to these people, to please them all in some way or other. Yozhov, sitting by his side, moved about on the ground, jostled him with his shoulder and, shaking his head, muttered something indistinctly.

Brethren!" shouted the stout fellow. "Let's strike up the student song. Well, one, two!"

"Swift as the waves,"

Someone roared in his bass voice:

"Are the days of our life."

"Friends!" said Yozhov, rising to his feet, a glass in his hand. He staggered, and leaned his other hand against Foma's head. The started song was broken off, and all turned their heads toward him.

"Working men! Permit me to say a few words, words from the heart. I am happy in your company! I feel well in your midst. That is because you are men of toil, men whose right to happiness is not subject to doubt, although it is not recognised. In your ennobling midst, 0h honest people, the lonely man, who is poisoned by life, breathes so easily, so freely."

Yozhov's voice quivered and quaked, and his head began to shake. Foma felt that something warm trickled down on his hand, and he looked up at the wrinkled face of Yozhov, who went on speaking, trembling in every limb:

"I am not the only one. There are many like myself, intimidated by fate, broken and suffering. We are more unfortunate than you are, because we are weaker both in body and in soul, but we are stronger than you because we are armed with knowledge, which we have no opportunity to apply. We are gladly ready to come to you and resign ourselves to you and help you to live. There is nothing else for us to do! Without you we are without ground to stand on; without us, you are without light! Comrades! we were created by Fate itself to complete one another!"

"What does he beg of them?" thought Foma, listening to Yozhov's words with perplexity. And examining the faces of the compositors he saw that they also looked at the orator inquiringly, perplexedly, wearily.

"The future is yours, my friends!" said Yozhov, faintly, shaking his head mournfully as though feeling sorry for the future, and yielding to these people against his will the predominance over it. "The future belongs to the men of honest toil. You have a great task before you! You have to create a new culture, everything free, vital and bright! I, who am one of you in flesh and in spirit; who am the son of a soldier; I propose a toast to your future! Hurrah!"

Yozhov emptied his glass and sank heavily to the ground. The compositors unanimously took up his broken exclamation, and a powerful, thundering shout rolled through the air, causing the leaves on the trees to tremble.

"Let's start a song now," proposed the stout fellow again.

"Come on!" chimed in two or three voices. A noisy dispute ensued as to what to sing. Yozhov listened to the noise, and, turning his head from one side to another, scrutinized them all.

"Brethren," Yozhov suddenly cried again, "answer me. Say a few words in reply to my address of welcome."

Again—though not at once—all became silent, some looking at him with curiosity, others concealing a grin, still others with an expression of dissatisfaction plainly written on their faces. And he again rose from the ground and said, hotly:

"Two of us here are cast away by life—I and that other one. We both desire the same regard for man and the happiness of feeling ourselves useful unto others. Comrades! And that big, stupid man—"

"Nikolay Matveyich, you had better not insult our guest!" said someone in a deep, displeased voice.

"Yes, that's unnecessary," affirmed the stout fellow, who had invited Foma to the fireside. "Why use offensive language?"

A third voice rang out loudly and distinctly:

"We have come together to enjoy ourselves—to take a rest."

"Fools!" laughed Yozhov, faintly. "Kind-hearted fools! Do you pity him? But do you know who he is? He is of those people who suck your blood."

"That will do, Nikolay Matveyich!" they cried to Yozhov. And all began to talk, paying no further attention to him. Foma felt so sorry for his friend that he did not even take offence. He saw that these people who defended him from Yozhov's attacks were now purposely ignoring the feuilleton-writer, and he understood that this would pain Yozhov if he were to notice it. And in order to take his friend away from possible unpleasantness, he nudged him in the side and said, with a kind-hearted laugh:

"Well, you grumbler, shall we have a drink? Or is it time to go home?"

"Home? Where is the home of the man who has no place among men?" asked Yozhov, and shouted again: "Comrades!"

Unanswered, his shout was drowned in the general murmur. Then he drooped his head and said to Foma:

"Let's go from here."

"Let's go. Though I don't mind sitting a little longer. It's interesting. They behave so nobly, the devils. By God!"

"I can't bear it any longer. I feel cold. I am suffocating."

"Well, come then."

Foma rose to his feet, removed his cap, and, bowing to the compositors, said loudly and cheerfully:

"Thank you, gentlemen, for your hospitality! Good-bye!"

They immediately surrounded him and spoke to him persuasively:

"Stay here! Where are you going? We might sing all together, eh?"

"No, I must go, it would be disagreeable to my friend to go alone. I am going to escort him. I wish you a jolly feast!"

"Eh, you ought to wait a little!" exclaimed the stout fellow, and then whispered:

"Some one will escort him home!"

The consumptive also remarked in a low voice:

"You stay here. We'll escort him to town, and get him into a cab and—there you are!"

Foma felt like staying there, and at the same time was afraid of something. While Yozhov rose to his feet, and, clutching at the sleeves of his overcoat, muttered:

"Come, the devil take them!"

"Till we meet again, gentlemen! I'm going!" said Foma and departed amid exclamations of polite regret.

"Ha, ha, ha!" Yozhov burst out laughing when he had got about twenty steps away from the fire. "They see us off with sorrow, but they are glad that I am going away. I hindered them from turning into beasts."

"It's true, you did disturb them," said Foma. "Why do you make such speeches? People have come out to enjoy themselves, and you obtrude yourself upon them. That bores them!"

"Keep quiet! You don't understand anything!" cried Yozhov, harshly. "You think I am drunk? It's my body that is intoxicated, but my soul is sober, it is always sober; it feels everything. Oh, how much meanness there is in the world, how much stupidity and wretchedness! And men—these stupid, miserable men."

Yozhov paused, and, clasping his head with his hands, stood for awhile, staggering.

"Yes!" drawled out Foma. "They are very much unlike one another. Now these men, how polite they are, like gentlemen. And they reason correctly, too, and all that sort of thing. They have common sense. Yet they are only labourers."

In the darkness behind them the men struck up a powerful choral song. Inharmonious at first, it swelled and grew until it rolled in a huge, powerful wave through the invigorating nocturnal air, above the deserted field.

"My God!" said Yozhov, sadly and softly, heaving a sigh. "Whereby are we to live? Whereon fasten our soul? Who shall quench its thirsts for friendship brotherhood, love, for pure and sacred toil?"

"These simple people," said Foma, slowly and pensively, without listening to his companion s words, absorbed as he was in his own thoughts, "if one looks into these people, they're not so bad! It's even very—it is interesting. Peasants, labourers, to look at them plainly, they are just like horses. They carry burdens, they puff and blow."

"They carry our life on their backs," exclaimed Yozhov with irritation. "They carry it like horses, submissively, stupidly. And this submissiveness of theirs is our misfortune, our curse!"

And Foma, carried away by his own thought, argued:

"They carry burdens, they toil all their life long for mere trifles. And suddenly they say something that wouldn't come into your mind in a century. Evidently they feel. Yes, it is interesting to be with them."

Staggering, Yozhov walked in silence for a long time, and suddenly he waved his hand in the air and began to declaim in a dull, choking voice, which sounded as though it issued from his stomach:

"Life has cruelly deceived me,
I have suffered so much pain."

"These, dear boy, are my own verses," said he, stopping short and nodding his head mournfully. "How do they run? I've forgotten. There is something there about dreams, about sacred and pure longings, which are smothered within my breast by the vapour of life. Oh!"

"The buried dreams within my breast
Will never rise again."

"Brother! You are happier than I, because you are stupid. While I—"

"Don't be rude!" said Foma, irritated. "You would better listen how they are singing."

"I don't want to listen to other people's songs," said Yozhov, with a shake of the head. "I have my own, it is the song of a soul rent in pieces by life."

And he began to wail in a wild voice:

> The buried dreams within my breast
> Will never rise again . . .
> How great their number is!"

"There was a whole flower garden of bright, living dreams and hopes. They perished, withered and perished. Death is within my heart. The corpses of my dreams are rotting there. Oh! oh!"

Yozhov burst into tears, sobbing like a woman. Foma pitied him, and felt uncomfortable with him. He jerked at his shoulder impatiently, and said:

"Stop crying! Come, how weak you are, brother!" Clasping his head in his hand Yozhov straightened up his stooping frame, made an effort and started again mournfully and wildly:

> "How great their number is!
> Their sepulchre how narrow!
> I clothed them all in shrouds of rhyme
> And many sad and solemn songs
> O'er them I sang from time to time!"

"Oh, Lord!" sighed Foma in despair. "Stop that, for Christ's sake! By God, how sad!"

In the distance the loud choral song was rolling through the darkness and the silence. Some one was whistling, keeping time to the refrain, and this shrill sound, which pierced the ear, ran ahead of the billow of powerful voices. Foma looked in that direction and saw the tall, black wall of forest, the bright fiery spot of the bonfire shining upon it, and the misty figures surrounding the fire. The wall of forest was like a breast, and the fire like a bloody wound in it. It seemed as though the breast was trembling, as the blood coursed down in burning streams. Embraced in dense gloom from all sides the people seemed on the background of the forest, like little children; they, too, seemed to burn, illuminated by the blaze of the bonfire. They waved their hands and sang their songs loudly, powerfully.

And Yozhov, standing beside Foma, spoke excitedly:

"You hard-hearted blockhead! Why do you repulse me? You ought to listen to the song of the dying soul, and weep over it, for, why was it wounded, why is it dying? Begone from me, begone! You think I am drunk? I am poisoned, begone!"

Without lifting his eyes off the forest and the fire, so beautiful in the darkness, Foma made a few steps aside from Yozhov and said to him in a low voice:

"Don't play the fool. Why do you abuse me at random?"

"I want to remain alone, and finish singing my song."

Staggering, he, too, moved aside from Foma, and after a few seconds again exclaimed in a sobbing voice:

"My song is done! And nevermore
Shall I disturb their sleep of death,
Oh Lord, 0h Lord, repose my soul!
For it is hopeless in its wounds,
Oh Lord, repose my soul."

Foma shuddered at the sounds of their gloomy wailing, and he hurried after Yozhov; but before he overtook him the little feuilleton-writer uttered a hysterical shriek, threw himself chest down upon the ground and burst out sobbing plaintively and softly, even as sickly children cry.

"Nikolay!" said Foma, lifting him by the shoulders. "Cease crying; what's the matter? 0h Lord. Nikolay! Enough, aren't you ashamed?"

But Yozhov was not ashamed; he struggled on the ground, like a fish just taken from the water, and when Foma had lifted him to his feet, he pressed close to Foma's breast, clasping his sides with his thin arms, and kept on sobbing.

"Well, that's enough!" said Foma, with his teeth tightly clenched. "Enough, dear."

And agitated by the suffering of the man who was wounded by the narrowness of life, filled with wrath on his account, he turned his face toward the gloom where the lights of the town were glimmering, and, in an outburst of wrathful grief, roared in a deep, loud voice:

"A-a-ana-thema! Be cursed! Just wait. You, too, shall choke! Be cursed!"

CHAPTER XI

"LUBAVKA!" said Mayakin one day when he came home from the Exchange, "prepare yourself for this evening. I am going to bring you a bridegroom! Prepare a nice hearty little lunch for us. Put out on the table as much of our old silverware as possible, also bring out the fruit-vases, so that he is impressed by our table! Let him see that each and everything we have is a rarity!"

Lubov was sitting by the window darning her father's socks, and her head was bent low over her work.

"What is all this for, papa?" she asked, dissatisfied and offended.

"Why, for sauce, for flavour. And then, it's in due order. For a girl is not a horse; you can't dispose of her without the harness."

All aflush with offence, Lubov tossed her head nervously, and flinging her work aside, cast a glance at her father; and, taking up the socks again, she bent her head still lower over them. The old man paced the room to and fro, plucking at his fiery beard with anxiety; his eyes stared somewhere into the distance, and it was evident that he was all absorbed in some great complicated thought. The girl understood that he would not listen to her and would not care to comprehend how degrading his words were for her. Her romantic dreams of a husband-friend, an educated man, who would read with her wise books and help her to find herself in her confused desires, these dreams were stifled by her father's inflexible resolution to marry her to Smolin. They had been killed and had become decomposed, settling down as a bitter sediment in her soul. She had been accustomed to looking upon herself as better and higher than the average girl of the merchant class, than the empty and stupid girl who thinks of nothing but dresses, and who marries almost always according to the calculation of her parents, and but seldom in accordance with the free will of her heart. And now she herself is about to marry merely because it was time, and also because her father needed a son-in-law to succeed him in his business. And her father evidently thought that she, by herself, was hardly capable of attracting the attention of a man, and therefore adorned her with silver. Agitated, she worked nervously, pricked her fingers, broke needles, but maintained silence, being aware that whatever she should say would not reach her father's heart.

And the old man kept on pacing the room to and fro, now humming psalms softly, now impressively instructing his daughter how to behave with the bridegroom. And then he also counted something on his fingers, frowned and smiled.

"Mm! So! Try me, 0h Lord, and judge me. From the unjust and the false man, deliver me. Yes! Put on your mother's emeralds, Lubov."

"Enough, papa!" exclaimed the girl, sadly. "Pray, leave that alone."

"Don't you kick! Listen to what I'm telling you."

And he was again absorbed in his calculations, snapping his green eyes and playing with his fingers in front of his face.

"That makes thirty-five percent. Mm! The fellow's a rogue. Send down thy light and thy truth."

"Papa!" exclaimed Lubov, mournfully and with fright.

"What?"

"You—are you pleased with him?"

"With whom?

"Smolin."

"Smolin? Yes, he's a rogue, he's a clever fellow, a splendid merchant! Well, I'm off now. So be on your guard, arm yourself."

When Lubov remained alone she flung her work aside and leaned against the back of her chair, closing her eyes tightly. Her hands firmly clasped together lay on her knees, and their fingers twitched. Filled with the bitterness of offended vanity, she felt an alarming fear of the future, and prayed in silence:

"My God! Oh Lord! If he were only a kind man! Make him kind, sincere. Oh Lord! A strange man comes, examines you, and takes you unto himself for years, if you please him! How disgraceful that is, how terrible. Oh Lord, my God! If I could only run away! If I only had someone to advise me what to do! Who is he? How can I learn to know him? I cannot do anything! And I have thought, ah, how much I have thought! I have read. To what purpose have I read? Why should I know that it is possible to live otherwise, so as I cannot live? And it may be that were it not for the books my life would be easier, simpler. How painful all this is! What a wretched, unfortunate being I am! Alone. If Taras at least were here."

At the recollection of her brother she felt still more grieved, still more sorry for herself. She had written to Taras a long, exultant letter, in which she had spoken of her love for him, of her hope in him; imploring her brother to come as soon as possible to see his father, she had pictured to him plans of arranging to live together, assuring Taras that their father was extremely clever and understood everything; she told about his loneliness, had gone into ecstasy over his aptitude for life and had, at the same time, complained of his attitude toward her.

For two weeks she impatiently expected a reply, and when she had received and read it she burst out sobbing for joy and disenchantment. The answer was dry and short; in it Taras said that within a month he would be on the Volga on business and would not fail to call on his father, if the old man really had no objection to it. The letter was cold, like a block of ice; with tears in her eyes she perused it over and over again, rumpled it, creased it, but it did not turn warmer on this account, it only became wet. From the sheet of stiff note paper which was covered with writing in a large, firm hand, a wrinkled and suspiciously frowning face, thin and angular like that of her father, seemed to look at her.

On Yakov Tarasovich the letter of his son made a different impression. On learning the contents of Taras's reply the old man started and hastily turned to his daughter with animation and with a peculiar smile:

"Well, let me see it! Show it to me! He-he! Let's read how wise men write. Where are my spectacles? Mm! 'Dear sister!' Yes."

The old man became silent; he read to himself the message of his son, put it on the table, and, raising his eyebrows, silently paced the room to and fro, with an expression of amazement on his countenance. Then he read the letter once more, thoughtfully tapped the table with his fingers and spoke:

"That letter isn't bad—it is sound, without any unnecessary words. Well? Perhaps the man has really grown hardened in the cold. The cold is severe there. Let him come, we'll take a look at him. It's interesting. Yes. In the psalm of David concerning the mysteries of his son it is said: 'When Thou hast returned my enemy'—I've forgotten how it reads further. 'My enemy's weapons have weakened in the end, and his memory hath perished amid noise. Well, we'll talk it over with him without noise."

The old man tried to speak calmly and with a contemptuous smile, but the smile did not come; his wrinkles quivered irritably, and his small eyes had a particularly clear brilliancy.

"Write to him again, Lubovka. 'Come along!' write him, 'don't be afraid to come!'"

Lubov wrote Taras another letter, but this time it was shorter and more reserved, and now she awaited a reply from day to day, attempting to picture to herself what sort of man he must be, this mysterious brother of hers. Before she used to think of him with sinking heart, with that solemn respect with which believers think of martyrs, men of upright life; now she feared him, for he had acquired the right to be judge over men and life at the price of painful sufferings, at the cost of his youth, which was ruined in exile. On coming, he would ask her:

"You are marrying of your own free will, for love, are you not?"

What should she tell him? Would he forgive her faint-heartedness? And why does she marry? Can it really be possible that this is all she can do in order to change her life?

Gloomy thoughts sprang up one after another in the head of the girl and confused and tortured her, impotent as she was to set up against them some definite, all-conquering desire. Though she was in an anxious and compressing her lips. Smolin rose from his chair, made a step toward her and bowed respectfully. She was rather pleased with this low and polite bow, also with the costly frock coat, which fitted Smolin's supple figure splendidly. He had changed but slightly—he was the same red-headed, closely-cropped, freckled youth; only his moustache had become long, and his eyes seemed to have grown larger.

"Now he's changed, eh?" exclaimed Mayakin to his daughter, pointing at the bridegroom. And Smolin shook hands with her, and smiling, said in a ringing baritone voice:

"I venture to hope that you have not forgotten your old friend?"

It's all right! You can talk of this later," said the old man, scanning his daughter with his eyes.

"Lubova, you can make your arrangements here, while we finish our little conversation. Well then, African Mitrich, explain yourself."

"You will pardon me, Lubov Yakovlevna, won't you?" asked Smolin, gently.

"Pray do not stand upon ceremony," said Lubov. "He's polite and clever," she remarked to herself; and, as she walked about in the room from the table to the sideboard, she began to listen attentively to Smolin's words. He spoke softly, confidently, with a simplicity, in which was felt condescendence toward the interlocutor. "Well then, for four years I have carefully studied the condition of Russian leather in foreign markets. It's a sad and horrid condition! About thirty years ago our leather was considered there as the standard, while now the demand for it is constantly falling off, and, of course, the price goes hand in hand with it. And that is perfectly natural. Lacking the capital and knowledge all these small leather producers are not able to raise their product to the proper standard, and, at the same time, to reduce the price. Their goods are extremely bad and dear. And they are all to blame for having spoiled Russia's reputation as manufacturer of the best leather. In general, the petty producer, lacking the technical knowledge and capital, is consequently placed in a position where he is unable to improve his products in proportion to the development of the technical side. Such a producer is a misfortune for the country, the parasite of her commerce."

"Hm!" bellowed the old man, looking at his guest with one eye, and watching his daughter with the other. "So that now your intention is to build such a great factory that all the others will go to the dogs?"

"Oh, no!" exclaimed Smolin, warding off the old man's words with an easy wave of the hand. "Why wrong others? What right have I to do so? My aim is to raise the importance and price of Russian leather abroad, and so equipped with the knowledge as to the manufacture, I am building a model factory, and fill the markets with model goods. The commercial honour of the country!"

"Does it require much capital, did you say?" asked Mayakin, thoughtfully.

"About three hundred thousand."

"Father won't give me such a dowry," thought Lubov.

"My factory will also turn out leather goods, such as trunks, foot-wear, harnesses, straps and so forth."

"And of what per cent, are you dreaming?"

"I am not dreaming, I am calculating with all the exactness possible under conditions in Russia," said Smolin, impressively. "The manufacturer should be as strictly practical as the mechanic who is creating a machine. The friction of the tiniest screw must be taken into consideration, if you wish to do a serious thing seriously. I can let you read a little note which I have drawn up, based upon my personal study of cattle-breeding and of the consumption of meat in Russia."

"How's that!" laughed Mayakin. "Bring me that note, it's interesting! It seems you did not spend your time for nothing in Western Europe. And now, let's eat something, after the Russian fashion."

"How are you passing the time, Lubov Yakovlevna?" asked Smolin, arming himself with knife and fork.

"She is rather lonesome here with me," replied Mayakin for his daughter. "My housekeeper, all the household is on her shoulders, so she has no time to amuse herself."

"And no place, I must add," said Lubov. "I am not fond of the balls and entertainments given by the merchants."

"And the theatre?" asked Smolin.

"I seldom go there. I have no one to go with."

"The theatre!" exclaimed the old man. "Tell me, pray, why has it become the fashion then to represent the merchant as a savage idiot? It is very amusing, but it is incomprehensible, because it is false! Am I a fool, if I am master in the City Council, master in commerce, and also owner of that same theatre? You look at the merchant on the stage and you see—he isn't life-life! Of course, when they present something historical, such as: 'Life for the Czar,' with song and dance, or 'Hamlet,' 'The Sorceress,' or 'Vasilisa,' truthful reproduction is not required, because they're matters of the past and don't concern us. Whether true or not, it matters little so long as they're good, but when you represent modern times, then don't lie! And show the man as he really is."

Smolin listened to the old man's words with a covetous smile on his lips, and cast at Lubov glances which seemed to invite her to refute her father. Somewhat embarrassed, she said:

"And yet, papa, the majority of the merchant class is uneducated and savage."

"Yes," remarked Smolin with regret, nodding his head affirmatively, "that is the sad truth."

"Take Foma, for instance," went on the girl.

"Oh!" exclaimed Mayakin. "Well, you are young folks, you can have books in your hands."

"And do you not take interest in any of the societies?" Smolin asked Lubov. "You have so many different societies here."

"Yes," said Lubov with a sigh, "but I live rather apart from everything."

"Housekeeping!" interposed the father. "We have here such a store of different things, everything has to be kept clean, in order, and complete as to number."

With a self-satisfied air he nodded first at the table, which was set with brilliant crystal and silverware, and then at the sideboard, whose shelves were fairly breaking under the weight of the articles, and which reminded one of the display in a store window. Smolin noted all these and an ironical smile began to play upon his lips. Then he glanced at Lubov's face: in his look she caught something friendly, sympathetic to her. A faint flush covered her cheeks, and she said to herself with timid joy:

"Thank God!"

The light of the heavy bronze lamp now seemed to flash more brilliantly on the sides of the crystal vases, and it became brighter in the room.

"I like our dear old town!" said Smolin, looking at the girl with a kindly smile, "it is so beautiful, so vigorous; there is cheerfulness about it that inspires one to work. Its very picturesqueness is somewhat stimulating. In it one feels like leading a dashing life. One feels like working much and seriously. And then, it is an intelligent town. Just see what a practical newspaper is published here. By the way, we intend to purchase it."

"Whom do you mean by You?" asked Mayakin.

"I, Urvantzov, Shchukin—"

"That's praiseworthy!" said the old man, rapping the table with his hand. "That's very practical! It is time to stop their mouths, it was high time long ago! Particularly that Yozhov; he's like a sharp-toothed saw. Just put the thumb-screw on him! And do it well!"

Smolin again cast at Lubov a smiling glance, and her heart trembled with joy once more. With flushing face she said to her father, inwardly addressing herself to the bridegroom:

"As far as I can understand, African Dmitreivich, he wishes to buy the newspaper not at all for the sake of stopping its mouth as you say."

"What then can be done with it?" asked the old man, shrugging his shoulders. "There's nothing in it but empty talk and agitation. Of course, if the practical people, the merchants themselves, take to writing for it—"

"The publication of a newspaper," began Smolin, instructively, interrupting the old man, "looked at merely from the commercial point of view, may be a very profitable enterprise. But aside from this, a newspaper has another more important aim—that is, to protect the right of the individual and the interests of industry and commerce."

"That's just what I say, if the merchant himself will manage the newspaper, then it will be useful."

"Excuse me, papa," said Lubov.

She began to feel the need of expressing herself before Smolin; she wanted to assure him that she understood the meaning of his words, that she was not an ordinary merchant-daughter, interested in dresses and balls only. Smolin pleased her. This was the first time she had seen a merchant who had lived abroad for a long time, who reasoned so impressively, who bore himself so properly, who was so well dressed, and who spoke to her father, the cleverest man in town, with the condescending tone of an adult towards a minor.

"After the wedding I'll persuade him to take me abroad," thought Lubov, suddenly, and, confused at this thought she forgot what she was about to say to her father. Blushing deeply, she was silent for a few seconds, seized with fear lest Smolin might interpret this silence in a way unflattering to her.

"On account of your conversation, you have forgotten to offer some wine to our guest," she said at last, after a few seconds of painful silence.

"That's your business. You are hostess," retorted the old man.

"Oh, don't disturb yourself!" exclaimed Smolin, with animation. "I hardly drink at all."

"Really?" asked Mayakin.

"I assure you! Sometimes I drink a wine glass or two in case of fatigue or illness. But to drink wine for pleasure's sake is incomprehensible to me. There are other pleasures more worthy of a man of culture."

"You mean ladies, I suppose?" asked the old man with a wink.

Smolin's cheeks and neck became red with the colour which leaped to his face. With apologetic eyes he glanced at Lubov, and said to her father drily:

"I mean the theatre, books, music."

Lubov became radiant with joy at his words.

The old man looked askance at the worthy young man, smiled keenly and suddenly blurted out:

"Eh, life is going onward! Formerly the dog used to relish a crust, now the pug dog finds the cream too thin; pardon me for my sour remark, but it is very much to the point. It does not exactly refer to yourself, but in general."

Lubov turned pale and looked at Smolin with fright. He was calm, scrutinising an ancient salt box, decorated with enamel; he twisted his moustache and looked as though he had not heard the old man's words. But his eyes grew darker, and his lips were compressed very tightly, and his clean-shaven chin obstinately projected forward.

"And so, my future leading manufacturer," said Mayakin, as though nothing had happened, "three hundred thousand roubles, and your business will flash up like a fire?"

"And within a year and a half I shall send out the first lot of goods, which will be eagerly sought for," said Smolin, simply, with unshakable confidence, and he eyed the old man with a cold and firm look.

"So be it; the firm of Smolin and Mayakin, and that's all? So. Only it seems rather late for me to start a new business, doesn't it? I presume the grave has long been prepared for me; what do you think of it?"

Instead of an answer Smolin burst into a rich, but indifferent and cold laughter, and then said:

"Oh, don't say that."

The old man shuddered at his laughter, and started back with fright, with a scarcely perceptible movement of his body. After Smolin's words all three maintained silence for about a minute.

"Yes," said Mayakin, without lifting his head, which was bent low. "It is necessary to think of that. I must think of it." Then, raising his head, he closely scrutinised his daughter and the bridegroom, and, rising from his chair, he said sternly and brusquely: "I am going away for awhile to my little cabinet. You surely won't feel lonesome without me."

And he went out with bent back and drooping head, heavily scraping with his feet.

The young people, thus left alone, exchanged a few empty phrases, and, evidently conscious that these only helped to remove them further from each other, they maintained a painful, awkward and expectant silence. Taking an orange, Lubov began to peel it with exaggerated attention, while Smolin, lowering his eyes, examined his moustaches, which he carefully stroked with his left hand, toyed with a knife and suddenly asked the girl in a lowered voice:

"Pardon me for my indiscretion. It is evidently really difficult for you, Lubov Yakovlevna, to live with your father. He's a man with old-fashioned views and, pardon me, he's rather hard-hearted!"

Lubov shuddered, and, casting at the red-headed man a grateful look, said:

"It isn't easy, but I have grown accustomed to it. He also has his good qualities."

"Oh, undoubtedly! But to you who are so young, beautiful and educated, to you with your views . . . You see, I have heard something about you."

He smiled so kindly and sympathetically, and his voice was so soft, a breath of soul-cheering warmth filled the room. And in the heart of the girl there blazed up more and more brightly the timid hope of finding happiness, of being freed from the close captivity of solitude.

CHAPTER XII

A DENSE, grayish fog lay over the river, and a steamer, now and then uttering a dull whistle, was slowly forging up against the current. Damp and cold clouds, of a monotone pallor, enveloped the steamer from all sides and drowned all sounds, dissolving them in their troubled dampness. The brazen roaring of the signals came out in a muffled, melancholy drone, and was oddly brief as it burst forth from the whistle. The sound seemed to find no place for itself in the air, which was soaked with heavy dampness, and fell downward, wet and choked. And the splashing of the steamer's wheels sounded so fantastically dull that it seemed as though it were not begotten near by, at the sides of the vessel, but somewhere in the depth, on the dark bottom of the river. From the steamer one could see neither the water, nor the shore, nor the sky; a leaden-gray gloominess enwrapped it on all sides; devoid of shadings, painfully monotonous, the gloominess was motionless, it oppressed the steamer with immeasurable weight, slackened its movements and seemed as though preparing itself to swallow it even as it was swallowing the sounds. In spite of the dull blows of the paddles upon the water and the measured shaking of the body of the vessel, it seemed that the steamer was painfully struggling on one spot, suffocating in agony, hissing like a fairy tale monster breathing his last, howling in the pangs of death, howling with pain, and in the fear of death.

Lifeless were the steamer lights. About the lantern on the mast a yellow motionless spot had formed; devoid of lustre, it hung in the fog over the steamer, illuminating nothing save the gray mist. The red starboard light looked like a huge eye crushed out by some one's cruel fist, blinded, overflowing with blood. Pale rays of light fell from the steamer's windows into the fog, and only tinted its cold, cheerless dominion over the vessel, which was pressed on all sides by the motionless mass of stifling dampness.

The smoke from the funnel fell downwards, and, together with fragments of the fog, penetrated into all the cracks of the deck, where the third-class passengers were silently muffling themselves in their rags, and forming groups, like sheep. From near the machinery were wafted deep, strained groans, the jingling of bells, the dull sounds of orders and the abrupt words of the machinist:

"Yes—slow! Yes—half speed!"

On the stern, in a corner, blocked up by barrels of salted fish, a group of people was assembled, illuminated by a small electric lamp. Those were sedate, neatly and warmly clad peasants. One of them lay on a bench, face down; another sat at his feet, still another stood, leaning his back against a barrel, while two others seated themselves flat on the deck. Their faces, pensive and attentive, were turned toward a round-shouldered man in a short cassock, turned yellow, and a torn fur cap. That man sat on some boxes with his back bent, and staring at his feet, spoke in a low, confident voice:

"There will come an end to the long forbearance of the Lord, and then His wrath will burst forth upon men. We are like worms before Him, and how are we then to ward off His wrath, with what wailing shall we appeal to His mercy?"

Oppressed by his gloominess, Foma had come down on the deck from his cabin, and, for some time, had been standing in the shadow of some wares covered with tarpaulin, and listened to the admonitive and gentle voice of the preacher. Pacing the deck he had chanced upon this group, and attracted by the figure of the pilgrim, had paused near it. There was something familiar to him in that large, strong body, in that stern, dark face, in those large, calm eyes. The curly, grayish hair, falling from under the skull-cap, the unkempt bushy beard, which fell apart in thick locks, the long, hooked nose, the sharp-pointed ears, the thick lips—Foma had seen all these before, but could not recall when and where.

"Yes, we are very much in arrears before the Lord!" remarked one of the peasants, heaving a deep sigh.

"We must pray," whispered the peasant who lay on the bench, in a scarcely audible voice.

"Can you scrape your sinful wretchedness off your soul with words of prayer?" exclaimed someone loudly, almost with despair in his voice.

No one of those that formed the group around the pilgrim turned at this voice, only their heads sank lower on their breasts, and for a long time these people sat motionless and speechless:

The pilgrim measured his audience with a serious and meditative glance of his blue eyes, and said softly:

"Ephraim the Syrian said: 'Make thy soul the central point of thy thoughts and strengthen thyself with thy desire to be free from sin.

And again he lowered his head, slowly fingering the beads of the rosary.

"That means we must think," said one of the peasants; "but when has a man time to think during his life on earth?"

"Confusion is all around us."

"We must flee to the desert," said the peasant who lay on the bench.

"Not everybody can afford it."

The peasants spoke, and became silent again. A shrill whistle resounded, a little bell began to jingle at the machine. Someone's loud exclamation rang out:

"Eh, there! To the water-measuring poles."

"Oh Lord! Oh Queen of Heaven!"—a deep sigh was heard.

And a dull, half-choked voice shouted:

"Nine! nine!"

Fragments of the fog burst forth upon the deck and floated over it like cold, gray smoke.

"Here, kind people, give ear unto the words of King David," said the pilgrim, and shaking his head, began to read distinctly: "'Lead me, Oh Lord, in thy righteousness because of mine enemies; make thy way straight before my face. For there is no faithfulness in their mouths; their inward part is very wickedness; their throat is an open sepulchre; they flatter with their tongue. Destroy thou them, 0h God; let them fall by their own counsels.'"

"Eight! seven!" Like moans these exclamations resounded in the distance.

The steamer began to hiss angrily, and slackened its speed. The noise of the hissing of the steam deafened the pilgrim's words, and Foma saw only the movement of his lips.

"Get off!" a loud, angry shout was heard. "It's my place!"

"Yours?"

"Here you have yours!"

"I'll rap you on the jaw; then you'll find your place. What a lord!"

"Get away!"

An uproar ensued. The peasants who were listening to the pilgrim turned their heads toward the direction where the row was going on, and the pilgrim heaved a sigh and became silent. Near the machine a loud and lively dispute blazed up as though dry branches, thrown upon a dying bonfire, had caught the flame.

"I'll give it to you, devils! Get away, both of you."

"Take them away to the captain."

"Ha! ha! ha! That's a fine settlement for you!"

"That was a good rap he gave him on the neck!"

"The sailors are a clever lot."

"Eight! nine!" shouted the man with the measuring pole.

"Yes, increase speed!" came the loud exclamation of the engineer.

Swaying because of the motion of the steamer, Foma stood leaning against the tarpaulin, and attentively listened to each and every sound about him. And everything was blended into one picture, which was familiar to him. Through fog and uncertainty, surrounded on all sides by gloom impenetrable to the eye, life of man is moving somewhere slowly and heavily. And men are grieved over their sins, they sigh heavily, and then fight for a warm place, and asking each other for the sake of possessing the place, they also receive blows from those who strive for order in life. They timidly search for a free road toward the goal.

"Nine! eight!"

The wailing cry is softly wafted over the vessel. "And the holy prayer of the pilgrim is deafened by the tumult of life. And there is no relief from sorrow, there is no joy for him who reflects on his fate."

Foma felt like speaking to this pilgrim, in whose softly uttered words there rang sincere fear of God, and all manner of fear for men before His countenance. The kind, admonitive voice of the pilgrim possessed a peculiar power, which compelled Foma to listen to its deep tones.

"I'd like to ask him where he lives," thought Foma, fixedly scrutinizing the huge stooping figure. "And where have I seen him before? Or does he resemble some acquaintance of mine?"

Suddenly it somehow struck Foma with particular vividness that the humble preacher before him was no other than the son of old Anany Shchurov. Stunned by this conjecture, he walked up to the pilgrim and seating himself by his side, inquired freely:

"Are you from Irgiz, father?"

The pilgrim raised his head, turned his face toward Foma slowly and heavily, scrutinized him and said in a calm and gentle voice:

"I was on the Irgiz, too."

"Are you a native of that place?"

"Are you now coming from there?"

"No, I am coming from Saint Stephen."

The conversation broke off. Foma lacked the courage to ask the pilgrim whether he was not Shchurov.

"We'll be late on account of the fog," said some one.

"How can we help being late!"

410

All were silent, looking at Foma. Young, handsome, neatly and richly dressed, he aroused the curiosity of the bystanders by his sudden appearance among them; he was conscious of this curiosity, he understood that they were all waiting for his words, that they wanted to understand why he had come to them, and all this confused and angered him.

"It seems to me that I've met you before somewhere, father," said he at length.

The pilgrim replied, without looking at him:

"Perhaps."

"I would like to speak to you," announced Foma, timidly, in a low voice.

"Well, then, speak."

"Come with me."

"Whither?"

"To my cabin."

The pilgrim looked into Foma's face, and, after a moment's silence, assented:

"Come."

On leaving, Foma felt the looks of the peasants on his back, and now he was pleased to know that they were interested in him.

In the cabin he asked gently:

"Would you perhaps eat something? Tell me. I will order it."

"God forbid. What do you wish?"

This man, dirty and ragged, in a cassock turned red with age, and covered with patches, surveyed the cabin with a squeamish look, and when he seated himself on the plush-covered lounge, he turned the skirt of the cassock as though afraid to soil it by the plush.

"What is your name, father?" asked Foma, noticing the expression of squeamishness on the pilgrim's face.

"Miron."

"Not Mikhail?"

"Why Mikhail?" asked the pilgrim.

"There was in our town the son of a certain merchant Shchurov, he also went off to the Irgiz. And his name was Mikhail."

Foma spoke and fixedly looked at Father Miron; but the latter was as calm as a deaf-mute—

"I never met such a man. I don't remember, I never met him," said he, thoughtfully. "So you wished to inquire about him?"

"Yes."

"No, I never met Mikhail Shchurov. Well, pardon me for Christ's sake!" and rising from the lounge, the pilgrim bowed to Foma and went toward the door.

"But wait awhile, sit down, let's talk a little!" exclaimed Foma, rushing at him uneasily. The pilgrim looked at him searchingly and sank down on the lounge. From the distance came a dull sound, like a deep groan, and immediately after it the signal whistle of the steamer drawled out as in a frightened manner over Foma's and his guest's heads. From the distance came a more distant reply, and the whistle overhead again gave out abrupt, timorous sounds. Foma opened the window. Through the fog, not far from their steamer, something was moving along with deep noise; specks of fantastic lights floated by, the fog was agitated and again sank into dead immobility.

"How terrible!" exclaimed Foma, shutting the window.

"What is there to be afraid of?" asked the pilgrim. "You see! It is neither day nor night, neither darkness nor light! We can see nothing, we are sailing we know not whither, we are straying on the river."

"Have inward fire within you, have light within your soul, and you shall see everything," said the pilgrim, sternly and instructively.

Foma was displeased with these cold words and looked at the pilgrim askance. The latter sat with drooping head, motionless, as though petrified in thought and prayer. The beads of his rosary were softly rustling in his hands.

The pilgrim's attitude gave birth to easy courage in Foma's breast, and he said:

412

"Tell me, Father Miron, is it good to live, having full freedom, without work, without relatives, a wanderer, like yourself?"

Father Miron raised his head and softly burst into the caressing laughter of a child. All his face, tanned from wind and sunburn, brightened up with inward joy, was radiant with tranquil joy; he touched Foma's knee with his hand and said in a sincere tone:

"Cast aside from you all that is worldly, for there is no sweetness in it. I am telling you the right word—turn away from evil. Do you remember it is said:

'Blessed is the man that walketh not in the counsel of the ungodly, nor standeth in the way of sinners.' Turn away, refresh your soul with solitude and fill yourself with the thought of God. For only by the thought of Him can man save his soul from profanation."

"That isn't the thing!" said Foma. "I have no need of working out my salvation. Have I sinned so much? Look at others. What I would like is to comprehend things."

"And you will comprehend if you turn away from the world. Go forth upon the free road, on the fields, on the steppes, on the plains, on the mountains. Go forth and look at the world from afar, from your freedom."

"That's right!" cried Foma. "That's just what I think. One can see better from the side!"

And Miron, paying no attention to his words, spoke softly, as though of some great mystery, known only to him, the pilgrim:

"The thick slumbering forests around you will start to rustle in sweet voices about the wisdom of the Lord; God's little birds will sing before you of His holy glory, and the grasses of the steppe will burn incense to the Holy Virgin."

The pilgrim's voice now rose and quivered from excess of emotion, now sank to a mysterious whisper. He seemed as though grown younger; his eyes beamed so confidently and clearly, and all his face was radiant with the happy smile of a man who has found expression for his joy and was delighted while he poured it forth.

"The heart of God throbs in each and every blade of grass; each and every insect of the air and of the earth, breathes His holy spirit. God, the Lord, Jesus Christ, lives everywhere! What beauty there is on earth, in the fields and in the forests! Have you ever been on the Kerzhenz? An incomparable silence reigns there supreme, the trees, the grass there are like those of paradise."

Foma listened, and his imagination, captivated by the quiet, charming narrative, pictured to him those wide fields and dense forests, full of beauty and soul-pacifying silence.

"You look at the sky, as you rest somewhere under a little bush, and the sky seems to descend upon you as though longing to embrace you. Your soul is warm, filled with tranquil joy, you desire nothing, you envy nothing. And it actually seems to you that there is no one on earth save you and God."

The pilgrim spoke, and his voice and sing-song speech reminded Foma of the wonderful fairy-tales of Aunt Anfisa. He felt as though, after a long journey on a hot day, he drank the clear, cold water of a forest brook, water that had the fragrance of the grasses and the flowers it has bathed. Even wider and wider grew the pictures as they unfolded upon him; here is a path through the thick, slumbering forest; the fine sunbeams penetrate through the branches of the trees, and quiver in the air and under the feet of the wanderer. There is a savoury odour of fungi and decaying foliage; the honeyed fragrance of the flowers, the intense odour of the pine-tree invisibly rise in the air and penetrate the breast in a warm, rich stream. All is silence: only the birds are singing, and the silence is so wonderful that it seems as though even the birds were singing in your breast. You go, without haste, and your life goes on like a dream. While here everything is enveloped in a gray, dead fog, and we are foolishly struggling about in it, yearning for freedom and light. There below they have started to sing something in scarcely audible voices; it

414

was half song, half prayer. Again someone is shouting, scolding. And still they seek the way:

"Seven and a half. Seven!"

"And you have no care," spoke the pilgrim, and his voice murmured like a brook. "Anybody will give you a crust of bread; and what else do you need in your freedom? In the world, cares fall upon the soul like fetters."

"You speak well," said Foma with a sigh.

"My dear brother!" exclaimed the pilgrim, softly, moving still closer toward him. "Since the soul has awakened, since it yearns toward freedom, do not lull it to sleep by force; hearken to its voice. The world with its charms has no beauty and holiness whatever, wherefore, then, obey its laws? In John Chrysostom it is said: 'The real shechinah is man!' Shechinah is a Hebrew word and it means the holy of holies. Consequently—"

A prolonged shrill sound of the whistle drowned his voice. He listened, rose quickly from the lounge and said:

"We are nearing the harbour. That's what the whistle meant. I must be off! Well, goodbye, brother! May God give you strength and firmness to act according to the will of your soul! Goodbye, my dear boy!"

He made a low bow to Foma. There was something feminine, caressing and soft in his farewell words and bow. Foma also bowed low to him, bowed and remained as though petrified, standing with drooping head, his hand leaning against the table.

"Come to see me when you are in town," he asked the pilgrim, who was hastily turning the handle of the cabin door.

"I will! I will come! Goodbye! Christ save you!"

When the steamer's side touched the wharf Foma came out on the deck and began to look downward into the fog. From the steamer people were walking down the gang-planks, but Foma could not discern the pilgrim among those dark figures enveloped in the dense gloom. All those that left the steamer looked equally indistinct, and they all quickly disappeared from sight, as though they had melted in the gray dampness. One could see neither the shore nor anything else solid; the landing bridge rocked from the commotion caused by the steamer; above it the yellow spot of the lantern was swaying; the noise of the footsteps and the bustle of the people were dull.

The steamer put off and slowly moved along into the clouds. The pilgrim, the harbour, the turmoil of people's voices—all suddenly disappeared like a dream, and again there remained only the dense gloom and the steamer heavily turning about in it. Foma stared before him into the dead sea of fog and thought of the blue, cloudless and caressingly warm sky—where was it?

On the next day, about noon, he sat In Yozhov's small room and listened to the local news from the mouth of his friend. Yozhov had climbed on the table, which was piled with newspapers, and, swinging his feet, narrated:

"The election campaign has begun. The merchants are putting your godfather up as mayor—that old devil! Like the devil, he is immortal, although he must be upwards of a hundred and fifty years old already. He marries his daughter to Smolin. You remember that red-headed fellow. They say that he is a decent man, but nowadays they even call clever scoundrels decent men, because there are no men. Now Africashka plays the enlightened man; he has already managed to get into intelligent society, donated something to some enterprise or another and thus at once came to the front. Judging from his face, he is a sharper of the highest degree, but he will play a prominent part, for he knows how to adapt himself. Yes, friend, Africashka is a liberal. And a liberal merchant is a mixture of a wolf and a pig with a toad and a snake."

"The devil take them all!" said Foma, waving his hand indifferently. "What have I to do with them? How about yourself—do you still keep on drinking?"

"I do! Why shouldn't I drink?"

416

Half-clad and dishevelled, Yozhov looked like a plucked bird, which had just had a fight and had not yet recovered from the excitement of the conflict.

"I drink because, from time to time, I must quench the fire of my wounded heart. And you, you damp stump, you are smouldering little by little?"

"I have to go to the old man," said Foma, wrinkling his face.

"Chance it!"

"I don't feel like going. He'll start to lecture me."

"Then don't go!"

"But I must."

"Then go!"

"Why do you always play the buffoon? "said Foma, with displeasure, "as though you were indeed merry."

"By God, I feel merry!" exclaimed Yozhov, jumping down from the table. "What a fine roasting I gave a certain gentleman in the paper yesterday! And then—I've heard a clever anecdote: A company was sitting on the sea-shore philosophizing at length upon life. And a Jew said to them: 'Gentlemen, why do you employ so many different words? I'll tell it to you all at once: Our life is not worth a single copeck, even as this stormy sea! '"

"Eh, the devil take you!" said Foma. "Good-bye. I am going."

"Go ahead! I am in a fine frame of mind to-day and I will not moan with you. All the more so considering you don't moan, but grunt."

Foma went away, leaving Yozhov singing at the top of his voice:

"Beat the drum and fear not."

"Drum? You are a drum yourself," thought Foma, with irritation, as he slowly came out on the street.

At the Mayakins he was met by Luba. Agitated and animated, she suddenly appeared before him, speaking quickly:

"You? My God! How pale you are! How thin you've grown! It seems you have been leading a fine life."

Then her face became distorted with alarm and she exclaimed almost in a whisper:

"Ah, Foma. You don't know. Do you hear? Someone is ringing the bell. Perhaps it is he."

And she rushed out of the room, leaving behind her in the air the rustle of her silk gown, and the astonished Foma, who had not even had a chance to ask her where her father was. Yakov Tarasovich was at home. Attired in his holiday clothes, in a long frock coat with medals on his breast, he stood on the threshold with his hands outstretched, clutching at the door posts. His green little eyes examined Foma, and, feeling their look upon him, Foma raised his head and met them.

"How do you do, my fine gentleman?" said the old man, shaking his head reproachfully. "Where has it pleased you to come from, may I ask? Who has sucked off that fat of yours? Or is it true that a pig looks for a puddle, and Foma for a place which is worse?"

"Have you no other words for me?" asked Foma, sternly, looking straight into the old man's face. And suddenly he noticed that his godfather shuddered, his legs trembled, his eyes began to blink repeatedly, and his hands clutched the door posts with an effort. Foma advanced toward him, presuming that the old man was feeling ill, but Yakov Tarasovich said in a dull and angry voice:

"Stand aside. Get out of the way."

And his face assumed its usual expression.

Foma stepped back and found himself side by side with a rather short, stout man, who bowed to Mayakin, and said in a hoarse voice:

"How do you do, papa?"

"How are you, Taras Yakovlich, how are you?" said the old man, bowing, smiling distractedly, and still clinging to the door posts.

Foma stepped aside in confusion, seated himself in an armchair, and, petrified with curiosity, wide-eyed, began to watch the meeting of father and son.

The father, standing in the doorway, swayed his feeble body, leaning his hands against the door posts, and, with his head bent on one side and eyes half shut, stared at his son in silence. The son stood about three steps away from him; his head already gray, was lifted high; he knitted his brow and gazed at his father with large dark eyes. His small, black, pointed beard and his small moustache quivered on his meagre face, with its gristly nose, like that of his father. And the hat, also, quivered in his hand. From behind his shoulder Foma saw the pale, frightened and joyous face of Luba—she looked at her father with beseeching eyes and it seemed she was on the point of crying out. For a few moments all were silent and motionless, crushed as they were by the immensity of their emotions. The silence was broken by the low, but dull and quivering voice of Yakov Tarasovich:

"You have grown old, Taras."

The son laughed in his father's face silently, and, with a swift glance, surveyed him from head to foot.

The father tearing his hands from the door posts, made a step toward his son and suddenly stopped short with a frown. Then Taras Mayakin, with one huge step, came up to his father and gave him his hand.

"Well, let us kiss each other," suggested the father, softly.

The two old men convulsively clasped each other in their arms, exchanged warm kisses and then stepped apart. The wrinkles of the older man quivered, the lean face of the younger was immobile, almost stern. The kisses had changed nothing in the external side of this scene, only Lubov burst into a sob of joy, and Foma awkwardly moved about in his seat, feeling as though his breath were failing him.

"Eh, children, you are wounds to the heart—you are not its joy," complained Yakov Tarasovich in a ringing voice, and he evidently invested a great deal in these words, for immediately after he had pronounced them he became radiant, more courageous, and he said briskly, addressing himself to his daughter:

"Well, have you melted with joy? You had better go and prepare something for us—tea and so forth. We'll entertain the prodigal son. You must have forgotten, my little old man, what sort of a man your father is?"

Taras Mayakin scrutinized his parent with a meditative look of his large eyes and he smiled, speechless, clad in black, wherefore the gray hair on his head and in his beard told more strikingly.

"Well, be seated. Tell me—how have you lived, what have you done? What are you looking at? Ah! That's my godson. Ignat Gordyeeff's son, Foma. Do you remember Ignat?"

"I remember everything," said Taras.

"Oh! That's good, if you are not bragging. Well, are you married?"

"I am a widower."

"Have you any children?"

"They died. I had two."

"That's a pity. I would have had grandchildren."

"May I smoke?" asked Taras.

"Go ahead. Just look at him, you're smoking cigars."

"Don't you like them?"

"I? Come on, it's all the same to me. I say that it looks rather aristocratic to smoke cigars."

"And why should we consider ourselves lower than the aristocrats?" said Taras, laughing.

"Do, I consider ourselves lower?" exclaimed the old man. "I merely said it because it looked ridiculous to me, such a sedate old fellow, with beard trimmed in foreign fashion, cigar in his mouth. Who is he? My son—he-he-he!" the old man tapped Taras on the shoulder and sprang away from him, as though frightened lest he were rejoicing too soon, lest that might not be the proper way to treat that half gray man. And he looked searchingly and suspiciously into his son's large eyes, which were surrounded by yellowish swellings.

Taras smiled in his father's face an affable and warm smile, and said to him thoughtfully:

"That's the way I remember you—cheerful and lively. It looks as though you had not changed a bit during all these years."

The old man straightened himself proudly, and, striking his breast with his fist, said:

"I shall never change, because life has no power over him who knows his own value. Isn't that so?"

"Oh! How proud you are!"

"I must have taken after my son," said the old man with a cunning grimace. "Do you know, dear, my son was silent for seventeen years out of pride."

"That's because his father would not listen to him," Taras reminded him.

"It's all right now. Never mind the past. Only God knows which of us is to blame. He, the upright one, He'll tell it to you—wait! I shall keep silence. This is not the time for us to discuss that matter. You better tell me—what have you been doing all these years? How did you come to that soda factory? How have you made your way?"

"That's a long story," said Taras with a sigh; and emitting from his mouth a great puff of smoke, he began slowly: "When I acquired the possibility to live at liberty, I entered the office of the superintendent of the gold mines of the Remezovs."

"I know; they're very rich. Three brothers. I know them all. One is a cripple, the other a fool, and the third a miser. Go on!"

"I served under him for two years. And then I married his daughter," narrated Mayakin in a hoarse voice.

"The superintendent's? That wasn't foolish at all." Taras became thoughtful and was silent awhile. The old man looked at his sad face and understood his son.

"And so you lived with your wife happily," he said. "Well, what can you do? To the dead belongs paradise, and the living must live on. You are not so very old as yet. Have you been a widower long?"

"This is the third year."

"So? And how did you chance upon the soda factory?"

"That belongs to my father-in-law."

"Aha! What is your salary?"

"About five thousand."

"Mm. That's not a stale crust. Yes, that's a galley slave for you!"

Taras glanced at his father with a firm look and asked him drily:

"By the way, what makes you think that I was a convict?"

The old man glanced at his son with astonishment, which was quickly changed into joy:

"Ah! What then? You were not? The devil take them! Then—how was it? Don't take offence! How could I know? They said you were in Siberia! Well, and there are the galleys!"

"To make an end of this once for all," said Taras, seriously and impressively, clapping his hand on his knee, "I'll tell you right now how it all happened. I was banished to Siberia to settle there for six years, and, during all the time of my exile, I lived in the mining region of the Lena. In Moscow I was imprisoned for about nine months. That's all!"

"So-o! But what does it mean?" muttered Yakov Tarasovich, with confusion and joy.

"And here they circulated that absurd rumour."

"That's right—it is absurd indeed!" said the old man, distressed.

"And it did a pretty great deal of harm on a certain occasion."

"Really? Is that possible?"

"Yes. I was about to go into business for myself, and my credit was ruined on account of—"

"Pshaw!" said Yakov Tarasovich, as he spat angrily. "Oh, devil! Come, come, is that possible?"

422

Foma sat all this time in his corner, listening to the conversation between the Mayakins, and, blinking perplexedly, he fixedly examined the newcomer. Recalling Lubov's bearing toward her brother, and influenced, to a certain degree, by her stories about Taras, he expected to see in him something unusual, something unlike the ordinary people. He had thought that Taras would speak in some peculiar way, would dress in a manner peculiar to himself; and in general he would be unlike other people. While before him sat a sedate, stout man, faultlessly dressed, with stern eyes, very much like his father in face, and the only difference between them was that the son had a cigar in his mouth and a black beard. He spoke briefly in a business-like way of everyday things—where was, then, that peculiar something about him? Now he began to tell his father of the profits in the manufacture of soda. He had not been a galley slave—Lubov had lied! And Foma was very much pleased when he pictured to himself how he would speak to Lubov about her brother.

Now and then she appeared in the doorway during the conversation between her father and her brother. Her face was radiant with happiness, and her eyes beamed with joy as she looked at the black figure of Taras, clad in such a peculiarly thick frock coat, with pockets on the sides and with big buttons. She walked on tiptoe, and somehow always stretched her neck toward her brother. Foma looked at her questioningly, but she did not notice him, constantly running back and forth past the door, with plates and bottles in her hands.

It so happened that she glanced into the room just when her brother was telling her father about the galleys. She stopped as though petrified, holding a tray in her outstretched hands and listened to everything her brother said about the punishment inflicted upon him. She listened, and slowly walked away, without catching Foma's astonished and sarcastic glance. Absorbed in his reflections on Taras, slightly offended by the lack of attention shown him, and by the fact that since the handshake at the introduction Taras had not given him a single glance, Foma ceased for awhile to follow the conversation of the Mayakins, and suddenly he felt that someone seized him by the shoulder. He trembled and sprang to his feet, almost felling his godfather, who stood before him with excited face:

"There—look! That is a man! That's what a Mayakin is! They have seven times boiled him in lye; they have squeezed oil out of him, and yet he lives! Understand? Without any aid—alone—he made his way and found his place and—he is proud! That means Mayakin! A Mayakin means a man who holds his fate in his own hands. Do you understand? Take a lesson from him! Look at him! You cannot find another like him in a hundred; you'd have to look for one in a thousand. What? Just bear this in mind: You cannot forge a Mayakin from man into either devil or angel."

Stupefied by this tempestuous shock, Foma became confused and did not know what to say in reply to the old man's noisy song of praise. He saw that Taras, calmly smoking his cigar, was looking at his father, and that the corners of his lips were quivering with a smile. His face looked condescendingly contented, and all his figure somewhat aristocratic and haughty. He seemed to be amused by the old man's joy.

And Yakov Tarasovich tapped Foma on the chest with his finger and said:

"I do not know him, my own son. He has not opened his soul to me. It may be that such a difference had grown up between us that not only an eagle, but the devil himself cannot cross it. Perhaps his blood has overboiled; that there is not even the scent of the father's blood in it. But he is a Mayakin! And I can feel it at once! I feel it and say: 'Today thou forgivest Thy servant, 0h Lord!'"

The old man was trembling with the fever of his exultation, and fairly hopped as he stood before Foma.

"Calm yourself, father!" said Taras, slowly rising from his chair and walking up to his father. "Why confuse the young man? Come, let us sit down."

424

He gave Foma a fleeting smile, and, taking his father by the arm, led him toward the table.

"I believe in blood," said Yakov Tarasovich; "in hereditary blood. Therein lies all power! My father, I remember, told me: 'Yashka, you are my genuine blood!' There. The blood of the Mayakins is thick—it is transferred from father to father and no woman can ever weaken it. Let us drink some champagne! Shall we? Very well, then! Tell me more—tell me about yourself. How is it there in Siberia?"

And again, as though frightened and sobered by some thought, the old man fixed his searching eyes upon the face of his son. And a few minutes later the circumstantial but brief replies of his son again aroused in him a noisy joy. Foma kept on listening and watching, as he sat quietly in his corner.

"Gold mining, of course, is a solid business," said Taras, calmly, with importance, "but it is a rather risky operation and one requiring a large capital. The earth says not a word about what it contains within it. It is very profitable to deal with foreigners. Dealings with them, under any circumstances, yield an enormous percentage. That is a perfectly infallible enterprise. But a weary one, it must be admitted. It does not require much brains; there is no room in it for an extraordinary man; a man with great enterprising power cannot develop in it."

Lubov entered and invited them all into the dining-room. When the Mayakins stepped out Foma imperceptibly tugged Lubov by the sleeve, and she remained with him alone, inquiring hastily:

"What is it?"

"Nothing," said Foma, with a smile. "I want to ask you whether you are glad?"

"Of course I am!" exclaimed Lubov.

"And what about?"

"That is, what do you mean?"

"Just so. What about?"

"You're queer!" said Lubov, looking at him with astonishment. "Can't you see?"

"What?" asked Foma, sarcastically.

"What's the trouble with you?" said Lubov, looking at him uneasily.

"Eh, you!" drawled out Foma, with contemptuous pity. "Can your father, can the merchant class beget anything good? Can you expect a radish to bring forth raspberries? And you lied to me. Taras is this, Taras is that. What is in him? A merchant, like the other merchants, and his paunch is also that of the real merchant. He-he!" He was satisfied, seeing that the girl, confused by his words, was biting her lips, now flushing, now turning pale.

"You—you, Foma," she began, in a choking voice, and suddenly stamping her foot, she cried:

"Don't you dare to speak to me!"

On reaching the threshold of the room, she turned her angry face to him, and ejaculated in a low voice, emphatically:

"Oh, you malicious man!"

Foma burst into laughter. He did not feel like going to the table, where three happy people were engaged in a lively conversation. He heard their merry voices, their contented laughter, the rattle of the dishes, and he understood that, with that burden on his heart, there was no place for him beside them. Nor was there a place for him anywhere. If all people only hated him, even as Lubov hated him now, he would feel more at ease in their midst, he thought. Then he would know how to behave with them, would find something to say to them. While now he could not understand whether they were pitying him or whether they were laughing at him, because he had lost his way and could not conform himself to anything. As he stood awhile alone in the middle of the room, he unconsciously resolved to leave this house where people were rejoicing and where he was superfluous. On reaching the street, he felt himself offended by the Mayakins. After all, they were the only people near to him in the world. Before him arose his godfather's face, on which the wrinkles quivered with agitation, and illuminated by the merry glitter of his green eyes, seemed to beam with phosphoric light.

"Even a rotten trunk of a tree stands out in the dark!" reflected Foma, savagely. Then he recalled the calm and serious face of Taras and beside it the figure of Lubov bowing herself hastily toward him. That aroused in him feelings of envy and sorrow.

"Who will look at me like that? There is not a soul to do it."

He came to himself from his broodings on the shore, at the landing-places, aroused by the bustle of toil. All sorts of articles and wares were carried and carted in every direction; people moved about hastily, care-worn, spurring on their horses excitedly, shouting at one another, filling the street with unintelligible bustle and deafening noise of hurried work. They busied themselves on a narrow strip of ground, paved with stone, built up on one side with tall houses, and the other side cut off by a steep ravine at the river, and their seething bustle made upon Foma an impression as though they had all prepared themselves to flee from this toil amid filth and narrowness and tumult—prepared themselves to flee and were now hastening to complete the sooner the unfinished work which would not release them. Huge steamers, standing by the shore and emitting columns of smoke from their funnels, were already awaiting them. The troubled water of the river, closely obstructed with vessels, was softly and plaintively splashing against the shore, as though imploring for a minute of rest and repose.

"Your Honour!" a hoarse cry rang out near Foma's ears, "contribute some brandy in honour of the building!"

Foma glanced at the petitioner indifferently; he was a huge, bearded fellow, barefooted, with a torn shirt and a bruised, swollen face.

"Get away!" muttered Foma, and turned away from him.

"Merchant! When you die you can't take your money with you. Give me for one glass of brandy, or are you too lazy to put your hand into your pocket?"

Foma again looked at the petitioner; the latter stood before him, covered more with mud than with clothes, and, trembling with intoxication, waited obstinately, staring at Foma with blood-shot, swollen eyes.

"Is that the way to ask?" inquired Foma.

"How else? Would you want me to go down on my knees before you for a ten-copeck piece?" asked the bare-footed man, boldly.

"There!" and Foma gave him a coin.

"Thanks! Fifteen copecks. Thanks! And if you give me fifteen more I'll crawl on all fours right up to that tavern. Do you want me to?" proposed the barefooted man.

"Go, leave me alone!" said Foma, waving him off with his hand.

"He who gives not when he may, when he fain would, shall have nay," said the barefooted man, and stepped aside.

Foma looked at him as he departed, and said to himself:

"There is a ruined man and yet how bold he is. He asks alms as though demanding a debt. Where do such people get so much boldness?"

And heaving a deep sigh, he answered himself:

"From freedom. The man is not fettered. What is there that he should regret? What does he fear? And what do I fear? What is there that I should regret?"

These two questions seemed to strike Foma's heart and called forth in him a dull perplexity. He looked at the movement of the working people and kept on thinking: What did he regret? What did he fear?

"Alone, with my own strength, I shall evidently never come out anywhere. Like a fool I shall keep on tramping about among people, mocked and offended by all. If they would only jostle me aside; if they would only hate me, then—then—I would go out into the wide world! Whether I liked or not, I would have to go!"

From one of the landing wharves the merry "dubinushka" ["Dubinushka," or the "Oaken Cudgel," is a song popular with the Russian workmen.] had already been smiting the air for a long time. The carriers were doing a certain work, which required brisk movements, and were adapting the song and the refrain to them.

"In the tavern sit great merchants Drinking liquors strong,"

narrated the leader, in a bold recitative. The company joined in unison:

"Oh, dubinushka, heave-ho!"

And then the bassos smote the air with deep sounds:

"It goes, it goes."

And the tenors repeated:

"It goes, it goes."

Foma listened to the song and directed his footsteps toward it, on the wharf. There he noticed that the carriers, formed in two rows, were rolling out of the steamer's hold huge barrels of salted fish. Dirty, clad in red blouses, unfastened at the collar, with mittens on their hands, with arms bare to the elbow, they stood over the hold, and, merrily jesting, with faces animated by toil, they pulled the ropes, all together, keeping time to their song. And from the hold rang out the high, laughing voice of the invisible leader:

> "But for our peasant throats
> There is not enough vodka."

And the company, like one huge pair of lungs, heaved forth loudly and in unison:

"Oh, dubinushka, heave-ho!"

Foma felt pleased and envious as he looked at this work, which was as harmonious as music. The slovenly faces of the carriers beamed with smiles, the work was easy, it went on smoothly, and the leader of the chorus was in his best vein. Foma thought that it would be fine to work thus in unison, with good comrades, to the tune of a cheerful song, to get tired from work to drink a glass of vodka and eat fat cabbage soup, prepared by the stout, sprightly matron of the company.

"Quicker, boys, quicker!" rang out beside him someone's unpleasant, hoarse voice.

Foma turned around. A stout man, with an enormous paunch, tapped on the boards of the landing bridge with his cane, as he looked at the carriers with his small eyes and said:

"Bawl less and work faster."

His face and neck were covered with perspiration; he wiped it off every now and then with his left hand and breathed heavily, as though he were going uphill.

Foma cast at the man a hostile look and thought:

"Others are working and he is sweating. And I am still worse than he. I'm like a crow on the fence, good for nothing."

From each and every impression there immediately stood out in his mind the painful thought of his unfitness for life. Everything that attracted his attention contained something offensive to him, and this something fell like a brick upon his breast. At one side of him, by the freight scales, stood two sailors, and one of them, a square-built, red-faced fellow, was telling the other:

"As they rushed on me it began for fair, my dear chap! There were four of them—I was alone! But I didn't give in to them, because I saw that they would beat me to death! Even a ram will kick out if you fleece it alive. How I tore myself away from them! They all rolled away in different directions."

"But you came in for a sound drubbing all the same?" inquired the other sailor.

"Of course! I caught it. I swallowed about five blows. But what's the difference? They didn't kill me. Well, thank God for it!"

"Certainly."

"To the stern, devils, to the stern, I'm telling you!" roared the perspiring man in a ferocious voice at two carriers who were rolling a barrel of fish along the deck.

430

"What are you yelling for?" Foma turned to him sternly, as he had started at the shout.

"Is that any of your business?" asked the perspiring man, casting a glance at Foma.

"It is my business! The people are working and your fat is melting away. So you think you must yell at them?" said Foma, threateningly, moving closer toward him.

"You—you had better keep your temper."

The perspiring man suddenly rushed away from his place and went into his office. Foma looked after him and also went away from the wharf; filled with a desire to abuse some one, to do something, just to divert his thoughts from himself at least for a short while. But his thoughts took a firmer hold on him.

"That sailor there, he tore himself away, and he's safe and sound! Yes, while I—"

In the evening he again went up to the Mayakins. The old man was not at home, and in the dining-room sat Lubov with her brother, drinking tea. On reaching the door Foma heard the hoarse voice of Taras:

"What makes father bother himself about him?"

At the sight of Foma he stopped short, staring at his face with a serious, searching look. An expression of agitation was clearly depicted on Lubov's face, and she said with dissatisfaction and at the same time apologetically:

"Ah! So it's you?"

"They've been speaking of me," thought Foma, as he seated himself at the table. Taras turned his eyes away from him and sank deeper in the armchair. There was an awkward silence lasting for about a minute, and this pleased Foma.

"Are you going to the banquet?"

"What banquet?"

"Don't you know? Kononov is going to consecrate his new steamer. A mass will be held there and then they are going to take a trip up the Volga."

"I was not invited," said Foma.

"Nobody was invited. He simply announced on the Exchange: 'Anybody who wishes to honour me is welcome!

"I don't care for it."

"Yes? But there will be a grand drinking bout," said Lubov, looking at him askance.

"I can drink at my own expense if I choose to do so."

"I know," said Lubov, nodding her head expressively.

Taras toyed with his teaspoon, turning it between his fingers and looking at them askance.

"And where's my godfather?" asked Foma.

"He went to the bank. There's a meeting of the board of directors today. Election of officers is to take place.

"They'll elect him again."

"Of course."

And again the conversation broke off. Foma began to watch the brother and the sister. Having dropped the spoon, Taras slowly drank his tea in big sips, and silently moving the glass over to his sister, smiled to her. She, too, smiled joyously and happily, seized the glass and began to rinse it assiduously. Then her face assumed a strained expression; she seemed to prepare herself for something and asked her brother in a low voice, almost reverently:

"Shall we return to the beginning of our conversation?"

"If you please," assented Taras, shortly.

"You said something, but I didn't understand. What was it? I asked: 'If all this is, as you say, Utopia, if it is impossible, dreams, then what is he to do who is not satisfied with life as it is?'"

The girl leaned her whole body toward her brother, and her eyes, with strained expectation, stopped on the calm face of her brother. He

432

glanced at her in a weary way, moved about in his seat, and, lowering his head, said calmly and impressively:

"We must consider from what source springs that dissatisfaction with life. It seems to me that, first of all, it comes from the inability to work; from the lack of respect for work. And, secondly, from a wrong conception of one's own powers. The misfortune of most of the people is that they consider themselves capable of doing more than they really can. And yet only little is required of man: he must select for himself an occupation to suit his powers and must master it as well as possible, as attentively as possible. You must love what you are doing, and then labour, be it ever so rough, rises to the height of creativeness. A chair, made with love, will always be a good, beautiful and solid chair. And so it is with everything. Read Smiles. Haven't you read him? It is a very sensible book. It is a sound book. Read Lubbock. In general, remember that the English people constitute the nation most qualified for labour, which fact explains their astonishing success in the domain of industry and commerce. With them labour is almost a cult. The height of culture stands always directly dependent upon the love of labour. And the higher the culture the more satisfied are the requirements of man, the fewer the obstacles on the road toward the further development of man's requirements. Happiness is possible—it is the complete satisfaction of requirements. There it is. And, as you see, man's happiness is dependent upon his relation toward his work."

Taras Mayakin spoke slowly and laboriously, as though it were unpleasant and tedious for him to speak. And Lubov, with knitted brow, leaning toward him, listened to his words with eager attention in her eyes, ready to accept everything and imbibe it into her soul.

"Well, and suppose everything is repulsive to a man?" asked Foma, suddenly, in a deep voice, casting a glance at Taras's face.

"But what, in particular, is repulsive to the man?" asked Mayakin, calmly, without looking at Foma.

Foma bent his head, leaned his arms against the table and thus, like a bull, went on to explain himself:

"Nothing pleases him—business, work, all people and deeds. Suppose I see that all is deceit, that business is not business, but merely a plug that we prop up with it the emptiness of our souls; that some work, while others only give orders and sweat, but get more for that. Why is it so? Eh?"

"I cannot grasp your idea," announced Taras, when Foma paused, feeling on himself Lubov's contemptuous and angry look.

"You do not understand?" asked Foma, looking at Taras with a smile. "Well, I'll put it in this way:

A man is sailing in a boat on the river. The boat may be good, but under it there is always a depth all the same. The boat is sound, but if the man feels beneath him this dark depth, no boat can save him."

Taras looked at Foma indifferently and calmly. He looked in silence, and softly tapped his fingers on the edge of the table. Lubov was uneasily moving about in her chair. The pendulum of the clock told the seconds with a dull, sighing sound. And Foma's heart throbbed slowly and painfully, as though conscious that here no one would respond with a warm word to its painful perplexity.

"Work is not exactly everything for a man," said he, more to himself than to these people who had no faith in the sincerity of his words. "It is not true that in work lies justification. There are people who do not work at all during all their lives long, and yet they live better than those that do work. How is that? And the toilers—they are merely unfortunate— horses! Others ride on them, they suffer and that's all. But they have their justification before God. They will be asked: 'To what purpose did you live?' Then they will say: 'We had no time to think of that. We worked all our lives.' And I—what justification have I? And all those people who give orders—how will they justify themselves? To what purpose have they lived? It is my idea that everybody necessarily ought to know, to know firmly what he is living for."

He became silent, and, tossing his head up, exclaimed in a heavy voice:

"Can it be that man is born merely to work, acquire money, build a house, beget children and—die? No, life means something. A man is born, he lives and dies. What for? It is necessary, by God, it is necessary for all of us to consider what we are living for. There is no sense in our life. No sense whatever! Then things are not equal, that can be seen at once. Some are rich—they have money enough for a thousand people, and they live in idleness. Others bend their backs over their work all their lives, and yet they have not even a grosh. And the difference in people is very insignificant. There are some that have not even any trousers and yet they reason as though they were attired in silks."

Carried away by his thoughts, Foma would have continued to give them utterance, but Taras moved his armchair away from the table, rose and said softly, with a sigh:

"No, thank you! I don't want any more."

Foma broke off his speech abruptly, shrugged his shoulders and looked at Lubov with a smile.

"Where have you picked up such philosophy?" she asked, suspiciously and drily.

"That is not philosophy. That is simply torture!" said Foma in an undertone. "Open your eyes and look at everything. Then you will think so yourself."

"By the way, Luba, turn your attention to the fact," began Taras, standing with his back toward the table and scrutinizing the clock, "that pessimism is perfectly foreign to the Anglo-Saxon race. That which they call pessimism in Swift and in Byron is only a burning, sharp protest against the imperfection of life and man. But you cannot find among them the cold, well weighed and passive pessimism."

Then, as though suddenly recalling Foma, he turned to him, clasping his hands behind his back, and, wriggling his thigh, said:

435

"You raise very important questions, and if you are seriously interested in them you must read books. In them will you find many very valuable opinions as to the meaning of life. How about you—do you read books?"

"No!" replied Foma, briefly.

"Ah!"

"I don't like them."

"Aha! But they might nevertheless be of some help to you," said Taras, and a smile passed across his lips.

"Books? Since men cannot help me in my thoughts books can certainly do nothing for me," ejaculated Foma, morosely.

He began to feel awkward and weary with this indifferent man. He felt like going away, but at the same time he wished to tell Lubov something insulting about her brother, and he waited till Taras would leave the room. Lubov washed the dishes; her face was concentrated and thoughtful; her hands moved lazily. Taras was pacing the room, now and then he stopped short before the sideboard on which was the silverware, whistled, tapped his fingers against the window-panes and examined the articles with his eyes half shut. The pendulum of the clock flashed beneath the glass door of the case like some broad, grinning face, and monotonously told the seconds. When Foma noticed that Lubov glanced at him a few times questioningly, with expectant and hostile looks, he understood that he was in her way and that she was impatiently expecting him to leave.

"I am going to stay here over night," said he, with a smile. "I must speak with my godfather. And then it is rather lonesome in my house alone."

"Then go and tell Marfusha to make the bed for you in the corner room," Lubov hastened to advise him.

"I shall."

He arose and went out of the dining-room. And he soon heard that Taras asked his sister about something in a low voice.

436

"About me!" he thought. Suddenly this wicked thought flashed through his mind: "It were but right to listen and hear what wise people have to say."

He laughed softly, and, stepping on tiptoe, went noiselessly into the other room, also adjoining the dining-room. There was no light there, and only a thin band of light from the dining-room, passing through the unclosed door, lay on the dark floor. Softly, with sinking heart and malicious smile, Foma walked up close to the door and stopped.

"He's a clumsy fellow," said Taras.

Then came Lubov's lowered and hasty speech:

"He was carousing here all the time. He carried on dreadfully! It all started somehow of a sudden. The first thing he did was to thrash the son-in-law of the Vice-Governor at the Club. Papa had to take the greatest pains to hush up the scandal, and it was a good thing that the Vice-Governor's son-in-law is a man of very bad reputation. He is a card-sharper and in general a shady personality, yet it cost father more than two thousand roubles. And while papa was busying himself about that scandal Foma came near drowning a whole company on the Volga."

"Ha-ha! How monstrous! And that same man busies himself with investigating as to the meaning of life."

"On another occasion he was carousing on a steamer with a company of people like himself. Suddenly he said to them: 'Pray to God! I'll fling every one of you overboard!' He is frightfully strong. They screamed, while he said: 'I want to serve my country. I want to clear the earth of base people.'"

"Really? That's clever!"

"He's a terrible man! How many wild pranks he has perpetrated during these years! How much money he has squandered!"

"And, tell me, on what conditions does father manage his affairs for him? Do you know?"

"No, I don't. He has a full power of attorney. Why do you ask?"

"Simply so. It's a solid business. Of course it is conducted in purely Russian fashion; in other words, it is conducted abominably. But it is a splendid business, nevertheless. If it were managed properly it would be a most profitable gold mine."

"Foma does absolutely nothing. Everything is in father's hands."

"Yes? That's fine."

"Do you know, sometimes it occurs to me that his thoughtful frame of mind—that these words of his are sincere, and that he can be very decent. But I cannot reconcile his scandalous life with his words and arguments. I cannot do it under any circumstances!"

"It isn't even worthwhile to bother about it. The stripling and lazy bones seeks to justify his laziness."

"No. You see, at times he is like a child. He was particularly so before."

"Well, that's what I have said: he's a stripling. Is it worth while talking about an ignoramus and a savage, who wishes to remain an ignoramus and a savage, and does not conceal the fact? You see: he reasons as the bear in the fable bent the shafts."

"You are very harsh."

"Yes, I am harsh! People require that. We Russians are all desperately loose. Happily, life is so arranged that, whether we will it or not, we gradually brace up. Dreams are for the lads and maidens, but for serious people there is serious business."

"Sometimes I feel very sorry for Foma. What will become of him?"

"That does not concern me. I believe that nothing in particular will become of him—neither good nor bad. The insipid fellow will squander his money away, and will be ruined. What else? Eh, the deuce take him! Such people as he is are rare nowadays. Now the merchant knows the power of education. And he, that foster-brother of yours, he will go to ruin."

"That's true, sir!" said Foma, opening the door and appearing on the threshold.

438

Pale, with knitted brow and quivering lips, he stared straight into Taras's face and said in a dull voice: "True! I will go to ruin and—amen! The sooner the better!"

Lubov sprang up from the chair with frightened face, and ran up to Taras, who stood calmly in the middle of the room, with his hands thrust in his pockets.

"Foma! Oh! Shame! You have been eavesdropping. Oh, Foma!" said she in confusion.

"Keep quiet, you lamb!" said Foma to her.

"Yes, eavesdropping is wrong!" ejaculated Taras, slowly, without lifting from Foma his look of contempt.

"Let it be wrong!" said Foma, with a wave of the hand. "Is it my fault that the truth can be learned by eavesdropping only?"

"Go away, Foma, please!" entreated Lubov, pressing close to her brother.

"Perhaps you have something to say to me?" asked Taras, calmly.

"I?" exclaimed Foma. "What can I say? I cannot say anything. It is you who—you, I believe, know everything."

"You have nothing then to discuss with me?" asked Taras again.

"I am very pleased."

He turned sideways to Foma and inquired of Lubov:

"What do you think—will father return soon?"

Foma looked at him, and, feeling something akin to respect for the man, deliberately left the house. He did not feel like going to his own huge empty house, where each step of his awakened a ringing echo, he strolled along the street, which was enveloped in the melancholy gray twilight of late autumn. He thought of Taras Mayakin.

"How severe he is. He takes after his father. Only he's not so restless. He's also a cunning rogue, I think, while Lubka regarded him almost as a saint. That foolish girl! What a sermon he read to me! A regular judge. And she—she was kind toward me." But all these thoughts stirred in him no feelings—neither hatred toward Taras nor sympathy for Lubov.

He carried with him something painful and uncomfortable, something incomprehensible to him, that kept growing within his breast, and it seemed to him that his heart was swollen and was gnawing as though from an abscess. He hearkened to that unceasing and indomitable pain, noticed that it was growing more and more acute from hour to hour, and, not knowing how to allay it, waited for the results.

Then his godfather's trotter passed him. Foma saw in the carriage the small figure of Yakov Mayakin, but even that aroused no feeling in him. A lamplighter ran past Foma, overtook him, placed his ladder against the lamp post and went up. The ladder suddenly slipped under his weight, and he, clasping the lamp post, cursed loudly and angrily. A girl jostled Foma in the side with her bundle and said:

"Excuse me."

He glanced at her and said nothing. Then a drizzling rain began to fall from the sky—tiny, scarcely visible drops of moisture overcast the lights of the lanterns and the shop windows with grayish dust. This dust made him breathe with difficulty.

"Shall I go to Yozhov and pass the night there? I might drink with him," thought Foma and went away to Yozhov, not having the slightest desire either to see the feuilleton-writer or to drink with him.

At Yozhov's he found a shaggy fellow sitting on the lounge. He had on a blouse and gray pantaloons. His face was swarthy, as though smoked, his eyes were large, immobile and angry, his thick upper lip was covered with a bristle-like, soldier moustache. He was sitting on the lounge, with his feet clasped in his huge arms and his chin resting on his knees. Yozhov sat sideways in a chair, with his legs thrown across the arm of the chair. Among books and newspapers on the table stood a bottle of vodka and there was an odour of something salty in the room.

"Why are you tramping about?" Yozhov asked Foma, and, nodding at him, said to the man on the lounge: "Gordyeeff!"

The man glanced at the newcomer and said in a harsh, shrill voice: "Krasnoshchokov."

Foma seated himself on a corner of the lounge and said to Yozhov:

"I have come to stay here over night."

"Well? Go on, Vasily."

The latter glanced at Foma askance and went on in a creaking voice:

"In my opinion, you are attacking the stupid people in vain. Masaniello was a fool, but what had to be performed was done in the best way possible. And that Winkelried was certainly a fool also, and yet had he not thrust the imperial spears into himself the Swiss would have been thrashed. Have there not been many fools like that? Yet they are the heroes. And the clever people are the cowards. Where they ought to deal the obstacle a blow with all their might they stop to reflect: 'What will come of it? Perhaps we may perish in vain?' And they stand there like posts—until they breathe their last. And the fool is brave! He rushes headforemost against the wall—bang! If his skull breaks—what of it? Calves' heads are not dear. And if he makes a crack in the wall the clever people will pick it open into gates, will pass and credit themselves with the honour. No, Nikolay Matveyich, bravery is a good thing even though it be without reason."

"Vasily, you are talking nonsense!" said Yozhov, stretching his hand toward him.

"Ah, of course!" assented Vasily. "How am I to sip cabbage soup with a bast shoe? And yet I am not blind. I can see. There is plenty of brains, but no good comes of it. During the time the clever people think and reflect as to how to act in the wisest way, the fools will down them. That's all."

"Wait a little!" said Yozhov.

"I can't! I am on duty today. I am rather late as it is. I'll drop in tomorrow—may I?"

"Come! I'll give a roasting!"

"That's exactly your business."

Vasily adjusted himself slowly, rose from the lounge, took Yozhov's yellow, thin little hand in his big, swarthy paw and pressed it.

"Goodbye!"

Then he nodded toward Foma and went through the door sideways.

"Have you seen?" Yozhov asked Foma, pointing his hand at the door, behind which the heavy footsteps still resounded.

"What sort of a man is he?"

"Assistant machinist, Vaska Krasnoshchokov. Here, take an example from him: At the age of fifteen he began to study, to read and write, and at twenty-eight he has read the devil knows how many good books, and has mastered two languages to perfection. Now he's going abroad."

"What for?" inquired Foma.

"To study. To see how people live there, while you languish here— what for?"

"He spoke sensibly of the fools," said Foma, thoughtfully.

"I don't know, for I am not a fool."

"That was well said. The stupid man ought to act at once. Rush forward and overturn."

"There, he's broken loose!" exclaimed Yozhov. "You better tell me whether it is true that Mayakin's son has returned?"

"Yes."

"Why do you ask?"

"Nothing."

"I can see by your face that there is something."

"We know all about his son; we've heard about him."

"But I have seen him."

"Well? What sort of man is he?"

"The devil knows him! What have I to do with him?"

"Is he like his father?"

"He's stouter, plumper; there is more seriousness about him; he is so cold."

"Which means that he will be even worse than Yashka. Well, now, my dear, be on your guard or they will suck you dry."

"Well, let them do it!"

"They'll rob you. You'll become a pauper. That Taras fleeced his father-in-law in Yekateringburg so cleverly."

"Let him fleece me too, if he likes. I shall not say a word to him except 'thanks.'"

"You are still singing that same old tune?"

"Yes."

"To be set at liberty."

"Yes."

"Drop it! What do you want freedom for? What will you do with it? Don't you know that you are not fit for anything, that you are illiterate, that you certainly cannot even split a log of wood? Now, if I could only free myself from the necessity of drinking vodka and eating bread!"

Yozhov jumped to his feet, and, stopping in front of Foma, began to speak in a loud voice, as though declaiming:

"I would gather together the remains of my wounded soul, and together with the blood of my heart I would spit them into the face of our intelligent society, the devil take it! I would say to them:

'You insects, you are the best sap of my country! The fact of your existence has been repaid by the blood and the tears of scores of generations of Russian people. 0, you nits! How dearly your country has paid for you! What are you doing for its sake in return? Have you transformed the tears of the past into pearls? What have you contributed toward life? What have you accomplished? You have permitted yourselves to be conquered? What are you doing? You permit yourselves to be mocked.'"

He stamped his feet with rage, and setting his teeth together stared at Foma with burning, angry looks, and resembled an infuriated wild beast.

"I would say to them: 'You! You reason too much, but you are not very wise, and you are utterly powerless, and you are all cowards! Your hearts are filled up with morality and noble intentions, but they are as soft and warm as feather beds; the spirit of creativeness sleeps within them a profound and calm sleep, and your hearts do not throb, they merely rock slowly, like cradles.' Dipping my finger in the blood of my heart, I would smear upon their brows the brands of my reproaches, and they, paupers in spirit, miserable in their self-contentment, they would suffer. Oh, how they would suffer! My scourge is sharp, my hand is firm! And I love too deeply to have compassion! They would suffer! And now they do not suffer, for they speak of their sufferings too much, too often, and too loud! They lie! Genuine suffering is mute, and genuine passion knows no bounds! Passions, passions! When will they spring up in the hearts of men? We are all miserable because of apathy."

Short of breath he burst into a fit of coughing, he coughed for a long time, hopping about hither and thither, waving his hands like a madman. And then he again stopped in front of Foma with pale face and blood-shot eyes. He breathed heavily, his lips trembled now and then, displaying his small, sharp teeth. Dishevelled, with his head covered with short heir, he looked like a perch just thrown out of the water. This was not the first time Foma saw him in such a state, and, as always, he was infected by his agitation. He listened to the fiery words of the small man, silently, without attempting to understand their meaning, having no desire to know against whom they were directed, absorbing their force only. Yozhov's words bubbled on like boiling water, and heated his soul.

"I will say to them, to those miserable idlers:

'Look! Life goes onward, leaving you behind!"'

"Eh! That's fine!" exclaimed Foma, ecstatically, and began to move about on the lounge. "You're a hero, Nikolay! Oh! Go ahead! Throw it right into their faces!"

But Yozhov was not in need of encouragement, it seemed even as though he had not heard at all Foma's exclamations, and he went on:

"I know the limitations of my powers. I know they'll shout at me: 'Hold your peace!' They'll tell me: 'Keep silence!' They will say it wisely, they will say it calmly, mocking me, they will say it from the height of their majesty. I know I am only a small bird, 0h, I am not a nightingale!

444

Compared with them I am an ignorant man, I am only a feuilleton-writer, a man to amuse the public. Let them cry and silence me, let them do it! A blow will fall on my cheek, but the heart will nevertheless keep on throbbing! And I will say to them:

"'Yes, I am an ignorant man! And my first advantage over you is that I do not know a single book-truth dearer to me than a man! Man is the universe, and may he live forever who carries the whole world within him! And you,'I will say, 'for the sake of a word which, perhaps, does not always contain a meaning comprehensible to you, for the sake of a word you often inflict sores and wounds on one another, for the sake of a word you spurt one another with bile, you assault the soul. For this, believe me, life will severely call you to account: a storm will break loose, and it will whisk and wash you off the earth, as wind and rain whisk and wash the dust off a tree I There is in human language only one word whose meaning is clear and dear to everybody, and when that word is pronounced, it sounds thus: 'Freedom!'"

"Crush on!" roared Foma, jumping up from the lounge and grasping Yozhov by the shoulders. With flashing eyes he gazed into Yozhov's face, bending toward him, and almost moaned with grief and affliction: "Oh! Nikolay! My dear fellow, I am mortally sorry for you! I am more sorry than words can tell!"

"What's this? What's the matter with you?" cried Yozhov, pushing him away, amazed and shifted from his position by Foma's unexpected outburst and strange words.

"Oh, brother!" said Foma, lowering his voice, which thus sounded deeper, more persuasive. "Oh, living soul, why do you sink to ruin?"

"Who? I? I sink? You lie!"

"My dear boy! You will not say anything to anybody! There is no one to speak to! Who will listen to you? Only I!"

"Go to the devil!" shouted Yozhov, angrily, jumping away from him as though he had been scorched.

And Foma went toward him, and spoke convincingly, with intense sorrow:

"Speak! speak to me! I shall carry away your words to the proper place. I understand them. And, ah! how I will scorch the people! Just wait! My opportunity will come."

"Go away!" screamed Yozhov, hysterically, squeezing his back to the wall, under Foma's pressure. Perplexed, crushed, and infuriated he stood and waved off Foma's arms outstretched toward him. And at this time the door of the room opened, and on the threshold appeared a woman all in black. Her face was angry-looking and excited, her cheek was tied up with a kerchief. She tossed her head back, stretched out her hand toward Yozhov and said, in a hissing and shrill voice:

"Nikolay Matveyich! Excuse me, but this is impossible! Such beast-like howling and roaring. Guests everyday. The police are coming. No, I can't bear it any longer! I am nervous. Please vacate the lodgings to-morrow. You are not living in a desert, there are people about you here. And an educated man at that! A writer! All people require rest. I have a toothache. I request you to move tomorrow. I'll paste up a notice, I'll notify the police."

She spoke rapidly, and the majority of her words were lost in the hissing and whistling of her voice; only those words were distinct, which she shrieked out in a shrill, irritated tone. The corners of her kerchief protruded on her head like small horns, and shook from the movement of her jaws. At the sight of her agitated and comical figure Foma gradually retreated toward the lounge, while Yozhov stood, and wiping his forehead, stared at her fixedly, and listened to her words:

"So know it now!" she screamed, and behind the door, she said once more:

"Tomorrow! What an outrage."

"Devil!" whispered Yozhov, staring dully at the door.

"Yes! what a woman! How strict!" said Foma, looking at him in amazement, as he seated himself on the lounge.

446

Yozhov, raising his shoulders, walked up to the table, poured out a half a tea-glass full of vodka, emptied it and sat down by the table, bowing his head low. There was silence for about a minute. Then Foma said, timidly and softly:

"How it all happened! We had no time even to wink an eye, and, suddenly, such an outcome. Ah!"

"You!" said Yozhov in an undertone, tossing up his head, and staring at Foma angrily and wildly. "Keep quiet! You, the devil take you. Lie down and sleep! You monster. Nightmare. Oh!"

And he threatened Foma with his fist. Then he filled the glass with more brandy, and emptied it again.

A few minutes later Foma lay undressed on the lounge, and, with half-shut eyes, followed Yozhov who sat by the table in an awkward pose. He stared at the floor, and his lips were quietly moving. Foma was astonished, he could not make out why Yozhov had become angry at him. It could not be because he had been ordered to move out. For it was he himself who had been shouting.

"Oh devil!" whispered Yozhov, and gnashed his teeth.

Foma quietly lifted his head from the pillow. Yozhov deeply and noisily sighing, again stretched out his hand toward the bottle. Then Foma said to him softly:

"Let's go to some hotel. It isn't late yet."

Yozhov looked at him, and, rubbing his head with his hands, began to laugh strangely. Then he rose from his chair and said to Foma curtly:

"Dress yourself!"

And seeing how clumsily and slowly he turned on the lounge, Yozhov shouted with anger and impatience:

"Well, be quicker! You personification of stupidity. You symbolical cart-shaft."

"Don't curse!" said Foma, with a peaceable smile. "Is it worthwhile to be angry because a woman has cackled?"

Yozhov glanced at him, spat and burst into harsh laughter.

CHAPTER XIII

"ARE all here?" asked Ilya Yefimovich Kononov, standing on the bow of his new steamer, and surveying the crowd of guests with beaming eyes.

"It seems to be all!"

And raising upward his stout, red, happy-looking face, he shouted to the captain, who was already standing on the bridge, beside the speaking-tube:

"Cast off, Petrukha!"

"Yes, sir!"

The captain bared his huge, bald head, made the sign of the cross, glancing up at the sky, passed his hand over his wide, black beard, cleared his throat, and gave the command:

"Back!"

The guests watched the movements of the captain silently and attentively, and, emulating his example, they also began to cross themselves, at which performance their caps and high hats flashed through the air like a flock of black birds.

Give us Thy blessing, 0h Lord!" exclaimed Kononov with emotion.

"Let go astern! Forward!" ordered the captain. The massive "Ilya Murometz," heaving a mighty sigh, emitted a thick column of white steam toward the side of the landing-bridge, and started upstream easily, like a swan.

"How it started off," enthusiastically exclaimed commercial counsellor Lup Grigoryev Reznikov, a tall, thin, good-looking man. "Without a quiver! Like a lady in the dance!"

"Half speed!"

"It's not a ship, it's a Leviathan!" remarked with a devout sigh the pock-marked and stooping Trofim Zubov, cathedral-warden and principal usurer in town.

It was a gray day. The sky, overcast with autumn clouds, was reflected in the water of the river, thus giving it a cold leaden colouring. Flashing in the freshness of its paint the steamer sailed along the monotonous background of the river like a huge bright spot, and the black smoke of its breath hung in the air like a heavy cloud. All white, with pink paddle-boxes and bright red blades, the steamer easily cut through the cold water with its bow and drove it apart toward the shores, and the round window-panes on the sides of the steamer and the cabin glittered brilliantly, as though smiling a self-satisfied, triumphant smile.

"Gentlemen of this honourable company!" exclaimed Kononov, removing his hat, and making a low bow to the guests. "As we have now rendered unto God, so to say, what is due to God, would you permit that the musicians render now unto the Emperor what is due to the Emperor?"

And, without waiting for an answer from his guests, he placed his fist to his mouth, and shouted:

"Musicians! Play 'Be Glorious!'"

The military orchestra, behind the engine, thundered out the march.

And Makar Bobrov, the director and founder of the local commercial bank, began to hum in a pleasant basso, beating time with his fingers on his enormous paunch:

"Be glorious, be glorious, our Russian Czar—tra-rata! Boom!"

"I invite you to the table, gentlemen! Please! Take pot-luck, he, he! I entreat you humbly," said Kononov, pushing himself through the dense group of guests.

There were about thirty of them, all sedate men, the cream of the local merchants. The older men among them, bald-headed and gray, wore old-fashioned frock-coats, caps and tall boots. But there were only few of these; high silk hats, shoes and stylish coats reigned supreme. They were all crowded on the bow of the steamer, and little by little, yielding to Kononov's requests, moved towards the stern covered with sailcloth, where stood tables spread with lunch. Lup Reznikov walked arm in arm with Yakov Mayakin, and, bending over to his ear, whispered something to him, while the latter listened and smiled. Foma, who had been brought to the festival by his godfather, after long admonitions, found no companion for himself among these people who were repulsive to him, and, pale and gloomy, held himself apart from them. During the past two days he had been drinking heavily with Yozhov, and now he had a terrible headache. He felt ill at ease in the sedate and yet jolly company; the humming of the voices, the thundering of the music and the clamour of the steamer, all these irritated him.

He felt a pressing need to doze off, and he could find no rest from the thought as to why his godfather was so kind to him today, and why he brought him hither into the company of the foremost merchants of the town. Why had he urged so persuasively, and even entreated him to attend Kononov's mass and banquet?

"Don't be foolish, come!" Foma recalled his godfather's admonitions. "Why do you fight shy of people? Man gets his character from nature, and in riches you are lower than very few. You must keep yourself on an equal footing with the others. Come!"

"But when are you going to speak seriously with me, papa?" Foma had asked, watching the play of his godfather's face and green eyes.

"You mean about setting you free from the business? Ha, ha! We'll talk it over, we'll talk it over, my friend! What a queer fellow you are. Well? Will you enter a monastery when you have thrown away your wealth? After the example of the saints? Eh?"

"I'll see then!" Foma had answered.

"So. Well, and meanwhile, before you go to the monastery, come along with me! Get ready quickly. Rub your phiz with something wet, for it is

450

very much swollen. Sprinkle yourself with cologne, get it from Lubov, to drive away the smell of the kabak. Go ahead!"

Arriving on the steamer while the mass was in progress, Foma took up a place on the side and watched the merchants during the whole service.

They stood in solemn silence; their faces had an expression of devout concentration; they prayed with fervour, deeply sighing, bowing low, devoutly lifting their eyes heavenward. And Foma looked now at one, now at another, and recalled what he knew about them.

There was Lup Reznikov; he had begun his career as a brothel-keeper, and had become rich all of a sudden. They said he had strangled one of his guests, a rich Siberian. Zubov's business in his youth had been to purchase thread from the peasants. He had failed twice. Kononov had been tried twenty years ago for arson, and even now he was indicted for the seduction of a minor. Together with him, for the second time already, on a similar charge, Zakhar Kirillov Robustov had been dragged to court. Robustov was a stout, short merchant with a round face and cheerful blue eyes. Among these people there was hardly one about whom Foma did not know something disgraceful.

And he knew that they were all surely envying the successful Kononov, who was constantly increasing the number of his steamers from year to year. Many of those people were at daggers' points with one another, none of them would show mercy to the others in the battlefield of business, and all knew wicked and dishonest things about one another. But now, when they gathered around Kononov, who was triumphant and happy, they blended in one dense, dark mass, and stood and breathed as one man, concentrated and silent, surrounded by something invisible yet firm, by something which repulsed Foma from them, and which inspired him with fear of them.

"Impostors!" thought he, thus encouraging himself.

And they coughed gently, sighed, crossed themselves, bowed, and, surrounding the clergy in a thick wall, stood immovable and firm, like big, black rocks.

"They are pretending!" Foma exclaimed to himself. Beside him stood the hump-backed, one-eyed Pavlin Gushchin—he who, not long before, had turned the children of his half-witted brother into the street as beggars—he stood there and whispered penetratingly as he looked at the gloomy sky with his single eye:

"Oh Lord! Do not convict me in Thy wrath, nor chastise me in Thy indignation."

And Foma felt that that man was addressing the Lord with the most profound and firm faith in His mercy.

"Oh Lord, God of our fathers, who hadst commanded Noah, Thy servant, to build an ark for the preservation of the world," said the priest in his deep bass voice, lifting his eyes and outstretching his hands skyward, "protect also this vessel and give unto it a guarding angel of good and peace. Guard those that will sail upon it."

The merchants in unison made the sign of the cross, with wide swings of their arms, and all their faces bore the expression of one sentiment— faith in the power of prayer. All these pictures took root in Foma's memory and awakened in him perplexity as to these people, who, being able to believe firmly in the mercy of God, were, nevertheless, so cruel unto man. He watched them persistently, wishing to detect their fraud, to convince himself of their falsehood.

Their grave firmness angered him, their unanimous self-confidence, their triumphant faces, their loud voices, their laughter. They were already seated by the tables, covered with luncheon, and were hungrily admiring the huge sturgeon, almost three yards in length, nicely sprinkled over with greens and large crabs. Trofim Zubov, tying a napkin around his neck, looked at the monster fish with happy, sweetly half-shut eyes, and said to his neighbour, the flour merchant, Yona Yushkov:

"Yona Nikiforich! Look, it's a regular whale! It's big enough to serve as a casket for your person, eh? Ha, ha! You could creep into it as a foot into a boot, eh? Ha, ha!"

The small-bodied and plump Yona carefully stretched out his short little hand toward the silver pail filled with fresh caviar, smacked his lips greedily, and squinted at the bottles before him, fearing lest he might overturn them.

Opposite Kononov, on a trestle, stood a half-vedro barrel of old vodka, imported from Poland; in a huge silver-mounted shell lay oysters, and a certain particoloured cake, in the shape of a tower, stood out above all the viands.

"Gentlemen! I entreat you! Help yourselves to whatever you please!" cried Kononov. "I have here everything at once to suit the taste of everyone. There is our own, Russian stuff, and there is foreign, all at once! That's the best way! Who wishes anything? Does anybody want snails, or these crabs, eh? They're from India, I am told."

And Zubov said to his neighbour, Mayakin:

"The prayer 'At the Building of a Vessel' is not suitable for steam-tugs and river steamers, that is, not that it is not suitable, it isn't enough alone. A river steamer is a place of permanent residence for the crew, and therefore it ought to be considered as a house. Consequently it is necessary to make the prayer 'At the Building of a House,' in addition to that for the vessel. But what will you drink?"

"I am not much of a wine fiend. Pour me out some cumin vodka," replied Yakov Tarasovich.

Foma, seated at the end of the table among some timid and modest men who were unfamiliar to him, now and again felt on himself the sharp glances of the old man.

"He's afraid I'll make a scandal," thought Foma. "Brethren!" roared the monstrously stout ship builder Yashchurov, in a hoarse voice," I can't do without herring! I must necessarily begin with herring, that's my nature."

"Musicians! strike up 'The Persian March!'"

"Hold on! Better 'How Glorious!'"

"Strike up 'How Glorious.'"

The puffing of the engine and the clatter of the steamer's wheels, mingling with the sounds of the music, produced in the air something which sounded like the wild song of a snow-storm. The whistle of the flute, the shrill singing of the clarionets, the heavy roaring of the basses, the ruffling of the little drum and the drones of the blows on the big one, all this fell on the monotonous and dull sounds of the wheels, as they cut the water apart, smote the air rebelliously, drowned the noise of the human voices and hovered after the steamer, like a hurricane, causing the people to shout at the top of their voices. At times an angry hissing of steam rang out within the engine, and there was something irritable and contemptuous in this sound as it burst unexpectedly upon the chaos of the drones and roars and shouts.

"I shall never forget, even unto my grave, that you refused to discount the note for me," cried some one in a fierce voice.

"That will do! Is this a place for accounts?" rang out Bobrov's bass.

"Brethren! Let us have some speeches!"

"Musicians, bush!"

"Come up to the bank and I'll explain to you why I didn't discount it."

"A speech! Silence!"

"Musicians, cease playing!"

"Strike up 'In the Meadows.'"

"Madame Angot!"

"No! Yakov Tarasovich, we beg of you!"

"That's called Strassburg pastry."

"We beg of you! We beg of you!"

"Pastry? It doesn't look like it, but I'll taste it all the same."

"Tarasovich! Start."

"Brethren! It is jolly! By God."

454

"And in 'La Belle Helene' she used to come out almost naked, my dear," suddenly Robustov's shrill and emotional voice broke through the noise.

"Look out! Jacob cheated Esau? Aha!"

"I can't! My tongue is not a hammer, and I am no longer young."

"Yasha! We all implore you!"

"Do us the honour!"

"We'll elect you mayor!"

"Tarasovich! don't be capricious!"

"Sh! Silence! Gentlemen! Yakov Tarasovich will say a few words!"

"Sh!"

And just at the moment the noise subsided some one's loud, indignant whisper was heard:

"How she pinched me, the carrion."

And Bobrov inquired in his deep basso:

"Where did she pinch you?"

All burst into ringing laughter, but soon fell silent, for Yakov Tarasovich Mayakin, rising to his feet, cleared his throat, and, stroking his bald crown, surveyed the merchants with a serious look expecting attention.

"Well, brethren, open your ears!" shouted Kononov, with satisfaction.

"Gentlemen of the merchant class!" began Mayakin with a smile. "There is a certain foreign word in the language of intelligent and learned people, and that word is 'culture.' So now I am going to talk to you about that word in all the simplicity of my soul."

"So, that's where he is aiming to!" some ones satisfied exclamation was heard.

"Sh! Silence!"

"Dear gentlemen!" said Mayakin, raising his voice, "in the newspapers they keep writing about us merchants, that we are not acquainted with this 'culture,' that we do not want it, and do not understand it. And they call us savage, uncultured people. What is culture? It pains me, old man as I am, to hear such words, and one day I made it my business to look up that word, to see what it really contains." Mayakin became silent, surveyed the audience with his eyes, and went on distinctly, with a triumphant smile:

"It proved, upon my researches, that this word means worship, that is, love, great love for business and order in life. 'That's right!' I thought, 'that's right!' That means that he is a cultured man who loves business and order, who, in general, loves to arrange life, loves to live, knows the value of himself and of life. Good!" Yakov Tarasovich trembled, his wrinkles spread over his face like beams, from his smiling eyes to his lips, and his bald head looked like some dark star.

The merchants stared silently and attentively at his mouth, and all faces bespoke intense attention. The people seemed petrified in the attitudes in which Mayakin's speech had overtaken them.

"But if that word is to be interpreted precisely thus, and not otherwise, if such is the case—then the people who call us uncultured and savage, slander and blaspheme us! For they love only the word, but not its meaning; while we love the very root of the word, we love its real essence, we love activity. We have within us the real cult toward life, that is, the worship of life; we, not they! They love reasoning' we love action. And here, gentlemen of the merchant class, here is an example of our culture, of our love for action. Take the Volga! Here she is, our dear own mother! With each and every drop of her water she can corroborate our honour and refute the empty blasphemy spattered on us. Only one hundred years have elapsed, my dear sirs, since Emperor Peter the Great launched decked barks on this river, and now thousands of steamships sail up and down the river. Who has built them? The Russian peasant, an utterly unlettered man! All these enormous steamers, barges—whose are they? Ours! Who has invented them? We! Everything here is ours, everything here is the fruit of our minds, of our Russian shrewdness, and our great love for action! Nobody has assisted us in anything! We ourselves exterminated piracy on the Volga; at our own expense we hired troops; we exterminated piracy and sent out on the Volga thousands of steamers and various vessels over all the thousands of miles of her course. Which is the best town on the Volga? The one that has the most merchants. Whose are the best houses in town? The merchants! Who takes the most care of the poor? The merchant! He collects groshes and copecks, and donates hundreds of thousands of roubles. Who has erected the churches? We! Who contributes the most money to the government? The merchants! Gentlemen! to us alone is the work dear for its own sake, for the sake of our love for the arrangement of life, and we alone love order and life! And he who talks about us merely talks, and that's all! Let him talk! When the wind blows the willow rustles; when the wind subsides the willow is silent; and neither a cart-shaft, nor a broom can be made out of the willow; it is a useless tree! And from this uselessness comes the noise. What have they, our judges, accomplished; how have they adorned life? We do not know it. While our work is clearly evident! Gentlemen of the merchant class! Seeing in you the foremost men in life, most industrious and loving your labours, seeing in you the men who can accomplish and have accomplished everything, I now heartily, with respect and love for you, lift my brimming goblet, to the glorious, strong-souled, industrious Russian merchant class. Long may you live! May you succeed for the glory of Mother Russia! Hurrah!"

The shrill, jarring shout of Mayakin called forth a deafening, triumphant roar from the merchants. All these big, fleshy bodies, aroused by wine and by the old man's words, stirred and uttered from their chests such a unanimous, massive shout that everything around them seemed to tremble and to quake.

"Yakov! you are the trumpet of the Lord!" cried Zubov, holding out his goblet toward Mayakin.

Overturning the chairs, jostling the tables, thus causing the dishes and the bottles to rattle and fall, the merchants, agitated, delighted, some with tears in their eyes, rushed toward Mayakin with goblets in their hands.

457

"Ah! Do you understand what has been said here?" asked Kononov, grasping Robustov by the shoulder and shaking him. "Understand it! That was a great speech!"

"Yakov Tarasovich! Come, let me embrace you!"

"Let's toss, Mayakin!

"Strike up the band."

"Sound a flourish! A march. 'The Persian March.'"

"We don't want any music! The devil take it!"

"Here is the music! Eh, Yakov Tarasovich! What a mind!"

"I was small among my brethren, but I was favoured with understanding."

"You lie, Trofim!"

"Yakov! you'll die soon. Oh, what a pity! Words can't express how sorry we are!"

"But what a funeral that is going to be!"

"Gentlemen! Let us establish a Mayakin fund! I put up a thousand!"

"Silence! Hold on!"

"Gentlemen!" Yakov Tarasovich began to speak again, quivering in every limb. "And, furthermore, we are the foremost men in life and the real masters in our fatherland because we are—peasants!'

"Corr-rect!"

"That's right! Dear mother! That's an old man for you!"

"Hold on! Let him finish."

"We are primitive Russian people, and everything that comes from us is truly Russian! Consequently it is the most genuine, the most useful and obligatory."

"As true as two and two make four!"

"It's so simple."

"He is as wise as a serpent!"

"And as meek as a—"

"As a hawk. Ha, ha, ha!"

The merchants encircled their orator in a close ring, they looked at him with their oily eyes, and were so agitated that they could no longer listen to his words calmly. Around him a tumult of voices smote the air, and mingling with the noise of the engine, and the beating of the wheels upon the water, it formed a whirlwind of sounds which drowned the jarring voice of the old man. The excitement of the merchants was growing more and more intense; all faces were radiant with triumph; hands holding out goblets were outstretched toward Mayakin; the merchants clapped him on the shoulder, jostled him, kissed him, gazed with emotion into his face. And some screamed ecstatically:

"The kamarinsky. The national dance!"

"We have accomplished all that!" cried Yakov Tarasovich, pointing at the river. "It is all ours! We have built up life!"

Suddenly rang out a loud exclamation which drowned all sounds:

"Ah! So you have done it? Ah, you."

And immediately after this, a vulgar oath resounded through the air, pronounced distinctly with great rancour, in a dull but powerful voice. Everyone heard it and became silent for a moment, searching with their eyes the man who had abused them. At this moment nothing was heard save the deep sighs of the engines and the clanking of the rudder chains.

"Who's snarling there?" asked Kononov with a frown.

"We can't get along without scandals!" said Reznikov, with a contrite sigh.

"Who was swearing here at random?"

The faces of the merchants mirrored alarm, curiosity, astonishment, reproach, and all the people began to bustle about stupidly. Only Yakov Tarasovich alone was calm and seemed even satisfied with what had occurred. Rising on tiptoe, with his neck outstretched, he stared somewhere toward the end of the table, and his eyes flashed strangely, as though he saw there something which was pleasing to him.

"Gordyeeff" said Yona Yushkov, softly.

And all heads were turned toward the direction in which Yakov Tarasovich was staring.

There, with his hands resting on the table, stood Foma. His face distorted with wrath, his teeth firmly set together, he silently surveyed the merchants with his burning, wide-open eyes. His lower jaw was trembling, his shoulders were quivering, and the fingers of his hands, firmly clutching the edge of the table, were nervously scratching the tablecloth. At the sight of his wolf-like, angry face and his wrathful pose, the merchants again became silent for a moment.

"What are you gaping at?" asked Foma, and again accompanied his question with a violent oath.

"He's drunk!" said Bobrov, with a shake of the head.

"And why was he invited?" whispered Reznikov, softly.

"Foma Ignatyevich!" said Kononov, sedately, "you mustn't create any scandals. If your head is reeling—go, my dear boy, quietly and peacefully into the cabin and lie down! Lie down, and—"

"Silence, you!" roared Foma, and turned his eye at him. "Do not dare to speak to me! I am not drunk. I am soberer than any one of you here! Do you understand?"

"But wait awhile, my boy. Who invited you here?" asked Kononov, reddening with offence.

"I brought him!" rang out Mayakin's voice.

"Ah! Well, then, of course. Excuse me, Foma Ignatyevich. But as you brought him, Yakov, you ought to subdue him. Otherwise it's no good."

Foma maintained silence and smiled. And the merchants, too, were silent, as they looked at him.

"Eh, Fomka!" began Mayakin. "Again you disgrace my old age."

"Godfather!" said Foma, showing his teeth, "I have not done anything as yet, so it is rather early to read me a lecture. I am not drunk, I have drunk nothing, but I have heard everything. Gentlemen merchants! Permit me to make a speech! My godfather, whom you respect so much, has spoken. Now listen to his godson."

"What—speeches?" said Reznikov. "Why have any discourses? We have come together to enjoy ourselves."

"Come, you had better drop that, Foma Ignatyevich."

"Better drink something."

"Let's have a drink! Ah, Foma, you're the son of a fine father!"

Foma recoiled from the table, straightened himself and continuously smiling, listened to the kind, admonitory words. Among all those sedate people he was the youngest and the handsomest. His well-shaped figure, in a tight-fitting frock coat, stood out, to his advantage, among the mass of stout bodies with prominent paunches. His swarthy face with large eyes was more regularly featured, more full of life than the shrivelled or red faces of those who stood before him with astonishment and expectancy. He threw his chest forward, set his teeth together, and flinging the skirts of his frock coat apart, thrust his hands into his pockets.

"You can't stop up my mouth now with flattery and caresses!" said he, firmly and threateningly, "Whether you will listen or not, I am going to speak all the same. You cannot drive me away from here."

He shook his head, and, raising his shoulders, announced calmly:

"But if any one of you dare to touch me, even with a finger, I'll kill him! I swear it by the Lord. I'll kill as many as I can!"

The crowd of people that stood opposite him swayed back, even as bushes rocked by the wind. They began to talk in agitated whispers. Foma's face grew darker, his eyes became round.

"Well, it has been said here that you have built up life, and that you have done the most genuine and proper things."

Foma heaved a deep sigh, and with inexpressible aversion scrutinized his listeners' faces, which suddenly became strangely puffed up, as though they were swollen. The merchants were silent, pressing closer and closer to one another. Some one in the back rows muttered:

"What is he talking about? Ah! From a paper, or by heart?"

"Oh, you rascals!" exclaimed Gordyeeff, shaking his head. "What have you made? It is not life that you have made, but a prison. It is not

461

order that you have established, you have forged fetters on man. It is suffocating, it is narrow, there is no room for a living soul to turn. Man is perishing! You are murderers! Do you understand that you exist today only through the patience of mankind?"

"What does this mean?" exclaimed Reznikov, clasping his hands in rage and indignation. "Ilya Yefimov, what's this? I can't bear to hear such words."

"Gordyeeff!" cried Bobrov. "Look out, you speak improper words."

"For such words you'll get—oi, oi, oi!" said Zubov, insinuatingly.

"Silence!" roared Foma, with blood-shot eyes. "Now they're grunting."

"Gentlemen!" rang out Mayakin's calm, malicious voice, like the screech of a smooth-file on iron. "Don't touch him! I entreat you earnestly, do not hinder him. Let him snarl. Let him amuse himself. His words cannot harm you."

"Well, no, I humbly thank you! "cried Yushkov. And close at Foma's side stood Smolin and whispered in his ear:

"Stop, my dear boy! What's the matter with you? Are you out of your wits? They'll do you—!"

"Get away!" said Foma, firmly, flashing his angry eyes at him. "You go to Mayakin and flatter him, perhaps something will come your way!"

Smolin whistled through his teeth and stepped aside. And the merchants began to disperse on the steamer, one by one. This irritated Foma still more he wished he could chain them to the spot by his words, but he could not find such powerful words.

"You have built up life!" he shouted. "Who are you? Swindlers, robbers."

A few men turned toward Foma, as if he had called them.

"Kononov! are they soon going to try you for that little girl? They'll convict you to the galleys. Goodbye, Ilya! You are building your steamers in vain. They'll transport you to Siberia on a government vessel."

Kononov sank into a chair; his blood leaped to his face, and he shook his fist in silence. Foma said hoarsely:

"Very well. Good. I shall not forget it."

Foma saw his distorted face with its trembling lips, and understood with what weapons he could deal these men the most forcible blows.

"Ha, ha, ha! Builders of life! Gushchin, do you give alms to your little nephews and nieces? Give them at least a copeck a day. You have stolen sixty-seven thousand roubles from them. Bobrov! why did you lie about that mistress of yours, saying that she had robbed you, and then send her to prison? If you had grown tired of her, you might have given her over to your son. Anyway he has started an intrigue with that other mistress of yours. Didn't you know it? Eh, you fat pig, ha, ha! And you, Lup, open again a brothel, and fleece your guests there as before. And then the devil will fleece you, ha, ha! It is good to be a rascal with a pious face like yours! Whom did you kill then, Lup?"

Foma spoke, interrupting his speech with loud, malevolent laughter, and saw that his words were producing an impression on these people. Before, when he had spoken to all of them they turned away from him, stepping aside, forming groups, and looking at their accuser from afar with anger and contempt. He saw smiles on their faces, he felt in their every movement something scornful, and understood that while his words angered them they did not sting as deep as he wished them to. All this had chilled his wrath, and within him there was already arising the bitter consciousness of the failure of his attack on them. But as soon as he began to speak of each one separately, there was a swift and striking change in the relation of his hearers toward him.

When Kononov sank heavily in the chair, as though he were unable to withstand the weight of Foma's harsh words, Foma noticed that bitter and malicious smiles crossed the faces of some of the merchants. He heard some one's whisper of astonishment and approval:

"That's well aimed!"

This whisper gave strength to Foma, and he confidently and passionately began to hurl reproaches, jeers and abuses at those who met his eyes. He growled joyously, seeing that his words were taking effect. He was listened to silently, attentively; several men moved closer toward him.

Exclamations of protest were heard, but these were brief, not loud, and each time Foma shouted some one's name, all became silent, listening, casting furtive, malicious glances in the direction of their accused comrade.

Bobrov laughed perplexedly, but his small eyes bored into Foma as gimlets. And Lup Reznikov, waving his hands, hopped about awkwardly and, short of breath, said:

"Be my witnesses. What's this! No-o! I will not forgive this! I'll go to court. What's that?" and suddenly he screamed in a shrill voice, outstretching his hand toward Foma:

"Bind him!"

Foma was laughing.

"You cannot bind the truth, you can't do it! Even bound, truth will not grow dumb!"

"Go-o-od!" drawled out Kononov in a dull, broken voice.

"See here, gentlemen of the merchant class!" rang out Mayakin's voice. "I ask! you to admire him, that's the kind of a fellow he is!"

One after another the merchants moved toward Foma, and on their faces he saw wrath, curiosity, a malicious feeling of satisfaction, fear. Some one of those modest people among whom Foma was sitting, whispered to him:

"Give it to them. God bless you. Go ahead! That will be to your credit."

"Robustov!" cried Foma. "What are you laughing at? What makes you glad? You will also go to the galleys."

"Put him ashore!" suddenly roared Robustov, springing to his feet.

And Kononov shouted to the captain:

"Back! To the town! To the Governor."

And someone insinuatingly, in a voice trembling with feeling:

"That's a collusive agreement. That was done on purpose. He was instigated, and made drunk to give him courage."

"No, it's a revolt!"

"Bind him! Just bind him!"

Foma grasped a champagne bottle and swung it in the air.

"Come on now! No, it seems that you will have to listen to me."

With renewed fury, frantic with joy at seeing these people shrinking and quailing under the blows of his words, Foma again started to shout names and vulgar oaths, and the exasperated tumult was hushed once more. The men, whom Foma did not know, gazed at him with eager curiosity, with approval, while some looked at him even with joyous surprise. One of them, a gray-haired little old man with rosy cheeks and small mouse eyes, suddenly turned toward the merchants, who had been abused by Foma, and said in a sweet voice:

"These are words from the conscience! That's nothing! You must endure it. That's a prophetic accusation. We are sinful. To tell the truth we are very—"

He was hissed, and Zubov even jostled him on the shoulder. He made a low bow and disappeared in the crowd.

"Zubov!" cried Foma. "How many people have you fleeced and turned to beggars? Do you ever dream of Ivan Petrov Myakinnikov, who strangled himself because of you? Is it true that you steal at every mass ten roubles out of the church box?"

Zubov had not expected the attack, and he remained as petrified, with his hand uplifted. But he immediately began to scream in a shrill voice, as he jumped up quickly:

"Ah! You turn against me also? Against me, too?"

And suddenly he puffed up his cheeks and furiously began to shake his fist at Foma, as he screamed in a shrill voice:

"The fool says in his heart there is no God! I'll go to the bishop! Infidel! You'll get the galleys!"

The tumult on the steamer grew, and at the sight of these enraged, perplexed and insulted people, Foma felt himself a fairy-tale giant, slaying monsters. They bustled about, waving their arms, talking to one another—some red with anger, others pale, yet all equally powerless to check the flow of his jeers at them.

"Send the sailors over here!" cried Reznikov, tugging Kononov by the shoulder. "What's the matter with you, Ilya? Ah? Have you invited us to be ridiculed?"

"Against one puppy," screamed Zubov.

A crowd had gathered around Yakov Tarasovitch Mayakin, and listened to his quiet speech with anger, and nodded their heads affirmatively.

"Act, Yakov!" said Robustov, loudly. "We are all witnesses. Go ahead!"

And above the general tumult of voices rang out Foma's loud, accusing voice:

"It was not life that you have built—you have made a cesspool! You have bred filth and putrefaction by your deeds! Have you a conscience? Do you remember God? Money—that's your God! And your conscience you have driven away. Whither have you driven it away? Blood-suckers! You live on the strength of others. You work with other people's hands! You shall pay for all this! When you perish, you will be called to account for everything! For everything, even to a teardrop. How many people have wept blood at those great deeds of yours? And according to your deserts, even hell is too good a place for you, rascals. Not in fire, but in boiling mud you shall be scorched. Your sufferings shall last for centuries. The devils will hurl you into a boiler and will pour into it—ha, ha, ha! they'll pour into it—ha, ha, ha! Honourable merchant class! Builders of Life. Oh, you devils!"

Foma burst into ringing laughter, and, holding his sides, staggered, tossing his head up high.

At that moment several men quickly exchanged glances, simultaneously rushed on Foma and downed him with their weight. A racket ensued.

"Now you're caught!" ejaculated some one in a suffocating voice.

"Ah! Is that the way you're doing it?" cried Foma, hoarsely.

For about a half a minute a whole heap of black bodies bustled about on one spot, heavily stamping their feet, and dull exclamations were heard:

"Throw him to the ground!"

"Hold his hand, his hand! Oh!"

"By the beard?"

"Get napkins, bind him with napkins."

"You'll bite, will you?"

"So! Well, how's it? Aha!"

"Don't strike! Don't dare to strike."

"Ready!"

"How strong he is!"

"Let's carry him over there toward the side."

"Out in the fresh air, ha, ha!"

They dragged Foma away to one side, and having placed him against the wall of the captain's cabin, walked away from him, adjusting their costumes, and mopping their sweat-covered brows. Fatigued by the struggle, and exhausted by the disgrace of his defeat, Foma lay there in silence, tattered, soiled with something, firmly bound, hand and foot, with napkins and towels. With round, blood-shot eyes he gazed at the sky; they were dull and lustreless, as those of an idiot, and his chest heaved unevenly and with difficulty.

Now came their turn to mock him. Zubov began. He walked up to him, kicked him in the side and asked in a soft voice, all trembling with the pleasure of revenge:

"Well, thunder-like prophet, how is it? Now you can taste the sweetness of Babylonian captivity, he, he, he!"

"Wait," said Foma, hoarsely, without looking at him. "Wait until I'm rested. You have not tied up my tongue."

But saying this, Foma understood that he could no longer do anything, nor say anything. And that not because they had bound him, but because something had burned out within him, and his soul had become dark and empty.

Zubov was soon joined by Reznikov. Then one after another the others began to draw near. Bobrov, Kononov and several others preceded by Yakov Mayakin went to the cabin, anxiously discussing something in low tones.

The steamer was sailing toward the town at full speed. The bottles on the tables trembled and rattled from the vibration of the steamer, and Foma heard this jarring, plaintive sound above everything else. Near him stood a throng of people, saying malicious, offensive things.

But Foma saw them as though through a fog, and their words did not touch him to the quick. A vast, bitter feeling was now springing up within him, from the depth of his soul; he followed its growth and though he did not yet understand it, he already experienced something melancholy and degrading.

"Just think, you charlatan! What have you done to yourself?" said Reznikov. "What sort of a life is now possible to you? Do you know that now no one of us would care even as much as to spit on you?"

"What have I done?" Foma tried to understand. The merchants stood around him in a dense, dark mass.

"Well," said Yashchurov, "now, Fomka, your work is done."

"Wait, we'll see," bellowed Zubov in a low voice.

"Let me free!" said Foma.

"Well, no! we thank you humbly!"

"Untie me."

"It's all right! You can lie that way as well."

"Call up my godfather."

But Yakov Tarasovich came up at this moment. He came up, stopped near Foma, sternly surveyed with his eyes the outstretched figure of his godson, and heaved a deep sigh.

"Well, Foma," he began.

"Order them to unbind me," entreated Foma, softly, in a mournful voice.

"So you can be turbulent again? No, no, you'd better lie this way," his godfather replied.

"I won't say another word. I swear it by God! Unbind me. I am ashamed! For Christ's sake. You see I am not drunk. Well, you needn't untie my hands."

"You swear that you'll not be troublesome?" asked Mayakin.

"Oh Lord! I will not, I will not," moaned Foma.

They untied his feet, but left his hands bound. When he rose, he looked at them all, and said softly with a pitiful smile:

"You won."

"We always shall!" replied his godfather, smiling sternly.

Foma bent, with his hands tied behind his back, advanced toward the table silently, without lifting his eyes to anyone. He seemed shorter in stature and thinner. His dishevelled hair fell on his forehead and temples; the torn and crumpled bosom of his shirt protruding from under his vest, and the collar covered his lips. He turned his head to push the collar down under his chin, and was unable to do it. Then the gray-headed little old man walked up to him, adjusted what was necessary, looked into his eyes with a smile and said:

"You must endure it."

Now, in Mayakin's presence, those who had mocked Foma were silent, looking at the old man questioningly, with curiosity and expectancy. He was calm but his eyes gleamed in a way not at all becoming to the occasion, contentedly and brightly.

"Give me some vodka," begged Foma, seating himself at the table, and leaning his chest against its edge. His bent figure look piteous and helpless. Around they were talking in whispers, passing this way and that cautiously. And everyone looked now at him, now at Mayakin, who had seated himself opposite him. The old man did not give Foma the vodka at once. First he surveyed him fixedly, then he slowly poured out a wine glassful, and finally, without saying a word, raised it to Foma's lips. Foma drank the vodka, and asked:

"Some more!"

"That's enough!" replied Mayakin.

And immediately after this there fell a minute of perfect, painful silence. People were coming up to the table noiselessly, on tiptoe, and when they were near they stretched their necks to see Foma.

"Well, Fomka, do you understand now what you have done?" asked Mayakin. He spoke softly, but all heard his question.

Foma nodded his head and maintained silence.

"There's no forgiveness for you!" Mayakin went on firmly, and raising his voice. "Though we are all Christians, yet you will receive no forgiveness at our hands. Just know this."

Foma lifted his head and said pensively:

"I have quite forgotten about you, godfather. You have not heard anything from me."

"There you have it!" exclaimed Mayakin, bitterly, pointing at his godson. "You see?"

A dull grumble of protest burst forth.

"Well, it's all the same!" resumed Foma with a sigh. "It's all the same! Nothing—no good came out of it anyway."

And again he bent over the table.

"What did you want?" asked Mayakin, sternly.

"What I wanted?" Foma raised his head, looked at the merchants and smiled. "I wanted—"

"Drunkard! Nasty scamp!"

"I am not drunk!" retorted Foma, morosely. "I have drank only two glasses. I was perfectly sober."

"Consequently," said Bobrov, "you are right, Yakov Tarasovich, he is insane."

"I?" exclaimed Foma.

But they paid no attention to him. Reznikov, Zubov and Bobrov leaned over to Mayakin and began to talk in low tones.

"Guardianship!" Foma's ears caught this one word. "I am in my right mind!" he said, leaning back in his chair and staring at the merchants with troubled eyes. "I understand what I wanted. I wanted to speak the truth. I wanted to accuse you."

He was again seized with emotion, and he suddenly jerked his hands in an effort to free them.

"Eh! Hold on!" exclaimed Bobrov, seizing him by the shoulders. "Hold him."

"Well, hold me!" said Foma with sadness and bitterness. "Hold me— what do you need me for?"

"Sit still!" cried his godfather, sternly.

Foma became silent. He now understood that what he had done was of no avail, that his words had not staggered the merchants. Here they stood, surrounding him in a dense throng, and he could not see anything for them. They were calm, firm, treating him as a drunkard and a turbulent fellow, and were plotting something against him. He felt himself pitiful, insignificant, crushed by that dark mass of strong-souled, clever and sedate people. It seemed to him that a long time had passed since he had abused them, so long a time that he himself seemed as a stranger, incapable of comprehending what he had done to these people, and why he had done it. He even experienced in himself a certain feeling of offence, which resembled shame at himself in his own eyes. There was a tickling sensation in his throat, and he felt there was something foreign in his breast, as though some dust or ashes were strewn upon his heart, and it throbbed unevenly and with difficulty. Wishing to explain to himself his act, he said slowly and thoughtfully, without looking at anyone:

"I wanted to speak the truth. Is this life?"

"Fool!" said Mayakin, contemptuously. "What truth can you speak? What do you understand?"

"My heart is wounded, that I understand! What justification have you all in the eyes of God? To what purpose do you live? Yes, I feel—I felt the truth!"

"He is repenting!" said Reznikov, with a sarcastic smile.

"Let him!" replied Bobrov, with contempt.

Some one added:

"It is evident, from his words, that he is out of his wits."

"To speak the truth, that's not given to everyone!" said Yakov Tarasovich, sternly and instructively, lifting his hand upward. "It is not the heart that grasps truth; it is the mind; do you understand that? And as to your feeling, that's nonsense! A cow also feels when they twist her tail. But you must understand, understand everything! Understand also your enemy. Guess what he thinks even in his dreams, and then go ahead!"

According to his wont, Mayakin was carried away by the exposition of his practical philosophy, but he realised in time that a conquered man is not to be taught how to fight, and he stopped short. Foma cast at him a dull glance, and shook his head strangely.

"Lamb!" said Mayakin.

"Leave me alone!" entreated Foma, plaintively. "It's all yours! Well, what else do you want? Well, you crushed me, bruised me, that serves me right! Who am I? 0 Lord!"

All listened attentively to his words, and in that attention there was something prejudiced, something malicious.

"I have lived," said Foma in a heavy voice. "I have observed. I have thought; my heart has become wounded with thoughts! And here—the abscess burst. Now I am utterly powerless! As though all my blood had gushed out. I have lived until this day, and still thought that now I will speak the truth. Well, I have spoken it."

He talked monotonously, colourlessly, and his speech resembled that of one in delirium.

"I have spoken it, and I have only emptied myself, that's all. Not a trace have my words left behind them. Everything is uninjured. And within me something blazed up; it has burned out, and there's nothing more there. What have I to hope for now? And everything remains as it was."

Yakov Tarasovich burst into bitter laughter.

"What then, did you think to lick away a mountain with your tongue? You armed yourself with malice enough to fight a bedbug, and you started out after a bear, is that it? Madman! If your father were to see you now. Eh!"

"And yet," said Foma, suddenly, loudly, with assurance, and his eyes again flared up, "and yet it is all your fault! You have spoiled life! You have made everything narrow. We are suffocating because of you! And though my truth against you is weak, it is truth, nevertheless! You are godless wretches! May you all be cursed!"

He moved about in his chair, attempting to free his hands, and cried out, flashing his eyes with fury:

"Unbind my hands!"

They came closer to him; the faces of the merchants became more severe, and Reznikov said to him impressively:

"Don't make a noise, don't be bothersome! We'll soon be in town. Don't disgrace yourself, and don't disgrace us either. We are not going to take you direct from the wharf to the insane asylum."

"So!" exclaimed Foma. "So you are going to put me into an insane asylum?"

No one replied. He looked at their faces and hung his head.

"Behave peacefully! We'll unbind you!" said someone.

"It's not necessary!" said Foma in a low voice. "It's all the same. I spit on it! Nothing will happen."

And his speech again assumed the nature of a delirium.

"I am lost, I know it! Only not because of your power, but rather because of my weakness. Yes! You, too, are only worms in the eyes of God. And, wait! You shall choke. I am lost through blindness. I saw much and I became blind, like an owl. As a boy, I remember, I chased an owl in a ravine; it flew about and struck against something. The sun blinded it. It was all bruised and it disappeared, and my father said to me then: 'It is the same with man; some man bustles about to and fro, bruises himself, exhausts himself, and then throws himself anywhere, just to rest.' Hey I unbind my hands."

His face turned pale, his eyes closed, his shoulders quivered. Tattered and crumpled he rocked about in the chair, striking his chest against the edge of the table, and began to whisper something.

The merchants exchanged significant glances. Some, nudging one another in the sides, shook their heads at Foma in silence. Yakov Mayakin's face was dark and immobile as though hewn out of stone.

"Shall we perhaps unbind him?" whispered Bobrov.

"When we get a little nearer."

"No, it's not necessary," said Mayakin in an undertone-"We'll leave him here. Let someone send for a carriage. We'll take him straight to the asylum."

"And where am I to rest?" Foma muttered again. "Whither shall I fling myself?" And he remained as though petrified in a broken, uncomfortable attitude, all distorted, with an expression of pain on his face.

Mayakin rose from his seat and went to the cabin, saying softly:

"Keep an eye on him, he might fling himself overboard."

"I am sorry for the fellow," said Bobrov, looking at Yakov Tarasovich as he departed.

"No one is to blame for his madness," replied Reznikov, morosely.

"And Yakov," whispered Zubov, nodding his head in the direction of Mayakin.

"What about Yakov? He loses nothing through it."

"Yes, now he'll, ha, ha!"

"He'll be his guardian, ha, ha, ha!"

Their quiet laughter and whisper mingled with the groaning of the engine did not seem to reach Foma's ear. Motionlessly he stared into the distance before him with a dim look, and only his lips were slightly quivering.

"His son has returned," whispered Bobrov.

"I know his son," said Yashchurov. "I met him in Perm."

"What sort of a man is he?"

"A business-like, clever fellow."

"Is that so?"

"He manages a big business in Oosolye."

"Consequently Yakov does not need this one. Yes. So that's it."

"Look, he's weeping!"

"Oh?"

Foma was sitting leaning against the back of the chair, and drooping his head on the shoulder. His eyes were shut, and from under his eyelids tears were trickling one after another. They coursed down his cheeks into his moustache. Foma's lips quivered convulsively, and the tears fell from his moustache upon his breast. He was silent and motionless, only his chest heaved unevenly, and with difficulty. The merchants looked at his pale, tear-stained face, grown lean with suffering, with the corners of his lips lowered downward, and walked away from him quietly and mutely.

And then Foma remained alone, with his hands tied behind his back, sitting at the table which was covered with dirty dishes and different remains of the feast. At times he slowly opened his heavy, swollen eyelids, and his eyes, through tears, looked dimly and mournfully at the table where everything was dirty, upset, ruined.

* * * * *

Three years have passed.

About a year ago Yakov Tarasovich Mayakin died. He died in full consciousness, and remained true to himself; a few hours before his death he said to his son, daughter and son-in-law:

"Well, children, live in richness! Yakov has tasted everything, so now it is time for Yakov to go. You see, I am dying, yet I am not despondent; and the Lord will set that down to my credit. I have bothered Him, the Most Gracious One, with jests only, but never with moans and complaints! Oh Lord! I am glad that I have lived with understanding through Thy mercy! Farewell, my children. Live in harmony, and don't philosophize too much. Know this, not he is holy who hides himself from sin and lies calm. With cowardice you cannot defend yourself against sin, thus also says the parable of the talents. But he who wants to attain his goal in life fears not sin. God will pardon him an error. God has appointed man as the builder of life, but has not endowed him with too much wisdom. Consequently, He will not call in his outstanding debts severely. For He is holy and most merciful."

He died after a short but very painful agony.

Yozhov was for some reason or other banished from the town soon after the occurrence on the steamer.

A great commercial house sprang up in the town under the firm-name of "Taras Mayakin & African Smolin."

Nothing had been heard of Foma during these three years. It was rumoured that upon his discharge from the asylum Mayakin had sent him away to some relatives of his mother in the Ural.

Not long ago Foma appeared in the streets of the town. He is worn out, shabby and half-witted. Almost always intoxicated, he appears now gloomy, with knitted brow, and with head bent down on his breast, now smiling the pitiful and melancholy smile of a silly fanatic. Sometimes he is turbulent, but that happens rarely. He lives with his foster-sister in a little wing in the yard. His acquaintances among the merchants and citizens often ridicule him. As Foma walks along the street, suddenly someone shouts to him:

476

"Eh, you prophet, come here!"

Yet he rarely goes to those who call him; he shuns people and does not care to speak with them. But when he does approach them they say to him:

"Well, tell us something about doomsday, won't you? Ha, ha, ha! Prophet!"

Lightning Source UK Ltd.
Milton Keynes UK
UKHW020155090223
416651UK00002B/490

9 781015 426337